TASTING LIFE TWICE

TASTING LIFE TWICE

Literary Lesbian

Fiction by New

American Writers

Edited by

E. J. LEVY

AVON BOOKS  NEW YORK

Permissions, which constitute an extension of the copyright page, appear on pages 343–344.

TASTING LIFE TWICE is an original publication of Avon Books. These works have never before been published together in book form.

AVON BOOKS
A division of
The Hearst Corporation
1350 Avenue of the Americas
New York, New York 10019

Copyright © 1995 by E.J. Levy
Cover art by Matt Mahurin
Published by arrangement with the editor
Library of Congress Catalog Card Number: 94-47010
ISBN: 0-380-78123-9

Library of Congress Cataloging in Publication Data:

Tasting life twice : Literary lesbian fiction by new American writers
   edited by E.J. Levy.
      p.   cm.
      1. Lesbians—United States—Social life and customs—Fiction.   2. American fiction—Women authors. 3. American fiction—20th century. 4. Lesbians' writings, American. I. Levy, E.J. (Ellen J.)
PS648.L47T37   1995   94-47010
813'.540809206643—dc20   CIP

First Avon Books Trade Printing: June 1995

AVON TRADEMARK REG. U.S. PAT. OFF. AND IN OTHER COUNTRIES, MARCA REGISTRADA, HECHO EN U.S.A.

Printed in the U.S.A.

OPM   10   9   8   7   6   5   4   3   2

For Alison Chi,
who dared me to,
and for my parents.

ACKNOWLEDGMENTS

I am grateful to all those who contributed to making this collection a reality. To the authors, for all they have written and will write. To Laurie Liss, who believed in this project and found it a good home. To Charlotte Abbott, for her unstinting efforts. To all those who allowed Charlotte and me to consider their work. To all those who took time to recommend and locate authors, including—but not limited to—Dorothy Allison, Laynie Browne, Victoria Brownworth, Christie Carr, Curtis Chin, Anne-christine D'Adesky, Tatiana de la Tierra, Dipti Gosh, Dorothy Randall Gray, Ellie Hernandez, Karla Jay, Terry Jewell, Jim Jones, Michelle Karlsberg, Sydelle Kramer, Sharon Him Ling, Tiffany Ana Lopez, Latika Malkani, Patricia Meono-Picado, Roz Parr, Micki Reaman, Julie Regan, Mattie Richardson, Sandip Roy, *SALGA*, Felix Sanchez, Charlotte Watson Sherman, Angie Slingluff, Barbara Smith, Frederick Smock, Linny Stovall, Urvashi Vaid, Judy Wenning, Marie-Elise Wheatwind, and Ron Whiteaker. To Alice Ro, Lynda McDonnell, and Margaret Beck, for terrific editorial advice. To Cottages at Hedgebrook and Norcroft, for time and space to work on this and other projects. To Lauren Fox, Gretchen Legler, Diana Saco, and Beth Rae Smith for moral support. And to Wendy Leavens, Sawnie Morris, Mei Ng, Debra Snow, Sasha Todorovic, Amy Weil, Suzi Winson, and Mark Harris for more than a phrase could ever acknowledge.

"We write to taste life twice,
in the moment and in retrospection."

—Anaïs Nin

CONTENTS

TASTING LIFE TWICE

INTRODUCTION

E.J. Levy

Several years ago at the Loft, a place for writing in Minneapolis, Minnesota, a panel of lesbian writers and critics gathered to discuss a controversial question: Why Is Lesbian Fiction So Bad? The query, while provocatively overstated, addressed a perception common among lesbian readers and writers that fictional representations of our lives often fall short of conveying the richness of our experience. At the same time, the question struck a nerve. Many women in the audience were offended by the topic; having been silenced by literary standards in the past, they rejected any attempt to assess the artistic merit of lesbian fiction. In subsequent years, when I have tried to raise the subject with other lesbians—well-read women, unafraid of debate—I have often met with the same chill hostility and a striking refusal to discuss the issue. The silence is significant; it is a silence that has reverberated in lesbian fiction, where the complex and ambivalent truths of our lives have all too often gone unrepresented, unrecorded.

In bringing together for the first time outstanding literary lesbian fiction by a new generation of American writers, this collection is deliberately provocative. It is my hope that it will provoke broader attention to and interest in lesbian fiction and inspire debate among writers and readers about what constitutes lesbian writing and literary fiction. Aesthetic standards have been a source of fierce contention among feminists: pitting those who would reject literary standards as elitist and patriarchal against those who desire more honest and compelling portraits of women's experience.

Because notions of good writing have traditionally been defined by those with power and used to bolster their claims to authority, many have been rightfully skeptical of efforts to evaluate artistic merit. When I mentioned this anthology to a young lesbian activist recently, she turned to me in horror. "You can't say some writing is better than others," she challenged. "It's all a matter of personal taste. It's purely subjective." To evaluate lesbian fiction, she believed, was to discredit some representations and enfranchise others. But there is another possibility: to recognize literary merit is to open up the possibility of taking our fiction seriously. And lesbian fiction deserves to be taken seriously: the writers whose work is collected here are producing some of the most interesting writing in America today.

Hidden in the current aesthetic relativism is a belief that art is not as important as our struggles for justice. Just as our fight for lesbian and gay rights depends on our ability to reframe familiar issues in new ways and to make meaningful distinctions about what is true and just, so we have to demand of our fiction a richness and complexity equal to our experience. Writing is, after all, a political act. Not simply because in the last decade censorship has pressed art to the front lines of political battles. Nor merely because its content can bolster our claims to justice. But because, through fiction, we mythologize our lives and our communities, and we live by those myths. We tell ourselves what is and what can be.

Novelist Dorothy Allison once joked that the phrase "lesbian fiction" brought to her mind an image of two female books in love. In truth, there is something a little unsettling about grouping works of fiction by the sexual preference of their authors. Our lives, any life, is more complex than a single label can suggest; such aggregations can inspire a false expectation of uniformity of experience or artistic expression. At the same time, there is a pressing need to identify literary lesbian fiction, precisely because it is assumed not to exist, and because as a category it has been excluded from the mainstream. If anything, this collection is likely to disprove any assumptions about lesbian *belles lettres* by demonstrating how various and very good lesbian fiction is.

The work in this collection is diverse in subject and in form—from Jan Ramjerdi's witty postmodern pastiche, "The Profound Theory of Complementarity," to the disquieting naturalism of Lee Ann Mortensen's "Not Quite Peru." What they share is artistic complexity and admirable craft. Each of these stories is able to transport the reader to see the world as the author would have it seen—from Carole Maso's *Bay of Angels*, which takes us on a sojourn among the dead, to Mary La Chapelle's "Anna in a Small Town," in which the complicated affections that bind two women culminate in a heroic confrontation between a mime and a bully in a Wisconsin tavern, in a struggle between conformity and honor.

What these works have in common is that each is written by a woman who knows what it is to love another woman—no small thing in a culture in which men and male perspectives dominate cultural narratives, particularly narratives of desire. Most of the authors represented here identify as lesbian, a few as bisexual, though these labels do not reflect the varieties of desire that a woman may feel for another woman, or that even a self-identified lesbian may feel for a man. The distinctions have never been easy or neat, nor should they be; our affections, after all, are never simple. Sappho, the seventh-century B.C. poet, had a child by her male lover and yet she wrote some of the greatest poems ever penned about love between women. What matters is that *all* these writers are women who love and desire women, a perspective too often elided in this culture enamored of men.

It is not surprising that lesbian fiction has often made the mainstream uncomfortable. While gay male fiction affirms our society's fascination with men, lesbian fiction, at its best, offers readers a chance to view our male-oriented culture with fresh eyes. Having made a conscious choice to love beyond the expectations of this society, lesbian writers possess a certain freedom of thought, a capacity to perceive alternatives to the way we live now, to disregard masculine pieties—not out of anger but pleasure. They have an opportunity to step beyond simple masculine-feminine dualism; to see the world in other terms than either-or.

Edmund White has said that gay fiction is marked by double vision, the result of passing as straight in society while feeling different; and the same can be said of sapphic writing, with the caveat that lesbians pass not just as heterosexuals but as women—

an identity which is itself an artificial construction in this culture. Sapphic writers know the distance between what is socially ordained and actual, what as women we are said to be and what we are, and their writing often gauges that gap, making it clear, so that we can see through to other possibilities. Some of the pieces in this collection exhibit the double vision White describes, offering an alternative to the familiar rules of the game. Others challenge readers' comfortable notions of narrative and story, and in so doing, the facile assumptions by which we often live. Still others radically reorient our perspective, as in C.W. Riley's "A Quiet Acre," in which an erotic attraction between sisters comes to seem natural in contrast to the stylized desire presented in popular magazines. Each has insights to offer the reader, whatever her or his sexual orientation.

Now as never before, there is interest in reading fiction by and about lesbians. For the first time, in 1992, a lesbian novel was a finalist for the National Book Award. Lesbian books, such as Jenifer Levin's *Sea of Light*, have been featured in the *New York Times Book Review*, and the *Washington Post* recently devoted an article to the new "lesbian literati."

Despite this growing audience for lesbian literature, the perception remains that there is little high-quality lesbian fiction available. In truth, many of the best contemporary lesbian writers are unknown to the general public. Even as lesbians are championed in the media as "chic," our literature has remained largely hidden. Some have found it difficult to publish literary fiction with openly lesbian content; others have been reluctant to be identified as lesbian authors, for fear their work would be dismissed as "merely lesbian." Still other lesbian writers—who have chosen to write about subjects other than women in love—have found their work stripped of a lesbian identity, as was the case for lesbian writer Dorothy Allison, whose novel *Bastard Out of Carolina*, was not nominated for a Lambda Literary Award because it was not "lesbian enough."

While gay male authors and explicitly gay fiction have recently found ready acceptance in prestigious mainstream venues such as the *New Yorker*—one thinks of David Leavitt, Michael Cunningham, Allen Barnett—the same cannot be said of lesbian authors, who have often had to choose between lesbian identity and liter-

ary aspirations. Rarely has fiction written about lesbians by lesbians
been published in the popular press. This exclusion has been possible in part because of the widespread perception that lesbian fiction is second-rate, a reputation that has been partially maintained
through the exclusion of lesbian literature from mainstream venues—and partially deserved. All too often lesbian fiction *has* been
poorly written, predictable, lacking complexity or subtlety of vision, favoring instead a preconceived notion of lesbian experience.

Given the dearth of lesbian fiction available in the past, it is
understandable that many lesbian writers and publishers have been
more concerned with representing lesbian lives than with artistic
sophistication. Misogyny and economic inequity, as well as racism
and homophobia, have long inhibited the development and expression of lesbian fiction, denying women the luxury of time and
liberty of mind that are prerequisites for the creation of art.

Since the 1970s, queer and women's presses have made enormous strides in providing a space for lesbian voices to be heard
and have paved the way for the current literary efflorescence.
Often these presses consciously emphasized raw and unedited experience. The lesbian fiction they published was more than fiction:
it has served as sociology, as history, as apologia, as philosophy.

But just as mainstream publishers have rejected overt lesbian
content, lesbian publishers have often imposed their own restric-
tions on lesbian writing. In place of artistic standards there have
been expectations that lesbian fiction would reflect positive images
of lesbian lives, address itself to "lesbian themes," eschew attitudes
considered inappropriate or distasteful to the "lesbian community."
In an effort to create and legitimize a lesbian vision of the world,
to define and affirm values and relationships in contrast to the
heterosexual mainstream, all too often writers, readers, and publishers have shied away from fiction that expresses the ambivalent
and complicated nature of lesbian lives or which addresses itself
to the spectrum of human experience.

The fact that lesbian fiction has been largely defined by its
content, rather than its authorship, has been nearly as damaging
to lesbian letters as the straight publishing world's demand that
sapphic elements be excised. Too often in the past, lesbian fiction
has been defined as fiction about lesbians, rather than fiction by
them. In her introduction to the *Penguin Book of Lesbian Short Stories,*

editor Margaret Reynolds defines lesbian fiction as ". . . writing which exhibits, within the confines of the text itself, something which makes it distinctly about, or for, or out of lesbian experience"—regardless of the author's sexuality.

The problem with this definition, of course, is that it assumes we know what lesbian experience *is*. All too often such definitions have led to a narrow definition of lesbian experience as simply desire between women. But to define lesbian fiction by some preconceived notion of appropriate lesbian subject matter grossly limits what lesbian writers—and lesbian fiction—can say. By insisting that lesbian fiction address only certain subjects, our fiction has been impoverished. By assuming we know what lesbian experience *is*, we have defined out much of the most complex fiction, that which starts with a question instead of an answer, which considers the whole of the human circumstance not just one aspect of it.

Besides, it is nothing new to read about lesbian characters in fiction. For centuries lesbians have been represented—and misrepresented—by straight authors for straight audiences. D.H. Lawrence, Guy de Maupassant, Émile Zola, Lillian Hellman are among the many straight writers who have written about lesbian characters. What we have seen far *less* often is a vision of the world through the eyes of an openly lesbian author. The reason, I think, is clear. In a culture enamored of men and rather fearful of women, the perspective of women who love women is—predictably—an uncomfortable one.

Surely if sapphic writing has any unique value in a patriarchal society, it has value in relation to all subjects. That is why in this collection the subject matter is as diverse as the authors themselves: the reader will find here stories about an American tourist bartering for sex in Spain; a female bodybuilder whose desperate quest for physical power parallels that of the declining American empire she inhabits; a family history from the point of view of an unborn child; and a young woman calling home for recipes for sea bass and the secret of love.

For all their diverse narrative strategies and subjects, these writers express what has traditionally been elided in literature—the vision of women who love women. Not all of these stories treat lesbian characters, but all describe the world from the perspective of women who have dared to challenge our culture's sexual proscriptions, and to see the world and write about it as their hearts dictate. From Judith Katz's folkloric tale of a Jewish whorehouse in turn-of-the-century Argentina, to Blake Aarens's deft navigation of the consciousness of an aging man and his middle-aged nurse, to Carol Anshaw's comic account of a modern urban love affair, these writers present us with stories we can return to again and again.

Any collection that purports to represent literary fiction is open to criticism of its standard, so let me make clear what mine has been: I have looked for work that seemed to me to possess the element of "transparence" critic Susan Sontag has said distinguishes works of art; or to put it less grandly, stories we live through, not merely read. I have looked for work that impressed me with its insights, the artfulness of its execution, above all that compelled me to read it.

Often I was startled to find in print a description of an experience that for me had been private and inchoate until that moment. That was the case with Stephanie Grant's story, "Posting-Up," about basketball, bigotry, and desire in a Catholic girls school in Boston during the era of forced busing. Written with the wry understatement of William Maxwell, the story put into words the vague perception I had had throughout school that certain students, but particularly the lesbian and gay students I knew, were somehow older, more certain, than everyone else. Or as Grant's narrator puts it, as she watches a high school basketball game, "There was something peculiar about them. Something I couldn't quite name. They were women, not girls. For the first time I saw the difference . . . There was a sturdiness about them, a sense of commitment to life, like at one point they each had made a conscious decision to stay alive. They had made choices."

In some cases, it was the sheer formal inventiveness that made the work a clear choice for inclusion. At other times I was moved by what Sontag calls the "pure, untranslatable, sensuous immediacy" of art, the ability to capture "the luminousness of the thing in itself." Still other pieces are included here simply because they are a great read: surely an essential criterion in any collection of writing.

And that is the real reason for bringing together these twenty-four writers in a collection of literary lesbian fiction: because theirs is some of the most engaging writing around and chances are you haven't read it. Although these women represent some of the most promising contemporary writers working in the country today, with few exceptions their work is not widely known. Many are emerging authors, for whom this is their first national publication. Others have published books, which despite awards and critical praise, have gone out of print. All deserve a wide and discerning audience.

Of course, no collection can be the last word on its subject: no doubt there are remarkable emerging lesbian writers whose work is absent from this book. What this anthology represents, then, is a sample of some of the literary lesbian fiction by contemporary American authors. Although the authors come from different geographical regions, different classes, ethnicities, and religions, collectively their work stands as a testament to the maturity of lesbian fiction, to its potential to entertain and to extend our understanding of literature and the human condition. Their distinctly literary fiction refutes the common criticism of lesbian fiction as poorly crafted. Often wry and sophisticated, it attests to the complexity of lesbian *belles lettres* and to its potential to reach a broad audience.

The French feminist theorist Monique Wittig has written that "A text by a minority writer is efficient only if it succeeds in making the minority point of view universal, only if it is an important literary text." Well crafted and humane, these literary fictions achieve such universality. They are relevant to all our lives.

Some seventy years ago, Virginia Woolf admonished writers to write beyond politics, beyond anger, beyond sex, to write androgynously, articulating in a single phrase the pervasive Western notion of art as rarefied and the artist as one transcending the fray. At the close of the twentieth century, it seems clear that we cannot write with the sort of objectivity Woolf prescribed. Even if it were desirable, it is a luxury not afforded this generation of writers, who confront unprecedented assaults on their lives and liberties—from environmental degradation to nuclear proliferation, from eating disorders to race hatred, from AIDS to Amendment 2. Ours is a politicized generation: versed in sexual politics, fluent in the language of annihilation, a language we should never have learned to speak. In a time of crisis, art cannot afford to be formulaic, to bow to convention, to play nice. The writers in this collection don't play nice. Women who love women, they describe a territory without the maps or compasses of social convention.

If, as Western literary tradition would have it, the outsider has a clearer view of society, then women loving women in a patriarchal culture are in a unique position to provide insights into human affairs. Certainly within academia, there has been a good deal of speculation about the potentially revolutionary nature of lesbian writing. Theoretical debate has been brewing for years about lesbian fiction as a source of literary invention. As the quintessential outsiders in a male-dominated society, lesbians are thought to inhabit an ideal position from which to formulate new literary strategies, to redefine character, plot, and subject matter in fiction.

Why then—to return to our original question—aren't lesbians producing more daring fiction? We are. This collection is a testament to that fact. The new lesbian writers whose work is represented here write vividly about human experience in all its variety. Theirs is a literature of striking originality, integrity, wit, and honesty. Taken collectively, these stories come close to fulfilling poet Muriel Rukyser's prophesy that if women told the truth of their lives, they'd break the world open. Certainly, these women are breaking ground.

POSTING-UP

Stephanie Grant

My senior year fourteen girls showed up to our first practice. The year before the team had been only half as strong: not enough bodies to scrimmage even. Which didn't bother our coach, Sr. Agnes, who had spent thirty of her seventy-odd years as a cloistered nun and who confused basketball with dodgeball. Sr. Agnes had retired at the end of last season. My dad said it was A Blessing In Disguise. Rumor was that our new coach, Sr. Bernadette, had gone to college on basketball scholarship. She was late getting to the first practice though, so we all stood around shooting baskets and checking each other out. I counted four, maybe five, point guards.

Every player in the city knew Kate Malone, if not by sight—she was six feet tall, with a mass of bright red hair—then by reputation. She led the Catholic league in total points scored for both boys and girls, and she had been kicked out of five Catholic schools in three years. Whatever school she ended up with, she took to the Catholic League Tourney; I'd watched her win with a different team all three years. Kate was the only new student at Immaculatta in 1973 who wasn't fleeing a court order: Immaculatta was her last hope for a parochial school education. The school before us—Sacred Heart—was in Dorchester, but not the Irish part. Kate had been the only white starter for Sacred Heart, which seemed more incomprehensible than her eighteen or nineteen points per game.

She stood at one end of the gym, shooting. Two other new girls waited beneath the basket for her to miss. Basketball etiquette required them to pass back the ball whenever she sank it. They looked pretty bored.

At the opposite hoop, Irene Fahey was practicing lay-ups. The rest of us stood in a rough semicircle around the basket, taking turns with the remaining ball. Irene wove in and out of us, charging from the left, then right, retrieving her own rebounds—whether or not she scored—dribbling out and flying back in, all the while asking questions about Immaculatta and the team.

"What was your record last year? I mean are you guys the losingest team in history? Who's your new coach? Is she a million and one years old like your last coach? I can't imagine losing all the time. I mean did you guys like to lose, or what?"

Irene was the second best basketball player and biggest mouth in the Catholic league. The year before she took Perpetual Faith to the playoffs with a 13-and-2 record. They lost to Kate's team in the next-to-last round by three points.

"You got a team this year, that's for sure. I've never seen so many freaking guards in one place before. I wonder who she's gonna start?"

Irene left Perpetual Faith, she confided in us at the top of her lungs, because her mother felt "the quality of education was deteriorating." Eventually I learned what that meant: Irene left because Perpetual Faith was one of the few Catholic schools in Boston that had black students, and it had accepted more blacks since the busing crisis began. Not only white parents took their children out of public school after the court order became final. Most of the black families removed their kids because they were concerned for their safety, which was exactly what the white parents said. Even I knew that the black people had real reason to worry. The first day of school a busload of black second-graders got stoned by white parents in Southie. We watched it on the news. My mom and dad were so disturbed they shut off the TV.

"Couldn't wait to get outta Perpetual Faith, that's for sure. Goin' downhill, you know what I'm saying?" Irene stomped on my toes on her way to the hoop.

Her lay-ups became so disruptive to our shooting that we were forced to join her. The girls who had been shooting with Kate (or hoping to shoot with Kate) left her to practice with us. Kate didn't budge, and Irene didn't ask.

Irene made me anxious. She sighed loudly at each of our mistakes, like somehow we were personally disappointing her. I missed every lay-up because I knew she was watching. We kept quiet during the drill and grew bored, but we were afraid to say anything. A tiny, dark-haired girl suggested we scrimmage. She was very serious looking. I had never seen her before, which was weird because I went to all the league games, Catholic and city, and I knew all the ball players. Irene was irritated.

"Ya, and who are you? Where'd you play? Not in this league, I don't think. Not too many guineas in this league. Not that I have anything against Italians. Don't get me wrong. Just never seen them play any kinda b-ball."

"Assumption," the girl replied, unflinching. I stared at the gym floor, nauseated; we didn't use words like *guinea* in my house.

"Assumption?" Irene looked puzzled. "Never heard of it. Where's Assumption?"

"Springfield," she responded, still indifferent. Her voice was low and steady.

"Ya, then how come I never heard of it? I got relatives in Springfield, and I've never heard of Assumption. You wouldn't be lying to me, would you? I hope not, lying is a cardinal sin, you know; it'll put a black mark on your soul, and guineas start out with half-black souls because of the Mafia. You can't afford too many cardinal sins."

"No, I wouldn't lie to you. You haven't heard of Assumption because it's not a high school. Assumption College." Ice edged the dark girl's words.

"I don't get it. What's your name?" Irene lost some of the color in her face.

"Bernadette. Sr. Bernadette. And you're Irene Fahey. That right?"

Irene nodded, ash-grey. All of us looked a little ill, except Kate, who was still shooting baskets. The bounce bounce of her ball kept time.

"Why didn't you tell us who you were?" Irene choked. "And how the hell old are you, anyway?"

Sr. Bernadette shrugged. "I just wanted to see you play relaxed, without knowing the coach was watching. And it's none of your

business how old I am. Just graduated from Assumption last spring
and took my vows at the same time. Any more questions?"

Silence. Then Irene: "Don't they have a height requirement for
nuns, for Christ's sake?"

There was a collective gasp. Everything I'd ever heard about
Irene Fahey was true.

"No, but there are requirements for being on this team." Sr.
Bernadette took a step toward Irene. "One of them is respect. If I
get any more lip from you, your behind is going to be warming
the bench all season. I don't care who you are or how good you
play. Got that?"

"Got it," Irene smiled a big, fake smile. "Got it, got it. I mean
you're the boss, right? You're about as big as my kid sister, but
you're the coach and whatever the coach says, goes."

I was sweating. Irene lived by the axiom that the best defense
is a good offense.

Sr. Bernadette fixed Irene with a glare so cold that every girl
within ten feet hugged her arms to her body. I remembered what
I had heard in school about Italians and the evil eye and was
instantly ashamed.

"Kate, come down here, will you? We're gonna scrimmage. I'd
like everyone to introduce herself first. Tell us your name, what
school you played for last year, and what position."

There did seem to be something sort of otherworldly about Sr.
Bernadette, I had to admit. Like how come she already knew
our names?

Everyone shifted her weight from leg to leg as we went around
the circle. There were six new girls.

"Maura Duggan, Dorchester High, point guard."

"Frances Fitzgerald, Southie, point guard."

"Peggy Gallagher, Charlestown High, forward."

"Pat Gallagher, Charlestown High, forward."

"Irene Fahey, Perpetual Faith, point guard."

"Kate Malone, Sacred Heart, point guard."

Point guard is like quarterback, only for basketball. She's your
best player. She controls the ball. My dad says point guards are
born, not made, that it's their disposition more than their skill
that a coach looks for. I had never seen so many in one room.

Sr. Bernadette bounced up and down on the balls of her feet.

All the guards stared at their hightops: only one of them would get to play point. Kate and Irene never looked at each other.

I started playing basketball because my dad wanted me to. He used to coach boys basketball at Most Precious Blood and coached my brother Tim when he went there. It was sort of like a dynasty, Dad and Tim together for four years. *The Meagher Dynasty* people called it. Dad insisted I play because of my height: I'm 5-foot, 11½ inches tall, and have been since eighth grade. My brother is 5-foot-7. Tim played guard at Most Precious Blood, but was too short for college ball. I think it made him crazy that I got the right body for basketball but didn't know how to use it. Of course, if Dad had given me one-fifth the attention he gave Tim growing up, I'm sure I'd have been a lot better. For a while I was hoping Tim and I were going to be the dynasty—*The Tim and Theresa Meagher Dynasty*. But it never worked out.

When I enrolled at Immaculatta in 1969, it was a small, egg-heady parochial school for girls who would rather read than do just about anything else. Our basketball team had had thirty-seven consecutive losing seasons. My senior year, everything changed. Busing doubled the enrollments of Boston's Catholic schools. Even though we were technically outside the neighborhoods designated for desegregation, we were close enough to absorb the shock of white students leaving the public schools. Not counting the incoming class, seventy-one new students matriculated in 1973. Six of them were basketball stars. The Sisters said it was God's will.

The whole first week of practice was like tryouts. Sr. Bernadette tried every possible combination of players. She ran very serious practices. The first hour we did drills: ball handling, lay-ups, shooting, and passing. The second hour we broke into teams and scrimmaged ourselves. When boys did this the two teams were called shirts and skins, because one team played bare-chested. When we scrimmaged, one team had to put on these horrible green smocks called pinneys. Everyone complained when they had to wear them. Irene said they looked queer. Sr. Bernadette called the team wearing pinneys "green" and the team without "white." Kate was always on the white team.

Tall people like Kate usually don't play point guard because more often than not they're lousy dribblers. The ball has so far to travel to get to the ground that it's easy to steal from them. Taller girls like me play underneath the basket, as forwards or centers. We spend most of our time fighting for good position and pulling down rebounds, so we don't get a lot of experience dribbling, faking people out, or setting up plays, which is what guards do. We mostly get a lot of experience hitting people. The few tall players who dribble are often so awkward that you don't have to guard against them very closely. Their Own Worst Enemy, as my dad would say. But Kate was not like that. She had a very low dribble for someone her height, and it was almost impossible to steal from her. She never seemed to crouch or bend over when dribbling, which left me with the impression that her arms were abnormally long. In fact, I would have sworn that her hands hung down past her knees. Though, when I saw her off the basketball court, her arms were normal: long, but in proportion with the rest of her.

Irene was built a lot more like your average high school point guard than Kate: short and skinny. Really skinny. No hips and breasts that were all nipple. (A terrific advantage on the basketball court, as in life.) In fact, if it weren't for her long, Farrah Fawcett hair and accompanying makeup, Irene could easily have been taken for a boy.

There were two schools of thought on eye shadow when I was in high school: some girls meticulously matched it to their outfits, being sure that their highlights—above the lid and below the eyebrow—corresponded to the contrasting color in their clothes. Others matched make-up with eye color, varying only the intensity of the shade. Irene was a renegade, defying both traditions, insisting on sky blue—despite her brown hair and eyes and rainbow assortment of J Crew polos. Irene's rebellion stopped here; in all else she was the standard bearer and enforcer of the status quo.

Irene also played more like your average high school point guard than Kate did. She was completely self-absorbed and unconscious of the rest of us. Irene shot whenever she had the ball. She dribbled too much (even if well) and she wouldn't pass. She tried endlessly to go in for lay-ups. She didn't think. Irene played like a one-person team, dribbling and shooting, dribbling and shooting.

Of course she got good at both because she had so much practice, but she was lousy to play with.

Friday afternoon after our first week of practice, Sr. Bernadette told us who would play where. We sat, as we had all week, far apart from each other on the bleachers of the gym listening to her comments about our play. She read without looking up from the notes she had taken on her coach's clipboard. We each had a towel and were conscientiously wiping away the day's sweat. Only Kate was still. She sat with her endless legs apart, one planted—knee bent—on the bleacher on which she sat, the other stretched out in front of her, ankle resting on the next, lower tier. Her freckled arms wrapped around the near leg, securing it to the seat. Sr. Bernadette looked up when she got to the end of her notes.

"Starting lineup will be as follows: Pat Gallagher, forward; Peggy Gallagher, forward; Theresa Meagher, center; Irene Fahey, off guard; Kate Malone, point guard. These are not lifetime memberships. If you play well, you keep your spot; if you don't, you rest a while. It goes without saying that everyone will play."

Before St. Bernadette finished her last sentence, Irene was in the showers. Her little body was rigid as she hightailed it across the gym, but her large mouth was open and slack, mumbling things we all tried not to hear.

Sr. Bernadette was the best coach I'd ever had. And the coolest teacher. Unlike most of the other nuns at Immaculatta, she was post–Vatican II, which meant she didn't wear a habit and she smiled at you when she spoke. But Sr. Bernadette was the most post–Vatican II nun I ever knew. She wore her hair short, but not severe. It was thick and black, stylishly cut in a shag. She had bright black eyes and smooth, almost-brown skin. During the day she wore jeans, and at practice she wore shorts and a tee shirt. Hers are the only nun's knees I've ever seen. She talked nonstop about basketball, and she shouted when she was angry or excited. She said "pissed off." She ran. Her last name was Romanelli, which was a big deal at the time because Irish people dominated the Catholic league then, and because what you were, like which Church you belonged to, mattered.

Her office was at the far end of the girls' locker room, next to the exit doors. Its walls were half wood, half glass, and you could see her working away at her desk as we got dressed to leave. The glass was opaque, with a bubbly texture, so you could see her outline. Sometimes girls went in to talk with her after practice if they were having trouble, or if Irene had said something particularly mean to them. I liked to take my time getting dressed so I could watch her move around her office.

There was a lot of talk about Kate's past. Particularly from Irene. Of special interest was why she had been bounced from five Catholic schools. Kate always left practice immediately, without showering; as soon as the door shut behind her, the discussion began. Irene would parade around the dressing room still pink-faced from practice, wet from the shower, and wrapped in a thick white towel. She would stop at practically every stall, grab onto the chrome curtain rod overhead and swing into our rooms unannounced as we changed.

"My cousin Mary Louise was at Our Lady of Mercy with Kate two years ago and she says Kate was expelled for refusing to go to religion class and disrespecting the nuns. She wouldn't even go to Mass."

Irene would pause, release one hand from the chrome bar to readjust the tuck and tightness of her towel, which was arranged to give the appearance of a bust, and continue talking and swinging one-armed.

"But my mother says her mother's just too cheap to pay tuition. Each year they pay half in September and promise to pay the rest by Christmas vacation. But never do. Can you imagine that, your mother lying to the nuns? Jesus Fucking Christ that's gross."

The first time Irene popped uninvited into my dressing room, I was mis-stepping into my underwear, damp from a hurried toweling-off. She stared at my body as I fumbled with leg holes.

"What do you think, Saint Theresa?" Irene always called me that. "I heard that our star player did it with black boys when she was at Sacred Heart."

Irene's mouth stayed open in a question mark as she surveyed my nakedness. I pulled on my jeans before answering. Somehow Irene always asked you questions that made you a jerk for just thinking about answering them. Her eyes traveled from my (now

covered) thighs to my bare breasts. The stall was too small for
me to go anyplace, so I stood there growing red, trying to come
up with an answer I could live with. Irene was discovering that I
had the biggest breasts on the team.

"Jesus Fucking Christ you've got big tits," Irene said. "Hey, Frances! Maura! Did you realize what big fucking tits Saint Theresa
has?" A small crowd gathered. My dad says that people like Irene
are a form of penance.

Our first game was against Irene's alma mater, Perpetual Faith. We
all were quiet on the bus ride over except Irene; she gave us a
pregame scouting report on her old teammates. We learned what
everyone's shooting percentage was and who shaved her arm pits.

When we climbed down off the bus at Perpetual Faith we could
see the other team watching us, but we pretended not to. They
were peering out of the small rectangular windows set high in the
walls of the gym. We knew that they had to be on tiptoe, standing
on top of the bleachers; we knew because we did the same thing
when the teams came to play us at Immaculatta. I could picture
their stretched arches as they leaned against the glass. They were
sizing us up, gauging their strength, laughing at the shrimpy girls,
worrying about the tall ones.

Sr. Bernadette had told us to look at the back of the head of
the girl in front of us as we filed into the gym. Kate led the
processional, followed immediately by Irene. Perpetual Faith's players were shooting when we entered, spread out in a fan underneath
the basket. Most of them knew Kate by sight, having lost to her
in the past. You could see them pulling aside the new players
to explain.

"No, no, the tallest girl's the point guard. The other one, the
next-to-tallest, she plays center. Watch out for the guard, that's
Kate Malone."

I was self-conscious, not being the tallest and playing center. I
knew I got the job because I was tall enough and because busing
had brought us only forwards and guards. I would have been
happier hiding out as a forward; I would have felt less responsible.
One of the Gallagher twins could have played center, they were
good enough, they were better than me. But Peggy and Pat had

played as forwards together all their lives. Choosing one as center over the other would have disturbed their equilibrium.

I wished I was a star center, the way Kate would have been. Lots of people thought that using her as a guard was a waste. But Sr. Bernadette knew that if Kate played center, Irene would be point guard, which meant that nobody but Irene (least of all Kate) would touch the ball.

My biggest shortcoming was that I wasn't aggressive enough, wasn't mean. I was taller than most of the centers I played, and I regularly got good position. I was a decent rebounder, although I've never been a great jumper, and frequently got outjumped by some little, but elastic girls. Offensively I was a nightmare. No guts. Most of my opportunities to score came from one-on-one matchups: me versus the other center in the middle of the key, smack underneath the basket. I was easily intimidated. If a girl played me close, if she bumped me or perhaps pushed me a little, just to let me know she was there, I would back right off. I would pass back out of the key, move the ball farther away from the basket. I was exasperating, really. Irene said so, right to my face, at practice. I guess I sabotaged a lot of good plays that way, by panicking.

I got constant advice from my teammates and Sr. Bernadette about posting-up, which is hoopster language for these one-on-one battles I kept avoiding. I got advice about staying firm, and wanting it bad enough, and going straight up or going up strong, and even, mixing it up with the big girls. But it was useless; the language alone confused me. Mixing what up? With whom? People assumed I couldn't post-up because I was afraid of the other girl, afraid she would hurt or humiliate me. But it wasn't true.

I played the entire first quarter on the verge of puking, praying no one would pass me the ball. Defensively, I was solid enough: mostly I just stood there and let girls run into me. Irene and Kate shot from everywhere. Swish, swish, swish, went the ball through the hoop. I didn't come close to scoring until the second half, when they substituted in a new center.

Kate and Irene had brought the ball up, and were weaving in and out of the key. I was directly underneath the basket, hands up, my back to the other center. She looked familiar, but I couldn't quite place her. I heard nothing but the sound of my own heartbeat and breathing. Sr. Bernadette waved wildly from the sidelines and I could see her mouthing directions. A play and then several plays unfolded around me. I tried to stay focused on the ball. My opponent and I do-si-doed for position. Finally, I heard a sound that didn't belong to me: the chink chink of Mary Jude McGlaughlin's cross and Virgin medallion hitting against each other.

Mary Jude was a friend of my cousin Anne, and from what Anne used to tell me, she was shy, devout, not overly intellectual, extremely sweet, and oppressively pretty. She had been warming the bench for Perpetual Faith for three years, and had scored twice during brief cameos, once for the opposing team. Mary Jude touched my soaked back lightly, just above my hip, with the tips of three fingers on her right hand. Her breathing was soft and even, and although I couldn't see her face, I knew she was smiling: Mary Jude never didn't smile.

I sighed. Here it was again. How could I possibly compete against such goodness? How could I fake left, all the while knowing that I would be moving to my right, digging my shoulder into Mary Jude as I pivoted, and lightly pushing the ball into the basket? How could I leave her standing there, as people had so often left me, mouth agape, embarrassed, wondering what had just happened? How could I press my advantage knowing the punishment she would take from her teammates, punishment I knew only too well? Worst of all, Mary Jude would smile through it all. This registered as sin to me. Something I would have to purge from my soul in order to receive communion next Sunday. Something, if left unattended, I would burn in hell for. So I didn't.

When the ball finally came to me, I was a knot of anxiety. I turned and faced Mary Jude. I held the ball high, above her head, and discovered I was right about her smile. She beamed at me. I smiled back. She had huge brown eyes. In the half second before I was going to pass the ball back to Kate, one of Mary Jude's teammates whacked the ball out of my hands and into the hands of their point guard. They scored before I turned around.

Irene was all over me.

"Jesus Fucking Christ, what was that? You plan to just give them the ball all day? Whose side are you on anyway?"

I blanched. The one legitimate basket Mary Jude had scored in the last three years was against me: I let her. It was as if I had no choice: it meant so much to her. I was terrified that Irene had figured it out, that she would tell about Mary Jude and the others like her. And there were others. Lots of others. I guess I knew the other centers wanted to win as much as I did, and I couldn't stand the thought of taking that away from them. It wasn't that I liked to lose, I hated to lose. But I guess I hated making other people lose worse. And besides, I was used to it.

I knew that this weakness was ten times worse than plain cowardice. I was My Own Worst Enemy. And now, potentially, the team's.

We won anyway. The first in an endless season of wins. We beat Perpetual Faith 59 to 36. Kate scored 23 points, Irene hit for 19. The team was ecstatic. Sr. Bernadette lectured us on the bus on the way home. I sat as far away from Irene as possible. Sr. Bernadette crouched in the aisle between the seats, pivoting left and right, facing each of us directly as she spoke. Sr. Bernadette had a custom of grabbing your shoulder or your knee or whatever was handy when she talked to you, so she was impossible to ignore. That day on the bus she got so close to me I could feel her breath on my face. I didn't hear a word she said, but I remember how she looked up close. Her hair was damp and limp from all the perspiring she had done during our game, her face glistened and the muscles on her neck stood out. Her black eyes were as black as her missing habit, and luminous.

Usually I hated the bus rides. If I could have, I would have sat right by Kate, who took the seat directly behind the bus driver and across the aisle from Sr. Bernadette. I was dying to be included in their conversations, to listen to Kate talk basketball, and to be on the receiving end of Sr. Bernadette's intensity. They sat at a slight angle to each other so that their knees touched, and Kate held the playbook on her lap. Sr. Bernadette gestured from the book to the air in front of them, with one hand going back periodically to Kate's shoulder to confirm her understanding. Kate stared closely at the invisible drawings in the air between them.

Irene occupied the very last bus seat by the emergency exit, the rest of us were staggered in the seats just before her. The cooler you were the farther back you sat and the closer to Irene you positioned yourself. I sat alone, as far away from Irene as I could get without leaving the group entirely. She talked nonstop about Kate. My ears burned red as I slumped forward in my seat pretending not to hear her, pretending to read the book in my lap, stealing glances at the front of the bus.

But I was, I knew, as guilty as Irene. Like her, I was obsessed with Kate. I wanted to know everything: what her family was like, why she kept changing schools, where she learned to play so well, whether she liked us, whether she liked me. In retrospect, I was infatuated with her, and it was my first big, stomach-wrenching infatuation. But I didn't know to call it that. I didn't even know enough to be embarrassed. Although, thank God, I knew enough to keep it from Irene.

I listened very closely to the horrible things Irene said. Each day she had a new story explaining Kate. Kate was on drugs; she was a kleptomaniac; her mother was a prostitute; her family was on welfare; they were really Protestant Irish; her father was a Jew; Kate was on the Pill; and, the worst possible slander for our immaculate ears, she had had two abortions. Everyone knew that Kate lived alone with her mother, and this in itself was extremely suspect. Some kids at Immaculatta had as many as ten brothers and sisters; most of us had at least four. I had never met an only child; Sr. Agnes said they were sins. And Catholic families were not families without fathers.

If Kate knew about the rumors Irene spread, she never let on. Kate rarely spoke. She had no friends on the team, or at Immaculatta, as far as I could tell. When Kate spoke it was b-ball talk. At practice she doubled as Sr. Bernadette's assistant coach, showing us moves and illustrating plays. One week Kate was assigned to demonstrate posting-up to the centers and forwards. That Monday we gathered around her underneath one basket, while Sr. Bernadette hollered at the guards at the opposite end of the court.

"First you have to find out where you are. Establish some territory. Take up some space. Back your butt into the other girl. See how much room she'll give you. Once you know where she is and how much she'll take, then you're ready. The first rule in posting-up is wanting it. Even if your hands are up like this for the ball, no guard's gonna pass it unless your face says you want it. The second rule is not thinking about it too much. Get ready and go. The longer you wait, the more likely it'll be taken away."

Was she talking just to me? Did she know? Had Irene told her something, or was I that transparent?

"Get out of your head, Theresa," Kate said on Tuesday. "I can see you thinking. Get out of your head."

"How?" I asked. "How can you see me thinking?" And to myself: *What can you see me thinking?*

"I just can," she shrugged. "And if I can, so can they. So lose it, whatever it is."

I struggled to empty my face. I struggled to eliminate Mary Jude and the others from my consciousness.

"Well you don't have to look like an idiot." Kate smiled at my vacant expression. The other girls laughed, and I was giddy with the attention. Emboldened, I asked her how come she knew so much about basketball.

"I don't really know," she said, completely serious. "It's like I was born knowing."

"Did your father teach you?" I ventured. "Or your brothers?" Heads turned, ears pricked expectantly.

She shook her head, No. Now her face emptied. End of conversation.

But I couldn't let it go. After practice, I followed her to her locker. She hadn't heard my footsteps over the noise of the girls taking showers, so she jumped when I said loudly into her left ear, "Uncles or cousins?"

"Uncles or cousins, what?" She looked angry.

I had never been this close to Kate, and now I saw the details of her face for the first time. Her skin was pale—red-head pale—and a pattern of soft brown freckles ran across the bridge of her nose and splashed onto her cheeks. Her eyes were clear blue. They widened with shock and anger as I persisted.

"Did your uncles or cousins teach you to play?"

"Why are you so anxious to know who taught me what? Maybe I taught myself. Maybe, like I said, I was born knowing. Maybe I couldn't help but learn. What's it to you?" She crossed her long arms in front of her chest and grew two inches. Her thin Irish lips pursed.

"I was just curious. Thought maybe if I knew what you did to get so good, I could learn a little faster. You know." Sweat collected on my eyelids.

"Look, lemme give you a tip, save you some time. The thing you need to do more than anything else is be in your body. I've seen it before. Lots of girls play in their heads. Get back here," one of her extraordinary arms flashed out and smacked me in the roundest part of my belly. The spot she touched burned, and I could feel little waves of heat fan out until my fingertips were warm. I knew the color was draining from my face. I nodded and bent forward a little, in an unintentional bow, and got stuck there. I tried to smile my thanks, but I couldn't move my muscles the way I wanted. Finally, I just backed away. We didn't speak again until Friday.

"Terry, come here."

Terry? No one called me Terry. It was always Theresa. I looked behind me; perhaps there was a new girl I didn't know.

"Yes, you, Terry. Come here. Come guard me."

We had had a week of posting-up lessons—we had practiced both offensive and defensive positions—and it was time to show Sr. Bernadette what we had learned. I couldn't move.

"Quit stalling, Terry. Get over here."

Terry. I said it over to myself. Kate had a name for me.

Slowly, anxiously, I got in position behind her. She grew taller and wider until I could see nothing but her muscled back and clump of braided hair. All week I had practiced against the Gallaghers and lost. How could I possibly defend against Kate?

She inched me back toward the basket with her butt. Her shoulders twisted left, then right, then left again. Finally Kate stepped away from me, turned, and shot. When I could at last see the ball, I started moving toward it, straight up into the air. My shoulder left its socket, released my arm, which floated up to touch the ball, and returned. Before I knew it, we were all three back on the ground.

"Not bad, Terry. Not bad at all." Kate looked surprised, but not displeased. "Now just stay there." She slapped one arm onto my shoulder, retrieved the ball with her free hand, and pumped it into my stomach. "Don't think about what you did, just stay here. In your body."

But I was already out, thinking about my new name, afraid of what I'd just done.

*   *   *

As we won more and more, I grew increasingly frustrated with my inability to score. I wanted to be part of the team in a way that I wasn't. I wanted to slap hands with everyone, triumphant, after an especially tough basket. Or, more truthfully, I wanted everyone to slap my hand, the way they slapped Kate's and Irene's. I wanted to be sought after. I wanted Kate to congratulate me in the same expressionless, monotone manner in which she congratulated Irene. I wanted the cool indifference of excellence.

So at the halfway point in the season, after we'd won twelve straight games, and we were looking like we couldn't lose, I began practicing on my own, mornings, before school. An hour and a half of shooting and dribbling (I set up those fluorescent orange cones and did figure eights around them) every day. I got a little better and a lot bored. Playing alone had its limitations; it's one thing to shoot from eight feet out, it's another thing to shoot from anywhere with someone's hand in your face. And I had no one to post-up against. So I started looking for a morning pickup game.

All the league stars played mornings. Many of them played nights, too, after regular practice or games, after dinner, under streetlights that had been rigged with hoops. I knew that Irene played early mornings in the school playground with a bunch of girls from Perpetual Faith. Girls-room girls. Smokers. They all wore eye shadow that matched their sweatpants and tons of St. Christopher medals and gold crosses that were constantly being tucked into ironed, white tee shirts. Irene was the best athlete there, and she tenaciously maintained possession of the ball, so after a few wasted efforts I decided to try a boys' game. I went to several boys' Catholic school playgrounds and found as many games. It didn't work. I realized that a girl's ability was always a problem for boys. If I wasn't as good as they were, they humiliated me by never passing me the ball; if I was as good, they humiliated me by never passing me the ball. Only girls who were as talented as Kate could play with boys without humiliation. Finally, I got up the courage to ask Sr. Bernadette. I tapped on the bubble glass of her office door one day after practice, after everyone had gone.

"Come in," she hollered, and swiveled in her chair. The office was warm and smelled of leather from balls and gloves and cleats.

I stood with my hands behind my back, one hand still on the doorknob.

"What's up, Theresa?" She smiled. She looked even smaller sitting down, her feet swung an inch above the ground.

"I, umm, I was wondering if you, umm, knew of a game I could play in mornings. Other than Irene's game." I turned the knob in my hand. It was slippery.

"What about my game?" she offered immediately.

"What about your game?" I was confused.

"My game." Sr. Bernadette stood up and jammed her hands in her sweatpants pocket.

"You coach a game? I'm looking for a pickup game, not another team." I leaned back into the door.

"No, I play in a game. A pickup game." She was still smiling.

"You play in a pickup game?" I didn't know nuns could do that. After all she had played in college before she took her vows.

"Theresa, what's the problem? Am I not being clear? I can't imagine being any more clear, really." Sr. Bernadette's smile waned and she seemed a little exasperated.

"No. It's just that, what do you mean, a game?"

"Jesus. I mean I play in a morning pickup game and would you like to play with us?"

For Christ's sake, I had made a nun swear. I opened the office door and took a half step out. "Well, yes, I mean, are you sure it's OK?"

"It's OK," Sr. Bernadette sighed. "Where are you going?"

"Then OK. All right. See you there. Where is it?" I was outside her office now. Only my head stuck into the warmth.

"Dorchester." Sr. Bernadette stepped toward me.

"Dorchester. OK. No problem. See you then. Tomorrow OK?" I closed the door. Then opened it. "How do I get there?"

Sr. Bernadette laughed and sat back down. "You can catch the bus on Randolph Avenue, right in front of Immaculatta."

"No problem," I lied and shut her door for good. I couldn't believe it! Sr. Bernadette invited me to her personal game. Her very own private game. I floated home. Maybe now I could sit in the school bus with her and Kate. Maybe now I would be protected from Irene.

The next morning I had to take two different buses to get there, and I had to lie to my parents about where I was going. Dorchester was off-limits.

I jumped off the bus three blocks too soon. My stomach knotted. It was a big, public school playground with several hoops. A handful of men played at the near corner. I stood by the fence in front of them, hidden by their moving bodies. I could see Sr. Bernadette and her friends warming up at the far end of the concrete park. I had imagined the way they might look several times: last night I dreamed that they played in full habits. My mind pictured every possible combination of athlete and cleric on the court. But I never guessed they would be a mixed group, even in Dorchester. I didn't know any black people, none of my friends knew any black people, so I hadn't imagined them in Sr. Bernadette's basketball game. I waited for everyone to start playing before I walked over.

Kate was there! I gasped at the sight of her, exhilarated and disappointed. Sr. Bernadette had invited another person from our team to share in her private life. I was not so special after all. I wondered how long they had been playing together, and if they had become friends. The knot in my stomach tightened.

There were ten women playing ball, including Kate and Bernie—which is what they called Sr. Bernadette. Two more women sat next to me on a green wooden bench that was rooted into the cement a few feet behind one of the hoops. I was sweating so much that my thighs slid off the bench and little pieces of green paint stuck to me when I stood up. The women at my side watched the game closely, calling out encouragements.

The first play I witnessed was a court-length pass to Kate, who was waiting underneath the basket. It took three seconds. They tried the exact same thing next possession but someone on the other team leapt into the air and stole away the play. I was out of breath just watching them.

They fought hard for rebounds and loose balls, and sometimes knocked each other down. One woman got roughed up three times in three consecutive plays. She was a forward and a very aggressive rebounder. She had the same coloring as Sr. Bernadette, another Italian I guessed. Her dark hair stood out every which way. Each time she hit the cement, whoever knocked her down helped her up. By the third fall everyone was laughing. She even smiled, although you could see she was hurt. Someone said it was a good thing she had so much padding, and they all laughed louder. The well-padded woman walked stiffly around the court, rubbing her behind. The others stopped to catch their breath, bending completely over, resting their hands on their knees so that their elbows jutted out and made shelves of their arms. Everyone's tee shirt was stuck to them.

After a minute or two, one of the point guards approached the injured forward and spoke to her. She massaged the woman's butt like it was her shoulder or something. They walked slowly over to the bench. We all stood up.

"Sub," said the guard, looking at me. "We need a forward."

The injured player lay out flat on the ground in front of the bench. She brought one knee up to her chest and held it there tightly. Her sore cheek lifted off the ground. One of the women who had been calling encouragements hustled onto the court.

"You sure look like a forward," the guard shrugged, letting her eyes travel up and down my full length. I felt that same funny heat wave I felt when Kate touched my stomach that time after practice.

"Center," I whispered.

"No kidding?" She smiled. "You're gonna play against Katie?" She shook her head. "Aren't you the brave one. I'd be whispering that too, if I were you." She sped back to the game.

I hadn't even noticed that Kate was playing center. I wondered if it was because they needed a center, or because there were guards who played better than Kate. I had never seen a guard better than Kate, so I watched the friendly woman play.

She reminded me of Irene—except that she was more friendly and she was black—they had the same build and the same jauntiness. She was everywhere at once. It was the kind of attitude you hate in people you don't like. It didn't bother me so much in her. She stole the ball five times in about eight tries.

I was used to seeing people steal a lot. Kate and Irene did it all the time, but against lesser players. This guard was something else again. The women she stole from were no pushovers; they could handle the ball, every single one of them. Where she edged them out was in speed and desire. Just a millisecond faster: she would attack the ball the instant after it was released from her opponent's hand, but before it touched the ground. She didn't grab the ball with both hands: that would have been too awkward, and too easy to defend against. She just tapped it lightly to one side and was gone. Like that. Desire so overwhelming you couldn't see it happening.

My dad had a drill test for desire. He said that desire was the most important thing in an athlete. Only he called it playing with heart. That's how he picked his starters: the five guys with the most heart played. At home, he would roll a basketball on the ground away from me and Tim. When it was a few feet out, he'd blow his coach's whistle and we'd lunge for it. On the cement driveway. We'd dive and grovel and kick for the ball. That was what I thought desire looked like. Desperation and skinned knees. I had trouble recognizing the smiling guard's desire: desire that left no room for alternatives. Desire that brought pleasure.

She was having a great time. Everyone was.

They were a strange-looking bunch. All different sizes and colors and abilities. I had expected them all to be the same. They were not. The guard who reminded me of Irene was 5-foot, 4 inches tall. The other point guard was equally as small, but had legs the thickness of fire hydrants. She could touch the rim of the basket; she could alley-oop.

There was something peculiar about them. Something I couldn't quite name. They were women, not girls. For the first time I saw the difference. I realized that this was what made Kate stand out so at Immaculatta; and that this, somehow, was why she had been thrown out of five Catholic schools. There was a sturdiness about them, a sense of commitment to life, like at one point they each had made a conscious decision to stay alive. They had made choices.

The longer I watched them play, the more inexplicable they seemed. I had never met women like them before. My mother, none of my friends' mothers, were like these women. Yet deep in my stomach they were familiar. I began to suspect I'd met them before and searched my brain for a memory. Nothing.

Kate was playing against a tall light-skinned black woman named Toni, who was as skinny as she was long. Kate seemed thickset by comparison. They spent most of their time about a hair's width apart, exchanging bruises. Fifteen minutes into the game, Kate elbowed her in the head, accidentally, while pulling down a rebound. It smarted. Toni staggered toward the bench, holding her head in her hands. "Sub," she hollered. Everyone else stopped moving.

"Toni, Toni, you okay? Talk to me, Toni." Kate's face was a mask of concern.

Toni turned to them, fingering the growing lump on her head. "You playing football out there, Malone, or what? No finesse, I tell you, Irish girls got no finesse."

Everyone smiled; a few giggles escaped. Kate tried not to laugh.

"Your concern is underwhelming, Malone, underwhelming." Toni resumed her stagger toward the bench and plowed directly into me. "Who are you? More Irish, I see. I need a sub. Go play against your cousin, will ya. You can beat up each other for a while." She shoved me onto the court.

Irene's look-alike came immediately to my rescue. She grabbed me by the shoulder.

"No problem, no problem. Maureen's here, and she's gonna take care of you. Mo's gonna help you out. What's your name, sweetheart? If you're gonna play with us, we need to know your name."

"Theres—Terry," I said, looking away from Kate. "Terry Meagher."

"Okay, Terry Meagher, it's two-one-two zone." She dragged me over to my new teammates. "You just stand in the middle with your arms up like this, okay?" Mo threw both of her arms into the air, her little body making a giant X. "Me and Bernie are your guards, Merril and Sam are behind you. Got that?" She stood frozen in a half–jumping jack. I nodded.

Everyone grunted hello, and Bernie—Sr. Bernadette—winked at me. Mo flung one arm over my shoulder and pulled me to her. She covered her mouth with her free hand and whispered loud enough for everyone to hear: "Don't let Katie get inside, okay? You're finished if she gets inside. Foul her if you have to."

I looked into Mo's eyes. Dark brown eyes in a dark brown face. Irene came to mind: how like Mo she was. How she would hate that. I thought about Mom and Dad. How grateful they were to have sent me to Catholic school, years ago, before it all started, before yellow school buses meant anything more than transportation. I pictured the busload of black second-graders that got stoned. I remembered the TV news clip my parents had kept me from watching; before they shut it off, I had recognized an Irish flag waving behind the mob of white parents.

Mo's left hand hung pink and brown over my shoulder, an inch from my face. I reached up and pressed it with both of my sweaty hands. "Cold hands," I smiled at Mo.

"They're always that way, even when I play." Mo looked directly at me.

"Cold hands, warm heart," I offered, and was instantly embarrassed. "It's an old Irish saying," I backtracked. What was I doing?

But Mo seemed charmed. "I like that. Cold hands, warm heart. Good for you. I like that. You're gonna do just fine. Well, let's go, Terry Meagher. And watch out for these cold-hearted women with hot shots." She laughed and shook her head.

The rest of the game seemed to go in slow motion. I knew it was faster than any other game I'd ever played in, but I could see every detail like it wasn't, like I was watching it under a magnifying glass.

I kept one eye on Kate, one eye on the ball, and one eye on Mo, who was never far from the ball. Then it happened. I was in the middle of the key, with Kate at my back. Mo brought the ball up and charged around me, into the key, making like she was going in for a lay-up. But instead of shooting, she dropped the ball back for me. Her move drew everyone with her, over to the right side of the key. Well, almost everyone. I was just left of center, with Kate between me and the basket.

So I did what Kate taught me. Fake right-left-right, turn, and up into the air. Kate was there, matching everything. A long, strong arm shot into the air and slapped the ball a second after it left my fingertips. We three thudded to the ground. The ball bounced hard, back into my hands. I held my breath. Kate was huge in front of me. Left-right-left, this time and up again, knees bent, arms stretched. Kate's arm grew longer than mine. She slammed the ball. We crashed down. People began murmuring encouragements. I heard my name. This time the ball dropped to Mo. She fired it back to me. I was shocked. She was closer to the basket than either Kate or me. Mo smiled and rolled her eyes up to the clouds. So I went up again, no fakes, just straight up into the air, Kate following.

She would beat me like this every time, I knew, so without ever having done it before, and a little off-balance, I hooked the ball. I had seen people do it before, mostly smaller players who were trying to get over big girls. Irene could hook, Sr. Bernadette could hook, and I had seen Mo do it once early that morning. But I myself had never tried it, not even in practice. It wasn't really a conscious decision, my right elbow just bent, all by itself, and let the ball go. It cleared Kate's fingers, smacked the backboard a little too hard, and fell into the hoop. This time we both landed on our butts.

From the ground, everything finally made sense. I knew what Kate meant by being in one's body: I was in mine. I looked up at the calves and thighs surrounding me. These women were in every inch of theirs. They seemed completely without fear: of their bodies, of each other, of their desires. I could see that they even liked their bodies, which is what at first seemed so peculiar. I had never met a woman who liked her own body.

I stayed on the ground, not wanting to get up. I knew that being in my body meant choosing myself. And choosing desire. So few women I knew had chosen themselves: Sr. Bernadette, Kate, and in her own evil way, Irene.

Sr. Bernadette walked over to Kate, who was still flat on her back, and extended both of her hands. Kate grabbed hold and Sr. Bernadette yanked her to her feet. Kate seemed about eight feet tall standing so close to Sr. Bernadette. They just looked at each other, and I could tell that they were, indeed, friends. But somehow it didn't bother me so much now.

Kate let go of Sr. Bernadette's hands and stepped over to me. She reached out one hand and pulled me up. She dusted my behind and shrugged, indifferent: "Nice move.... Who taught you that?"

"No one," I said. "No one taught me that." And she nodded.

Anna in a Small Town

Mary La Chapelle

I'm waiting in the car outside the Waupaca County jail. My cousin Anna left me here five minutes ago. She needs to check on Mike's bail and to see if she can talk with him awhile. I had started to get out of the car to go with her, but she said, "Wait here, Jane. I feel so bad about your being involved already." I couldn't be sure what she really wanted, or what I wanted, so I made one of those faces I know how to make, where each of my eyebrows goes in a different direction.

And after she got out, she came over to my side of the car and bent far down to peer into my window. "Really," she said. "He's so hung over, he won't mind sleeping until the bail comes through. Besides, Sunday is the best time to see the zoo; I'd still like to give you the tour."

She straightened up, and all I could see were her log-size legs until she walked away. Her softball jacket was shiny blue and said BALDY'S AND MARY'S on the back. I thought about how there wasn't much reason for her to wear it anymore, and then I could see her from behind pulling at the material in the front of her jacket. Adjusting, not because she was cold, or because it was raining, but because adjusting was second nature to her, always making herself fit, into her clothes, into other people's cars, or the next room she might enter.

My cousin is a giant, and you can't forget that fact while looking at her. I watched her set her feet on the steps to the jail with a sliding motion, smoothly and softly, the way I imagine Indians were taught to step so as not to disturb the forest. Her purse looked like a toy over her wrist, and she took the steps two at a time. But these are details anyone might notice.

There are yellow leaves stuck to the windshield. One leaf is sliding down a drip of water. It could make me think of a tear, but I don't want to think about tears, or the gloom inside this car, or the gloom outside of it. I want to know how I got into this? I came here to see Anna; well, this is partly true. I came to direct a mime workshop at the college in Steven's Point, which is only a stone's throw from Waupaca. The two of us have exchanged a few cards, but basically we haven't seen each other since her sister's wedding six years ago. She urged me in every one of her cards to stop in Waupaca if I should happen to pass through. I never encouraged her to visit me, however; I suppose because I was doubtful about her fitting into my little box of an apartment, but also because I am on tour so much of the time.

Anna called me a week ago. My sister, she said, had mentioned in her last note that I would be coming through. I had forgotten about her voice: it's like birch bark, rough and smooth at the same time. And we chatted together with the strained feelings of two people who were once close and now aren't sure why. Finally, she talked me into driving up for the weekend since my workshop didn't begin until Monday.

We estimated that the leaves would be peak color for my drive from Chicago, but I was disappointed. If they had changed at all, it was only to a dull yellow like these leaves on the windshield— no reds, no ambers. In fact, there wasn't a tree along the road that didn't seem somehow listless in its response to autumn.

I had hardly come onto her property and out of my car before Anna was there, bending over me. She gave me a kind of hug by putting a hand around each of my shoulders. "Sorry about the leaves," she said.

"Why?"

"Because the rain's been bringing them down before they've had a chance."

"That's not your fault, Anna. It's been raining in Chicago too."

I'd forgotten how different she was from anyone else. She was standing back from me, smiling, but trying not to smile too much.

Sometimes her body has an enormous energy of expectation you can almost see, like mercury in a thermometer. It makes me very uncomfortable. When she sensed I was feeling this way, she let go of her excitement and became still before slowly bending at the waist into the trunk of my car. I noticed once again how the movements of her hands were delayed, as if it took longer for intentions to travel the lengths of her arms.

Her fingers were too large to fit into the grips of my suitcases. And after she had gathered up all my bags under one arm, I had to tell her I only needed one for the weekend; she blushed and put two of them back. "This is it," she said, extending her other arm over the property. Three years ago she sent me a card on which she had sketched a picture of her land. It was drawn as if from an aerial view, a square, cut into the front of a forest of small, friendly pine trees. Standing in the lot, I could see the pines were not as proportionally small as they had been drawn, and they weren't friendly. They were stiff and had been planted in rows. The bottom branches were scraggly on every tree, creating, at eye level, a scratched, gray haze. And the upper bulk of the trees was massed together in a unified plan to keep the light out.

If I ever lived in a forest—and I have thought about it—I wouldn't live in a pine forest. I've never seen much else grow in pine forests, except pines. Whether this is because of the piles of needles, or the lack of light, I don't know. The kind of forest I would live in would be a great mixture of plants and trees. And if I couldn't identify everything that grew there, I think I might even find a comfort in that.

I didn't know what to say to Anna, so I said, "Just smell that pine."

We walked up to the house, which isn't quite a house yet. She had explained this on the phone, and now she was explaining it again. "Everything's in the basement while the rest of the house is being built. It's sealed off, though, and warm."

A door was cut into the front blocks of the basement, which were all exposed. It was too small for Anna, as most doors are, so she needed to bow her head and pull in her shoulders to go through. I stopped behind her and waited. When she was inside, I said, "Anna, look." Then I imagined a door much smaller than my body, and I mimed my way through it. She was laughing as she watched, but her eyes were troubled. My imitation wasn't right; I could feel it, and she knew it too. And I imagined, even in this case, that she probably felt it was her own fault.

I tried to smooth it over by switching my attention to her place. Since it wasn't completely a house yet, it seemed to me a basement apartment. The floors and walls were cement. She had tried to warm it up with rugs and hangings, but still the color and the smell of basement blocks were everywhere.

"This is nice, Anna. And look! A wood stove."

"This little fellow," she said, tapping her knuckles on the pipe, "is going to heat the whole house eventually."

"Really!" I made a big deal of it because I knew she must have paid a lot of money for it, and because it was an uncommon thing in the city.

We drank Leinenkugels, brewed locally. The afternoon was so gray, we needed to turn the lights on, and I wondered if I could already feel so fuzzy from the beer. There was an illustration of an Indian maiden on the label with her arms winding up toward the neck. I was sitting on the couch, and Anna was sitting on an unpacked crate of books she had pulled up to the coffee table, her legs set wide apart with her feet flat on the floor. This is the way I remembered her sitting whenever she had pants on. After many of our exchanges she would say, "God, it's been a long time." She would punctuate this by jabbing a little knife into a nut-covered cheese ball she had made, spreading the cheese over another cracker. "Your hair's so short," she finally seemed comfortable enough to say to me.

"Once a harlequin, always a harlequin," I said deadpan.

"Harlequin?" she said. "I forget what that is."

We talked about Chicago, her old neighborhood and my old neighborhood, high school, and the times we slept at each other's houses. We didn't talk about her being a giant. In my family the policy was not to call attention to her differences, but we talked about her among ourselves. Grandma would cluck, "Poor Nanna," after each visit. I was only eight months younger than she, but even when we were babies, Anna was three times my size. I can still hear my aunt, calling after her as she ran into the yard to play, telling her to be careful of the other children, as if she were a Great Dane loping into the midst of us.

After Anna told me about her promotion and transfer to the post office in Waupaca, and I tried to explain the different ways I was able to make a living as a performer, there was a lull in the conversation, and the noise of Anna shifting her weight on the book box sounded the way a tree groans just before it falls.

"I hear you have a boyfriend." I knew this was going to embarrass her, but I didn't know how else to break into it.

She put her hands palms down on her knees. "Mike," she said.

"Tell me about him."

"He was one of the carpenters working on the house. We got friendly, and then we got close."

"Close?"

She hugged her knees, looked down, and smiled, like it was high school and this was her first boyfriend. I was the one with boyfriends in high school, not Anna. When I slept at her house, she'd pump me for every detail. "What did he say? What did you say?"

And when I first learned to kiss, I promised I would show her. Setting the stage for her that night was far more dramatic than any real kiss I'd had up to then. I put some red gym shorts over the lamp and a 45 on the player called "The Look of Love." Her cocker spaniel, Puddles, named because his eyes were muddy pools of devotion, watched the record go around. I had Anna sit on the edge of her bed while I went out of her room to come back in again. Then I walked up to where she was waiting and put a hand on each side of her big face, looked into her eyes and said, "I'm going to kiss you." She fell backwards on her bed laughing, which was a long fall for her and hard on the bed. Puddles jumped onto her stomach and barked at her. I climbed onto her and tried to throttle her, pleading for her to get serious. The needle came to the saddest part of the record. She sat up and set Puddles on the floor. I imagined I was the most serious kisser. I put my face close to hers. "The first one is the most important. Dry your mouth on your sleeve like I am; our lips have to be dry. Don't open your mouth and don't breathe."

Even then I knew it wasn't experience that Anna needed. She never had a boyfriend, she didn't pretend that she didn't want one. She approached her makeup like a science. She set her hair, painted her nails, pulled away her eyebrows with melted wax. I remember her identifying the shape of her face from a makeup diagram in *Seventeen* magazine. She was pleased to find that hers was heart-shaped and from then on would point out other people with heart-shaped faces whenever she saw them.

I looked at her with her tiny knife poised in the air. She was looking back at me, as if to say, "Don't think what you're thinking." She picked at the label of her beer bottle, sucked in her breath, then let it out. "None of you ever thought I'd be with anyone, did you?"

"Well, I think we expected it would be harder for you than for some people."

"It was. Mike's the first one, and Mom and Dad won't admit he exists."

"Why?"

"Because he's older, because he's been married more than once, because he's had some trouble along the way."

"He's not what they expected," I said.

"They didn't expect *anything*. But now that I have someone, they don't approve. They're looking into some book for the right person for me. You'd never find me in those books in the first place. But that's enough, we don't have to spend our whole wad on this kind of talk." She dug into the cheese ball. "It'll be good just to have some time together. I planned things out. We can change anything you don't like. Tonight I'll take you to a good fish fry."

"When am I going to meet Mike?"

"He's hoping to make it to the fry, but he's always stuck with a lot of overtime this part of the year, trying to get things built before the cold sets in. Tomorrow we're going to play an out-of-season softball game."

"Why are you going to play out of season?"

"Baldy's and Mary's, the bar that sponsors us, is having a closing-out party tomorrow night."

"A what?"

"When a bar closes, they can't sell their liquor to the next owner—tax reasons, or something like that. So they have a party and serve it free."

"Sounds as though people may be getting a bit drunk."

"A bit," she said. "Then on Sunday I want to take you to the zoo."

"Waupaca has a zoo?"

"Well, it's a little one, but yeah. It was a community effort. The Lions Club sponsored the lions. Other groups sponsored other parts. The hardware store donated cans and cans of paint. The high school kids have done a lot of the painting and help keep up the grounds. I'm surprised you didn't hear about it in the papers last year."

"About what?"

"Someone tried to kill one of our elks."

"I'm not sure what elks are."

"They're like deer here, only bigger. I think these came from Wyoming."

"Someone tried to kill one?"

"Yeah, it was in the paper here for two weeks. A twelve-point male, a gorgeous animal, something they could have used in a beer commercial. Everybody was shook up. Someone went out there in the night and filled it full of arrows. Three of the high school kids found him when they were doing their chores in the morning. He was still alive, heaving with all these arrows in him, and blood coming out of his nostrils. One of the high schoolers ran to get help. When the vet and the sherrif and the kid came back, they found the other two kids fighting with each other. One of them, it seems, had been running in circles, trying to find a rock or something to end it for the buck. The other one was standing his ground over the thing, telling him he wouldn't let it be killed . . ."

"So the buck's okay?"

"Well, he's alive."

I'd been looking forward to a fry at a Wisconsin tavern: the knotty-pine kind we found when we summered at the lake as kids. I'd even mentioned this to Anna on the phone. But she chose a more modern place in Stevens Point, something I might have found on any strip in the Chicago area, a place with anchors on the walls, a circular salad buffet, and a huge fish-tank wall that separated the bar from the restaurant.

Anna had dressed up in an orange silk top she had sewn for herself, and orange earings that looked diminutive on her ears. While she took great care to make up her face, I decided to follow the cue and bring my black suit out of the car along with an orange bow tie I use in some of my performances.

We went together as an odd couple to the Schooner Inn, where it seems the locals were proud to come. Many of the ladies looked as though they had had Friday afternoon hair appointments. Anna, who wears a hairstyle reminiscent of the bouffant she wore in high school, had fluffed hers up, too. She didn't try to understate her visibility in the way she used to. She did not slouch or talk softly. And there was even one point where she spoke up to me as if I had said something on the subject that needed to be corrected. "All the upstairs doors in my house are going to be custom fit. It's expensive, but Mike figured out a shortcut, some way that he can use standard doors and add on to them." I realized she was still troubled by my imitation of her that afternoon.

In the salad line, she introduced me to two married women with perfectly stiff hairdos. She said, "This is my cousin Jane from Chicago. She's a visiting teacher at the college." She didn't tell them I was a mime, but I had a great inclination to waddle away from the buffet like Charlie Chaplin. When the ladies returned to their table, I could see they were telling their husbands what the story was. The husbands nodded, chewing, and went back to their steaks, reassured. I had the keen feeling throughout the evening that we were being watched, but whenever I looked around, people would look away.

Anna went to the bar several times to call Mike. Each time she came back to the table flushed. And when I finally asked her what was wrong, she said there were troublemakers in there. I tried to look through the aquarium wall of the bar to see who these troublemakers were, but all I could make out were the reflections in the glass of all the people in the lighted restaurant, as if they were sitting at little tables inside the tank, and the fish were swimming around them.

"I'll go make the call for you."

"Not with the bow tie and all," she said. "They're tanked up. They'll give you just as much of a hard time." So neither of us made another call to Mike and he must have gotten tied up, because he never came.

*   *   *

I slept on the couch near the stove that night. Before I went to sleep, my thoughts wandered through the reasons I felt Anna had been showing me off at the restaurant. Maybe Anna thought that if the people in the restaurant could see that we had known each other for a long time, it would make her more real to them.

But did I know her? When I tried to do her in the doorway, it wasn't her *at all*. I realized it was only the smallness of the doorway that I had been imitating. I've done so many people and animals and household appliances, she should have been an easy subject.

When the adults weren't around, my brothers and sisters used to say, "Do Anna! Come on, do Anna!" But walking into a mime is like walking the length of a diving board. On the first bounce you know if you're going to pull it off. I tried a few times to make the approach with Anna, but couldn't get her. At the last minute, I would be unsure, and the sense I had of her would swell into something impossible and painful. I couldn't contain her. I fell asleep with the idea of standing on the edge of the diving board.

I've slept on couches before, in many people's houses, so when I heard Mike come in, I barely stirred. I heard the talking, and later I heard the bed moving in the other room. It registered that two people were making love. But in the dark there, almost asleep, I wasn't expecting to hear Anna's voice. I don't suppose it was so different from other women's cries at those times, but it was surely Anna's voice, and then I was awake and disturbed. For all the pleasure associated with it, there is also a beseeching quality in this sound. It has to do with coming to the edge of loneliness, being helpless in the face of it. There is that moment where you can be everything—or nothing—depending on how the other cares for you.

Even after they were quiet, I couldn't go back to sleep. What was it like to sleep with Anna? I should know; I'd spent enough nights in her room. I'd hook my arm over the side of her bed to avoid rolling into the crater her weight made in the mattress. Her bed was really two mattresses, a double bed and a single bed strapped crosswise to the end of it. Puddles would try to sleep between the two of us, but he would be delegated to the bottom of my side of the bed, since there was still a lot of room left there, and even though it was hard to see him in the dark, it seemed that he would be sitting up and watching us, as if he could make sense of our conversations.

She'd ask me questions, not wanting me to fall asleep. Questions about what I thought of her, and if I thought there was a way she could make friends. Because of her longing, I found the simplest ways to mislead Anna about the world. I painted possibilities for her that I didn't believe. It was just a matter of people getting to know her I would say—just a matter of time.

I had stopped sleeping over by my sophomore year. I was involved with my own friends. In Anna's junior year she maintained that her height was seven feet six inches. But I'm sure she was at least eight. She stopped going to school. My mother would say, "Call your cousin. She's depressed." I hated this. Sometimes my aunt would call. "Talk to Anna," my mother would whisper with her hand cupped over the phone. But I'd shake my hand and wave her away.

Close to that time we were all shocked by a feature story about Anna in the *Tribune*. My mother saw it first. She pushed the paper in front of me at the breakfast table and stood up abruptly to call my aunt.

GIANT GIRL RESOLVED TO BECOME MONUMENT AT EL was the headline in the local section. My mother was on the phone, "Helen, they say she has been loitering in the El station for weeks. The same stop every day."

I stared, bleary-eyed, at a photograph of Anna in the paper. Anna, whom I had never thought of as part of the world, had been photographed at the busiest El stop in Chicago, and this picture was printed in hundreds of thousands of newspapers across the state.

"Helen!" my mother hissed into the phone. "You knew she wasn't in school. Didn't you wonder where she was? They say she stands right where the doors of the train open up. People have to walk around her to get off and on. She won't answer the guards when they question her."

I won't forget that photograph, Anna's back to the camera, her head and shoulders standing out of the crowd like a tree in a marsh. The absurdity—what made it a good photograph, and perhaps also a good story—was that not one face or body in the crowd was acknowledging Anna's enormous presence amidst them.

Only the photograph recognized her power—the frozen image of the impression she made in a crowd of bodies, and how the crowd had no choice but to stream around her.

I still have that photo tucked away in my performance scrapbook. Even when I was sixteen, looking at that picture for the first time, I wanted my cousin to turn and face her photographer. I wanted to see her realize that, at least for that moment, she was being understood.

The publicity caused the police to be involved, and she ended up in a psychiatric unit. I don't know if they talked to her about the difficulties of being a giant. I'm sure they talked about "fitting in," because her behavior turned around. She got a starting position in the post office through Job Corps. When I went to college, Anna started a checking account, got raises and promotions. Eventually she was transferred to Waupaca in a supervisory position. I received a card from her in my dormitory one day. "Puddles died," she wrote, "and I'm still sad about it. I won't be getting another until I'm more settled here. This is a very small town. I see the same people over and over again and they see me. I figure eventually they're going to get used to me. . . ."

Anna and Mike were up before I was. They were making breakfast sounds, and the smell of coffee eventually drew me out from beneath my covers. The stove had gone too far down. I put my coat on and my wool socks because the cement was cold.

"Here's Jane, Mike," Anna said with great enthusiasm.

He was perhaps in his mid-forties, stout in his work clothes. His hands were short-fingered and ruddy around his coffee cup. I think he probably thought that he smiled. But it was really just a quick nod.

"Hello," he said, clearing his throat.

My short hair, after it has been slept on, tends to resemble that of a hedgehog's. I wished I could look less bizarre.

"Why don't you stoke that thing, Mike, while I start the eggs," Anna said.

The smell of bacon frying and the burning of new wood in the stove began working against the dampness of the cement, making it more like a home.

After breakfast, Anna showed me some wooden figures Mike

had carved. Most of them were of wildlife: a squirrel running over
the branch of a tree, a duck in flight. He was very good at conveying the motion in the bodies. Mike stood near the stove with
his coffee cup and thumbed through the morning paper while we
commented on each figure. But he was paying enough attention
to realize we were finished because he pulled out another shoe
box. "I've started to do some people too," he said. They were not as
true to form, but there was an earnestness in some of his detail—an
apron bunched in a woman's hand, a boy with bulging pockets—
that made the figures appealing in their own way.

The Waupaca Township field is like other small-town athletic
fields. It is in a prominent location on the highway into town.
The town marker (POPULATION 3,862) is directly across the road.
Except for the two cyclone-fence backstops, the two diamonds,
two trash barrels, and a pair of six-tier bleachers, the park is grass.
Standing in the field, one can see the surrounding businesses: an
auto body shop in a large aluminum prefab building; a house with
a lot full of school buses; a co-op with two grain elevators like
shoulders on either side of it. Nothing was too far away. As people
began gathering in the field, I imagined I could almost hear the
doors of their houses slamming and cars starting as they left home
to come there.

The sky was a gray canopy, bulging, heavy, and holding water
over our heads. The few spectators and the team members stood
in hopeful but uncertain postures; it could so surely rain in the
next minute. Some of the people dusted the paths between bases
with sand to make them less muddy.

Anna started the women's softball team three years ago. That
was how she made her first friends in town. Mike is on the men's
team. Since they were playing a casual game, the two teams mixed
together. Mike and Anna were split up, so one or the other came
to stand with me while they waited to bat. Mike brought me a
plastic cup filled with beer, which was cold in my already cold
hand. Anna was playing first base. She stood with her feet wide
apart, calling at plays, yodeling and yelling, having a good time.

"How'd she ever find a mitt to fit her?" I asked Mike.

"Had it custom made," he said.

I was having trouble thinking of conversation. But there was always the game to watch, and Mike, though taciturn, was comfortable to be with. He had the slightest overbite, giving a touch of vulnerability to an otherwise rough face.

"She looks absolutely frightening," I said.

"Yeah." Mike laughed for the first time, letting his teeth jut out. "You gotta believe. No batter can run as fast as he might when he's got Anna waiting for him on first."

"You should carve her like that," I said.

He looked out at her from underneath the visor of his cap. "No," he said. I knew he wasn't finished. He seemed to need to spend a certain amount of time between words. "It would have to be Michelangelo," he said. "I bought a book of him in Milwaukee. It cost a hundred and twenty-five dollars."

He was right. We could see it in the muscles in her legs, as she strained forward waiting for the next play, and in her hands, which were both like a man's and a woman's and then like something else. Mike couldn't carve her into a figure that fit into a shoe box any more than I could make my own hands resemble hers simply by copying the movement of them.

When I was nine, I used to stand on the sidelines with my friends and watch her play touch football with the older boys. She was fascinating to all of us, and I played the part of her representative. "She's only ten," I would say, defying our family taboo about calling attention to her size. "She ate forty-seven pancakes for breakfast last Saturday."

Anna stood for the possibility of myth in our daily lives. And for a while, I earned a certain admiration from the others because I knew her. This was when I first realized that I had a special knack for pointing out certain details in life. But eventually Anna was no longer an amusing wonder. She was as real and floundering in her adolescence as we were. And I suppose, where she was once an ideal, she later became only an exaggeration of what was painful in ourselves.

A thin man with long sideburns got caught in a pickle between first and second. Anna had the ball and shuffled toward him. He headed back to second. Anna whipped the ball over his head. He spun round and made it back to first before she could touch him or the base.

"Go, man! Get past that big hog!" A fist came up out of a group of five men standing on the sidelines.

"Jesus, what's he doing here?" Mike muttered.

"What? Who?" I said.

"That guy in the letter jacket."

After some of the men in the group shifted their positions, I could see the man in the letter jacket. Levis, boots, about thirty years old. The men around him were different ages, mostly older. Some wore hunting clothes, a couple wore jeans and flannel shirts like Mike. All of them seemed affected by the diffuse charisma of the younger man. One would chuckle and pass some joke on to another, who would laugh and spit on the ground. But the flow of their interaction seemed to originate always from this young man, who was very handsome. He stood with the tips of his fingers in his jeans' pockets. He kept his eyes on Anna, and he must have been saying things under his breath, because the others would laugh and look toward her.

"What does he have to do with her?" I asked.

"Good question," Mike said. "He's a troublemaker. He's out for her. He was at the Schooner Inn last night. Didn't she tell you? This has been a problem since she came."

"What do you mean out for her?"

"Out for her. Can't let her be."

"Why?"

"Who knows? Anna's convinced herself that the guy applied for a job at the post office and didn't get it or something. That's not it, though. There've been others like him, drawn to her in a hateful way."

The game ended in rain, with Anna standing on first base. She stood out there longer than anyone, as if the umpire might change his mind. Her wet clothes were becoming translucent and defining the lines of her body. Her makeup was running. She would be embarrassed, I thought, if she could see how she looked. Mike and I waited for her, getting water in our beer. The man in the letter jacket stood around. The blond hair on his head got dark in the rain. His friends shifted their weight on their feet, blew on their hands. It was getting colder by the minute.

*   *   *

I took a Saturday afternoon nap in Anna's room, while she and Mike watched a football game on TV. I think the smell of the cement made me dream about the El station. I was walking along the tracks. Someone had sent me to find Anna. I still hadn't found her but met the man in the letter jacket everywhere, coming down the stairs, hoisting himself up onto the platform from the tracks. I spent the whole dream trying to get to her before he did.

Anna woke me hours later. She had a bag of burgers and some milk. "You've slept a long time. Fill your stomach now, or you won't keep up with the drinking tonight."

It was dark, and I was groggy and disoriented. "Where's Mike?"

"He has a roof in Steven's Point to finish. He'll meet us later."

Anna and I went early to the closing-out party. This way we were able to get a table before the crowds piled in. I thought I had known what to expect: there would be more men than women, many farmers and mill workers. I expected that people would get very drunk, and I'd get a little drunk and watch them. I looked forward to it. I hadn't expected to get involved.

Baldy's and Mary's was downtown. When we came to the door, Anna stopped for a minute and adjusted herself. She brought out a mirror that looked as tiny as a postage stamp in her hand, checked her lips, her eyes, and the blush on her cheeks. Cars, driving by, made a sticky sound on the wet pavement. A banner cut out of a bed sheet with the word WELCOME hung over the door. The paint was running. Pale red drops of water beaded from the edges and dripped on the sidewalk. When Anna opened the door, there was a vacuum sound like one's ears being unclogged.

The bar was dark. We were the first ones there. As we walked, the sound of our heels echoed over the wooden floor. There was one long bar with a mirror behind it. The bartender was bald, as I would have expected. He watched Anna and me as we came in. "Wait, I'll introduce you," she said. During her introductions, Baldy looked at me with the studied indifference I've seen in many bartenders. But he had small, brown, wary eyes. Mary, a wiry, middle-aged woman, wearing a T-shirt and an apron, pointed her finger like she was shooting us and went on working at a grill behind the bar. I expected this was another friendly sort of bartender's greeting.

"Baldy, your bottles are already gone?" Anna said, gesturing toward the empty shelves in front of the mirror.

He looked up at Anna. "We'd a gone crazy—pouring out individual drinks. We made Wapatui."

There were five tables on the floor constructed out of wooden cable spools. Two stacked together made them high enough to put stools around them. In the center of each table was a steel tub. We walked over to one of the tables and looked into the tub.

"What's in here?" Anna called back to the bar.

"Everything," Baldy answered.

It was hard to tell what color the punch was. It seemed a sort of amber red. Maraschino cherries and canned pineapple rings floated in it. As we settled onto stools, Anna pulled two plastic cups from a stack and filled them with a ladle. It tasted sweet and very strong.

We were joined shortly by three young women, each of them wearing a shoulder bag. They didn't remove their purses, as if they hadn't decided they would stay. Anna knew one of them slightly. A young man, whom no one knew, and his girlfriend sat down. The last two stools were taken by an older man and his wife.

People kept coming through the doors. I realized I'd better pace my drinking. The liquor was much stronger than it tasted. Anna huddled over me, and we were able to talk in the privacy of the noise. We became used to people standing near our table reaching around us to fill their glasses.

"What do you think?" Anna asked.

"It's wild. How come they're selling out?"

"Baldy's had two heart attacks. Mary gave him an ultimatum— no bar, or no wife."

Sometimes we were quiet, and I could listen to the snatches of conversation about gardens, or factories, or casseroles. Sometimes there would be hick Wisconsin syntax shouted across the room. "Com'on over—why don't cha, hey?" and I'd want to nudge Anna to share the distinction between this place and Chicago. But then I remembered that Anna felt no kinship for Chicago. She was less a part of that than I was of this.

"Do you like Mike?" She was bending close to my ear.

"Yeah," I shouted.

I was telling Anna about the Mardi Gras in New Orleans, because the crowd reminded me of my time there. She began to seem distracted as I was talking. We were facing the bar, and she kept looking in the mirror behind it. I finally looked into the mirror too. It was the man in the letter jacket. He was leaning over his glass on the bar, but he was watching Anna. She had turned away from him and was laughing with the girl next to her—trying to ignore him. His cronies were standing around him on the floor, but he had his back to them. They were all laughing and drinking together. One or another would look over at him, make some mental note, and then look again into his drink.

Anna seemed resolved to ignore him. She had struck up a conversation with the husband and wife. I stared at him, trying to lock his eyes, the way people will do with cats. But his eyes wouldn't leave Anna. I looked around the room. Little dramas were developing throughout the crowd that wouldn't have happened an hour ago. A woman crying in her hand while her boyfriend tried to talk to her. A young man pleading into the pay phone, waiting, nodding his head, opening and closing his fist against the wall. Many people making a point with each other, emphatically pointing their fingers, carefully slurring the words, trying to explain something.

Anna wasn't drunk. It took a lot to get her there because of her size. I was on my way. So was the man in the letter jacket. Now he was leaning his back against the bar and facing us. He had begun to mix with his friends again. They all seemed glad of it. Then I heard what he was saying.

"What a sow! Look at her. They shouldn't let things like that out of the cave."

Anna's hand was tight around her glass. He was getting louder.

"Hey! You big sexy thing. Hey! Look at me when I talk to you." Anna wouldn't look up, but I did. He was quiet, weaving a little on his feet, waiting for Anna to look at him. He began chipping little pieces off his plastic cup, throwing them in her direction. The woman next to me was murmuring her disapproval to her husband.

"Somebody should round that fellow up," the husband said.

The young couple watched the man in the letter jacket the way they might watch someone on TV. The three women next to Anna looked down at their hands.

The little pieces of plastic were collecting in Anna's hair. I looked over at Baldy. He had decided he wasn't going to do anything yet. He had a heart condition. The man in the letter jacket had chipped away his entire cup—started a new one. Anna's hair was full of the pieces. She wouldn't look up. People all around us were getting drunk. Perhaps it seemed this was just a part of it.

Anna clamped the table edge so hard there were white streaks on the top of her hands. I felt sick.

"I have to go to the bathroom."

Anna pinned my wrist to the table. "Don't go."

I broke away, grabbed my bag, and pushed through the crowd to the ladies' room. A woman was coming out of the stall. I shoved ahead of the other women in line, said, "Let me by. I'm going to be sick!" Closed myself in the stall, leaned over the toilet. Nothing would come. There was sweat in my eyes, my face was burning. I kept thinking about Anna and how she would bear anything— she would bear it until he was all played out. She had hopes for this town, thought she could rely on her own durability, just like she relied on that little stove to heat her house. I'm sure she believed it was just a matter of time before most of them stopped being afraid of her. But it was taking too long; it hurt her. It was hurting me, and reasons as simple as these are the reasons that make you brave.

Mime is an art of absorption. If one day I find that I imitate a rooster rather well, it means that somewhere along the lines of my life I have seen roosters and taken in the impressions they have made. But I mustn't think too much about those roosters, not about why they lift their feet in a certain way or what they can see out of each side of their head, because all those thoughts confuse me and cause me to lose confidence in my particular talent. This has seemed excuse enough for my detachment. But there's been another reason.

I left the stall and pushed ahead of the women at the sink. I rubbed cold water over my face, dried it with my sleeve. In my bag I found my tin of whiteface, my grease pencils. The white spread quickly, changed my face to nothing. A girl in the corner said, "What's she doing?" I put the little bit of red on my mouth, a long vertical line through each of my eyes. I pressed my bag

into the arms of a girl in the corner and told her to watch it
for me.

I moved through the crowd quickly, before anyone had a chance
to really see me. I'd see surprise begin to register on a man or
woman's face, then I was past them.

The man in the letter jacket was still standing a few paces in
front of our table. His feet were apart. He was pointing at Anna.
His friends had backed away from him. His litany sounded frightening, even from a distance. My face was turned so he couldn't
see it. One of the girls at the table gasped and covered her mouth
when I stepped up from the rung of her stool onto the table.
"Hey!" he shouted. I stood with my back to him facing Anna.

The voices in the crowd were still rubbing together, like pieces
in an engine. She looked up at me. With my hands, I made a
square around my face. A face just for her. I made the sign for a
tear. I gave my face the expression of great sadness, none of which
could be said in words. It was all in my face, what I gave to Anna.

He was shouting into my back. I could hear him. As I looked
at Anna, he seemed so weak compared to her. But I didn't think
so much about him. I wasn't thinking about how some people
need to be the master of their world—not just their life, but their
little world and every perceivable object in it—and how that is
another difference between people and animals. An animal would
never just destroy something because he didn't understand it. Or
misunderstand it only because it was different, or because it was
something great and beautiful, but not exactly the same as itself.
Or how the difference can be as small as the difference between
a man and a woman. But the differences were all there, and they
made up the engine in that room, and that was the sound like a
roar in my ears. I was standing, drunk, on a table in a Wisconsin
bar. Not too drunk to know it, but drunk enough to do what I
was doing. And everyone else was drunk. But I didn't think about
everyone else, how all of us in that room, including me, are unset-
tled by our own humanity, how we bleed it but can't stand the
sight of it.

So, I have to say again that, standing there facing Anna, I wasn't
thinking. I was a mime, on the edge of the diving board, poised
for a backward dive. And when I had looked at her long enough,
I was ready to take in the man in the letter jacket. He kept

shouting. I could feel him behind me. But it really didn't matter, because many of his traits I'd absorbed before I'd ever seen him. I mean they weren't unique to him. I was ready to do him. As I turned, I felt I had his body now. And when I faced him, I *was* him; if a man could be a clenched fist with white knuckles that held nothing, that's what he was. It was right.

I hadn't seen anything after I had turned on the man. In that moment my vision had reversed, like a movie camera turned into a projector. I became a short film of his miserable life. I became handsome, gave myself a letter jacket, stood in the center of every-thing, just the way he did; and then slowly, I became ugly, just the way he was, the way a lot of us are. The engine sound died. No crowd, just one man screaming—a faraway call like an angry crow's. The air was being pushed out of me. I felt faint, then weightless.

Anna said he had lunged for my legs. She had picked me up by the waist and carried me out the backdoor of the bar. She carried me to an abandoned pickup, which was leaning against a wet telephone pole. She pulled me up with her into the back. I had to hang over the side to vomit something that had been creeping up my esophagus. I coughed and cried, came back to where Anna was and punched her in the chest. She laughed and put her hands around my shoulders.

"That was good," she said.

I was still crying.

"Animals wouldn't do that to each other," I said. "They wouldn't do what he did."

"They do it too," Anna said. "I've read about it. Animals do it too."

So it was hopeless.

"When are we going to be happy, Anna?" I was trying to find a place in the truck bed to lay my head. And I think I was trying to find a way to ask her forgiveness. But all I could say was, "I hate the rain. It feels like it's been raining for weeks." Sometimes I cry like that when I've been drinking and when I become too much a part of the world.

Now I'm sitting in the car in front of the Waupaca County jail. And I'm waiting for Anna. For a moment I had a fantasy that she might come back down those steps as an average-sized person, and I tried to imagine what would be different about the way we were together. But I realized that was a trick I was playing on myself, as usual, making things simpler than they are or even should be.

Mike's in jail because he and some of his friends went back to the bar to fight for Anna. The man in the letter jacket had already vanished before he got there. So they ended up fighting with everyone, making it into a kind of free-for-all. Anna says he feels like a jerk. But I think if he had the option, he would have made a life-size sculpture of Anna as beautiful as a Michelangelo and set it up in the middle of Baldy's and Mary's. I know how it feels to want to show everyone exactly what is so hard to see.

Those who were in that crowd at Baldy's and Mary's will be talking about this for weeks. Most of them will say the man in the letter jacket started it. Some will think it was me, or they'll think it was Mike. No one would blame Anna, but many are angry with her without knowing why. "My God! She's a human being," my grandmother used to say. It was a refrain we heard so regularly it stopped having meaning. And as long as she was out of our lives, in some other place, the enormous fact of her couldn't hurt us. But the fact has always been in us.

And whatever is happening with Mike, Anna still intends to show me the zoo. "I'm so tired," I'll tell her, "and don't feel like looking at another thing." But I know her heart is set on showing me these places. The leaves are still dripping down the windshield, gathering one by one in my view, and it's all silence here except for that dripping. She tells me that the kids have painted everything on the zoo grounds bright colors, the picnic tables and even the tree stumps. We'll see lions, she says, peacocks, reindeer, the heroic elk.

The Profound Theory
of Complementarity

Jan Ramjerdi

*If one is inside the other
will be outside or vice versa.*[1]

Joy and Alice do not always maintain a harmonious and balanced relationship.

When the fog rolls in, Alice is afraid to open the back door.

When the fog rolls in what Alice does is she does not let the
back door slam shut like it does if she does not hold it by the
handle and it slams shut and Joy wails "O my mortal body." What
she does is she holds it by the handle this way with her thumb
on the knob until the latch catches with an undisturbing click that
is such a soft unobtrusive click that it could not possibly disturb
a word on the page Joy was reading.

What Joy was reading when the fog rolled in was:

---

[1]Avatamsaka Sutra (Japanese: *Kegon*, "Flower Garden"): Doctrine of the World
of Totalistic Harmony Mutually Relating and Penetrating.

Walburga Oesterreich, a dark, plumpish, deeply-emotional woman who was in the thirty-second year of her life.[2]

Like Alice, thinks Joy, like Alice is in the thirty-second year of her life like Alice is dark like Alice is deeply emotional (Joy is not deeply emotional, Joy is rational, deeply rational) but Alice is not, Alice is not plumpish like I am. I am plumpish.

"Do you think I'm getting fat?" Joy had said that morning rolling over and over in their bed and the bed boards had creaked and Alice had groaned and said "Shhhhh. Be quiet. I want to hear this," and the radio downstairs had said, "the pod of two hundred and forty-three whales on Cape Breton's Chetticamp Beach. Hundreds of volunteers worked feverishly through the night to roll them back in the water, but by this morning they had beached themselves again. They are keeping the whales wet and rolling them from side to side to keep the blood circulating. Experts say if they do not get them back in the water by tonight, they will all perish. Ten have died already." "The poor things," Alice had said. "What about me?" Joy had said. "You belong on land." "You don't care," Joy had said. "You don't care if my blood keeps circulating." (The indifference of her hair, Joy had thought, the indifference of the deep dark sea.)

Lately Joy was feeling that way, lately she was envying the most abject animal: the mottled cat howling at the bedroom window last night. (It's Fellini," Alice had said. "It's my baby." "No it's not," Joy had said. "It's me. I'm your baby.") Lately there was between them every night this wailing, these rats coughing everywhere, these two hundred and forty-three beached whales spouting sand.

Lately Joy was feeling this way, like her body could swell to overwhelming proportions ("To be in any form—what is that?"[3]): multiply and divide and multiply and divide and mass all its selves in a fogbank (Chalk everywhere), abandon the deep deep oceans of Joy within ("I hate you ocean."[4]), and thus thud like a maddened

[2]Alan Hynd, *The Case of the Attic Lover and other true crime stories* (New York: Pyramid Books), p. 9.
[3]Walt Whitman, "Song of Myself."
[4]Charles-Pierre Baudelaire, "Obsession," *Les Fleurs du Mal.*

herd thud like a maddened herd of whales upon the sand. ("This is the emerging monster to whom I am attached."[5])

Lately Joy was feeling that way. Lately she was hard to satisfy. "You're never satisfied." The bedroom door slams. "Where are you going?" The bathroom door slams. "Where are you going?" The kitchen door slams. "WHERE ARE YOU GOING?" Alice said she was going to Paris. "I'll bring you back our nuptial shadows." The back door slams. "Bring them back in black silk," Joy had said. "Bring them back in black silk crepe."

When the fog rolls in what Joy does is she lies down on the fainting couch and reads:

Walburga Oesterreich, a dark, plumpish, deeply-emotional woman who was in the thirty-second year of her life, in the year of Our Lord nineteen hundred and three, was, according to several doctors who examined her, a nymphomaniac in the classic tradition. The woman was, purely and simply, sex mad. She thought of nothing but.[6]

Alice.

Alice at the back door.

Alice on the fogbound beach working feverishly through the night pushing pulling rolling Joy in the sand to keep the blood circulating, keep the blood circulating, you need to keep the blood circulating—or it stops, Joy thinks, I am that old ("the same old blood"[7]).

Joy is forty, that is, she thinks she could see out the window if the fog ever lifts she could see there was a hill, she was over it, she was on the other side of it, it was a blueberry moor she had walked there not long ago, it seemed not very long ago, maybe it was only two weeks ago she had walked there with Alice, they had picked pints, quarts, metric litres, of blueberries when she was ripe, when they were ripe, they had picked so many they had given them away to the neighbors to the old old neighbors,

[5]Herman Melville, *Moby-Dick, or The Whale* (New York: Penguin Books), p. 684.

[6]Hynd, *The Case of the Attic Lover*, p. 9.

[7]Walt Whitman, "I Sing the Body Electric."

none of them were under seventy-five ("I'll be like them soon, soon I will be saying 'I've had a hard life.' ") and now they were all over, all the blueberries, all that urgent fruit, and youth, and Joy was over, the blueberry moors, that were all those hills, that hill, she was over it, it was behind her, she could see if the fog ever lifts it was there still there but it was behind her, and Alice was their ("She plays and she melts in all her prime."[8]) summer, it was almost over, soon they'd be old ladies, the leaves were curling up, soon they'd have to learn how to crochet fancywork, she was in a state, she was in a state of decline, soon they'd have to sell pies at church fairs ("I am not happy about this."), soon they'd have to have their hair dyed blue.

Joy reads:

It would appear that in the year 1903, Mrs. Oesterreich's sex graph was still very much in the ascendant while her husband at forty, had, unfortunately begun to run downhill. Now, as practically any doctor can tell you, a combination like that bodes no good. And it certainly didn't in the case of the Oesterreichs.[9]

She'll leave me I know for some body young some body young and macrobiotically svelte with whole grain breasts and no body fat. Some body comfortable with a diet high in fiber, a diet of bok choy and tofu, tamari and mullet, dried kelp and brown rice, some body who's examinate for instance, yes, as brown rice and dried kelp. Yes. The lady at the health food store, for instance, she's that type, all bones and feather—she could live her whole life in a birdbath, she does, she lives her whole life in a birdbath, she splashes daily in the ice-cold sea, "It's good for your circulation," she says. "I run five miles each morning on the beach."

"What would you like for dinner?" Alice had asked Joy the night before. Joy wanted scalloped fettuccine Alfredo à la lobster gambado and a Caesar salad, a real Caesar salad with Parmesan

---

[8]William Blake, "Couplets and Fragments," *Ideas of Good and Evil.*
[9]Hynd, *The Case of the Attic Lover,* p. 9.

cheese and anchovies and a raw egg yolk, that would be good.
"Too much cholesterol, too much fat, too much sodium, and no
raw egg yolk, raw egg yolk gives you salmonella poisoning." Alice
had made brown rice and lentils. She mashed the lentils with
boiled turnips and carrots. Joy thought it tasted like the ground
must taste to leguminous plants. "Here, put some cayenne pepper
on it," Alice had said. "I'm sick of cayenne pepper," Joy had said.
"The lady at the health food store says it's good for your circulation." "Sex. Sex is good for my circulation."

Joy had said this like a beached whale ("A whole Leviathan
could decay!"[10]), she was that dry. She dreamed that night a dream
about dried-out eggs. She told Alice in the morning: "There were
two of them in the pan, two fried eggs in the frying pan. They
were overcooked the way I hate them—all crispy with the yolk
hard and one yolk was cracked, a trickle of egg yolk oozing out.
It was disgusting." "You're just a little bit depressed," Alice had
said. "It's the fog." "It's not the fog," Joy had said. "It's the fog,"
Alice had said. "It's not the fog," Joy said. "It's not the fog. It's
menopause and then death. That's what it is."

Joy was on the fainting couch, she was reading in a glaucous fog,
she was thinking flocks of whales beach themselves in similar condi-
tions, she was thinking: What happened to their migratory patterns?
("Oh the beautiful patterns of my blood.") What happened to their
migratory patterns? It's not youth something has to happen it's time
passing something has to happen it's time passing plain ordinary time
passing fog time time in which a whole Leviathan could decay ("I
am nearly half sand!") time something has to happen. What do they
do if two hundred and forty-three whales perish on the beach?

Such was the situation with Walburga Oesterreich when one
of the sewing machines in the apron factory broke down
one day and the Singer Sewing Machine Company, which
serviced the machines, sent a repairman to the factory. Well,
not exactly a man.[11]

---

[10]Arthur Rimbaud, "The Drunken Boat."
[11]Hynd, *The Case of the Attic Lover*, p. 10.

Alice.
(Alice sexually wanting anything.)
Alice.
(Have you ever loved the body of a woman?)
Alice.

Joy reads:

A boy, rather. He was only seventeen, his name was Otto
Sanhuber, and he was an undersized squirt with watery blue
eyes, an open, guileless countenance and practically no chin
at all. But the moment Walburga Oesterreich laid eyes on
little Otto she, connoisseur of the male animal that she was,
saw something in the boy that everybody else had
overlooked.[12]

Alice.
(My *Deus ex Machina*.)[13]
Alice.
(Call any body Alice and she gets to be Alice.[14])

She saw to it there was plenty of repair work for him at the
factory. And then one raw morning in the autumn, she con-
trived to have Otto call at the Oesterreich home—a top-
heavy mustard-colored frame house—to fix a sewing machine
in, of all places, the bedroom.[15]

Alice at the back door.
("A threshold is a sacred thing."[16])
"What will make you happy?" Alice had asked.

---

[12]*Ibid.*, p. 10.
[13]"Latin: 'god out of the machine.' In Greek drama the use of a god lowered
by a mechanism of some sort onto the stage to rescue the hero or untangle
the plot. Serious modern writers avoid the *deus ex machina* though it has sometimes been used in comedy." (Beckson and Ganz, *A Dictionary of Literary Terms*).
[14]See, for instance, Gertrude Stein, *The Autobiography of Alice B. Toklas*.
[15]Hynd, *The Case of the Attic Lover*, p. 10.
[16]Porphyrus, *The Nymph's Cave*.

("Why not think that, incarnated in the door, there is a little threshold god?"[17])

"What will make you happy?"

She answered the door wearing only a bathrobe and bedroom slippers, and led the way to the bedroom.[18]

"What will make you happy?" Alice had asked.

"The flood of passion, divine possession, desire, desire, desire, the sun, the sun, the sun. 'O drop like a liana into my arms.'[19]"

Something has to happen. This, this is what happens:

A truck pulls up and stops in the drive. Who's that? Joy is at the window. Who's that? Joy is at the door. Who's that. What it says on the truck in bold red letters is "DEUS EX MACHINA— 24 HOUR EMERGENCY SERVICE." Just in time, Joy thinks, I couldn't stand it any longer, and out she comes: this Goddess and the sun.

"Approach me with a slightly indolent walk, anklets languorously clanging."[20]

She is disrobed, but heavily ornamented.

"I am here to repair you, she says. She smells like sandal powder. It is difficult to be beneath her dusted arms. And, of course, that did it.

She sat on the edge of the bed, watching little Otto as he went to work on the machine.[21]

A kindly present, thinks Joy. There is some use in giving, there is no use in a rectangular ribbon. There is so much difference to surrender to one another.

---

[17]Gaston Bachelard, *The Poetics of Space.*
[18]Hynd, *The Case of the Attic Lover,* p. 10.
[19]Jayadeva, "The Song of the Cowherd," Ode Two: "The Penitence of Krishna," (c. A.D. 1175).
[20]*Ibid.,* Ode Eleven: "The Union of Radna and Krishna."
[21]Hynd, *The Case of the Attic Lover,* p. 10.

When late in the afternoon, little Otto Sanhuber got into his clothes and left the house, he was no longer a boy.[22]

I inhabit this body, Joy thinks, this is my form of constraint, she was thinking flocks of whales on the sand, their mystic eyes, their dualistic vision, the absolute bothness of this and that of sea and sand of outside and inside (unbutton Alice) of male and female (Otto identical) of sand sand sand, "Is it possible most of the parts of animals come into being by chance?"[23] Otto: A female body with the head of a whale. Otto: A birdlike musician with a male head. Otto: Alice, this could be true, we could possess a myriad of bodies, it's hard to know what will make me happy, what will make me happy.

The lady, loath to so much as think of letting go of little Otto now that she had found him, thought up a way to keep the intrigue in motion—in fact, step it up, if anything—and at the same time run no risk of being found out. There was a trapdoor in the bedroom ceiling that led to an unused room in the attic. She would fix up that room, with an oil lamp, a cot, food, reading matter, and other conveniences, and Otto could make that his permanent headquarters. Otto was, in fact, enthusiastic about it. His every want would be supplied, and, when the Oesterreichs were out at night, he could sneak out for a little exercise. Then, during the day, when Mrs. Oesterreich was at home, feigning illness, he could come down through the trapdoor and spend the whole day in illicit love and to hell with the winter winds that whistled outside. The lady, taking no chances on her husband ever going up through the trapdoor, put a padlock on it and always carried the key herself. Why the padlock? asked Oesterreich. "I want to keep my furs in a safe place."[24]

Alice, would you do this for me, would you keep your furs in a safe place, would you, would you lock me up in your attic?

---

[22]*Ibid.*, p. 10.
[23]Aristotle, *Physics: Book II.*
[24]Hynd, *The Case of the Attic Lover*, pp. 11–12.

Joy thinks it is a very hard thing to know if you are a real living thing, a really living thing, if you are really living inside the thing you have always been living in ("We all have our bodies."): we all have our Otto, our One and our Other, inside out and outside in Otto is the same Otto, our Other and our One Otto, our sea selves and sand, like whales can't know ("Joy, why are you reading this junk?") whales can't know they are living in the sea until they are dying on the sand when they are living in the sea they are not conscious of any Other any Otto rolling them back and forth and back and forth ("Joy, why are you reading this junk?) they are the same thing ("Alice, this is the truth, this is not junk.") they are the same thing they are the same as the sea in the sea they are not Other they are Otto-identical they are alike they are like you Alice like me Alice do you still like me Alice? Unbutton me Alice.

"I am the daughter of the Milky Ocean, too."
Alice.
"Fog, what is fog, is it everything we speak?"
Alice.
"Cloudiness, what is cloudiness, it is melting."
Alice unbuttoned and the sun.
Alice arrayed as a goddess in the deepest sense. (Only she can fix me.) A divine vision, a wayward angel with the sign of the sun on her forehead. ("O, I haven't seen you for days.")

Unbutton Alice and what you find is Joy.

THE ESCAPE ARTIST

Judith Katz

A Proposal

Tutsik Goldenberg didn't look like a weasel, he looked like a man, but a weasel he was, and a coward too.

He was handsome enough, although that wasn't the first thing you noticed. First you noticed how clean he was, how he shimmered, you thought, from cleanliness, for his European-cut clothes were spotless, his white teeth sparkled, and underneath his fingernails there was never a speck of dirt. Even Tutsik Goldenberg's shoes glistened; they carried, it seemed, none of the dust that burdened other men. And always, a gleaming white handkerchief sat in Tutsik Goldenberg's breast pocket, plumped and ready to dab a lady's tearful eye.

Yes, a person thought Tutsik Goldenberg shimmered from cleanliness but only until they realized that he shimmered also from the diamonds he wore—on the stickpin that held his tie in place, the cuff-links that stuck out from his pressed linen jacket, the fat gold rings that jumped from the pinkies of both his hands.

Why was it, some wondered, that a man so clean and not at all hard to look at could seem so oily on closer view? Surely it wasn't the pomade he used only lightly to work his mass of curly hair back from his forehead, nor the tiny bit of imported cologne he sprayed about himself as rich gentile men sometimes did. It certainly wasn't the well-blocked derby which he wore at a slight angle tilting to the left, nor the slim short cigars he smoked, but never in the company of ladies.

Tutsik Goldenberg always looked like he stepped out of a bandbox but he was no fop. In polite company he always comported himself like a gentleman. It wasn't until he opened his mouth that a clever person realized how slippery indeed Tutsik Goldenberg was, and so slippery was he that some people sensed trouble (but only vaguely) and patted their wallets unconsciously just after Tutsik Goldenberg left the room. Yes, there was a certain chill one felt, an iciness that caused a person to pull up his or her scarf, a shudder that went down the spine as Tutsik Goldenberg passed by.

But it wasn't wallets Tutsik Goldenberg stole. If you dropped a *gulden* or a few *pesos* fell from your pocket, he was the first to pick them up and hand them back to you. If he for once won a hand of pinochle it was always on the up-and-up because he didn't cheat at cards, in fact he could hardly play. He never showed off with knives or brass knuckles, he paid all his European debts on time and with interest. No, by all outward appearances Tutsik Goldenberg was an honest man.

And yet a person couldn't help feeling after eating *Shabbas* dinner with him or smoking one of his fancy cigars, that Tutsik Goldenberg was up to no good, though no one in any of the small ghetto synagogues where he appeared on *Shabbas* eve during the European summer months could put a finger on why. And then after he left your table and you felt for your wallet and it was still there, often fatter than it was before, you thought perhaps you were imagining things. For Tutsik Goldenberg was a rich man and he had come to pray in your synagogue and eat at your table on a Friday night. And best of all, even on the *Shabbas*, he had offered you the sweetest deal.

All the Jewish men in the little cities in Poland and Russia, Hungary and Lithuania fell over themselves to be the first to invite Tutsik Goldenberg home for *Shabbas* dinner. He had his pick of perfectly cooked chickens and *cholent* potatoes. He had his pick

of any of their daughters. For he was a modern Jew who looked
to all like a high-class salesman. One thing bothered them, though.
If he was a salesman, where were his cases?

"Ah," Goldenberg would say, but only to the men of the house,
as he sat at their well-laid tables, "I'm in the export business."

The men scratched their beards and nodded approval. The fathers of the house signaled the daughters to bring forth the good
brandy. "And what do you export," the fathers always asked, pouring the brandy themselves for their fancy stranger.

"Diamonds and other fine jewels," Goldenberg told them in
earnest.

"If you are an exporter of diamonds and other fine jewels, Reb
Goldenberg—pardon my ignorance but—what could possibly
bring you to our little town? We are honest working men, but
practically paupers. If you knew what this chicken cost me—"

"Ah," Goldenberg would say, looking sadly into the eyes of
the father of the house, "I am a rich man, but I am a
lonely man. I am looking in your little city for a fine and
wholesome wife."

"A Jewish wife?" the father of the house asked, just to be certain,
for Goldenberg, as a modern Jew, wore no beard, and might not
wish to be encumbered with the weight of women's piety.

"A Jewish wife," Goldenberg concurred. "I have tried all the
usual routes, the matchmakers and *shadchens*, I've met rich daughters
from here to Chernigov (or Kovno or Plock), but all anyone is
interested in is filling their own pockets. Ah, my friend, my host,
if you only knew how my heart aches for a good Jewish wife . . ."

With that the fathers' eyes twinkled and their minds worked
fast. "Have you met my Rachel? My Merle? My little Sophia?" the
fathers asked. "Of course our dowries are quite small—"

"A dowry? My good man, I have told you already. Money means
nothing to me. But can your Racheleh cook? Does Merle sew?
Will Sophia follow the Jewish laws to make me a happy man, in
the home and in the bedroom? For I have been lonely lo these
many years and what I really want is the companionship of a
Jewish daughter, righteous and pure."

"This daughter is a saint among women," the fathers were always
so quick to say. "The *challah* you ate tonight, this is a *challah* that
she made with her own hands while my wife stood and only

watched. This chicken soup? Her own creation. And as to the
challab cover, the tablecloth, the napkin on your lap, my daughter
finished these with her own dainty hands. Look, Reb Goldenberg,
look here Pan Salesman, Mr. Broker in Diamonds and other fine
jewels, my daughter is a feast among women. You have only
to gaze upon her luscious cherry of a mouth, her delicious
green eyes, her delectable breasts to see what a fine wife she
will be."

.True enough, no matter how exaggerated the fathers' claims to
their daughters' household abilities, the daughters of the houses
where Tutsik Goldenberg was treated like an honored *Shabbas*
guest were always *zaftik,* flirtatious, and under twenty. Before the
brandy glasses were emptied and the dinner dishes cleared, wedding arrangements were practically made.

And this was no accident. For before Tutsik Goldenberg made
his way to the Western Wall of any synagogue in Slutsk, Brody,
Tarnopol, or Minsk, before he took a seat at the table of a down-
and-out but upright citizen of Lodz or Lublin, Zamosc or Belz,
Tutsik Goldenberg had done his homework. He came into a town
on Monday and got himself a room in a respectable inn, then he
spent the next three days quietly shopping and watching the
goods. He sat in the kosher bakeries and the Jewish bars with a
Yiddish newspaper in front of his face as the men and women
came and went, so busy with their own daily business they hardly
noticed him. He listened to the people talk about themselves and
their neighbors. When he wanted to know more about a particular
young woman, he sprang for a sandwich or a glass of schnapps.
By Thursday afternoon he understood the lay of the land—he
figured out what tasty dish belonged on which table, so to speak,
so that by Friday night, when he presented himself to the *shammes*
for a synagogue seat, he knew exactly which of the generous
fathers he was about to take advantage of.

Dinner over, marriage contract all but signed, Tutsik Goldenberg always ended his first evening with his would-be in-laws
the same way. "Imagine it, Reb Ansky, Reb Mordkhe, Reb Teitelbaum—here I have traveled all this way, for how many months,
in search of just the woman who would make me happy—me, a
man who does business in South America, Constantinople, and all
of Europe. And where do I find my love and my heart? Just here,

in Chudnov, Praga, in Kotsk, only miles from my little hometown. Ah, God has surely blessed me tonight." And the father of the bride-to-be, the soon to be *shver* of Tutsik Goldenberg, importer/exporter of diamonds and other fine jewels, was sorely tempted to break the sabbath law and smoke one of his prospective *aidim's* fine cigars. For he was soon to be a happy man, a rich man himself, by association and because of the bride-price Tutsik Goldenberg had generously offered to pay, no dowry necessary, no none at all, for he had been searching his life long and just imagine it, Tutsik Goldenberg found his own beloved here.

This was the web he caught me in, that Tutsik Goldenberg, with his big talk about South America and his diamond-covered hands. It seemed so perfect, there I was, the oldest of three daughters at the table one April night just a week before *Pesach*. Wasn't it my *challah* cover that the father of the house was showing off to his honored guest at this *Shabbas* dinner? My meager chicken cooked to a turn? My lovely bosom and sweet red lips? And didn't I want to get out of Poland more than life itself?

Goldenberg never once looked at me, but I wasn't discouraged. He never looked at my mother or my two younger sisters either. He spent his entire dinner staring straight into my father's eyes. He told him jokes and stories of his life in faraway Argentina, as if we, the women of the house, were invisible and that his food and drink appeared by magic.

I found him boring until he said the words Buenos Aires, but even then I was hardly impressed. In the kitchen where we piled plates with chicken and potatoes my mother, Bayla, whispered he was a cold fish. My sisters giggled agreement as I pulled my lips up and down like a perch. But my father was obviously fascinated with him, and soon he, too, was looking past my mother and my sisters and me, only into Tutsik Goldenberg's lively eyes.

After dinner, when my father called me into his study for the brandy, I came right away. "Set the brandy down," he said, "put the bottle on the table. Now turn around and show Reb Goldenberg your stuff." He winked at our guest. "If you do it right, daughter, you may get your wish and leave this town better off than you are now."

I looked at my father and then at my mother, who stood behind me with a plate full of honey cake. My younger sisters were absolutely silent in the other room. My father motioned with his hand. "Let him see what you look like for God's sake," he said impatiently. "Do you want to go to South America or not?"

"Must I, Mama?"

She shrugged her shoulders and looked the other way.

I didn't want to but I did it. When my backside was to Goldenberg my father said, "Hold, hold up."

"Yakov," my mother started, but my father snapped his fingers at her and told her to *shah*. "Now look," he said to Goldenberg, "haven't I told you the truth?"

"As far as I can tell," said Goldenberg with a wink and the two men burst out laughing. I ran from my father's study, shaking with shame. The men were still laughing. My father banged his glass down on the table and yelled to my mother, "Pour us more brandy! You know, Reb Goldenberg, we shouldn't be making such arrangements on a Friday night, but times being as they are—"

"And also, Reb Teitelbaum, consider the *mitzvah*—me, a lonely man, successful in business with no one to share it, and suddenly, through the virtue of your generous hospitality, a miracle! No, Reb Teitelbaum, this is a *mitzvah*, a double *mitzvah* since it happened on the *Shabbas*, and God will remember your goodness, and I will remember your goodness, mark my words."

Then there was much backslapping and more drinking. I sat in the dark, staring out the window. I could hear the men mumbling and laughing. Then my father roared my name. "Sophia! Sophia! Reb Goldenberg is leaving us for tonight! Come bid him good-bye."

I didn't budge. My father kept calling me. Then my mother appeared. "Your rudeness is absolutely beyond belief," she whispered, "now go out there and say good-night to the man and do it with respect." I could not move. She pulled me by the arm and dragged me into the front room.

Goldenberg was adjusting one of his diamond rings with no interest. My father was agitated and when I appeared was full of false cheer. "Ah, here she is, Reb Goldenberg. Our blushing bride . . . Sophia, please, say good-night to your fiancé. You're engaged to be married." Then he looked nervously at Tutsik Goldenberg, who looked up from his ring and smiled at my father.

"What? Engaged to him? We don't even know who he is!" My mother slapped me then and there.

"You ingrate, Sophia! You with all your big talk about leaving for America. Here is Reb Goldenberg offering to do it for you, to take you there himself and treat you like a lady, and this is how you pay him back?"

"My apologies, Reb Goldenberg," my father practically bowed to him, "the shock of good news—my daughter is usually the most compliant of girls—"

Goldenberg got up from the table and for the first time all evening really looked at me, looked me up and down and with a sly smile. He took the hand I held over my stinging cheek. "Don't think about it twice, Reb Teitelbaum. I am only surprised that a girl so lovely as your daughter has not been snatched up much sooner." Then he kissed my hand but looked straight at my father. A trip to Argentina, I thought, but as this man's wife? A horrible shudder ran through me.

In his usual custom, Tutsik Goldenberg took his leave of our table and disappeared from us for several weeks. He was to spend *Pesach* with us, his fiancé's new family, but then a note came to my father by messenger the next day. Sudden business troubles had developed and he was leaving for Odessa on the first train after *Shabbas*. A maiden aunt was kind enough to take him in for the *seder* and his company would return her *mitzvah*. He hoped the enclosed money would make a start for my trousseau. He would pay the balance of the bride-price at their next meeting, which he hoped would not be too far in the future, perhaps a week or two after *Pesach*. In the meantime, again many thanks for the fine dinner, how honored he felt to be a future member of the Teitelbaum family, so sorry he could not be there to say his thanks in person, with much respect, etc. etc., Tutsik Goldenberg.

I was greatly relieved that he was gone. Even as my mother began to sew my bridal gown and my father began to make plans for the wedding I hoped against hope that Tutsik Goldenberg would never return. Yes, Argentina was better than here, and with *Pesach* of course there were more tales of smashed synagogues and murdered grandmothers. But my intention was to escape with my family beside me, my two sisters, my parents. The thought of

going off alone with a man who never spoke to me, even to exotic
South America, was not what I had in mind at all.

Goldenberg did come back, of course, three *Shabbas* evenings
later, on the arm of my father, the two of them slapping each
other on the back like oldest drinking pals. "Bayla! Sophia! Our
diamond seller is back, our son-in-law! Set another place at the
table, our bridegroom has arrived!"

My mother quickly sent me out of the kitchen to greet him.
"Treat him with respect now," she spat, "he's about to make you
rich."

I curtsied to him and against all instincts, offered my hand. He
kissed it briefly and then stood back and examined me with his
hands on his hips as if I were a piece of livestock. "Oh, she's
sweeter than I remembered her. She'll do quite nicely. Now, *Froy*
Bayla," Goldenberg looked at my father, not my mother, "I'm starving. What's to eat?"

At dinner, although Goldenberg referred to my parents as *shviger*
and *shver*, my sisters as his future treasures, and me as his little
bride to be, not one word was said about the actual wedding.
Finally, when my mother and I left the table for cake and brandy,
my father meekly said, "Reb Goldenberg, dear—"

"*Shver* Teitelbaum—"

"The summer is fast approaching. I've announced our lovely
Sophia's fortunate engagement and now, the whole town wants to
know—"

"Ah, the balance of the bride-price. *Shver* Teitlebaum, I'll bring
it myself first thing Sunday morning—"

"—bride-price, nothing, Reb Goldenberg. I'm a shrewd man. I
know you're good for it. What the town wants to know is—"

"—when's the wedding?" My mother put the cake plate right in
front of Tutsik Goldenberg.

"Yes, well . . . the wedding." Tutsik Goldenberg adjusted his
diamond cuff links and looked blankly at my mother. He turned
to my father and said, "Reb Teitelbaum, you are a scholar and a
man of business. Out of nowhere, with an empty pocketbook, you
provide for your family each *Shabbas* with a little chicken, a few
potatoes, an onion, some salt—"

"It's my wife who manages that, actually—" I was surprised to hear my father give a woman credit. Goldenberg, however, continued without hearing.

"I am a man of business only. My studies are as scant as the food on this table. But as a man of business I can turn a little chicken and some honey cake into fat geese and fabulous strudels. I can snap my fingers and bring gold and chocolate to your table, even this table on the outskirts of Warsaw. On Sunday morning, Reb Goldenberg, you will be a rich man. But in order to make you rich, I must deprive you of a very great pleasure. As you know, three weeks ago I was called away to Odessa for a business emergency. That emergency now requires that I take myself back to the home office before winter settles in. The home office is in Buenos Aires, and winter there commences in June." Tutsik Goldenberg took my hand into his own. He looked in my direction but his eyes never settled. "I will pay you our agreed-upon brideprice on Sunday, but on Monday I must come and get our little Sophia and take her with me to Argentina."

"Without a wedding?" my mother's mouth hung open. "I won't hear of it!"

Tutsik Goldenberg let go my hand and sat back in his seat. "*Froy* Teitelbaum, then you mean to tell me the whole thing is off?"

My father stood up and banged the table with his fist. "She means no such thing. If you don't intend to marry Sophia here in Warsaw, Reb Goldenberg, when do you intend to do it?"

"Why on the ship, Reb Teitelbaum. There is a rabbi on the ship. It will be wedding and honeymoon all in one. My only regret is that you will not be there to give the bride away. And as for Sophia, she has quite a life ahead of her in Argentina. I share an apartment with my sister on Talcahuano Street that is the envy of the entire Jewish community. I will provide her with servants, pamper her with sweets, she will have little to do all day but lie about like a lady."

"Couldn't we arrange to have the Warsaw rabbi perform the ceremony here, tomorrow evening?" my mother was frantic.

"I'm afraid that's impossible, *Froy* Teitelbaum. I have a thousand loose ends to tie up."

"And well you should," said my father, "well you should. A man

who can turn honey cake into chocolate must certainly take care
of his own business and make room for more."

"But to prove to you, my future *machutonim*, that I am a man of
my word, let me show you what I am forbidden to give our
cherished Sophia on this Sabbath eve." Goldenberg reached into
his pocket and brought out a velvet box. He opened it and even
I was dazzled by the stone on the ring within. "This is the first
thing I will give your eldest daughter as our ship sails away. Mark
my word, *Shver* Teitelbaum. You won't be sorry. And as for our
darling Sophia, she'll be safe in Buenos Aires in a way she could
only imagine in Warsaw. Her fragile Jewish life will never be
the same."

Romance

. . . several years later in Buenos Aires . . .

It is quiet as can be in Madame Perle's kosher whorehouse, the
shutters still closed, only the faintest sunlight squeezing through
the blinds. The cats on the street have stopped howling, the parrots in the courtyard click their beaks and claws and all of the
women are fast asleep, all but we two, locked in one another's
arms. Me, Sophia Teitelbaum, most tasty morsel on the menu at
Talcahuano 745, this month's most valuable *nafkeh*, earner of most
pesos per minute, spitfire, whore most likely to bite back when
slugged in the stomach or punched in the mouth. Here am I with
the escape artist, Hankus Lubarsky, a man no longer in these
desperate arms.

In truth, I had planned to extort her. I am after all a whore
with many months' practice, a quick study who knows a golden
opportunity when one falls down drunk on the floor in front of
me. Get me out of here is what I imagined I'd tell her, take me
with you the next time you go. And when she asked me how did
I think she, a woman dressed like a man, could do more than I,
a woman dressed like a slut could do for myself, I was going to
tell her to buy me, trade me for a week of magic show profits,
rescue me with her quickest wits. Because what I had on her was
huge, huge, what I had on her was huge. For if Tutsik Goldenberg

and his thug cronies got wind of the fact that their *wunderkind* Hankus Lubarsky was a woman in disguise, she was no better off than I, and even more despised. She too would know the feel of a fist against the eye, a hard *shlang* shoved up the *toches*, one two three boom, and all one had to show for it was an asshole full of kosher cum, and then they spit on you besides.

I spent my afternoons scheming. I would one day trap Hankus Lubarsky into showing me her secret self, seduce her into opening her shirt for me and then at my mercy she would be. Then one night, long after *Pesach*, two years to the day since I first set foot on the slippery ground of Buenos Aires, such an opportunity fell into my lap.

Perle Goldenberg was long gone to Rumania in order to spend the European summer in the Carpathian Mountains with a new and rich lover. "It's strictly business, you understand, with a modicum of pleasure," for the new lover, a lapsed follower of the Wonder Rabbi Nachman of Bratislava, was not much to look at but had piles of money and had hinted strongly at buying in. Against her better judgment and all of ours, Madam Perle left her brother Tutsik in charge of the house on Talcahuano Street and went off to take the air.

As brother of the boss, Goldenberg was obnoxious enough, but as boss of the brothel he was impossible. He ordered us around as if we were maids as well as *nafkehs*, and then we weren't just *nafkehs*, we were his *nafkehs*, and he thought he was at liberty to make us do anything that suited his fancy. More than ever I wanted to kill him or get out.

Then as if by magic, I was passed a key:

Tutsik Goldenberg and his boys loved Hankus Lubarsky like a little brother and a son and they all felt bad for him. "Poor guy," Benya Sharf became teary one afternoon over coffee, "He's a virgin still, at twenty."

"We really ought to show him some fun," said Dov Hirsch, slapping Mordechai Dorfman on the back.

"He works so hard, day and night on those tricks of his," Tutsik Goldenberg placed a slim cigar into his greedy mouth. "He's got one now, you can tie him up any way you want—with your own rope even, you can bring it yourself, tie his hands, his feet, in two minutes, he's free. Hang him upside down when he does it, alright it takes him maybe five minutes, but face facts, the boy is a genius. When his show opens at the Royal, he'll be the hit of Jewish Buenos Aires, you mark my words, it's a sure thing. But he needs to relax more."

"We really ought to get him a woman," Mordechai Dorfman sighed as he signaled Marianna to pour him another cup.

"Well," said Dov Hirsch, pinching my ass, "this is certainly the place to get one."

"We've tried," whined Benya Sharf, "I've offered to spring for one myself, he says nothing doing. If you ask me he's *faigeleh*. Look at those little wrists."

Tutsik Goldenberg pounded the table. His eyes popped out of his head. "Hankus Lubarsky is no fag! He's a respectable, talented boy with old world ways, and it's our job as elders of the community to teach him how to have a good time." He wrenched my arm and pulled me on to his lap. He ran his eyes over my bare breasts. I wanted to spit in his face. "Sophia will teach him I think. She's still got some juice in her. I'll insist, a gift of the house. He's too polite to refuse." He pushed me off his lap and stood up.

"Where are you going," Mordechai Dorfman asked, shuffling a fresh deck of cards "I'm all set to beat your pants off at pinochle!"

"Start without me," Goldenberg said resolutely, "I'm going over to Tucuma'n to get Lubarsky. We'll give him a Bar Mitzvah he won't soon forget."

And so they did. Sharf ordered Marianna to put up a dinner of *klops* and cabbage and Mordechai Dorfman went over to the cantina on the corner for one liter of red wine and two of champagne. Dov Hirsch went up and dragged poor sliced-up Eva out of her room and ordered her downstairs to play the beat-up piano. "Some Yiddisheh tango," he insisted, "We want a good atmosphere."

"A good sexy atmosphere," Sharf chimed in. "That boy's got to come to his senses about women once and for all."

One or two early customers came before Goldenberg returned with Hankus Lubarsky, they wanted to dance with Rachel and Merril, me they wanted to take upstairs. I was done with both of them in less than an hour. I took their tokens and we all went downstairs.

The seduction of Hankus Lubarsky had already begun. She was

sitting at a table in the kitchen, a linen napkin tied around her neck, a plate piled high with Marianna's Spanish-Jewish cooking before her. Goldenberg was sitting almost in her lap.

"Marianna, more wine, the boy needs a drink—"

"No more" said Hankus, lifting her glass, "look here, I've barely drunk this—"

"Drink it up," ordered Goldenberg, "it's all on the house. Dear boy, it's the middle of winter, our most dismal time of year. Drink up, drink up, enjoy!"

After dinner there was more coffee served up by Marianna, Spanish style, into which Benya Sharf tipped a little schnapps. Dov Hirsch took Mordechai Dorfman into his arms and the two of them proceeded to dance the tango, first with each other, then one at a time with a squirming Lubarsky, who they then thrust into my arms.

Hankus pulled herself away horrified but the men pushed her back to me. "Relax," I whispered in her ear, "I know everything." Lubarsky looked into my eyes, clearly frightened. "You've nothing to worry about, Mameh," I whispered, "your secret's safe with me."

The men opened up bottles of champagne, poured it over each other's heads, down one another's throats. When Lubarsky waved the foaming bottle away, Tutsik Goldenberg grabbed her by her tie and slurred, "Don't resist it, *yingeleh,* it's all for you!"

Goldenberg's cronies danced with each other, they danced with us, they stood on the tables and when Marianna begged for them to get down, God forbid they should break them and then what would Madam Perle say on her return? The men grabbed her in their arms and danced her around the parlor as well.

By the early Argentine hour of 12:30 in the morning Hankus Lubarsky was flat on her face, drunk. "Marianna," Goldenberg ordered, "bring more coffee!" Dov Hirsh and Benya Sharf heaved Hankus up to standing and each pulled an arm onto one of their shoulders and hauled her up the stairs. Marianna followed with a tray of coffee things just as the two men dumped Lubarsky onto my bed. The two of them stood around. "What are you *shmucks* waiting for?" I snarled.

"He's out cold," Benya Sharf said, "we gotta revive him."

"I'll take care of that," I said, "and I'll give you *shlubs* a full report

in the morning." Then I took them by the hand and led them out
of my room. When they were gone I locked the door.

I poured myself a cup of coffee and sipped at it while I watched
Lubarsky sleep. Passed out, her collar open, her tie askew, she
looked womanly indeed. The light from my lamp fell softly on
her white and open throat. I wanted to bury my face in it at once.
I took my coffee and sat beside her on the bed. "Hey, you, Lubarsky," I whispered, take a sip of this, for me." She sat up for a
minute, opened her eyes, then fell back flat.

I set the cup down and took off her men's shoes and socks, got
her out of her jacket, slid off her trousers. I slipped off her well-
made shirt then unwrapped the binding that held her lovely
breasts flat. She was a beautiful woman, and I felt myself wanting
her, not like I wanted Perle or even Rachel. I wanted to burrow
into the body of Hankus Lubarsky, now asleep and snoring. I
draped a blanket over her and kissed her lightly on the forehead.
I wanted into her as I wanted to be free.

An hour passed, then two. I lay beside the sleeping magician, ran
my fingers through her hair, brushed my lips over her arms and
fingers. Suddenly Goldenberg was pounding on the door. Lubarsky
sat up in my bed with a start. "Keep yourself covered up, I'll get
rid of him," I whispered.

I pulled my kimono around me and opened the door a crack.
Hirsh, Dorfman, and Sharf stood behind Goldenberg salivating.

"So, *nu*," Tutsik Goldenberg slurred, "you got him up here all
night. What's going on?"

"Give him a chance, the *petseleh* is new at it, remember. I'm
trying to teach it to him slow, not the way you *chazzers* taught it
to me."

"So he's the sensitive type, so *nu*." Dov Hirsh tried to push his
way into my room.

"He's the sensitive type and he's shy," I said, pushing Hirsh back.

"Just so long as you show him a good time," Tutsik Goldenberg
said, "because after tonight, he'll pay for it like everyone else."

"Sure, sure," I told him, "now get out of here so I can get back
to work."

They all four of them grumbled as I shut them out. I opened
the door again to find them all scrambling for a bit of ear space

at the door. "What's with you *alter kuckers*, can't a girl have some privacy?" Then I slammed the door and turned the key.

Lubarsky sat up in bed and held her head. She fumbled for her jacket, then fished her cigarette case out of the pocket. "Do you want one?" she asked without looking at me.

"The coffee is cold, I'll ring Marianna if you want some hot."

"I detest Marianna's coffee. I detest all coffee." Lubarsky took a long drag of her smoke. "This is catastrophe," she muttered in Polish. "This is disaster."

"What disaster? So I know you're a woman now, all of us knew it months ago."

"Everyone?" Lubarsky looked at me alarmed.

"Not those imbecile men. They see what they want to see. You are their *goldeneh yingeleh*, Lubarsky, the son most of them left in Poland and never met."

Lubarsky blew a stream of smoke and glanced down at her breasts. "Yes, well . . . so much for that."

Now was the time I should have threatened Hankus Lubarsky, now I should have promised exposure if she would not comply with my plan to escape. "Get me out of here," I wanted to whisper into her tender ears, "buy me from the Goldenbergs, tell Tutsik you want me for a gift." But when Hankus Lubarsky left her cigarette to smolder on the edge of the marble table at my bedside, I was struck mute. Moved by the sorrow in her brown eyes, the tender curve of her generous lips, I was able only to bend over the girl magician's most handsome face and kiss her with the passion of my whole heart.

TINY, SMILING DADDY

Mary Gaitskill

The phone rang five times before he got up to answer it. It was his friend Norm. They greeted each other and then Norm, his voice strangely weighted, said, "I saw the issue of *Self* with Kitty in it."

He waited for an explanation. None came so he said, "What? Issue of *Self*? What's *Self*?"

"Good grief, Stew, I thought for sure you'd of seen it. Now I feel awkward."

"So do I. Do you want to tell me what this is about?"

"My daughter's got a subscription to this magazine, *Self*. And they printed an article that Kitty wrote about fathers and daughters talking to each other, and she well, she wrote about you. Laurel showed it to me."

"My God."

"It's ridiculous that I'm the one to tell you. I just thought—"

"It was bad?"

"No. No, she didn't say anything bad. I just didn't understand the whole idea of it. And I wondered what you thought."

He got off the phone and walked back into the living room, shocked. His daughter Kitty was living in South Carolina working in a record store and making pots, vases, and statuettes which she sold on commission. She had never written anything that he knew of, yet she'd apparently published an article in a national magazine about him without telling him. He lifted his arms and put them on the window sill; the air from the open window cooled his underarms. Outside, the Starlings' tiny dog marched officiously up and down the pavement, looking for someone to bark at. Maybe she had written an article about how wonderful he was, and she was too shy to show him right away. This was doubtful. Kitty was quiet but she wasn't shy. She was untactful and she could be aggressive. Uncertainty only made her doubly aggressive.

He turned the edge of one nostril over with his thumb and nervously stroked his nose-hairs with one finger. He knew it was a nasty habit but it soothed him. When Kitty was a little girl he would do it to make her laugh. "Well," he'd say, "do you think it's time we played with the hairs in our nose?" And she would giggle, holding her hands against her face, eyes sparkling over her knuckles.

Then she was fourteen, and as scornful and rejecting as any girl he had ever thrown a spitball at when he was that age. They didn't get along so well anymore. Once, they were sitting in the rec room watching TV, he on the couch, she on the footstool. There was a Charlie Chan movie on TV, but he was mostly watching her back and her long, thick brown hair, which she had just washed and was brushing. She dropped her head forward from the neck to let the hair fall between her spread legs, and began slowly stroking it with a pink nylon brush.

"Say, don't you think it's time we played with the hairs in our nose?"

No reaction from bent back and hair.

"Who wants to play with the hairs in their nose?"

Nothing.

"Hairs in the nose, hairs in the nose," he sang.

She bolted violently up from the stool. "You are so gross you disgust me!" She stormed from the room, shoulders in a tailored jacket of indignation.

Sometimes he said it just to see her exasperation, to feel the adorable, futile outrage of her violated girl delicacy.

He wished that his wife would come home with the car so that he could drive to the store and buy a copy of *Self*. His car was being repaired and he could not walk to the little cluster of stores and parking lots that constituted "town" in this heat. It would take a good twenty minutes and he would be completely worn out when he got there. He would find the magazine and stand there in the drugstore and read it and if it was something bad, he might not have the strength to walk back.

He went into the kitchen, opened a beer and brought it into the living room. His wife had been gone for over an hour, and God knows how much longer she would be. She could spend literally all day driving around the county doing nothing but buying a jar of honey or a bag of apples. Of course, he could call Kitty, but he'd probably just get her answering machine, and besides, he didn't want to talk to her before he understood the situation. He felt helplessness move through his body like a swimmer feels a large sea creature pass beneath him. How could she have done this to him? She knew how he dreaded exposure of any kind, she knew the way he guarded himself against strangers, the way he carefully drew all the curtains when twilight approached so that no one could see them walking through the house. She knew how ashamed he had been when, at sixteen, she had announced that she was lesbian.

The Starling dog was now across the street, yapping at the heels of a bow-legged old lady in a blue dress who was trying to walk down the street. "Dammit," he said. He left the window and got the afternoon opera station on the radio. They were in the final act of *La Bohème*.

He did not remember precisely when it had happened, but Kitty, his beautiful, happy little girl, turned into a glum, weird teenager that other kids picked on. She got skinny and ugly. Her blue eyes, which had been so sensitive and bright, turned filmy, as if the real Kitty had retreated so far from the surface that her eyes existed to shield rather than reflect her. It was as if she deliberately held her beauty away from them, only showing glimpses of it during unavoidable lapses, like the time she sat before the TV, daydreaming and lazily brushing her hair. At moments like this, her dormant charm broke his heart. It also annoyed him. What did she have to retreat from? They had both loved her. When she was little, and she couldn't sleep at night, Marsha would sit with her in bed for hours. She praised her stories and her drawings as if she were a genius. When Kitty was seven, she and her mother had special times, during which they went off together and talked about whatever Kitty wanted to talk about.

He tried to compare the sullen, morbid Kitty of sixteen with the slender, self-possessed twenty-eight-year-old lesbian who wrote articles for *Self*. He pictured himself in court, waving a copy of *Self* before a shocked jury. The case would be taken up by the press. He saw the headlines: Dad Sues Mag—Dyke Daughter Reveals . . . reveals what? What had Kitty found to say about him that was of interest to the entire country that she didn't want him to know about?

Anger overrode his helplessness. Kitty could be vicious. He hadn't seen her vicious side in years, but he knew it was there. He remembered the time he'd stood behind the half-open front door when fifteen-year-old Kitty sat hunched on the front steps with one of her few friends, a homely blond who wore white lipstick and a white leather jacket. He had come to the door to view the weather and say something to the girls, but they were muttering so intently that curiosity got the better of him, and he hung back a moment to listen. "Well, at least your mom's smart," said Kitty. "My mom's not only a bitch, she's stupid."

This after the lullabies and special times! It wasn't just an isolated incident either; every time he'd come home from work, his wife had something bad to say about Kitty. She hadn't set the table until she had been asked four times. She'd gone to Lois's house instead of coming straight home like she'd been told to do. She'd worn a dress to school that was short enough to show the tops of her panty hose.

By the time Kitty came to dinner, looking as if she'd been doing slave labor all day, he would be mad at her. He couldn't help it. Here was his wife doing her damnedest to raise a family and cook dinner and here was this awful kid looking ugly, acting mean and not setting the table. It seemed unreasonable that she should turn out so badly after taking up so much time. Her afflicted expression made him angry too. What had anybody ever done to her?

He sat forward and gently gnawed the insides of his mouth as he listened to the dying girl in *La Bohème*. He saw his wife's car pull into the driveway. He walked to the back door, almost wringing his hands, and waited for her to come through the door. When she did, he snatched the grocery bag from her arms and said, "Give me the keys." She stood open-mouthed in the stairwell, looking at him with idiotic consternation. "Give me the keys!"

"What is it, Stew? What's happened?"

"I'll tell you when I get back."

He got in the car and became part of it, this panting, mobile case propelling him through the incredibly complex and fast-moving world of other people, their houses, their children, their dogs, their lives. He wasn't usually so aware of this unpleasant sense of disconnection between him and everyone else, but he had the feeling that it had been there all along, underneath what he thought of most of the time. It was ironic that it should rear up so visibly at a time when there was in fact a mundane yet invasive and horribly real connection between him and everyone else in Wayne County: the hundreds of copies of *Self* magazine sitting in countless drugstores, bookstores, groceries and libraries. It was as if there were a tentacle plugged into the side of the car, linking him with the random humans who picked up the magazine, possibly his very neighbors. He stopped at a crowded intersection, feeling like an ant in an enemy swarm.

Kitty had projected herself out of the house and into this swarm very early, ostensibly because life with him and Marsha had been so awful. Well, it had been awful, but because of Kitty, not them. As if it wasn't enough to be sullen and dull, she turned into a lesbian. Kids followed her down the street jeering at her. Somebody dropped her books in a toilet. She got into a fistfight. Their neighbors gave them looks. This reaction seemed only to steel Kitty's grip on her new identity; it made her romanticize herself like the kid she was. She wrote poems about heroic women warriors, she brought home strange books and magazines which, among other things, seemed to glorify prostitutes. Marsha looked for them and threw them away. Kitty screamed at her, the tendons leaping out on her slender neck. He hit Kitty, Marsha tried to stop him and he yelled at her. Kitty leapt between them, as if to defend her mother. He grabbed her and shook her but he could not shake the conviction off her face.

Most of the time though, they continued as always, eating dinner together, watching TV, making jokes. That was the worst thing; he would look at Kitty and see his daughter, now familiar in her withdrawn sullenness, and feel comfort and affection. Then he would remember that she was a lesbian and a morass of complication and wrongness would come down between them, making it impossible for him to see her. Then she would just be Kitty again. He hated it.

She ran away at sixteen and the police found her in the apartment of an eighteen-year-old body builder named Dolores who had a naked woman tattooed on her sinister bicep. Marsha made them put her in a mental hospital so psychiatrists could observe her, but he hated the psychiatrists—mean, supercilious sons of bitches who delighted in the trick question—so he took her back out. She finished school and they told her if she wanted to leave it was all right with them. She didn't waste any time getting out of the house.

She moved into an apartment near Detroit with a girl named George and took a job at a home for retarded kids. She would appear for visits with a huge bag of laundry every few weeks. She was thin and neurotically muscular, her body having the look of a fighting dog on a leash. She wore her hair like a boy's and wore black sunglasses, black leather half-gloves and leather belts. The only remnant of her beauty was her erect martial carriage and her efficient movements; she walked through a room like the commander of a guerrilla force. She would sit at the dining room table with Marsha, drinking tea and having a laconic verbal conversation, her body speaking its precise martial language while the washing machine droned from the utility room and he wandered in and out trying to make sense of what she said. Sometime she would stay into the evening to eat dinner and watch *All in the Family*. Then Marsha would send her home with a jar of homemade tapioca pudding or a bag of apples and oranges.

One day instead of a visit they got a letter postmarked San Francisco. She had left George, she said. She listed strange details about her current environment and was vague about how she was supporting herself. He had nightmares about Kitty, with her brave, proudly muscular little body, lost among big fleshy women who danced naked in go-go bars and took drugs with needles, terrible women who his confused romantic daughter invested with oppressed heroism and intensely female glamour. He got up at night and stumbled into the bathroom for stomach medicine, the familiar darkness of the house heavy with menacing images that pressed about him, images that he saw reflected in his own expression when he turned on the bathroom light over the mirror.

Then one year she came home for Christmas. She came into the house with her luggage and a shopping bag of gifts for them and he saw that she was beautiful again. It was a beauty that both offended and titillated his senses. Her short spiky hair was streaked with purple, her dainty mouth was lipsticked, her nose and ears were pierced with amethyst and dangling silver. Her face had opened in thousands of petals. Her eyes shone with quick percep-tion as she put down her bag and he knew that she had seen him see her beauty. She moved towards him with fluid hips, she em-braced him for the first time in years. He felt her live, lithe body against his and his heart pulsed a message of blood and love. "Merry Christmas, Daddy," she said.

Her voice was husky and coarse, it reeked of knowledge and confidence. Her T-shirt said, "Chicks With Balls." She was twenty-two years old.

She stayed for a week, discharging her strange jangling beauty into the house and changing the molecules of its air. She talked about the girls she shared an apartment with, her job at a coffee shop, how Californians were different from Michiganders. She talked about her friends: Lorraine, who was so pretty men fell off their bicycles as they twisted their bodies for a better look at her; Judy, a martial arts expert; and Meredith, who was raising a child with her husband, Angela. She talked of poetry readings, ceramic classes, celebrations of spring.

He realized, as he watched her, that she was now doing things that were as bad as or worse than the things that had made him angry at her five years before, yet they didn't quarrel. It seemed that a large white space existed between him and her, and that it was impossible to enter this space or to argue across it. Besides, she might never come back if he yelled at her.

Instead, he watched her, puzzling at the metamorphosis she had undergone. First she had been a beautiful, happy child turned homely, snotty, miserable adolescent. From there she had become a martinet girl with the eyes of a stifled pervert. Now she was a vibrant imp living, it seemed, in a world constructed of topsy-turvy junk pasted with rhinestones. Where had these three different people come from? Not even Marsha, who had spent so much time with her as a child, could trace the genesis of the new Kitty from the old one. Sometimes he bitterly reflected that he and Marsha weren't even real parents anymore, but bereft old people rattling around in a house, connected not to a real child who was going to college, or who at least had some kind of understandable life, but a changeling who was the product of only their most obscure quirks, a being who came from recesses that neither of them suspected they'd had.

There were only a few cars in the parking lot. He wheeled through it with pointless deliberation before parking near the drugstore. He spent irritating seconds searching for *Self* until he realized that its airbrushed cover girl was grinning right at him. He stormed the table of contents, then headed for the back of the magazine. "Speak Easy" was written sideways across the top of the appointed page in round turquoise letters. At the bottom was his daughter's name in a little box. "Kitty Thorne is a ceramic artist living in South Carolina." His hands were trembling.

It was hard for him to rationally ingest the beginning paragraphs which seemed, incredibly, to be about a phone conversation they'd had some time ago about the emptiness and selfishness of people who have sex but don't get married and have children. A few phrases that stood out clearly: ". . . my father may love me but he doesn't love the way I live." ". . . even more complicated because I'm gay." "Because it still hurts me."

For reasons he didn't understand, he felt a nervous smile tremble under his skin. He suppressed it.

"This hurt has its roots deep in our relationship, starting, I think, when I was a teenager."

He had a horrible sensation of being in public so he paid for the thing and took it out to the car with him. He slowly drove to another spot in the lot, as far away from the drugstore as possible, picked up the magazine, and began again. She described "the terrible difficulties" between him and her. She recounted, briefly and with hieroglyphic politeness, the fighting, the running away, the return, the tacit reconciliation.

"There is an emotional distance that we have both accepted and chosen to work around, hoping the occasional contact—love, anger, something—will get through."

He put the magazine down and looked out the window. It was near dusk; most of the stores in the little mall were closed. There were only two other cars in the parking lot, and a big, slow, frowning woman with two grocery bags was getting ready to drive one away. He was parked before a weedy piece of land at the edge of the parking lot. In it were rough, picky weeds spread out like big green tarantulas, young yellow dandelions, frail old dandelions, and bunches of tough blue chickweed. Even in his distress he vaguely appreciated the beauty of the blue weeds against the cool white and grey sky. For a moment the sound of insects comforted him. Images of Kitty passed through his memory with terrible speed: her nine-year-old forehead bent over her dish of ice cream, her tiny nightgowned form ran up the stairs, her ringed hand brushed her face, the keys on her belt jiggled as she walked her slow blue-jeaned walk away from the house. Gone, all gone.

The article went on to describe how Kitty hung up the phone feeling frustrated and then listed all the things she could've said to him to let him know how hurt she was, paving the way for "real communication," all in ghastly talk-show language. He was unable to put these words together with the Kitty he had last seen lounging around the house. She was twenty-eight now and she no longer dyed her hair or wore jewels in her nose. Her demeanor was serious, bookish, almost old-maidish. Once he'd overheard her talking to Marsha and heard her say, "So then this Italian girl gives me the once-over and says to Joanne, 'You 'ang around with too many Wasp.' And I said, 'I'm not a Wasp, I'm white trash.' "

"Speak for yourself," he'd said.

"If the worst occurred and my father was unable to respond to me in kind, I still would have done a good thing. I would have acknowledged my own needs and created the possibility to connect with what therapists call 'the good parent' in myself."

Well, if that was the kind of thing she was going to say to him, he was relieved she hadn't said it. But if she hadn't said it to him, why was she saying it to the rest of the country?

He turned on the radio. It sang: "Try to remember, and if you remember, then follow, follow." He turned it off. He closed his eyes. When he was nine or ten an uncle of his had told him, "Everybody makes his own world. You see what you want to see and hear what you want to hear. You can do it right now. If you blink ten times and then close your eyes real tight, you can see anything you want to see in front of you." He'd tried it rather half-heartedly and hadn't seen anything but the vague suggestion of a yellowish-white ball moving creepily through the dark. At the time, he'd thought it was perhaps because he hadn't tried hard enough.

He had told Kitty to do the same thing, or something like it, when she was eight or nine. They were on the back porch sitting in striped lawn chairs, holding hands and watching the fire-flies turn on and off.

She closed her eyes for a long time. Then very seriously, she said, "I see big balls of color, like shaggy flowers. They're pink and red and turquoise. I see an island with palm trees and pink rocks. There's dolphins and mermaids swimming in the water around it." He'd been almost awed by her belief in this impossible vision. Then he was sad because she would never see what she wanted to see.

His memory flashed back to his boyhood; he was walking down the middle of the street at dusk, sweating lightly after a basketball game. There were crickets and the muted barks of dogs and the low, affirming mumble of people on their front porches. He felt securely held by the warm light and its sounds, he felt an exquisite blend of happiness and sorrow that life could contain this perfect moment, and sadness that he would soon arrive home, walk into bright light and be on his way into the next day, with its loud noise and alarming possibility. He resolved to hold this evening walk in his mind forever, to imprint all the sensations that occurred to him as he walked by the Oatlanders' house in a permanent place, so that he could always take it out and look at it. He dimly recalled feeling that if he could successfully do that, he could stop time and hold it.

He knew he had to go home soon. He didn't want to talk about the article with Marsha, but the idea of sitting in the house with her and not talking about it was hard to bear. He imagined the conversation grinding into being, a future conversation with Kitty gestating within it. The conversation was a vast, complex machine like those that occasionally appeared in his dreams; if he could only pull the switch everything would be all right, but he felt too stupefied by the weight and complexity of the thing to do so. Besides, in this case, everything might not be all right. He put the magazine under his seat and started the car.

Marsha was in her armchair reading. She looked up and the expression on her face seemed like the result of internal conflict as complicated and strong as his own, but cross-pulled in different directions, uncomprehending of him and what he knew. In his mind he withdrew from her so quickly that for a moment the familiar room was fraught with the inexplicable horror of a banal nightmare. Then the ordinariness of the scene threw the extraordinary event of the day into relief and he felt so angry and bewildered he could've howled.

"Everything all right, Stew?" asked Marsha.

"No, nothing is all right. I'm a tired old man in a shitty world I don't want to be in. I go out there, it's like walking on knives. Everything is an attack, the ugliness, the cheapness, the rudeness, everything." He sensed her withdrawing from him into her own world of disgruntlement, her lips drawn together in that look of exasperated perseverance she'd gotten from her mother. Like Kitty, like everyone else, she was leaving him. "I don't have a real daughter and I don't have a real wife who's here with me because she's too busy running around on some—"

"We've been through this before. We agreed I could—"

"That was different! That was when we had two cars!" His voice tore through his throat in a jagged whiplash and came out a cracked half-scream. "I don't have a car, remember? That means I'm stranded, all alone for hours and Norm Pisarro can just call me up and casually tell me that my lesbian daughter has just betrayed me in a national magazine and what do I think about that?" He wanted to punch the wall until his hand was bloody. He wanted Kitty to see the blood. Marsha's expression broke into soft open-mouthed consternation. The helplessness of it made his anger seem huge and terrible, then impotent and helpless itself. He sat down on the couch and instead of anger felt pain.

"What did Kitty do? What happened? What does Norm have—"

"She wrote an article in *Self* magazine about being a lesbian and her problems and something to do with me. I don't know, I could barely read the crap."

Marsha looked down at her nails.

He looked at her and saw the aged beauty of her ivory skin, sagging under the weight of her years and her cock-eyed bifocals, the emotional receptivity of her face, the dark down on her upper lip, the childish pearl buttons of her sweater, only the top button done.

"I'm surprised at Norm, that he would call you like that."

"Oh, who the hell knows what he thought." His heart was soothed and slowed by her words, even if they didn't address its real unhappiness.

"Here," she said, "let me rub your shoulders."

He allowed her to approach him and they sat sideways on the couch, his weight balanced on the edge by his awkwardly planted legs, she sitting primly on one hip with her legs tightly crossed. The discomfort of the position negated the practical value of the massage, but he welcomed her touch. Marsha had strong, intelligent hands that spoke to his muscles of deep safety and love and the delight of physical life. In her effort, she leaned close and her sweatered breast touched him, releasing his tension almost against his will. Through half-closed eyes he observed her sneakers on the floor—he could not quite get over this phenomenon of adult women wearing what had been boys' shoes—in the dim light, one toe atop the other as though cuddling, their laces in pretty disorganization.

Poor Kitty. It hadn't really been so bad that she hadn't set the table on time. He couldn't remember why he and Marsha had been so angry over the table. Unless it was Kitty's coldness, her always turning away, her sarcastic voice. But she was a teenager and that's what teenagers did. Well, it was too bad, but it couldn't be helped now.

He thought of his father. That was too bad too, and nobody was writing articles about that. There had been a distance between them too, so great and so absolute that the word "distance" seemed inadequate to describe it. But that was probably because he had only known his father when he was a very angry young child; if his father had lived longer, perhaps they would've become closer. He could recall his father's face clearly only at the breakfast table, where it appeared silent and still except for lip and jaw motions, comforting in its constancy. His father ate his oatmeal with one hand working the spoon, one elbow on the table, eyes down, sometimes his other hand holding a cold rag to his head, which always hurt with what seemed to be a noble pain, willingly taken on with his duties as a husband and father. He had loved to stare at the big face with its deep lines and long earlobes, its thin lips and loose, loopily chewing jaws. Its almost godlike stillness and expressionlessness filled him with admiration and reassurance, until one day, his father slowly looked up from his cereal, met his eyes and said, "Stop staring at me, you little shit."

In the other memories, his father was a large, heavy body with a vague oblong face. He saw him sleeping in the armchair in the living room, his large, hairy-knuckled hands grazing the floor. He saw him walking up the front walk with the quick, clipped steps that he always used coming home from work, the straight-backed choppy gait that gave the big body an awesome mechanicalness. His shirt was wet under the arms, his head down, the eyes abstracted but alert, as though keeping careful watch on the outside world in case something nasty came at him, while he attended to the more important business inside.

"The good parent in yourself."

What did the well-meaning idiots who thought of these phrases mean by them? When a father dies, he is gone, there is no tiny, smiling daddy who appears, waving happily, in a secret pocket in your chest. Some kinds of loss are absolute. And no amount of self-realization or self-expression will change that.

As if she heard him, Marsha urgently pressed her weight into her hands and applied all her strength to relaxing his muscles. Her sweat and scented deodorant filtered through her sweater, which added its muted woolliness to her smell. "All righty!" She rubbed his shoulders and briskly patted him. He reached back and touched her hand in thanks.

Across from where they sat had once been a red chair, and in it had once sat Kitty, gripping her face in her hand, her expression mottled by tears. "And if you ever try to come back here I'm going to spit in your face. I don't care if I'm on my deathbed, I'll still have the energy to spit in your face," he had said.

Marsha's hands lingered on him for a moment. Then she moved and sat away from him on the couch.

Not Quite Peru

Lee Ann Mortensen

*Exiled from yourself, you fuse with everything you
meet. You imitate whatever comes close. You
become whatever touches you.*

—Luce Irigaray, *This Sex Which Is Not One*

At night I sleep without movement in the suburbs of a Phoenix
desert having dreams of hot plants in the Andes, dreams filled
with parents as they talk to me through moldy Peruvian phone
lines from Lima. I dream of their typed letters on fine onionskin
paper, filed, unopened because I don't want to hear or read about
them telling me they know God. When it's closer to morning and
the Arizona desert is already getting hot, I dream of Peruvian boot
prints in short grass, and of wet apples covered in chocolate that
reflect the Aymara faces and the Aymara bodies who stand in
weeds before the picking season begins. And if I've run too far
the day before, trying to lean out, I sometimes dream of white
women's bodies that don't look like bodies, that are steely and
like machines. My mother, with her white skin and white
clothes, will occasionally call from a Peruvian village she is

visiting to tell me none of these things are in the South America she knows.

"It's just windy," she says. "It makes people shoot guns."

"I keep dreaming of chocolate-covered apples. I dream of machines," I say.

"We live here. Your father and I should know. Chocolate and industry are American things."

My mother calls me Terry and so do all her relatives, but I tell them it's Teresa now.

"I'm taking Spanish classes," I tell my parents, long-distance to Peru. "*Hola*," I say for thirty dollars. I imagine my mother, dressed in white, sits on velvet chairs when we talk, that her voice echoes over polished marble floors.

"You're always Terry, no matter what," my mother says.

Sometimes I try to speak to her in Spanish, tell her I want to live in downtown Phoenix and buy tortillas cheap and hot from the *tortilleria*. I tell her I want to sell things on street corners, things I can make myself, with my fingers, with these callused hands I use to lift weights and turn myself into something not quite human. I try not to tell my mother about my body, though. I try not to tell her that every day I lift so many barbells, do so many squats that my clothes fit tighter and men stare. I try not to tell her that I sit in my Spanish classes, trying to become foreign, wanting to pack a gun in a leather shoulder holster and walk stiffly past those barrio boys who take the same classes to laugh at the stilted language their parents speak. I try not to tell my mother that I want to walk past these same boys on the street, sneering and flexing myself at them until they faint. I don't say anything to her about the scar I now have on my stomach from a short knife fight in a fake cantina. I don't tell my parents about the barrio boy I look for every day, the barrio boy who held his gun so close to my face when I was alone once, lifting heavy objects in an old weight room downtown close to where I work.

These things happen to women with muscles, I told myself then, and I keep saying it. So when my parents call, there is little I can say.

"My biceps are bigger," I tell them, touching the scar on my stomach. Lately, muscles are the safest things I can tell my parents about, though I try to play it down. "I win things by flexing in public. I'll send you a picture."

"I hope you win money," my mother says. "What's the point if it doesn't give you something to invest?"

"It'll keep her out of trouble," my father says from another line. He is a former Latino made over by money.

"Have money so you won't need it," my mother says. "And remember, white people don't have to sell tortillas."

Their financial advice is good, but the rest I try to ignore. I lie outside in the sun and inside on tanning booths until my white skin doesn't look white. I eat tortillas before and after my heavier workouts, sitting in the sauna with a rag full of corn ones, chewing their dry, yellow textures. I sweat and think of yellow, the yellow of the barrio boy's shirt, the way the color reflected off his gun, the way his teeth reflected everything.

I try to think of other things, like the way the color yellow looks so very deep and bright on the school bus I see every morning on my way to the bank, the bus full of children scream-ing, my bank boss's children waving at me, making muscles at me through the thick windows that keep them all from jumping. When men in Jeeps and suits stare at me as we drive to the downtown where we all work, I kiss my rolled-up window and leave lipstick stains there to make them think twice. And as I drive into the basement of the bank, I stare back at the staring Latinos waiting for the morning grapefruit trucks.

"If you eat too many tortillas soon you'll be speaking nothing but Spanish," my mother says during another long-distance conver-sation where bad connections require us to repeat everything we say.

"You should know about Spanish and tortillas," I tell her.

"Spanish is good," my father says. "I speak it. I eat tortillas. I was born in Juárez you know." Each time I call, my father tells the story of his father's goats being buried by sand in the Sonoran desert. And I always laugh.

"Goats move too much," my mother says. "Anyway, if your daughter came down here, I bet she'd be shooting guns with the rest of them. I bet she'd be one of those communists."

"They're Maoists," I say. I try to think of the word for "bour-geois" in Spanish, but nothing comes. My Spanish book doesn't

list it, and only has words like "dog," "rain," "apartment," "rent."
Because I don't think the Maoists would care much for my textbook Spanish, I tell my mother I could never visit them there in
that place where people shoot and touch you too much, where
people get too close to you with guns.

"Moving around isn't for me," I tell my parents. "I have to
stay where it's warm and people understand what I'm talking
about."

"Of course you can move. People are the same everywhere," my
mother says. My father hums on the other line, reading.

Sometimes, I can't move from the dusty chair I'm sitting in right
now, I want to tell them, but I don't. Sometimes all I can do is
sit here, and if it is spring, I will watch desert tornados start to
swirl. And when the dust in the sky turns yellow, like the yellow
of his shirt so close to my face, I do push-ups, I do sit-ups,
I grab the bar in the kitchen doorway and pull until my head
is too full and I almost want to kill like Maoists who shoot
with quiet faces.

These parents of mine, they move and talk so much their motions upset the balance of things. At least that's what Linda tells
me, Linda, my trainer, who once lifted herself, who says she is
partly Navajo. Linda, whose blond, muscular words make my body
something other. And I do believe everything she says with her
promises of bulk, cuts, and trophies. I do believe her as she gives
me half kisses between the strain of power-lifting sets, or when
I'm pushing at weight until my skin is about to rip open.

This is what I try to think of when I remember the boy in
yellow.

"Balance is all there is," Linda says one day, using her pinky to
pull slightly at the middle of the bench press bar I'm straining
with in the middle of this weight room, a room I sometimes have
dreams about at night as my large muscles twitch. When we first
started here, when I had a body no one noticed, a body without
veins, when Linda was still competing, and pushing her muscles
at thin-haired judges, that was when the men who lift here used
to ignore us. But now they stare as I strain, as my arms get bigger
than theirs, as muscle striations start to make me look like the
metal I lift.

"You must have everything in alignment," Linda says as we sit in her suburban home, as she massages me, and then, as she carefully folds my socks, placing them in a circle around me as I sit on the bed waiting for her to use the spiritual Navajo phrases that will help me win trophies and money and fear with my body.

This is how Linda and I spend our nights, concentrating on the things that prepare us and our muscles for competition. We used to watch television when I first moved in. I was thin and unspectacular and never wanted to speak Spanish. Linda even used to kiss me, uncertain about what or who to love. Now she is more certain and kisses no one. Now I am told to sit on the bed and breathe in powerful words as she surrounds me with socks or with food, anything that is round, and thus, more spiritual. Eternal, she says. This almost-Navajo woman turns out lights and makes me watch the ritual candle she holds, the blue flame of it, the way it moves back and forth when we breathe. It will, she says, make me forget the judges who grope and stare during competitions. When asphalt is melting outside on Phoenix streets, and Linda is saying her Navajo power words over me, the words that will make the judges know I am perfect, I always feel a small sweat moving over my shoulders as if I were coming down from a sugar binge.

But this is not the time for a binge, Linda tells me. We have to be flexing and hard in the morning. We have to be completely without fat or sweat.

"We have to be mechanical," she likes to say, and I like to hear it. Machine words make me feel like I am made of small, perfect molecules. Some nights she'll even say I'm "steely" as she reads aloud from her Navajo books, trying better to learn the language she thinks her father spoke.

"We do not eat chocolate or fatty foods," she says in English, and then in Navajo. She tries to translate everything she says into this Indian language, sometimes making me repeat after her as I strain my deltoids with dumbbells. She is always saying words I will never know or be able to pronounce.

But this is how a bodybuilder gains spirituality, and we are bodybuilder people she tells me. She makes me watch myself flex in the bedroom mirror every night before we go to bed, celibate and tingling with spent muscle cells and incense and Navajo incantations.

"There are lots of jobs I have to do here," I tell my parents when they ask me, again, to visit them in their Andean jungle, to tour the mountains of cocaine and poppy fields with them during the spring mists. "I lift weights, you know. My possessions are here. My car, my mascara, my Spanish class, my pets." Of course, I have no pets, but mothers like them. Pets, like muscles, make them feel like their daughters will live through anything.

"You shouldn't have too many things. You're still young," they say, sounding almost like the Maoists they despise. They themselves are in denial, always saying "no" to things, "no" to materiality, "no" to new paint for the flaking walls I see in the pictures they send. They say "no" to new shoes, they tell me, and put their Mercedes up on blocks, refusing to drive it anywhere out of a fear of God and things man-made.

"When you're dead, objects won't matter," my mother says. "We can't take our Mercedes with us. So why should we drive it now?"

"You should buy something, paint the house, live in a condo," I tell them, but they don't listen. Their walls keep flaking. Their pool gets holes in the plaster as the water evaporates, unused. Their grass gets diseases.

"We're just like monks," they say.

"Monks are good," Linda tells me later. "They know what they need and they know how to get it."

These spare parental conversations from Peru make me dream at night of the Latin women my mother talks about, the ones I want to be like. Or I dream of a Linda who kisses my lips with real kisses. Of course I don't tell my parents any of this. And I don't tell Linda. She always makes symbols out of things. If I dream of Oreos she says it means there is a black woman named Carla whose muscles I will beat someday soon in competition.

"We are in training so everything is meaningful," Linda would say. "The sand we run on swirls to make patterns that tell us things. The air particles tell us how close we are to becoming bigger."

"Some people don't want to be big," I tell her. "Some people want to go unnoticed, be blank and invisible."

"Only the holy can be invisible," she says. But I have never wanted to be holy.

At the bank where I work, I speak in numbers. My boss looks hard at me when the loan season is slow, when men aren't borrowing money to finance a boat or a mistress or a desert pool. My boss looks hard at me and I can tell he is one of those who thinks I am too big.

"That suit, it doesn't look right on you," he says. And it's true. I look at myself in the building windows at lunch, my rippling reflection walking past mirrored glass, my well-defined calf muscles pushing against the pantyhose I will soon stop wearing. My legs are men's legs. Drag queens who walk downtown, pretending their husbands have sent them out to shop, stop and ask me for advice as I eat enchiladas outside by noisy pigeons. I invite them to sit and have lunch, and this is how I end up in cafés eating with people who are more beautiful than me, their transvestite faces more perfect than the gloss of magazine faces, their waists thin and ready for photographs. We talk about makeup and posture, and I nod at their questions as the outside heat saps me of what little moisture Linda has allowed me to have. When these men walk with me back to the bank, the barrio boys whistle at all of us.

Once I sent my now-Peruvian parents a picture, me in a posing bikini, my body oiled, my G-string tight, my gluteals twice the size they were when my parents last saw me three years ago. They called to say I looked nice.

"Things sure change," my father said.

"Yes," my mother said. "In my day even the men were flabby."

"I was skinny like a fence," my father said.

"My father was big, but he didn't have muscle," my mother said. "His voice was very muscular, though."

"It sure is nice to talk to you," my father said.

"Is that oil on you?" my mother asked. "You look wet. Is your bikini wet? I didn't even know you wore bikinis."

"I saw a woman like that at the fair once," my father said.

"If we had those kinds of women here, they would live in the hills," my mother said. "They would shoot guns."

Without thinking, I told them what I had been telling them for years about all my activities. "It's normal. Everyone does it."

"If you were here, you would live in the hills. You would shoot guns too. You just like to fight," my mother said, and for a moment I felt exposed. I touched my stomach scar, the scar I should get removed, Linda tells me, the scar that reminds me of the real anger I saw that night in the cantina I went to looking for the yellow shirt, for the barrio boy and his gun, but only finding an angry man with a knife. He had the kind of anger, the kind of face I so seldom see at my air-conditioned job or at Linda's desert home. He was yelling at the wall when I walked in after seeing the *Cervezas* sign flash from the road, thinking I might like to look around after a long day of bank meetings and numbers.

"*Pendejos*," he yelled. He was sweating, drinking from a bottle, spinning around to make sure no one was behind him. Everyone else was standing against the wall farthest from the man, drinking or staring. I stood at the door, understanding his intensity, wanting to touch the man, to taste some of his emotion. He looked at me, and then my shirt was split, and there was blood staining my expensive suit as everyone ran.

And so it is difficult to have this scar removed, even though the judges at bodybuilding events tell me they can't see my abdominals clearly enough with a scar like that in the way. They say it looks like cheating, like I have muscles where I shouldn't.

Because I have scars I don't want my parents to see, because I sometimes believe what my mother says about guns, that I would shoot them if I were there, because of this I tell them I will never visit them, never fly three thousand miles away from the sandy dryness of this Phoenix desert. But sometimes I do imagine living in Peru. Sometimes I imagine coming out of bushes surrounded by mist and rain, wearing green camouflage, wearing large earrings and someone else's muddy boots that don't fit. I would be a *guerrillera* with muscles, and go to villages to tell people they must stop buying food with English or Japanese writing on the labels. I will tell them that potatoes are better, more natural, more Peruvian and less capitalistic. But when I dream of this, they all say they're bored with potatoes. They say they hate imported beans.

"We aren't Peruvians either," they say in my dreams.

While I'm awake, after workouts, I sit in locker room saunas, imagining that in South America I would be a woman with a shoulder-slung AK-47. I would have to keep pushing it out of the way as I tell the villagers how to cook different potato dishes through frying and basting and breadifying. But these Aymaras don't listen. They draw pictures of cars and curvy women in the dark Peruvian mud and look at each other. Sometimes I imagine flexing for them when I help lift boxes full of market vegetables ready to sell for guns. When I'm flexing they touch my white, muscled skin with their fingernails. I want to name my muscles for them, say "deltoid" and "latissimus," but those words don't come to me without dictionaries.

These people call me transparent in my dreams.

"You look like coca leaves," they tell me. I smile because they say that is the highest compliment to give a white person in Peru, even if I am really a Mestizo.

Sometimes as I lie on the carpeted weight room floor, the one that is safe from guns and full of white men who want to do things to me but never will, that is when I think of Peru. I like to imagine letting the Indian women there put lipstick on my lips and arms so they can see it stain.

"You are like rocks at low elevations," they say. "Large and smooth." They seem to like this drawing time we share. They smile as their lipstick leaves marks like dark berries on my skin.

"You've got to get that out of your mind," Linda says, rubbing my scar, trying to make it fade before the judges complain. "Peru is no place for a woman with muscles."

I am sitting on an old examination bed in the auditorium hallway before my first competition, before my first time flexing in bikini, in oil, in public. This will be the picture I send my parents later, the one they will think is nice, the one where I'm oiled in bikini, on a bed with a hand over my scar as if I were laughing so hard I had to hold my stomach in. I tell Linda to take the picture. This way my parents will never see her face that is so thin and ravaged by the life and cigarettes they would call evil.

Men in dark suits walk by as Linda takes pictures of me and my muscles so my parents can see what I am doing to myself. She puts oil on my lats as men ask me questions about my body-building past, how long I've competed, how much I weigh, what the circumference of my biceps is.

"You are a big one," these men tell me, making me get on a scale. It says 142, the most I have weighed without fat.

"She has to concentrate," Linda says, moving in front of them, snapping her fingers at me to help me focus.

In the bathroom she opens a makeup kit for me and we start to put powders and colors on my face, bits at a time. She puts eyeliner in my hand, but all I do is hold it.

"A little charcoal would look good here," she says, pointing at my eyelid.

"A little charcoal," I say. I am dazed, staring and hot from a lack of food, not sweating from a lack of water, nervous about showing my body off in front of yelling crowds, in front of suited men. My fingers are twitching with shaky nerves and a low supply of electrolytes. This is normal, everyone says, and everyone does it, they all say, so there must be some kind of safety.

"You can't afford to bloat," they say.

I have learned that safety is not a word for them. Food and bloated stomachs and saturated skin cells are foreign, evil things. I think of bloating, my skin swelling a little, my muscle cuts fading into a mush like Darryl's body, the man I once almost loved, especially for his cooking. My stomach growls as I think of his recipes, so I think of the Andes instead, of bodies bloating in bushes, of their muscles fading too, but for different reasons. These would be the ones who got too close to people with guns on a windy day, my mother might tell me. Maybe if it were windy here, I too would want to get a gun out, a gun I will maybe buy later, or take from a barrio boy. I think of him again, the boy in yellow, even though I know Linda would not approve if she knew. I think of the way he touched my arm, pushed his fingernails into the muscle, leaving red marks.

"You think you're big," he said. I lay there on a dusty bench, still holding the barbell above in its metal support arms, feeling the pressure of veins in my neck as I became speechless and angry. "If you were a woman, I'd fuck you." He laughed, then looked at the door as if someone he had been running from might come in, blasting.

And if there is a day when I go by a gun store downtown, I might get the same kind of gun he had, and if I take it out, I may try to blow away some sneering boy in yellow who thinks he can touch me and laugh. I would leave this kind of boy in the weeds close to a baseball field, later to be found by children.

But in Phoenix, the winds are hot and slow, and seldom do white women like me shoot hot bullets.

"Your eyes are slightly dilated. Make a fist for a few minutes," Linda tells me now, her voice so quiet. I can feel heat rising in my neck. All colors and objects at this cheap bodybuilding contest seem far away. I'm beginning not to care what my face looks like or what kind of color Linda is putting on me.

"I don't care," I tell Linda. "Everything is fuzzy." I look at her, and her eyes are dark blue but speaking foreign languages. Navajo, she says. But still, she is American, she is blond and does her laundry at home while watching the news, while wishing for the cigarettes she gave up years ago. When she sits in the kitchen, wanting to smoke, her mouth says unspiritual things about sex and hate no matter how much she burns sage and reads her Navajo books, telling me she wants to live in Sedona, Arizona, and become holy like her Navajo relatives.

"That's why we can't kiss," she tells me at night. "You and I need to be empty and clean. We need to be invisible." She sits on the carpet and, instead of smoking, paints her nails in un-Navajo fruit colors as I fall asleep on her bed and feel my large quads twitching.

"Close your eyes," she tells me now in the auditorium bathroom that smells of sweaty competition and chlorine. These are the smells of powders and perfume that muscular women use to make their faces look less like machines. In front of me, in Linda's hand, there is that sharp point of a pencil eyeliner that drags against my skin and clumps when I do it myself. But Linda's fingers are cool as they hold my chin. She spritzes my forehead and puts on the sweet-smelling base. Light rouge is brushed on thickly, the brush pricking my cheeks. Then the sparkling powder she says the judges will like in those lights is blown on to hold it all in.

"That's not me," I say at the mirror. My face has changed. It looks like the face I see on so many other women as they try to do what their bosses tell them.

"That's much more you," my mother says when she sees the close-up photo, me in makeup and an almost real hairdo with small curls. I would not go to a barrio with this kind of makeup. I would not pack a gun with this hair.

"You are so pretty," my parents say. But no one ever calls me pretty. And I don't want them to. My muscles get in the way, and when I flex them, I think of flaky pastries and Irish Cream, things I cannot eat. I think of Peruvian villagers touching me with charcoal fingers. I think of clenching my buttocks for the judges. I don't think of being pretty.

Now, onstage for the first time, I unprettily flex for the first time in front of a large audience, and the dizziness of bright lights and cigarette smoke make me want just to stop moving and fall onto the stage floor in front of the judges. But I know Linda is out there looking at me, saying magical words for me, so I avoid falling by not moving my feet or doing any twisting or turning. I flex in place, and still, I get applause.

When I work I am corporate, letting my barbell callused hands finesse bank statements, allowing my muscular lips to tell people if they can have ten thousand dollars or not. At work, I wield the power of finance, and I feel guilt because of it.

"You are so bourgeois," Linda says, though she herself wields power with the governor of our Arizona. She is his supreme executive secretary. She helps him understand that the blueprints he makes have an effect on his spirituality. She points out that the way he walks and thinks can put holes where they weren't meant to be in a desert that doesn't want them.

"But you wear two-hundred-dollar suits," I tell Linda, trying to find inconsistencies in a woman who lives for contradiction.

"My suits are natural. Yours are not," she says.

This is sometimes the only thing we talk about anymore when weights aren't being pulled or magical Navajo words aren't being invoked or I'm not watching yellow desert storms.

Still, I do feel sorry when I'm in my expensive and unnatural power suits, sitting over oak desks with clients. Last month I tried to buy some suits in donation centers, but the woman at the cash register looked at me too much. She saw my clean, tanned, white skin, my impractical leather shoes, my too-finely combed hair, all in somebody else's unwanted, crumpled suit. She knew I was a fraud.

At work, I've created nothing but problems with my occasional discount suits and bulging body.

"No one has thighs like that," my boss says. He calls me in a lot now. Lately I've had trouble saying no to men in cowboy hats and large belt buckles who want ten thousand dollars to start iguana purse factories in Peoria. I want to tell my boss that money doesn't mean that much, that people should be able to buy any kind of purse they want, and that I should be able to help them do it.

"I think people like unique accessories," I tell my boss.

"This isn't California." He always breathes a lot when I'm in his office, wanting to ask me to flex for him, I know, but he doesn't ask. When I leave, he watches my calf muscles as I walk.

Though I have been at the bank for years, now that I am big, the cameras there follow me more often as I walk clients to the outer offices, or take copy jobs to the secretaries, or stop to stare at the women and men in yellow shirts. As I walked up and down with spreadsheets and financial profiles, these cameras quietly spin in any direction on high-tech hydraulics, zooming in on parts of my legs, I'm sure, or my thick neck with the turn of a lens. Linda tells me it's just jealousy, that people have always wanted to look at what they can't have.

"Even I still get stares," she tells me, almost flexing her thin arm. "A body like this can hypnotize."

"I don't think it's jealousy," I tell her. I always look behind me now when I walk around the office, trying not to turn as I imagine the hum of cameras coming into focus.

In the early evenings when Linda is working late at the capitol, telling the governor how to behave, I watch as the sun bleaches the yards in our neighborhood, turns all the cactus gardens full of painted rocks white, and all the lawns light yellow. Linda's house is too close to the desert for such civilized things to survive. Dust and jackrabbits eat away at any hints of excess or careful pruning. Javelinas with their wild pig snouts and black hair lie dead and bloating on the eighteenth hole of nearby executive golf courses, unaware of the havoc their smelling bodies cause.

I clean my short, practical nails while the dust storms of late summer hit, burying newly planted sod, blowing quartz crystals from rock gardens into the road, bending the tall yuccas people have brought in from our backyard desert to see if they would grow next to roses and purple snapdragons. Our neighbors pat manure around the base of their yuccas, but still their hollow stalks bend, still their pods blow down the street past station wagons trying to get in out of the dust and swirling desert bushes.

When it's dark and the monsoon lightning storms are flashing by South Mountain, I read makeup magazines to improve my skills for Linda and the judges, or at least that is what I tell Linda. Lately, I've become more interested in the bras than the eyeliners or lipsticks. There is always a lure to a piece of clothing you haven't worn for years, the containment of it unneeded for so long. I look at the advertising photos, trying to remember if I ever had breasts like that, and what it might have felt like to hold them, even to be able to lift them up or see them sway. Linda made my breasts disappear long ago with all her reps and diets. Now these magazine bras and women's bodies seem so foreign, they pull my eyes in. Sometimes, when the models all look pillowy and full of curves, I have to cut out pictures of them in their Maidenform and Balis, put them in a file I keep at the office so Linda won't see. She would say they were a distraction.

"Women's bodies will break you," she would say.

When it's lunchtime and the office is eating in, licking fallen mayonnaise off their desks while clients wait outside, I look at my bra pictures, and at these bra models without stomach muscles. Their mammaries would shock the bodybuilding world. I touch the glossy pages where the bras are highlighted. I tabulate interest rates for my next client, and think of calling the phone number at the bottom of one bra ad, a 1-800 number for sharing bra mishaps and complaints about fit and color and unnatural rashes, problems I haven't had for years.

There are days when I watch my clients waiting, sitting and

cleaning their own nails as they hope they have told me the right things to receive the big loans. I watch the camera in front of my office as it zooms in on them and their fidgeting, their crossing legs, their constant physical readjustments. As the camera in the outer office focuses on me through my executive window, I tabulate figures more rapidly, and think of phoning that number, of calling up the bra receptionists who no doubt have big breasts, who I'm sure wear nothing but a bra when they talk to their callers so assuredly.

One day, after a night full of starvation dreams and yellow-shirted hispanic men, I do call, right there after lunch, my boss walking by my door every so often to try and look at my leg muscles hidden by the desk. I listen to the computerized messaging service and push buttons until a real person talks.

"Service Center," a woman says.

"I have a lot of questions. Do I just start asking them?" I look up and wave first at my client, then at my boss.

"That's what we're here for."

"Do you know about underwires? Mine doesn't fit very well." I try to remember a conversation I had with my favorite transvestite last week, and I try to talk like him. The camera lens above my secretary moves slightly, so I cover the ad on my desk with my hand, turn in my swivel chair to face the outside window.

I try to imagine what this phone woman looks like as I listen to her explain the styles I could try to get my breasts to cooperate, if only I had them. I want to ask her what her body looks like, if it is like the model on the page in my hand. I want to tell her I lied, that I don't have the kind of body that requires the extra support of bras, but I don't say anything about this.

"Do you enjoy talking to women?" I ask her.

"I like my job very much," she says.

At night when Linda's house moves in slow motion around my starving and breastless body, when Linda is working late with the governor, when all I can think about is the food she won't let me have, and the way that her deprivations and the barrio boy's violence make me feel so weak, I start to make phone calls I don't tell anyone about.

"Have you ever tried a Maidenform Bra?" I ask the women when they answer, drinking soda water after soda water that Linda has told me will make me bloat. No doubt tomorrow she will see it, the bloating, the soda waters coming out of my pores, the empty bottles covered over in the kitchen trash can. This is all I can do when Linda won't let me binge, when she tells me bloating would be like death for someone with a body like mine.

But there are times when being reckless is all that keeps me from lying on the couch for days without moving just to feel the slow atrophy of muscle, and the invisibility of being still.

When I talk about bras to these phone book women, I drink mineral waters with abandon, using my best corporate voice to make them talk.

"We are doing a bras survey this evening," I say, sipping.

"Are you selling them?" the woman on the phone asks. When I tell them I'm not selling, they always want to buy, they always want to ask me the questions I wanted to ask the woman with the hotline service.

"What stores do you usually buy your brassieres in, madam?" I try to remember the days when I would walk into a store and try bras on, the saleswoman bringing me different sizes and colors, asking me if she could come in to see how they fit.

"Bra stores?" says the woman on the phone. "Frank will only buy me red ones, but they stain my skin." I look at the front door to make sure Linda isn't opening it as I ask for more details, as I pry into another woman's life. Sometimes I can keep them on the phone for half an hour as I tease them with a potential sale or a new bra that would drive any man or woman crazy. This is all I can think to do some nights when it's too hot for kissing or knife fights, and my body seems so big and unnecessary, so fearful of movement, so unholy it starts to disappear beneath me.

After a workout of fast-moving squats, and the pull-downs needed to emphasize my obliques, I walk slowly up the weight room stairs to the grey company car I will drive to Linda's desert house, my muscles acid-filled and heavy. As I walk, I think of Darryl my lovely, fat ex, and his cooking, his sticky sweet kisses many month's away now, but living only a few blocks down from Linda.

"Darryl will make you bloat," Linda tells me, afraid her former bodybuilding partner will do to me what he did to her, make me bloat, make me want to lie in a bed for days and smoke.

"Linda will starve you," Darryl says. "She'll sap your muscles right out from under you." He is always chewing on the phone. His cooking noises make my holy and deprived stomach squirm.

"Darryl will kill you," Linda says. "Darryl has killed many things." She always goes into the kitchen when she speaks about him. She talks about his bloated body while holding imaginary cigarettes between her fingers.

Sometimes I see Darryl outside on his sandy desert lawn, walking around his house in flowered shirts, his legs strangely white, and smooth like a woman's. These legs of his make me want to talk to him, smell the richness of his cooking, binge once again with him until we are in comas.

"I'm thinner now," I tell Darryl on the phone, secretly, hiding in the bathroom while Linda makes lettuce sandwiches.

"I could make you the most incredible chocolate cheesecake," he says. "Syrup dripping off the top."

"God," I say.

Linda knocks on the door.

"I can see the cord," she says. "Tell Darryl to fuck off."

"Fuck off, honey," I tell my old boyfriend, who wants to make me fat so I will stay with him.

"That wasn't a very holy thing to say," I tell Linda later after I've hung up. I walk into the kitchen and pinch at my very thin skin for her, slap at my heavy quads for her to see my transparent leanness. "He says I'm too thin."

"That's the idea," Linda says. "Lean and nothing but sinew and fiber. That's the only way to win." She touches my cheek with a fingernail, pinches at my gluteals, but there is nothing to pinch when I'm flexing.

At night when Linda is painting her nails or learning new Navajo words, I sometimes think of Darryl kissing me in the desert like he once used to, the 110° sand sticking to our legs as snakes watched from under bushes. That is sometimes what I think of as I fall asleep with celibate, but muscular lips, trying to feel the imaginary sand between my fingers, and the kiss of Darryl's sweetness. As I dream of Darryl instead of the color yellow, as I think of his fat lips, Linda and her nail polish smells fade.

In the afternoons after a day of banking and bra phone calls, after yelling *"pendejo"* at every barrio boy I see from the safety of my car, I like to run through the tall saguaros and junipers in the desert behind Linda's house, the desert Darryl once kissed me in, sand and dead lizards hitting the backs of my calves like they used to hit the back of Darryl's calves when he would run, when his body was as hard as mine. I like the way the sand sticks to my shoulders and hair, and I do sprints as snakes sidewind patterns on the trail in front of me. This is where children play behind our neighborhood houses, hide behind prickly pears, throw dead yuccas at each other, and watch the skin of their hands melt on anything they touch.

This is the place where I watch these children as I run on a circular path, the one all the husbands and ex husbands run on in the mornings when the snakes have receded. They tell me their running makes them more aggressive at work. But for me, it is a way of celebrating, of knowing I am more powerful than others. My boss himself lives down the street by Darryl, and he runs here in the mornings, but his eyes make me nervous. His children watch Linda and me in the kitchen as we almost kiss over tabouli salads on the weekends, Linda always pulling away and smiling.

Still, my boss knows I'm a banker who can kill with a look, who can bleed loan payments out of clients with a word on the fax that makes their secretaries feel fear. And so he hesitates to fire me. What he doesn't know is that I'm a loan officer almost packing a .44 I will buy to shoot at things when the heat is pushing in on me, when the winds are blowing in Peru, when my body is even more of a foreign thing my parents will not have any words for.

Maybe when I have a gun, and I have sat polishing its blueness for hours, and felt the movement of its parts, maybe then I will even shoot at people in South Phoenix during the sandy season if Linda and her constant flow of words and starvation tactics keep pushing my adrenaline to new highs. Maybe if I can't stop thinking of that sneering barrio boy in the empty weight room, of being alone with him, his gun in my face, my large muscles immobilized, unmoving, useless, if I can't stop thinking of the yellowness of that, maybe then shooting will be the only release.

"I kill with a flex," I say before every competition, and in every mirror, trying to believe it. "My muscles can flatten you," I say before every loan appraisal. "My hands are dangerous," I say as I drive by cantinas in South Phoenix, wishing it were true.

No Soap Radio

Pamela Shepherd

Dear Christian,

When we were kids you'd get sick and vomit each time you saw a dead dog on the road. It was just too much somehow, the knowledge that things die. Mama used to lie to you and say the dog was sleeping, when it was flat as a flounder and anyone with eyes could see that. You never could believe her, and it seemed as if even the lie was too much.

"That dog is dead!" you'd scream, and then throw up all over the back seat of the station wagon.

Once we saw a dog that was in fact sleeping. You threw up anyway. "Christian," I said. "It really was sleeping. How come you threw up?"

"It's going to die," you answered. "You know it's going to die!"

Mama wept at that. She pulled off the road and sat with her arms around us, crying for the longest time.

"So what," I said. "It's only a dog."

Mama pushed me away from her and slapped my face. Then she wiped her eyes, pressed you to her breast one more time, and pulled back onto the highway.

I sat back satisfied. Like I'd given you something, a gift maybe. Later Mama tried to tell me why she'd hit me. I didn't care. You never puked at dead things after that.

*   *   *

I want to tell you about frost and ice, I want to tell you about melting. I will mention church songs here, our childhood God and falling. Ruby's tumble from Black Mesa, the fall from grace, dead trees, the sound an old man's body makes skidding down an icy roof, wool coat against tin. The Thud. Soft. Sickening. Shall I tell you about geometry? The triangle, the three-sided structure of the four-membered family. Or circles. The Acme Ace Pace Race, our bikes returning again and again to the same banked curve.

After Tupper was murdered Angus said that he'd been trying to figure out who was to blame. Each time he'd think he understood it; just as he'd want to say Tupper or Gresh; he'd hear this other voice speaking, and that voice would say, "Angus, look in the mirror."

I've been trying to understand what really brought me to that mountain cabin in the Jarbridge Range, with Angus dead and Ruby mad at me and missing. Bad luck, I want to say, but this voice I keep hearing, she says, "Patch honey, look in the mirror."

There was a myth I heard one time, how the God, Vulcan, had built humans but forgot to build a window to the heart. I picture a heart like a coffin under glass. You could watch it pump; you could understand. I can look in the mirror: the last years in the desert have shaped me, melted down my flesh until I find myself stretched skin to bone, all lines and angles, my life mirrored in geometric patterns nose to chin to cheek to jaw. I remember Ruby tracing the first lines cutting at my eyes. "The story of your life," she said. "Too bad you don't know how to read."

I feel myself stretched taut in time, a strand of paper chain dolls formed. And is memory then the accordion fold through which I at last come face to face with every girl child woman I have been? Perhaps time bends. Memory bends it, or else it lies, those teething misconceptions, those memories we make from who we were, to who we hope to someday be. Perhaps time bends, memory slings it round us like an old thong and rock.

Make sense! you say. What makes you think that any life makes sense? I try to find the line that leads from Gettysburg to here, some path, some patterned map of choices I have made. I find nothing. Memories circle like vultures or crows: I feel the sweep of them, the momentary darkening of the sky. And though I mean to tell a story I find no thread to lead you through. Only the repetition of my past, only long months frozen into place. Perhaps it really is that simple. I can't go forward unless I go back. I will circle myself, vulturous, trying to find some window to the heart.

"The question is," Angus used to say. "How is one to live?" Only being Angus he never said it that way. He said, "Patch, honey. Sometimes you get yourself to a place where all the choices are wrong ones. I always figured you could judge a man by what he does then."

Ruby always said it was just a matter of cleaning up after yourself. She said all morality boiled down to that. "Just live," she said, "And remember to pick up after yourself."

Images repeat themselves. The fake windmill in the rain, your soft buffed shoes, wet carpet, pitch and lime. Ruby on the mesa, gathering seeds from coyote tobacco. She kneels over spindly green stalks, her fingers rubbing seed pods. Tiny seeds roll like ball bearings into the palm of each hand.

Angus on the wool rug before the wood stove, peering over his glasses at our domino game, the umpteenth version, the third glass of wine. His eyes like blue ball lightning, flashing from the leather of his face.

Christian, deadly still in an oxygen tent; your face drained white. Steel pins jut from your wrists and your knees.

Ruby standing at the bar of a Nevada ghost town tavern, her hand a dark red-brown against my own. The bar smells of stale tobacco, sweaty hats and beer, Ruby beside me, amber scented, her breath like peaches and sweetgum sap.

The sound of a ladder skidding against the frozen tin roof. Angus twisting sideways. The thud, muffled by new snow.

And you again, six this time, crying in the front seat of a station wagon. Weeping and puking because things die.

Things die, Christian.

Shall I begin with Angus? Angus, my mentor and friend, though forty years my elder. There? Not there. With love? Wrong love. Oh Christian, in the world you know I have been wrong in my loving, even wronger than this. Ask a woman about life and she will tell you about love. I don't know why.

Vocabulary records. You remember. Mama's purchase of RCA

WORDPOWER BUILDERS. One hundred record albums containing, in the words of Art Linkletter, all the words YOU'LL ever need. All of them, Christian. Have they failed you yet?

Mama bought the set from a door to door salesman in 1957. I was one, you were two, she felt we had no time to waste. What I remember is the drone of that one man's voice, speaking to us through every breakfast I ever ate at home. One hundred long playing records, two sides: all the words you'll ever need. Mama'd start side one, record one in September, every year on the first day of school. She had a way of spacing them so that June came and school let out just as we reached the last Z. Zygote. (a cell formed by the union of male and female gametes; a fertilized egg cell before cleavage.) One hundred long playing records, seventeen years.

The school year began with A's, moved on through the E's by Thanksgiving (embrocate/embrangle). By Christmas we'd be somewhere between gyral/gyrate and halidom. January ran through the LM's, February the NO's; March the P's (I loved the P's). April raced through the QR's and sank into the S's. It took all of May to get through the S's, while T through Z could be finished in the first two weeks of June.

Our most important childhood scenes were played against the backdrop of that one man's voice. My fights with Mama, your loss of faith. He droned on through Father's leaving. Father standing by the front door, his tinplate voice raised to be heard. "Someday, you'll understand. Your mother and I, we can't . . ."

Father. Let me dispose of him once and for all. My Daddy was a shoe salesman who one day took a walk. My daddy left us with one last piece of advice. "Remember," he said, "your shoes are the second thing a man looks at when he meets you. Be sure your shoes are always cared for."

"Not you, Patch," you whispered. "That's just for men. For girls it's the tits, so you better grow some."

We said good-bye in a deserted Gettysburg miniature golf course in the rain. It must have been March of my seventeenth year. I left home during the P's (Palimpsest). I'd been gone almost three days when I called you to meet me at the Funtime Golforama off Pickett Street. (It was the one place I could think of that you could get to in your wheelchair.) It had been raining for days; the green felt carpet was completely waterlogged and covered with puddles. From my seat inside the plywood windmill I could lay my cheek on the only dry spot remaining and stare out past the cyclone fence surrounding the golf course, down Pickett Street to the rain-drenched cemetery on Cemetery Ridge. The wind blew hard from the east, bringing the rain in gusts and torrents, splattering the windmill and sending its plywood blades churning through their rounds.

When you found me I was balanced on your paperback copy of *Look Homeward Angel*, trying to keep my Levi's dry. I'd been waiting for an hour or more and was content watching the rain splatter against the sides of a pink papier mache elephant lumbering across Hole 7. By laying my head carefully on the one dry spot remaining, I could watch the world sideways; Pickett Street forming a vanishing point somewhere lost among the rolling graves of Cemetery Hill, the enormous pink elephant facing into the rain, its underside mud splattered, its trunk held in place with silver duct tape.

I heard the sear of hard rubber wheels across wet carpet, but it was your shoes I spotted first. For some reason you'd worn your dress shoes and they were soft burnished brown. (Burnt Sienna, you'd called it after we'd decided all the color names in the world were found in the large Crayola box.) Your shoes were so absurdly shining, resting above wet carpet, your oldest bluejeans buckling over them almost covering the foot rests for your chair. You lit a Marlboro from the box in your jean jacket and passed me one. We smoked quietly for a while, ignoring the rain on our faces, plastering hair to our scalps.

"You know I loved that girl, Christian. So I kissed her. I never meant to make a scene."

You nodded, running one calloused hand along your wheelchair's wheels. "They'd let you back in school I think, if you apologized maybe."

The hair above your lips looked bristly and red, darker than your head. A few stray hairs grew randomly on your cheeks and chin, not many but long, as if you hadn't shaved for days and were trying to cover that up with lime cologne. I traced figure eights in the air with my cigarette; bluish smoke twisted and rose like streamers between us. "You think I'm a pervert?"

"Nah." You stared down at your impossible shoes. "I think it's hard."

"Chris, I made a mistake. I know that."

You shrugged and looked away. "I don't know. I mean. If it's girls you like. I don't know if you can help that."

I stubbed my cigarette out on wet carpet. The air smelled like burning tires for a second and then cleared. "That's not what I was thinking." I leaned back against the plywood wall. "Margaret Lee, that girl. She didn't have any lips. I think, next time I kiss a girl, I want her to have lips."

You laughed hard, sending your cigarette butt arcing out onto the rain-soaked 6th hole, where it bounced off a plywood tugboat and went out. "You've got three months to finish school, Patch. I think you ought to come home and at least finish school."

I stared down at Hole 9 trying to imagine how anyone could hit a golf ball along a ramp only an inch and a half wide. "I can't go back there, Chris. It's making me crazy, trying to stay, trying to be so pushed down all the time. There's got to be, you know there's got to be some place that makes more sense."

"You can't leave like this. You can't just run off. Finish school at least. It's only three more months."

I tried to tell you then, about three months. How it can seem the longest time of all. How everywhere I looked in Gettysburg, there were the dead, the near dead, monuments to the dead. How even you were stuck, working in a box factory, the dirty brown of Doe Creek crawling beside the railroad tracks, the smell of hot tar and asphalt from the alley behind our house. I tried to tell you and I think maybe that you knew because along toward late afternoon, once the rain had stopped and the sun made tentative pushes against the breaking mass of gray, you stopped with your persuading and began to let me go.

We left the miniature golf course together, you carrying my rucksack, my hands clutching your now soaked copy of Thomas Wolfe. At the corner of Pickett Street and the Boulevard out, you set down my pack and hugged me, wrapping me in your scarecrow arms, your hair falling from your face, blond. Blonder than it would ever be again. I handed you your now soaked book. "It's true you know. You can't go home again."

You laughed and gave me wizard kisses. "I grant you," you said, "Courage, Hope. Decency. And all the words you'll ever need."

I rested my head on your now soaked lap and tried hard not to cry. You said, "Plagioclase. A cleaving fracture."

What did I bring to Ruby while I thought I brought her love? Betrayal, finally. It was my lack of faith which failed us. I was nineteen when I came to Jarbridge. The pass above the town had just been cleared of the last winter storm and mounds of rotten snow towered above the narrow roadbed. From the summit I could see the town below me, a dozen clapboard houses, a couple of stores and an old barnwood saloon. Beside the saloon two antique gas pumps stood before a run-down trailer, and though the trailer door stood open, the shades were drawn and the sign said, *Closed*. In the back, behind the bar and gas pumps, four or five trailers were set up on concrete blocks, looking desolate and lonely against the rabbit brush and greasewood.

I parked my truck next to the Last Chance Saloon, and hung a bright red, yellow, and blue banner off the side of my camper and eight or ten kites on hooks along one wall. I'd been traveling and selling kites all the way into Nevada, and now my newest and biggest, an American Three Stick, I propped out from my roof at an angle, forming a brilliant green and yellow shade against the intense desert sun. Business was steady through the morning, and by two o'clock I'd sold ten kites and was laying patterns to cut more.

"How much are you asking for that parafoil?"

I looked up from my cutting to see a lanky-looking Indian woman in blue jeans and scuffed boots, a man's snap button shirt with the sleeves ripped off. She pointed casually to the stayless backpacking kite draped over the doorjamb.

"Fifteen dollars." I unhooked the parafoil from the door and laid it flat where she could see it.

She glanced up at me once and then back to the kite, letting her fingers run along the seams as if her hands would tell her what the eyes had missed. "I was looking for something to take backpacking. Do you have any others?"

I shook my head. "Just that. But I can make another if you want."

"How much?"

"Fifteen," I said again, wondering if she hadn't heard me.

She shifted and rubbed at the back of her neck. "Fifteen dollars for a kite? For something that could hang up on a power line or drop off a cliff?"

"What do you want," I said, "A guarantee? You want everything to work out perfect, maybe you should take up bookkeeping."

She glanced up at me then, and I noticed that her eyes weren't brown like I'd first thought. They were black, blue-black like chipped obsidian. I looked down at her worn boots again and then back to her face. It was an almost-frightening face, the angles so austere and perfect, her cheekbones so sharp they seemed sculpted from stone. She was about my height, older by ten years I guessed, and she wore her hair carelessly twisted into a bun, which she held loosely in place with a chopstick. "You live in that thing?" She gestured toward the camper.

I nodded.

"And you travel. You travel all around?"

"So. What of it?"

She went back to inspecting the kite, removing the pinpoint of her gaze from my overheated face. "I was just thinking," she said. "All that moving around. Kind of helps you live without a guarantee, doesn't it?"

She grinned then, the sculpted planes of her face broken by white, wide-gapped teeth which seemed to jut from her jaw like a jack-o'-lantern.

"Your bracelet." I pointed to the intricate silver band around her wrist which held a clear blue turquoise the size of a quarter. "I was admiring your bracelet. Maybe we could make a trade."

She pushed a strand of hair behind one ear and smiled a little. "A trade then, but not the bracelet. It belonged to my mother and it isn't for sale. How about this?" She pulled a silver cigarette case out of her shirt pocket. "Do you smoke?"

I shook my head. "Not anymore." But I examined the case anyway: hand-formed silver, engraved along the sides and top and inlaid with garnets along the lid. "But I like this. Maybe we can deal."

She laughed. "Not the case. That's not for sale either. But this . . ."

She opened the case and held out five hand-rolled cigarettes, each with a series of brown initials stamped along one end.

"Marijuana?"

She laughed. "Cigarettes. They're mine. A special blend. I grow the tobacco on my farm south of town. These are from my most special plants."

She grinned that jack-o'-lantern grin again and I almost couldn't stand to say it. "Yeah. That's nice, but I don't smoke so why don't we just say fifteen for the kite and forget the barter."

"I thought you wanted to deal?"

"I do. I do. But I'm not trading a kite for five cigarettes, I mean, get real here."

"Get real yourself!" She pulled one cigarette from the case and lit it, blowing a stream of smoke into the air, before handing it to me. "This tobacco is amazing! the best! and another thing . . ." She leaned closer. "It's the only kind there is that doesn't kill you."

I swallowed and looked toward the closed gas station behind me and then toward the empty saloon. "Sure. Well. How about ten dollars and the cigarettes and we'll call it a deal?"

She took the cigarette from me and clipped it with a pocketknife before placing it back inside the case. "Ten dollars. I don't know . . ." She started to replace the kite on the doorjamb and then stopped. "I know. How about the cigarettes, five dollars and this?" She reached into her jeans pocket and pulled out a bright green river stone about the size of a silver dollar. "Look at the stripes on this thing!" She licked one finger and drew it across the stone, slightly darkening it in places. Dissatisfied with that effect, she placed the entire stone in her mouth and sucked on it before dropping it suddenly into my hand, where it shone almost like emerald, the black lines like ebony rivers winding their way across its face.

I stared down at the wet rock in the palm of my hand. "I don't know, I mean, it's just a rock . . ."

"Just a rock! Are you crazy?" She grabbed my outstretched hand and waved it in my face. "For one thing, I'm sure it's magic, and for another it's beautiful! What the hell do you want for five dollars?"

I turned the rock into her hand and closed it. "It's a nice rock. I just can't eat it. Ten dollars if you want the kite. You keep the rock and the cigarettes and the magic and whatever else is in your pockets."

She adjusted her hat down over her eyes and put the rock back in her pocket. "That's just like a white girl. You offer her magic and she'd rather have money. I don't think I want a kite after all." She shoved her hands in her pockets and strolled out into the street. I stared after her, feeling suddenly responsible for everybody from Kit Carson to the Trail of Tears. I had the momentary image of a forked tongue darting from the base of my mouth.

"Wait." I called after her. "How about five bucks, the cigarettes and the stone?"

She stopped and tipped her hat back, raising her face toward the sky. "Five cigarettes, the magic stone, and dinner. I don't have five dollars."

I watched her walk down Main Street with her new parafoil draped over one shoulder and flowing down her back. In my hand I held a green stone still damp from her mouth, five hand-rolled cigarettes, and a map to her house. I shrugged and turned back to the shade of the camper.

"Miss. Excuse me, Miss. Are you selling them kites?"

"No, I'm just flying them off my truck for entertainment . . ." I stared down at gnarled little man in his late fifties, chunky and broad as a normal-sized man but maybe five feet tall at the most. His chest seemed massive but was probably only full-size, his legs were so short they were almost adorable, tiny little bowed things in Wranglers and boys' boots. His head, as broad and weathered as any man's, seemed enormous hovering above that stumpy body, and was topped with a ten-gallon Stetson adding another nine inches to his height, but in the wrong direction. I wondered how short a man had to be to be considered a dwarf. What the cutoff point was, so to speak.

"The reason I was askin', I thought my boss might be interested in a banner like this. Something to fly over the station when we was open." He reached out toward the red-orange banner flying from the side of the truck but let his fingers pause just short of it. "Mind if I touch it?"

"That's all right. Go ahead."

He reached closer toward the fabric but again stopped, holding his hand steady until the wind caught the banner and it fluttered against the back of his fingers and then went limp. He grinned suddenly, his mouth splitting the lower half of his face into an enormous smile. He ran the back of his hand slowly across the nylon fabric and then, holding the fabric, ran the fingers of his other hand across the sewed-on image of a castle keep. "Look it," he said. "The castle's flying the same banner as this one." He squinted and held the fabric up close to his face. "Then there ought to be another castle and another banner on this one. And then there ought to be . . ."

"Sure there are. They're just too small to see."

He let the banner flutter from his hands and hitched at his jeans. "Kind of reminds me of something. I don't recollect just what. . . ."

"The Borden Milk can."

He snapped his fingers and grinned again. "That's it. Them damn cows going on forever."

I was starting to really like his grin. "You want a beer?"

He grew serious, almost solemn, nodded, and touched his hat. "Why thank you much, I believe that would be just the thing in this weather."

I lifted a couple of cans of Rainier from my cooler and handed him one.

"Why it's an import, isn't it?"

I laughed. "From Washington State. I guess that's kind of imported."

He nodded. "I believe it is. I never had a Rainier Beer." He balanced the beer in the crook of his arm and removed his hat, so that I looked down on a completely bald sunburned head, peeling and freckled across the top. "John Staunt." He bowed his head toward me.

I nodded back. "Leviticus Patch. People call me Patch."

"Folks most always call me Shorty. I guess that's no surprise, is it?"

I opened my beer and took a sip. It was almost cold after riding all week on a single block of ice, now melted into a thin pool of cool water on the bottom of my ice chest. Next to me the four and a half cigarettes huddled against a flat river stone. "Like a cigarette, Shorty?" I held one out to him.

"Thank you much, Miss Patch, I believe I will." He took the

cigarette and rolled it slowly between his fingers. "Why it's Ruby's, isn't it?"

"I beg your pardon."

"The tobacco. RBJ." He held the cigarette so that I could see the tiny initials in dark brown against the white paper. "Ruby B. Jaynes, Tobacconist." He grinned and ducked his head. "That's what her sign says anyway."

"I got them from an Indian woman."

"Yeah. That'd be Ruby. Tall. Kind of skinny and big hipped."

"Yeah." I rooted around in my change box and found him a matchbook.

"She's a fine woman, that Ruby. Real fine. I always thought the world of her, I don't care what they say about her." He dragged carefully on his cigarette and flicked the match into the dirt.

"What do they say?"

"Huh?" He turned slightly redder and looked at the ground. "Why nothing, they don't say nothing, and I don't believe a word of it anyway." He glanced up toward the banner again and then back at his boots. "She sure is growing some fine tobacco up at her place. There's nothing funny about that."

I looked down again at the map in my hand and then back toward the canyon. "You know what time it is?"

Shorty pulled out a strapless wristwatch tied with a shoelace to his belt loop. "Ten to six, just exactly."

I stared down the road to the base of the canyon. "If you'll excuse me. I've got to get closed up here and go to dinner. Did you want that banner?"

"You know, I wish it had a horse or something on it. I'll just talk to my boss about it."

"Sure."

He set down his can and touched his hat again in that charming TV cowboy way. "A pleasure to converse at you." He backed out from the shade, tracing his fingers across the banner one last time, and hobbled off toward a dilapidated old trailer next to the saloon, which seemed to serve as the office for the two antique gas pumps just outside.

I set to work, folding up the stock before driving down past town to a sunny spot on the bank of the Jarbridge River. Though it was still too cold to swim, I splashed around in the shallows until I was reasonably clean, put on my least-wrinkled shirt and tried to make my hair lay down before heading west to dinner.

Ruby's house sat up a canyon about three miles off the pavement. Coming up on it slowly along the heavily rutted lane, I first spotted the greenhouse and a quarter acre garden, fenced with something that looked like wire mesh and old window screens. To the right of the garden, two large fields of about ten acres each had been plowed and turned over, and sat peaceably awaiting their spring planting. The main house sat back from the lane surrounded by giant cottonwoods and bordered by wild roses and Russian olives. The house had been built to face south and its front wall was all glass, or rather, not so much all glass as old windows salvaged from other places and hung together to form the southernmost wall. There were large picture windows and old fourpanes, sixpanes, bay windows and even sections of French doors hung sideways. All the windows had been set on top of each other and end to end until the entire wall became glass and frame, held together by old sashes and two-by-fours and shaded by a homemade awning of dirty red and silver canvas. The side walls were log, chinked with gray-white plaster and cut in places with more traditional–looking windows opening out onto the garden and a postage stamp lawn. Ten feet of stovepipe cut through the back wall and rose over the pitched tin roof, held in place by loose guy wires. A thin ribbon of smoke worked its way out the chimney cap and angled back to the steep box canyon behind the house.

A note taped to the screen door said, "Come in and be careful." I knocked anyway and took a step into the living room, ducking as a gray-and-green cockatiel dive-bombed my head. The bird flapped twice around the living room, and then came to rest on the open front door of a Mexican bird cage, arching his wings and puffing his orange cheek patches while admiring himself in a tinplate mirror.

"That's Carlo. He's showing off for company." Ruby's voice came from a doorway off to my left, from what seemed to be the kitchen. "Make yourself at home, I'll be right out."

I wandered around, inspecting everything. The house was cool and dark in spite of its southern glass wall. The interior walls were stuccoed a light earth color and an adobe banco lined two walls, forming an L-shaped couch covered with bright red pillows and multicolored cushions. Along one wall bookshelves rose from floor to ceiling, partially filled with books but also loaded with rocks, shells, bits of glass, and clay pots of all sizes. Next to the bookcase a collection of arrowheads had been mounted on a faded piece of red velvet and covered by cracked glass.

"Would you put Carlo in his cage for the night? He'll go right in, just shove that chopstick through the door latch once he's in there. I'll be right with you; I'm in the middle of some prospecting."

I put the bird into his cage and locked the door. He chirped once, ruffled his feathers, and began to eat some pieces of broccoli knocked onto the cage floor. I went back to surveying the room: the floors were plank, heavily varnished, and covered in places with throw rugs and Navajo blankets. The kitchen opened to my left; a door to the right was closed and when I tried the handle discovered it was locked.

"That's the lab. Off-limits!" Ruby called out. "Would you double-check the bird's cage. I want to let the cats out of the broom closet."

"The bird seems fine. I like your house." I let go of the door handle and shoved my hands into my pockets.

"Thanks." She leaned against the doorjamb, wiping her hands on a dish towel. "I built most of it myself."

"Yeah. I could tell. I mean. It feels like you."

She laughed. "How do I feel?"

I turned back to the bookcase and began to intently examine a book off the shelf. It turned out to be a U.S. Department of Agriculture publication entitled, *The Boll Weevil and Your Crop.*

"I don't know. I guess I meant . . . It's a little eccentric, you know. Cool. Dark. Chinked walls . . . just, you know. Stuff." I waved vaguely about me, toward walls inlaid with pieces of old shell and dried starfish, chipped dishes and fried marbles. The book in my hand began, "In 1967, in the Southern Atlantic states alone, the Boll Weevil was responsible for the loss of three million dollars in cash crops."

I set the book back on the shelf.

"Come on in the kitchen. You can keep me company while I dig."

Ruby knelt in the middle of the kitchen, hacking at the floor with a hand ax. Next to her, a wiry contraption of hangers and fishing line sprawled across the table like a bad joke, a Tinkertoy of enormous proportions. From the center of a wire hoop formed out of clothes hanger, a quartz crystal dangled six inches off the table and hung perfectly still. Ruby'd cut a hole in the floor about two feet square and was digging into the dirt below with a large spoon.

"What are you doing?" I circled the ripped-up linoleum and growing mound of dirt and found a seat at the table next to the crystal contraption.

She sat back on her heels and grinned that gap-toothed grin again. "Treasure! I was playing with the crystal reader and it said there was treasure under here. I'm not sure how deep though, I forgot to ask it that."

I looked at the contraption on the table and then back at Ruby. "What do you mean, it told you. What *exactly* did it say?"

Ruby hacked up another chunk of linoleum and began to chop at the floorboards below. "Well, nothing *exactly*. I mean, it doesn't talk! I asked it a question and then it told me where to dig."

"You asked? What *exactly* did you say?"

She laughed and set the ax down. "I said, 'Where shall I dig for buried treasure?' Then I touched the crystal and it spun around and pointed right here!" She reached over and flicked the crystal with one finger, watching intently as it spun around on its nylon thread, coming to rest this time pointing toward the front door. "Now look, we've confused it. But that's okay, we've already got the real info. I'm pretty sure I got that first spin right."

"Pretty sure!" I said, looking down at her ransacked linoleum, the kitchen floor half-excavated, a hole in the dirt already two feet deep. "Look at your linoleum!"

I half shouted the last, rising to my feet and pointing stupidly at the hole in the center of the kitchen. Ruby started to laugh. "Who would have thought," she said, "that we'd discover in you such a passion for linoleum."

I shook my head. "Do you always do things like this to your kitchen?"

"Only when there's buried treasure. Would you hand me that crowbar? There's another spoon if you want to help dig."

We dug for another hour or more, prying up floorboards and digging into the dirt below. Suddenly Ruby's spoon hit something. We both stopped and stared at the spot in the earth. Ruby worked carefully, using her spoon to clear away the dirt, revealing bright blue medicine glass, a bottle that was obviously old, with raised print near the base. Ruby held it up to the light so we could both admire it. "God, I bet it's worth a fortune!" She kept turning the bottle in her hands and grinning wider and wider. Then she thrust it at me. "Here. You keep it. I bet it's worth a million dollars!"

"A million?" I turned the bottle carefully until I could read the print along one side.

"A thousand, anyway. I bet it's worth a thousand easy."

"Phillips Milk of Magnesia." I read, staring at Ruby over the top of the bottle.

"Imagine!" She looked even more delighted. "I bet it's the first one ever made!"

We ate dinner outside on the patio. I admired the herringboned bricks mortared into place and was secretly grateful for all the places that crystal hadn't pointed. The table rested next to a small patch of grass, bordered by a white picket fence and shaded by a cherry tree just beginning to leaf out. An old tiger tomcat lay stretched along the lowest branch, letting one paw dangle toward the ground.

"Nice cat."

"Oh scat, you! I caught him this morning eating a sparrow under Carlo's cage. He's a bit of a sadist, I think. Cats, dogs, one bird. I used to have chickens but I gave them to a friend of mine."

Ruby set down the stewpot and wiped her hands. "I hope you like chili."

"Sure. Great. Anything. . . ." I trailed off as she disappeared back into the house for the salad and then returned, placing it on the table between us.

I ate slowly while we talked casually, easily about kites, the weather, the relative joys of a Chevy slant six. Ruby's homemade wine was thick and smooth and went down like syrup. We finished the bottle before I noticed its subtle kick. ("Kung Fu Wine" she called it. Saying it could knock you on your butt before you knew you'd been hit.) I stood slowly, my head thick and spinning. Far off I could hear the sound of marsh frogs, the occasional coo of the poorwill and the slight flutter of bats around the door to the barn.

"Great dinner." I stretched slowly, trying to regain my sense of balance.

"Good company." She sat back in her chair and grinned at me, a hand-rolled cigarette dangling from her fingers like a lance.

"So . . ." I said, trying to keep the world in focus. "You like kites."

"I liked the kitemaker anyway." Her face was in shadow. I could see only a brief flash of teeth and the outline of her lips.

"What do you mean?"

"Nothing. I wanted to meet you. That's all. So I bought a kite." She grinned briefly and lit her cigarette.

I leaned across the table at her, balancing on two fists. "You bought a kite to meet me? You didn't buy it, you stole it! Why didn't you just walk up and shake hands like normal people?"

"Oh come on. You liked our barter! It made you feel . . . what? Like you were being very smooth." She laughed and poured another glass of wine for each of us. "Besides, I liked the way you looked."

"How'd I look?"

She laughed. The tip of her cigarette glowed briefly brighter. "Sort of like a cross between P.T. Barnum and Joan of Arc. Like you know there's a sucker born every minute and you're just beginning to suspect it might be you."

I sat back down rubbing my stomach and pulling my shirttail into place. "I'd better go."

"Does that offend you?"

"Of course not. It doesn't even mean anything."

"Yeah, you're right." She laughed and began to clear the table. "It was just a thing. You know. A thing to say."

She carried the dishes into the kitchen while I stumbled up the path to the outhouse. The view was lovely from up there and I sat quietly watching the stars while waiting for my head to clear. Below me, by the river, I could hear the bullfrogs blow and trumpet. The wind blew down from the canyon smelling of juniper

and sage. The screen door to the house slammed shut and I heard
Ruby in the kitchen talking to someone. I hitched up my jeans
and staggered back down the path to the kitchen. Ruby crouched
in the doorway to the living room talking earnestly to a small
black dog. "This is Bright. I've got another, Burley, around here
somewhere. The little squirt won't eat again. Bright, sit up and act
your age!"

The dog stared at Ruby with one ear half-raised, ignoring an
untouched bowl of mashed vegetables and brown rice. "Look. I
better go. Thanks again for dinner."

"I don't think you ought to drive, Patch. We had an awful lot
of wine."

"I'm okay. I'll just drive to the river and . . ." I stumbled down the
two steps into the living room, landing on my hands and knees.

Ruby picked me up by the arm and hauled me back into the
desecrated kitchen. "I'll make some tea, and then you can just
leave your truck parked here, okay?"

I said, "Ruby, I think I'm a little drunk, maybe."

She laughed and sat me back down at the table.

I said, "You know what. I think if I lived here, in this town, I
think if I lived here, we'd have probably been friends. Don't you
think so? Don't you think we might have been friends. If there'd
been time, I mean."

"Sure. I think that. I think that if you lived here, and we had
time, we might have been friends. We'd probably like all sorts of
things about each other."

I drank the tea she made me and let her help me out the front
door and up the steps to my camper. "It's been fun," I said. "Like
a friendship . . . but quick and complete."

"Clean." Ruby tilted her head like she wanted to laugh. "That's
what you mean isn't it. Clean."

I didn't have an answer. It wasn't a question that made sense. I
said, "Maybe we'll . . ."

She shook her head. "Endings are good. Say good-bye."

So I did. It felt sadder than I thought it should. It felt strangely
final, like a death.

She left me balanced in my doorway and I hovered there, listening to her footsteps in the dark. "Ruby, wait. I want you to
know something."

"What?"

"I really like it . . . what you did to your linoleum."

I heard her laugh from somewhere in the dark. "I'll bring you coffee in the morning."

"Yes," I said. "Coffee. First thing."

LOVER BOYS

Ana Castillo

Two boys are making out in the booth across from me. I ain't got nothing else to do, so I watch them. I drink the not-so-aged house brandy and I watch two boys make out. It's more like they're in the throes of passion, as they say. And they're not boys, really. I think I've seen them around before, somewhere on campus maybe. Not making out though.

One gets up to get them each another drink I guess, and he and I check each other out briefly as he passes me up on his way to the bar. He's a white boy wearing a t-shirt with a graphic of Malcolm X on it.

This is the way my life is these days or maybe it's a sign of the 90s: a white boy with a picture of Malcolm X on his t-shirt and me, sitting here in a gay bar trying to forget a man.

Well, okay. He must not have been just any man and I'm sure not just any woman. Before him there were only women. Puras mujeres—(sino mujeres puras)! A cast of thousands. Women's music festivals, feminist symposiums, women of color retreats and camp outs, women's healing rituals under a full moon, ceremonies of union and not-so-ceremonious reunions, women-only panels and caucuses at conferences, en fin, women ad infinitum.

And then one day a boy—not much older than either of these two loving it up in front of me—nor the half dozen other clientele here on a dead Monday night for that matter—comes into my store asking for a copy of *The Rebel*. I point in the direction of

Albert—whom once I was so fond of we were on first name basis—
and he, the boy in my store, kind of casually goes over to check
out what we got on the shelf. We're always stocked up on the
existentialists, so I didn't bother to offer assistance.

My partner, who used to be my partner in all senses of the
word and whom I bought out a year ago, and I opened up the
store about ten years ago. We thought about making it a woman's
bookstore, a lesbian bookstore, a gay and lesbian bookstore, a
"Third World" bookstore or even an exclusively Latina bookstore.
Heaven knows, any town could use at least one of each of those
kind of book shops—stocked up on alternative press publications
that inform you about what's going on with the majority of the
population when you sure don't hear it from the mass media. You
know? But no, spirituality won out—since all roads eventually lead
to one place, we reasoned.

So along with Camus, Sartre, and Kirkegaard, we ... I carry
almost anything you can imagine that comes out of the East and
Native imaginations and ancient practices.

I sat back and picked up the book I was reading. I let the boy
browse. I saw him leafing through some other things and finally,
he came over with a copy of *The Stranger*.

"Didn't you see *The Rebel* up on the shelf?" I asked not really
looking at him, just taking the book and ringing it up.

"Yeah. But I don't think I'm ready for it," he answered. "I read
this in high school. I think I'll read it again ... I really like this
translation anyway," he said, referring to the edition he had
chosen.

I rang it up. But he didn't pick up his package right away. Just
kept looking at me. I looked back and smiled, a little cockily. I'm
a mirror that way. You look at me a certain way and I respond
in kind. Just like with this white guy here who just passed me by
again with two Coronas. He looks. He doesn't smile. He just looks
like I don't belong here. *I* don't belong here? I helped start this
joint about twelve years ago when you couldn't find a gay bar
within ten miles of this town.

Me and Rosie and her compadre, who's over there tending bar—
the big guy with the Pancho Villa charm and beer belly. He looks
like someone's father, right? Not the kind of bartender you would
expect to find in a gay bar. Well, just for the record he *is* some-

body's father. His oldest son enlisted in the Air Force—overcompensating for his dad's dubious machismo or patriotism, if you ask me. He just got shipped off to the Middle East last week. His daughter, Belinda, Rosie's godchild, got married last summer.

That's the way it goes.

Yeah. His wife knows he owns this bar. And she knows all the rest, too. But she's pretty religious and would never have thought to divorce him. Besides, Rosie told me that his wife really doesn't find the men in her husband's life a threat to her marriage. He's got it pretty good, huh?

Anyway, I say to this young man with Indian smooth skin like glazed clay, and the off-handed manner of a chile alegre if I ever saw one, after he's been staring at me for a good minute or so without saying anything, "Is there anything else I can help you with?"

His dark face got darker when he blushed, and he laughed a little. "Naw, naw . . ." he said, shaking his head. "Actually, I *did* wanna get that one of his, too, but I can't afford it 'til payday'," he admitted, referring to *The Rebel*.

Liking his white, uneven teeth, although I'm not very good with quotes, except to massacre them usually, I said, " 'I was placed halfway between poverty and the sun.' " With that he got this expression like I had just done a wondrous thing by quoting Albert spontaneously. I was ready to part the sea if I could continue to elicit that gaze of a devotee from those obsidian eyes so I dared to continue quoting: " 'Poverty kept me from thinking all was well under the sun and in history: the sun taught me that history was not everything . . .'"

He laughed out loud. He laughed like he had just discovered he was in the presence of Camus himself and he slapped his thigh, as if to say, 'what a kick!' He stared at me some more and then he left, still laughing.

After that it was all out of our hands. He came back a few more times that week and finally one evening just before I closed. He wasn't buying anything, just browsing and talking with me when I had a minute between customers. By this time we were old chums—talking about all kinds of things, literature mostly. He likes poetry. He writes poetry. Well, at least he says he does. He never showed me anything. But who am I to question or to judge?

So we went to get a taco down the street at my favorite taco joint.

I'm really a creature of habit, no doubt about it. There's only one place where I go for tacos and only one place where I go to get loaded. And there's my store. In between is home and sleep.

Anyway, then we came here, as you might have guessed, to have a drink—where I used to come just on week-ends but since about the time when we stopped hanging out I am here just about every night of the week it seems.

That night we got pretty "hammered," his favorite word for what we used to do very well together—besides make love. We made love anytime, any place, as often as we could—like a happy pair of rabbits—with the one big difference that I don't reproduce—never did when I could and now I never will.

He's really gonna hate me for telling you all this (and I don't doubt that he'll find out someday that I have, since it was the very fact that I'm kind of a public person around here), but little by little, his PMS started to get the better of him. You know, his "Pure Macho Shit." Maybe it's not fair to call what he started to feel towards me that but I don't know what else it was. I can't explain none of it. I don't know why he's gone, why I'm here worrying about it . . . why *you're* here, for that matter . . .

Except to drink. And we know how far that will get you. It's just like that Mexican joke with the two drunks just barely hanging on to their bar stools. "Well, why do *you* drink?" One asks the other. "I drink to forget," the other guy replies. "And what's it you're trying to forget?" the first guy asks. The other looks up, kind of thinking for a bit, then says, "I dunno. I forgot."

Well, it's a lot funnier in Spanish. Or maybe you have to be Mexican. But for sure, you have to be a drunk to get it . . . or maybe just drunk.

I went over to the payphone when I first got here and tried to call him. Although I promised myself never to look for him again, I broke down finally—because between books and drinks, there's only him in my head, like one of those melodies where you only know half the words. I called him without thinking about it, like I had done so many times before, and him always on the other end, and pretty soon, he would be with me.

I called the gas station where he *used* to work 'cause I can't call his house, but apparently he's not gigging there anymore. The guy that answered couldn't tell me anything. High turnover in those places is all the consolation he could give me.

Where do you think my boy went? Fired, most likely. Left town, maybe? I doubt it. He's not ready for that kind of wandering, the kind of wandering his soul takes when he's alone and the kind of wandering loving me gave his imagination. Unless I really underestimated him.

Well, see, in the beginning he seemed very cool about my life. The fact that I had not been with a man since college, just women . . . one woman mostly. Considering himself a sensitive, progressive, politically conscious, self-defined young male of color—*of course* he was cool about my life, he said. How could he not be, he insisted.

But that didn't stop him from jumping on top of me the first night we were alone, did it?—when he came over to my place with the excuse to drop off a copy of Neruda's *"Veinte poemas de amor y una canción desesperada"* that he bought in Mexico where he lived for a semester as an exchange student.

A bright young man, he was. Is. A bright, splendid ray in my life. But like Picasso said, "When you come right down to it, all you have is your self. Your self is a sun with a thousand rays in your belly. The rest is nothing." But for a while, he was all mine. *Mio. Mio. Mio.*

Then his brothers started telling him about running around with a lesbian—or worse, a bisexual, nothing more shady or untrustworthy (except for a liberal)—who plays soccer and who knows how to do her own tune-ups and oil change. And his mother, about me being a woman with a past. And his father, about me being an independent businesswoman, and what could he teach an older woman?

As if my loverboy were not tormenting himself well enough on his own day and night over all this as it was. Once he was reading a book by a male psychologist that talked about the history of goddess worship and said that in early times the pig and cow represented the female and were considered powerful deities. So one night we were sleeping and his body gave a great jerk and we both woke up. "I was dreaming that I was at home in the kitchen and I was telling my brothers that a pig was after me . . .

and suddenly this huge pig leaped right through the window at me . . . and I jumped!" He told me.

Well, of course it didn't take a genius to figure out who the pig was but I was pretty impressed by his metaphorical interpretation of what I was in his life. He was cool about us for a while, as I said, although he did spend the first months doing some hard drinking over it. Then he sobered up so that he could sort it all out with a clear head, he said.

And then he left.

I went on with my business without missing a beat. You know, I got the store to run. And I spoke at a pro-choice rally last weekend. I started dating a woman I met some time back who had asked me to go out with her before, but I was too busy being in love with an existentialist Catholic pseudo poet *manito* fifteen years younger than me to have noticed even Queen Nefertiti herself gliding by on the shoulders of two eunuchs. *¡Jijola!* Was I cruisin' for a bruisin'—*o ¿qué?*

I stopped drinking too. You know? For about a week. I couldn't take the hangovers. I told my new friend, who was already frowning pretty seriously on the extent of my alcohol consumption. "You drink too much," she told me at the end of our first date as she walked me to my door. Then she turned around and left me standing there feeling bare-assed with my drunkenness showing and my broken heart, which I would not admit to no matter what. Like everybody, she comes from a disfunctional family and all that brings up too much stuff for her, she said.

But the funny thing was that when I stopped drinking, I didn't feel any better about him, but I did feel worse about *her*. I just took a good, hard sober look at her one day and thought, who wants someone around who's gonna be telling you about yourself all the time? Especially when you haven't asked her for her opinion in the first place.

So I told her last Sunday that we were gonna have to be just friends and we talked about it for a while on the phone, (I didn't have it in me to tell her to her face) and she said, "Fine, I understand."

Yeah, yeah, yeah. After we hung up, I went out. I came here, naturally, and around closing time I made it back home, seeing cross-eyed and hardly able to find the key-hole to get my key in the door when I jumped back and would have screamed like a banshee except that nothing came out of my mouth I was so scared by something moving suddenly out of the darkness coming right at me. And there she was. She had been sitting on the front porch all night waiting for me.

Now, I ask you: Is there justice to this life at all? Or maybe the question should be, is life even supposed to make sense? Or maybe we shouldn't bother trying to figure it out, just go about our business tripping over it like that crack in the sidewalk that sends you flying in an embarrasssing way and when you look back to see what tripped you, and everybody's looking at you, there's nothing there.

I mean, I have been half out of my mind since I said good-bye to my loverboy and I ain't heard nor seen hide nor hair of him since; and meanwhile this woman, whom I forgot the moment I hung up the phone saying good-bye, is convinced that God has put her on this planet for the sole purpose of rescuing me from myself!

Yeah, you heard right just now. I know I said earlier that he left me. But it was me who suggested we not see each other anymore. I mean, it was just a suggestion, right? A damn good one I thought at the time, driven by my self-respect as I am, since he had just told me that he was gonna take a trip and travel around South America with a college friend of his, and didn't know exactly when we'd see each other again. So I decided to give him a head start on feeling what it was to not see me anymore and said I was gonna be pretty busy myself, and as of that moment didn't know when I could see *him*.

Well, let me tell you how it was with us. We had done all the hokey things people in love do. We stayed up in bed for hours after making love, just talking, confessing all our childhood traumas to each other: we cried together about a lot of things. We went to the zoo, the movies; we took walks and had picnics. We even kissed in the rain, making out in the downpour like nobody's business.

Which of course, it wasn't. He said to me once, "You are the kind of woman who deserves to be kissed in front of everybody."

We had only one fight in all those months. I don't remember what stupid thing started it, but the next thing I know I threw a cushion at him that must've been tearing already because it hardly had an impact and there was fluff all over the place like it was snowing in the room. Well then, he throws a cushion at me. And before you know it, we're laughing and pounding each other with *almohadas destripas*, a flurry of feathers and fluff all over the room.

That's the way it was with us. A lot of laughs. A lot of good times. It's real hard to find someone to laugh with, you know?

Like, you see those two guys still sitting there in the dark? Now they're not smooching anymore. In fact, it looks like they're a little pissed off at each other. Who knows why? I was sitting here since before they came in and never once did those two laugh with each other. They came in, sat down without a word, and as soon as the one got the other a drink, they started making out. Now, they're mad at each other.

But those two will probably grow old together because they really know how to be mad at each other, while me and my loverboy who didn't have a bad moment together have already gone up in smoke—with the force of burning copal and all the professed tragedy of "La Noche Triste"—succumbing to our destiny. Between the sun and poverty there was us for a little while.

Well, someone had to take my lunch away. I don't mind admitting it. I hurt Rosie pretty bad after being with her all our adult lives, practically. I just fell out of love with her and even out of like, since we fought so much toward the end. Actually, I know by then that she was seeing that woman who she ran off to Las Cruces with. But she would never admit to that. I couldn't prove it, but I knew it in my heart—the little emaciated excuse for a heart I had left when she took off. But I can't say I blame her for leaving since it wasn't happening with us anymore.

Anyway, I don't really know why I'm telling you about Rosie. That's all over with. But it's like the one who matters is too hard to talk about. I can't talk about it without thinking I look ridiculous—like the classic jilted older woman. Of course it wasn't going to work out. *I* knew that. *He* knew that. And his family didn't help it any either. But even so. Somewhere in the middle of all its fatality, *we*, me, him, even his mother, who was busy having Masses said for her son's salvation—and I'm not putting down his mother either, in case you ever run into him and tell him any of this— *she* knew that what we had was indelible.

I'm gonna stop drinking. This time not because someone is shaming me out of it. And not because I can stand to go to bed at night thinking of him or waking up alone remembering waking up with him. But because it doesn't help anymore.

I'm gonna stop torturing myself in all the ways that I've been doing, I'll even stop playing all those Agustin Lara records he brought over—for us to make love to. And we did, over and over again.

I saw Agustín Lara perform in Mexico City when I was a kid. Did you know that? He was gaunt and very elegant. My mother was swooning. I was just a little kid, so I was just there. But when I mentioned it to my loverboy, he gave me the sign of *la bendición*—implying that I was among the blessed to have laid eyes on the late, great inimitable saint of Mexican music:

Santa, santa mia, mujer que brilla en mi existencia . . . His saint he called me, his saint and his treasure. His first and only love.

I've been thinking about renting the storefront next to my bookstore and extending my business to include a cafe. You know, caffe latte, avocado and sprout croissant-sandwiches and natural fruit drinks. I think this town is ready for a place like that. Maybe I'll exhibit local artists there, not that there are too many good ones around. But there are a few who are going places—I'll get them to show in my establishment before they do . . .

I think he already split town with his friend, he's probably somewhere in Veracruz at Carnival at this very moment—having a great old time. Well, at least for his sake, I hope so.

You think that maybe he misses me a little bit?

Probably the saddest boy in Mexico right now, you say?

I hope so.

Let me tell el compadre over there to send those two unhappy lovers a couple of beers, on me. There's something insupportable about being pissed with the one person on this planet that sends your adrenaline flowing to remind you that you're alive. It's almost like we're mad because we've been shocked out of our usual comatose state of being by feeling something for someone, for ourselves, for just a moment.

He made me feel alive, cliché or not. Drunk or sober. If he ever finds out I told you all this, he'll really be furious. I guess he felt like he was living in a glass bowl with me. Not that I'm not discreet, but everyone in town seems to know me, or at least think that they do. But I like my privacy, too, you know? *Mis cosas son mis cosas.* I just had to talk to somebody about it. Been carrying it around inside me like a sin, a crime, like that guy in *Crime and Punishment.* And it wasn't like that at all—far from it.

Anyway, I haven't used any names, in case you didn't notice, not even yours—even though people'll figure it out soon enough. And everybody already knows who I am. I run the only bookstore in town that deals with the question of the soul. All roads sooner or later will lead you there.

Joshua's Visit

Kristina McGrath

Overlate, because of new birth at his place, Joshua comes in feeling okay in his mercy of the surplus dirt and walking rather well. His ankles are doing fine today. He sets down in the kitchen, in the silence of stacked pots, and sometimes the world is so far off the plates look like buttons. So Joshua says, There's your manure, and I'm brought back by the good dirt smell of his clothes, the color of his jacket that tints the curtains green, and I'm grateful.

I ask after him and he says he's about as usual, except for new birth. A single lamb, and that he'll give to the freezer since it's male. Disappointed, Joshua crosses his arms and legs and fusses in the stuffed chair by the table. I offer coffee.

Honey

It takes concentration to give Joshua coffee, decipher the cups from the cupboard walls, the black pot from the stove top, the spoons from their dark nest in the drawer, because my mind, for as far as I remember, was always got by other things, not things.

More the ghost of things, or real things but only after they leave. Things at a distance like those hills that border these ten acres, where I'd like to throw myself sometimes, onto distant slopes. Though to do it, slopes would vanish. The women in them would go away. The gentleness would vanish as the earth faced you flat.

A great blue heron came and went tonight, I'd like to tell him, but I take two cups from the drafty cupboard, two white saucers. I set them on the cold sinkboard, wet from washed plates. The cups sit there, silent, and I make myself see them, white on the white sinkboard, with their squat satisfied shape.

Joshua lifts an inch, moving himself and his chair closer to the table. He reaches for the reading stack, a yellow pencil from the sill, and flips through the pages of a seed catalog, taking notes on slips of crumpled paper from his shirt pocket where he's already figured lambs: what's been bled, scalded, skinned, and gutted. Now he adds the beans and turnips to his place, planning rows on slips of paper. I stare out at those hills.

I lift the pot from the cold back of the stove to the sink, I take the spoons from the drawer, but it's the far off I've loved, more the cloudy days and not how the sun cuts everything clear, more the pond color shadowed on the curtains by a jacket. It's more the ghost of the world. Like waking up mystified in someone's arms. Someone who's not there. Somebody small with perfect positions and light curly hair maybe. Something about that person makes you think of honey, like honey skin, or the shadows on that person's body are the color of dark honey, especially at the neck. Is it the chin that makes that tiny shadow just below?

I stare out at those hills because the earth is an answer to a lot of questions. A landscape is a message, and in its rise and fall tonight, it keeps returning Bode. Half-there, half-given, but grateful it was me who wandered in, Bode wakes, her honey-colored legs in a wrestle with the bedclothes, trying to swing one of them over me, she does. So huh, says Bode, and falls back again, her face vanished to the pillow.

Even when you live with her, all you get of Bode is glimpses. In the middle of the night you find her in the bed. You find her face for an instant in the gray of Cornby's porch light, her right leg in porch light, the top of her hand, and with your face you find the back of her shoulder, her thighs. Sunlight streams through the front door, and you find her in the hallway with your coat in her hands. In the kitchen you find her behind you, making tea in two gray cups, somehow her arms are around your waist. You stand at the sink washing cups, and she has placed her left foot between your feet. You find it there in its shoe. But then she has flung herself onto the sofa, where you find her staring at its pattern of blue leaves, and her shirt is blue also, loosened around the honey color of her neck, with four buttons undone.

Late Beans

I'm tempted to ask Joshua about that particular area where bones meet to form that tiny hollow at the center of a person's neck, but he seems absorbed, his head filled with late beans. Besides, it's too odd anyways, Mazelle. That's odd, Mazelle. Odd Mazelle. I've heard it so all my life that I took to writing the *Creek County Bell*, "At The Homefront" column. Seeing my letters to the editor, Miss May Kaney, made Mazelle real.

> *Dear May,*
>
> *After raising 1 genie bean a year as my hobby for over 40 years, I ought to know they're too slow to grow fast, and that over 5 foot in 20 days is just a story you've been told. You can tell Mr. Billy Jameson of Oven Fork, who claims that span of time and bean, for Mazelle Back, that life or genie beans are not that possible, as my achievement in genie blue ribbons does testify.*
>
> *Yours in Creek County,*
> *Mazelle Back*

Now water rattles into the pot. Joshua fiddles with his hat. Near everyone he knows knows how to work a car insides and out. He holds his blue Ohio Valley baseball cap lightly by the brim in his fingertips as if he would set it free, his hands at rest on his knees, his feet planted firm, slips of paper forgotten in his lap. I let go the heron, the shadows on a person's neck, the pond color, Bode. I make coffee so hard with all my might that the heron really is ancient history, though it feels a little like losing somebody when you don't know how they died or where they were buried.

I grind the new earth of the coffee beans. Heat pours up from the wood stove and Joshua's eyes fall shut. Mazelle, I say. Thought is a luxury like angels. It's no use looking up to a heaven you can't afford. Look at that new ready-to-be-plowed earth and give Joshua coffee. Everyone he knows is from Ohio.

Water rattles into the pot, bubbles up and clears. That always reminds me of something nuclear, particles mushrooming upward, and I pray for the Japanese. For the current generations with something in their blood or memory. Or maybe for the ones that died near fifty years ago. Then I pray for the Jewish people because I'm always praying for the Jewish people. A prayer is something you have no control over, it goes off. Into the past, if it still needs it, which it usually does the most. Into the somewhere of the bushes.

I set the pot down cold on the hot wood stove. The black top of it hisses to a flatter black and I take some comfort in that. The room is touched with the smell of new shoes. Why coffee is new shoes I don't know. Except Daddy was always noted for them both, drinking sugared coffee and wearing new shoes. I don't think that man ever walked more than fifty miles a pair, which is not much to note about a life, though maybe I'll think of something later. To be startled by the smell of home, that's the first effort, Mazelle.

I sit down across the table from Joshua Day. His eyes fall shut again, then open onto mine without meaning to.

"The new pup's beginning to trot," he says, "she's a full-time job."

"She's as pretty a dog as you could get anywhere," I say. And his eyelids blink shut. I stare out the window, planning beans and a trellis at the back of the lot.

"That fool cousin of mine, Billy Cotton, Jeannie's boy from Marietta," says Joshua suddenly back from sleep, "run out the road last week after his dog gets hit; got his hand bit near up to the elbow; dog got his pelvis smashed. A body should know not to get that close to something wild with pain," he says. "Hit dog'll lash out at anything, including what it loves."

"A body should know better," I say.

"Dog in pain like that . . . But my mother's people are a mixed-up lot," he says, gathering up his slips of paper, his last dream of beans and turnips, into a thin neat stack on the table. He sets back his head and his eyes fall shut.

Joshua and the day are lost and drifting out into darkness, where the sky arrives at nothing but Ohio night, where the sleepy ones float off all the way down Cottonwood Road, nodding in their easy chairs, lost in the shipwork of their sleep. The front yard elm stares into window glass. A curved branch, grown earthward, bends down, low to the ground, like Billy Cotton.

Preserves

Now Joshua wears his hat as he sleeps in my sagged chair, its pattern of flowers rubbed out from the years. The chair is the color of Joshua's chin and cheeks grizzled with a three-day beard, and I make a note of that in my mind. I try to see Joshua sleeping. I try to see him with my eyes the way I would a heron, a genie bean, or the windward side of the barn, seeing how it weathers, standing out there an hour, peering at things, learning what the wind has done. His cheeks are grayish blue. The cushion is puffed like Joshua's stomach, and I make a note of that. The chair will be Joshua when he rises. In the wind from the window cracks, the slips of paper flutter down into his lap again. His lips part with a puff of air and curl out like he was just about to read them to me. But his head falls slightly to one side, then another, as if he's on a ship and slowly going out to sea. The fire cracks with sap. His head listens against the air, then steadies itself, upright again. With his legs crossed and his hands crossed in his lap, Joshua has a polite way of sleeping at my kitchen table.

He's used to chairs. Some nights at home he sleeps in a chair with his shoes on. No use disturbing an otherwise fine piece of bed, he's fond of saying.

With its two unmatched chairs, a table, and an undressed bed, Joshua's house is near naked. Sometimes I think Joshua Day couldn't be happier than having nothing but a Chevy with just wind in it. Chairs and bureaus won't stand around his feet, telling him he's here, belonging to a place, and been hurt by Ivory, first-and-only, gone-for-good wife, he calls her. Joshua reminds me of somebody pretending to be the sea. Like to move when I like, with just what's on my back, he's fond of saying. Now his head falls sideways. He arches his back into the chair, backing away from something, something that peers into his face.

I take the pot from the black stove top. Joshua starts from the weight of his big head that falls to the side and straightens itself awake. His eyes open. "Nella Mae Owens died last week," I tell him.

"Almost blind for years," says Joshua, "but she had a nice-looking family."

"Her eldest son, poor thing," I say.

"Hear he's doing well after that cave-in at Dorsey; already he can walk with braces and drive a truck with hand controls."

"He's a fine boy," I say. The fire cracks with sap. Then Joshua asks can he put on a little bit of radio. I know he likes the noise. Sometimes he sits out front a while after he pulls up the drive, gunning the motor of his Chevy pickup. I see him with his head bent down, listening to the steering wheel, with a smile on his lips, perfectly satisfied. So I tell Joshua yes, "That's fine." I like it all right, it's a comfort.

Joshua puts on the radio. A woman sings of radial tires, which is pleasant enough. The room is deep with the smell of new shoes. Wandering through my living room as if he were lost in a foreign country, Joshua looks like he needs preserves and bread. So I get that ready, thinking. Bread is defiance. Preserves are defiance, their colors lined on root cellar shelves. Canning in five rows, two jars deep is defiance: red beets, green kale, yellow squash. Feeding yourself or someone else, that's defiance. I've got it in me. Though I've never been much for hungry.

Still I get that ready, counting trees from the window. While Joshua searches the Ohio airwaves for another station, I accept the necessary of the lost maples from the clearing done for the pond. Two exactly, ten years old, where the seasons invested. Plus all the pines I'm not going to be sorry about. That's just the way it is, Mazelle. Certain losses you can count on and go on from. Your eye will stray from the emptiness they leave, go on to other things, dig deeper into other colors. Losing the maple, your heart receives the elm.

Joshua finds his weather report, then wanders over to the window, expecting night and finding it. "Cloudy, with cool temperatures, highs in the mid-40s." I smile at his body bent there at the window, peeking into open space. "Preserves," I tell him. His face nods up with a look of satisfaction now he knows night is as night is, and coffee's near ready. He studies the darkness for the dogs, a rambling fence, a red barn side, weaving from three windows a picture of what's out there. He stands back and makes it whole. He walks backward a few steps, raises the volume on the radio, then strolls back into the kitchen with a swing to his shoulders, as if everything is the way he wants it to be. He stands in the doorway, roots himself like a tree from his heavy feet, his boots cracked with Ohio dust almost forever.

A Victim of Desire

Sometimes I wish Joshua Day Anderson from the Tuscarawas Valley, an able speaker when he wants to be, would tell me about his childhood. Better yet, I wish it was still standing. Most childhoods are all knocked down by this time of life. I wish he'd sit here at the table and tell me his real true mental philosophy or about Ivory, his share of sorrow, first-and-only wife.

Joshua cleared out the house after Ivory Anderson, his wife of twenty years, went off in '73. Left everything on the roadside with a sign:

Good Stuff   Free
U-Haul

I couldn't have touched the stuff. Not that they were sorry things, but because it was the furniture of sorrow. Ivory's weight in the sagged pillows. Ivory's sweat in the black-handled pots and hoe. The course of their days in the flattened-down faces of colored rugs. How a chair, where Ivory sat, still creaked with Ivory in the wind at roadside.

But Joshua Day cheats at rummy and conversation. So I don't hear a word, not more than twice, about a life that once called itself Ivory Anderson.

I'm not much better when it comes to talking, but I know what's in my head. I don't know what Joshua has in his. When I first knew Joshua, I asked him: Have you ever had a love? A love is a person, ain't it? he says. And sometimes I wonder if Joshua Day feels a terrible injustice in not being able to express himself, except about a Chevy. Most people can't, not even finally or at long last. And if you want to know the truth, you may as well listen to a chicken opera as to Joshua Day.

As for Ivory, she was what she was and things are as should be, or so said Joshua once, who sat in my house, flipping through magazines, from noon till dawn a few months back, twenty years to the day that Ivory left, pretending to be a simple man, all settled with his heart.

Bode was what she was, spilled flat out and given against me, wanting the rooms lit, loving dogs, listening to Mozart, swearing she'll take French, dreaming she was seventeen, her legs dangling through the bedposts, dreaming of some lighter thing, chasing after Eden on a bus route in her dreams, her head at rest on my back.

Life has its steps, only some of them are ours. I could never make her stay or leave, give an inch or go. It was only just Ivory, says Joshua. It was only Bode. It was only a heron came and went tonight. And those are only hills. If I repeat that word "only" forty times in a row, it begins to sound like holy or alone, and either's fine. Just maybe.

Instead of Ivory or childhood, Joshua tells me plans for a second-hand motor home. He sits right down at my table and tells me his wish of driving off to God knows where, counting freighters, up along the Cuyahoga to Cleveland of all places, a spider's web of highways, railways, power lines, a mill every two seconds for the express purpose of machine tools, food processing, and cement. And I'm sorry, Joshua Day, I don't understand the exact appeal. He says, "Just curious." He'd like some nice eating places with self-service along the way. And I think he must be a victim of desire.

Coffee Cups

I'd like to ask Joshua over coffee. I'd like to ask Joshua Day. About that person I thought of with honey skin? Somebody you could be a little afraid of when you smelled them coming across the yard or down the hall in a sugar of blossoms something like oranges? And suddenly you're mindless except for the colors of that person's shirt? Ever felt that, Joshua?

But I'm not much for telling stories. Especially about Bode. It's hard to find the facts it takes to tell your place on earth, let alone it was another woman. You don't tell that to Ohio.

Besides, I don't know how to make Bode walk across the room to me in a story the way Joshua can tell a ton of motor home he doesn't even own yet barreling down the road so real you step away. Besides, I haven't thought of her in years.

I'm too busy wondering at how things in this world are arranged: a mutt against the sky, a fence post tangled with vines, man and woman, sun and moon, salt and pepper, wondering why it all didn't turn out some other way. I'm too distracted by the colors of things, as if there weren't a thing there, only deeper color.

I give Joshua coffee. I set down two cups, two saucers, in that way, and Joshua divides them. Says, "So there's your manure; guess you'll be starting up that second lot." Or, I'm interested in not so much what people say, but the fact their voices make a sound. I wonder why you arrive, what you left behind, not how you manage to stay. Not where you sleep, in what bed or town, but what do you dream. I get the coffee. I give Joshua coffee. I pick up the cup. That, I touch. That, I pour into. But it all comes down to not to me. Whether we sit here having coffee saying one word or not: those hills in green darkness are out there silent, curving into more of the same.

Brown and scruffy, or full green and ticking with the legends of horseflies—I wish they were just hills for at least a week. I'd look out and see that's only hills, mud darkness, not answers or grace, not Bode asleep, not dreams or questions about the width of the sky, the height of a person, or the span of a wing, but just hills where our lives take place in the comings and goings of light, hills with true stories in them. Stories so plain you might pass them by like pennies, but wild in all their plainness: how people are born and come to settle down below, come to dream, know Chevies, love birdcall or somebody small with perfect positions and honey skin. I wish they were just hills with only sky and wind above them. I wish I didn't recall parts of God or women in near everything I see. Even a round white cup, with the silence of the sky whipping through it. And that, I set down.

THE JETSAMS

E.J. Graff

"Flotsam and jetsam," Kate singsongs beside me, "Flo-otsam and jetsam."

"Ka-ate, shut up!" pleads Webb, squeezed in the back seat. "Shut the fuck up!"

The moon echoes off the steely hood, which looks as ghostly and pine-green as the surrounding trees. Mud from three days of sullen Ohio rain splatters up through the VW's rusted floorboards onto our bare feet: mine, Kate's, her boyfriend Jo-Jo's. Jo-Jo is staring out the window, elbow out. He's got a bottle to himself. The three in back are sharing.

"Flo-o-o-o-tsssum," repeats Kate, head pressing into Jo-Jo's shoulder.

"And the Jetsams," I say quickly, to cut off Webb. Webb is a question mark of a guy, skinny and quiet and curled up inside, but you never know what he'll do when he's high. "That famous TV family! That crazy 21st century bunch!" Quickly I turn the wheel to avoid a bad bump.

Kate takes a strand of my hair and runs it slowly through her fingers. The sensation hurries down my spine and burns my bare soles, pressing the clutch and the gas. The car lurches, slightly. No one can tell this lurch from the others.

"Geeeooooorge Jetsam!" chants Blond Suzette—Kate and I declared that her official name—in back. "Jane, his wife!" She leans over the seat. Beside me her fingers make explosions to show little flying saucers zooming across the tube.

"Oh no," I say. "Melissa, his ex-wife. Lila, Ben, and Lizzie, his ex-children. Captain Kirk, his ex-dog. How does the rest go?"

"Dear Lizzie," says Kate, stretching behind me to take the joint. "Our good Princess Elizabeta. When are you going to learn? So hung up on the nuclear family. Don't you get it? It's history! It's over! Flotsam, noun: the wreckage. See also: parents. Jetsam, noun: what's jettisoned, or thrown overboard. Nous. Les peoples. *We're* your family now."

"I wasn't thrown," says Blond Suzette. "I jumped." We've all heard how many times she ran away.

"Jetsams," says Webb. "Hey." He props his chin on the seat beside my shoulder. "I never realized that before? Did you ever realize that before? That we're all divorced kids?"

"Speak for yourself," says Jo-Jo. His mother's dead. He thrusts himself out the window and does his "Werewolves of London" howl at the sky. His little barks and howls are his radio trademark. He drags himself back in like a backwards chin-up.

"Les divorcois: nom, enfants des divorces," Kate intones.

"Les enfants *divins*," says Blond Suzette. I glance in the mirror and catch her fluffing out her long, curled tresses. That's what actresses have, she told me once: tresses. She was serious.

"How much farther?" I ask Harriet.

"Left up here where it forks," Harriet says, between drags on her cigarette, "then straight about half a mile." She grew up in Athens County, and has been telling me about the quarry all quarter. She promised to take me after exams. I dragged along everyone else.

We've already passed so many clusters of rural mailboxes and hairpin dirt roads I haven't a clue how far we are from campus. I hate the driving. If I go too slow we'll get stuck. Too fast, we'll be thrown into the swampy weeds. But I'm the only one who doesn't drink or drug. Unlike the rest of them, I don't like being out of control.

We turn into a clearing. The misshapen moon stares at us twice, above and in the black water. Black trees sweep the bottom of the sky.

"Lordy," says Webb.

Doors open and slam. The car lightens and rises out of the mud. By the time I cut the engine, I'm the only one in the car.

In the quiet, bodies pale with moonlight return to the car, dropping clothes through the windows. The door slams behind me, a large metallic sound. Mud oozes cool through my toes. The dark smell of algae and weeds makes me sneeze. I pull off my shirt and shorts, exposing the blubber at the edges of my swimsuit.

"Coward," whispers Kate in my ear. Despite myself I glance at her tiny breasts, dark nipples stiffened by the breeze, and the burnished wire between her thighs. I look at the black water, lapped by moonlight.

A hand reaches over my shoulder and grabs Kate. I startle. She closes her eyes. I look up at Jo-Jo's stark cheekbones and skull, blue under the moon. His hair is the length of a three-days' beard. He looks like a concentration camp survivor, even more so than in daylight. It's his official protest against his father's marrying a stranger, only two months after his mother died. He shaved it the day after he got the letter. Once a week Kate shaves it again.

"Jo-Jo, I swear to God," I say, "you look pre-dead."

"Aren't we all?" Jo-Jo opens his eyes that extra width that makes him look uncanny and bare. It was seeing that look across the back of French class, Kate says, that made her fall in love. Beyond vulnerable, she says. How many men, she says, can be as nearly naked as that? Her voice wasn't a question, it was a shiver.

"We are the hollow men," says Kate.

"Is it like this in death's other kingdom?" quoth Jo-Jo. You can imagine him thinking that to himself: 'quoth Jo-Jo'.

He heaves a rock at the water, as if to skip it. It explodes beside Harriet's muscular bottom.

"Hey!" she calls back over her naked shoulder, accompanied by her orange ember. "Watch out for innocent bystanders!"

"Innocent?" I call. I'm the only virgin. In January we all had a slumber party in Webb's room. For weeks afterwards I had flashbacks to all those sleeping bags squirming around us on the floor. I could barely stand being near the rest of them. Except that being separated was just as bad. When someone touches your skin, I found out, it unwraps your insides. After that I decided the safest policy was not even to kiss.

Jo-Jo walks toward Kate. I have to look away to not see his

penis. Kate wraps herself around his arm. Out of the corner of my eye I see her nipple press against his arm's black hairs.

I splosh through the mud toward Harriet, who's now dragging what looks like a raft, a rope pulling against her heavy breasts. Beyond her, white arms appear occasionally above the water, like sharks' fins, or maybe like angels' wings. A head bobs up, spouting water and a truncated laugh.

"It's eerie out here." My voice wavers in the dark.

Harriet's bulldog face tightens as she pulls on the rope. Even in daylight you can barely see her pale red eyelashes. "I helped build this raft. My uncles said if I did a good job, they'd let me help fix my cousin's barn."

"Oh, great." I get behind the raft and push.

"Yes, great. Haven't you noticed? I'm a civil engineering major." After she told her major in our women's history class—she was the only engineer—I started hanging out with her, to see how she could stand being different.

"Did they let you help with the barn?"

"I got tonsillitis. But I snuck into the truck and watched from the cab."

Under my feet, the waterlogged wood is soft as a carpet. It sways slightly in the water. The cool air laps over me, a relief from the swollen heat of the three-day rains.

"Wait for me!" Kate sploshes toward us, sans Jo-Jo, to my relief. I step off, and the three of us walk the raft in. I try not to think about rusty fishhooks or snakes. The water is soft, rising up my legs. When it ripples against my pubes, I flush. As the raft clears the rocks, we climb on. We lie watching the moon drift through the haze. At a distance from its white blur a few stars waver, like uncertain messages.

Webb taught me to look closely and see they're not all white. I pick out some bluish, one winking green, one pale orange. Wood knots press my back. A fresh smell drifts above the water. Harriet and Kate pass a bottle.

The raft rocks gently, Blond Suzette's long skinny arms straining as she climbs on. When Webb follows, slight and dark, I'm relieved he's wearing trunks. He hunches at the edge, his back to Suzette, his legs trailing. The raft is so big no one has to shift to make room.

The talk is quiet, and drifts back into darkness.

The raft takes another dip, and holds still at a tilt. Near Kate's ankles rests Jo-Jo's grinning head, as if decapitated. I stare at the stars' wiggling colors.

"Above us you see mathematics," says Webb, "the first and purest language." Which means the mushrooms have hit. It's the only time Webb talks physics, his major. He deals drugs to put himself through school. "Equations swimming out from the very first equation, the one that said: Let there be light."

"What about, let there be black holes?" asks Suzette. She's propped across the raft like a sphinx, pointing her breasts at Webb.

He keeps his back to her, staring into the blurry sky. "Equations collapsing into a nothing so heavy it's something."

"The nothing that is not there and the nothing that is," says Kate.

"A whirlpool of nothing that can flush you like shit down a toilet," says Jo-Jo. He grabs the bottle.

"We're all fallout from those equations," says Webb. "Made of stars, every one of us. Even Jo-Jo."

His gentleness relieves me. It means he's not letting Suzette get to him. At his best he can distract Jo-Jo from what Kate calls his morosity: like viscosity. But sometimes Webb lies on my floor for hours, asking why Kate stays with Jo-Jo when he treats her like shit, and why Suzette flirts with Webb and drops him if he acts interested, but only gets serious about her married drama professor. He wants to know: are women insane?

Harriet takes over in her matter-of-fact voice, telling how when she was a kid, her family would come down to watch the stripmining. Her cousin operated one of the big machines; she was too little to remember its name. She points out what we can see now, with our eyes adjusted to the dark: sheer rock that cuts into the water at the south side. The mining company got off without a slap, she says, after an explosion off that cliff killed two miners.

We drift under the influence of the blue rock for a minute.

"So we're floating over dead people?" says Kate.

Harriet's orange ember glows, then arcs over us through the quivering black. It sizzles as it hits.

Maybe it wasn't an accident," says Jo-Jo. "Maybe they said to hell with the rest of you, I've fucking had it."

"If you had a choice," says Blond Suzette, "would you kill some-one or be killed?"

"Be killed," I say. I've been a vegetarian since I was ten. "*Was* it the mining company's fault?"

Harriet snorts. "What do you think?"

"You'd stand aside and let the Nazis take over the world?" Webb says. "Pol Pot?"

"Weber!" I say. "Et tu?"

"What about Gandhi?" Kate says. "Or Martin Luther King?"

"Dead," says Jo-Jo. "And their factions are killing or being killed in the streets."

"So that's what they teach in pre-law?" I say. "That everything's hopeless? 'If I am for myself alone, what am I?' "

"An amoeba?" asks Webb. "A quark?"

"No, seriously, Lizzie," says Suzette angrily. The raft rocks un-pleasantly as she grabs the bottle from Webb and takes a swig. "If someone was attacking your family, coming at you and your kids with a broomhandle or a—a—a—telephone ripped out of the wall, would you just lie there like mold?"

Suzette refuses to visit or call home. With her hair damp and tangled around her face, her eyes look drowned.

"I'd run away," I say.

Harriet says, "One of the miners was my mother's cousin."

"So what does that mean?" asks Jo-Jo. "The big bad owners smoke cigars and plot death for profit? Join the union and sing Pete Seeger songs? A vote for Stalin is a vote for the people?" He switches from his Radio EclectoMania voice into his marble-mouthed imitation of his history prof. "The people. First invented in the late-nineteenth century by that remarkable, remarkable co-median, first among Marx brothers, Karl. Degenerated now to a remarkable few, jammed on a lumpen raft, doomed to disperse, or die first." He mock-salutes the stars.

"Jo-Jo," Kate says, "it was her cousin."

The raft rocks as Jo-Jo shoves away. We hear the angry splash-ing of his arms.

"He's just upset because tomorrow he meets his father's new wife," Kate says.

"Like anyone *likes* it," Suzette says. "Nobody says you *like* it." She tosses her hair back with both hands, not looking at me.

"The day my mother got married," I say, "she says I held up the chuppah. She has pictures of me shaking people's hands. I don't remember a thing. I can remember when Dad was in the house. Then comes the part where Mom's husband is telling me to get off the phone, he has an important call coming in. It's like the movie broke in the middle."

"Tell me about it," says Harriet. Her parents got divorced, but moved back in together.

"My dear Jetsams," says Kate, "we are gathered here today to remind ourselves to forget those foolish Flotsams."

I stick my toes in the water, hoping a fish will nibble.

Suzette stands up fast, rocking the raft. "Marco Polo!" she yells, and dives off.

Webb dives after her. Harriet's dive is a strong arc, leaving hardly a splash where her feet disappear. I swing my legs over to join them.

"Don't." Kate puts a hand on my arm.

Splashing water and voices calling "Marco Polo!" echo through the quarry.

Kate says, "I'm afraid of the water. I don't know how to swim."

"You're kidding!" I've been swimming since I was four. I lie back, looking up at the blue mists.

She turns over on her belly facing me, propping her chin in her hands. Her face looks like a heart-shaped moon.

"So what are you doing out here?"

"I wanted to be with everybody." She touches my shoulder.

Shifting my butt against the wood, I stare at the moon. Before Jo-Jo, Kate and I were inseparable. We studied together in the library. We walked home together after student government. We even binged together, although I would sneak off to eat more, and sometimes heard her vomiting in the toilet. She was the only person I ever told about waiting up all night for my mother to come home, the year after the divorce. Kate used to wait up for hers, too, hoping she'd come home alone. When Kate had nightmares, she'd come into my dorm room and curl up with me. I'd prop myself on my elbow, holding myself stiff so I didn't brush her skin, and watch her eyes flutter under her eyelids.

We lie together in the blurry dark. Her breath is warm on my shoulder.

"Marco Polo!" Their splashing and squealing almost drown out the peepers. I pick out heated stars behind the haze, trying to see them as equations. It's light moving at different speeds, Webb explained once, that makes the stars different colors. Scientists like to tell you they know what's happening with the stars. But most of it is a mystery: that's what he likes about it. Once, when Webb was very tripped out, he said: God speaks in mathematics. Learn the language and you know God.

Kate leans over and kisses me.

The sensation spreads through me like a star. When she lifts her head, I want to cry.

A Tarzan howl echoes over the water. We sit up.

"Oh Christ! What an idiot!" Harriet's pointing toward the blue rock.

I make out a figure poised on top. Judging by how small he looks from here, Jo-Jo is maybe fifty feet above the water. Maybe a hundred.

He dives. We watch the silent splash.

I realize I'm counting my breaths: ten, fifteen, twenty.

"Jo-Jo!" Kate's voice is so loud I wince. "Jo-Jo!" As she jumps up I spread my arms to steady the raft.

Voices join in. "Jo-Jo! Where are you!" "You! Asshole!"

Kate shrieks his name, flapping her arms like a drunken air controller. Under the moonlight, the others' white arms lap toward us, punctuated by irregular cries.

Fifty, fifty-five.

I picture the five of us under a police station's blue fluorescence. My chest feels like cement. Remember this feeling, I think, to use in drama class. Immediately I'm ashamed. "Jo-Jo!" My voice is raw.

Kate puts her hand on my head, steadying herself. "His mother didn't die of cancer last fall, like he said," she whispers. "She killed herself."

Harriet climbs on the raft. Kate grabs her wrist. "We have to swim out to save him!"

I realize how stoned they all are. "Let's push the raft back to shore, and turn the headlights on the water."

"Asshole!" Webb's shoved himself onto the raft and is hopping across, yelling through his cupped hands. "Where the fuck are you, asshole!"

"Webb," I say, "help us kick." Obediently he climbs down. Suzette joins us, her long body trailing the raft. Her eyes are big as frogs. We all kick or paddle toward shore, our voices banging against the half-mined cliffs. Kate weeps, quietly as hiccups.

Mud sucks at my ankles. While Harriet drags in the raft, Webb and Kate shout at the trees and clouds. Suzette holds herself, standing in mud like a rag doll.

I hurry toward the car. Without thinking, I slap a mosquito whining against my wrist. When its blood and body smear my skin, I almost start to cry.

The solidity of the car door steadies me. The plastic smell inside turns my stomach. I flick on the lights.

Light erases most of the quarry. A few spotlit trees wash back and forth in a breeze overhead. The gunning engine shuts out the world. I back up and return at a different angle. Flattening the water, light slithers out like a whistle, dissolving into the dark.

Kate screams.

I back up, grinding through mud, to shift my spotlight onto her. Jo-Jo holds up Kate's wrist like a victory sign. Her hand dangles helplessly. He is laughing, head back. I cut the engine. Framed by the windshield, the glare turns their bodies into a police lineup, unreal.

I cut the lights.

A bullfrog bellows, its warning huge and useless. Then, like an art history slide appearing through the windshield, two sets of bodies appear on the shore, marbled by moonlight. I grab the doorhandle and lean into the dark.

That's when I realize I've seen Jo-Jo's penis. It looks exactly like what you'd expect.

Two of the statues are walking toward me, becoming women. The tall stringy one is streaked with mud, walking like an ungainly duck. The short one strides, brushing herself off, brisk. Beyond them a pair of blue-white arms is lifting over the black water, aiming toward infinity. How will I ever get us all home?

I swing open the car door, wincing at the flash of light, and walk toward them, feet sinking again in the mud. Arms wrapped around myself, I look away from the two who keep kissing, like headless bodies trying to disappear into the dark.

THE HOUSE WITH THE HORSE AND
THE BLUE CANOE

Cheryl Strayed

Dan liked to tell us about the rats. He promised, in a jolly and threatening kind of way, to get his hands on a pair of good binoculars and then he'd show us. This is when we lived in the trailer on a low ridge overlooking the town of Chaska, Minnesota. Below us there was a pickle factory, and alongside it an enormous field of vats full of cucumbers, vinegar and, Dan said, rats. He knew because he'd worked there twice.

We had the best trailer, one on the edge of a whole spiraling ring of trailers. There was a patio where Dan sat with us and tried to hush us up long enough so rabbits would come out to sit in the weeds where we could see them. He made us memorize the capital cities of all the states in the entire nation. He'd say, "Kentucky." We'd yell, "Frankfort!" Dan would think a good while, then, trying to catch us. "Maine." "Augusta!" He stood us up and tried to show us things from the patio. The Minnesota River where it curved out of Chaska, coursing bravely away from the Mississippi. The high steeple of the Catholic church and school where he had been made to go to mass every morning and had nuns for teachers who rapped him on the hands with rulers. He pointed out the other factories beyond the pickle factory. The sugar factory, the egg plant, and the plastics factory where my mother worked until she made a mistake and got her pinky finger burned and broken. After that my mother had both of her pinky fingers broken. She would hold them together to show us. They jutted and bumped away from one another like carrots planted in rocky soil. The other finger was broken by my real dad when he got mad at her for baking a birthday cake for the guy who lived next door to us. I was four, but I remember. He dragged her around the kitchen and she got away from him—all but her pinky finger. He twisted it until it snapped. It sounded clean and painless like when you crack a chicken wing apart at the joint.

Dan was not our father, or anybody's father, though we loved him as one.

He was eight years younger than our mother. He had thick glossy hair that went down to his waist when we met him. At Halloween he dyed it green and let it slowly fade out by Thanksgiving. Later, a year or two after he'd married my mother, he fell off a roof and hurt himself. They shaved all of his hair off in the hospital because they thought his head was cut, though it ended up being just blood from where he'd touched it with his bloody hand. A nurse gathered it all together in a white string and set it on the hospital dresser in front of the television as if it were a bouquet.

Dan was a carpenter. He'd started at a new company after giving up on making it on his own. They gave him all the work that nobody else wanted to do because he was the newest guy. Jobs like sheetrocking and scraping glue off a floor and roof work in the winter. He slipped on ice and fell off the roof of a mansion three stories high. The woman who owned the house found him huddled under a bush in front, mumbling and moaning, sucking on a gash in his hand. He'd crawled there from the place where he hit the ground, searching for shelter by pure instinct like an animal.

At the hospital we could see him two at a time. My mother went in to see him first, pulling Joshua along with her nervously. When they came out my sister Leah and I were shuffled in. He was wrapped in white gauze across his middle. He had a neck brace on and a complicated sling came down from the ceiling, suspending him from the bed in several places.

Dan had a hard time staying awake. He said, "Hey! What's your name?"

Leah and I stood on opposite sides of the bed. "You know," I said, drawing my words out, teasing. I touched his hand then, the one on my side of the bed. I touched it barely, with one finger. Dan was a hardworking man. His hands were thick and rough as tree bark. At night he cut the calluses off with a jackknife. But then, in the hospital, his hands looked sore and swollen. I thought if I held one the way I wanted to he might cry. "I'm Stephanie." I rested my small hand on top of the mountain of his knuckles then, delicate as a spider's web.

"Oh, right, right, Jesus, how are you? How the hell are you?" He wagged his head around, not focusing on either of us. "Can I get a cigarette off you?"

Leah twirled her hair the way she did when she was nervous or bored. Dan tried to lift his head from the pillow but couldn't. He said, "Oh boy." His glasses were on the table beside me. One lens was missing, the other had a thin crack straight across it. He clenched his eyes shut and trumpeted out a little tune between pursed lips.

Leah said, "We're here to see you, Dan. To see how you are."

He opened his eyes then and stared at the ceiling. He didn't make a sound. What he did was let one of my fingers fall from his knuckles down in between two of his own and held it there.

All of this happened before we lived in the trailer. When Dan fell off the roof we lived in a two-story farmhouse on Highway 41 going out of Chaska. Besides for the highway we were fairly secluded. There were woods and fields all around and a hill behind the house that went down to a muddy abandoned lake named Grace. There were seven colors of paint on the outside of the house, though you could only see two at a time when you stood in one spot. There was a long porch on the back with a cement floor and old-fashioned pictures painted right on the wall. Pictures of roosters and young women with assertive behinds and breasts and plump forearms holding baskets of brown eggs.

By the time we lived here—it was the late 1970s—it hadn't been a real farm for years. We had cats and dogs and one horse named Lady Highland Stonewall Jackson, who we called Nancy for short. She drank her water from a blue canoe that we'd smashed when we used it as a toboggan the first winter we lived in the house. The blue canoe sat on the edge of her pasture, in plain view of the highway. When people asked where we lived all we had to say was the house with the horse and the blue canoe and everyone knew exactly where we meant.

It was the first house Leah, Josh, and I had lived in. Before that it was apartments. And once, when we still lived in Pennsylvania with our real dad, we lived in a boxcar that was converted into a house of sorts. It was in a whole row of boxcars parked in a field by the coal mine where our father and grandfather were working. This was when the mining jobs were getting slim, when we had to go on the road after such jobs. There was a huge structure at the end where we all ate and took showers, in shifts. Later, after we were long gone from there, my mother liked to make a big deal of us having lived in such a way. She called Joshua Boxcar Willie. She imitated the sound of a train whistle for us when she talked about that time of our lives. The miners with families lived on one end and the single men on the other end. Those men, the ones without families, drank after work without showering. They sat on their steps with mangy hair and spit and drank and smoked. They howled at my mother when she walked by, or cheered when she hung clothes on the line wearing her bathing suit. My mom would laugh and wave them away or scold them kindly.

So besides for the boxcar, this house—the house with the horse and the blue canoe—was the first for Leah, Joshua, and me. We had a good deal in the way of rent because the place was so run-down. Paint was splattered on the wood floors and there were garish brown stains on the walls and ceiling. The floorboard heat didn't work well enough to keep the dog's water from freezing into a thin layer of ice on the top.

Dan unhooked the heat altogether and made a gigantic wood stove by welding two metal barrels together. He set it up in the middle of the kitchen in a wooden sandbox. My mother macraméd hangings full of feathers and beads to put on the walls to cover the stains. Together they painted a mural on the ceiling of the living room. Dan did the golden lions and parrots and a rainbow lizard and my mother followed behind him, painting in the vines that twisted among them, the roses and thorns that sprouted up near the waterfall, snakes and bugs and lily pads. When it was finished it covered half the ceiling, rounding out from two corners. The five of us took turns standing on a stepladder to press our palms, full of yellow paint, into the place on top they left bare. Each of our handprints touched the next, forming a sun.

That is how it was for a brief time in our lives, when I was ten, eleven, twelve.

My mom and Dan bought two canoes—new ones to replace the one we'd wrecked. On Saturdays we'd canoe the Minnesota River. We bolted them together so we wouldn't tip over. We floated down the river, slow and wide as a pontoon. Dan knew the river, he'd grown up on that river. He called the names of the towns out to us as we floated by: Carver, Jordan, Belle Plaine. When we went far enough, we came to a place where there was a herd of cattle with no fence on the riverside. Dan would shut the motor off then, or if we were paddling, he'd tell us to stop and sit quietly. We'd let the river carry us down, sideways, backward. My mother would take her sunglasses off. We'd look at the cows; they'd look back at us. The cows would lift their heads and stop chewing the way rich people do in movies when someone says something startling at dinner: mouths open, forks in midair. Dan whispered that these cows belonged to a very wealthy man who owned that side of the river for miles. We weren't allowed to stop there. The cows would watch us float away from them, craning their necks lazily. Joshua wondered why the cows didn't jump in the river and escape and Dan would ask, "From what?"

Dan told stories of the river in a way that made me associate him with Tom Sawyer, only Dan's stories seemed even more legendary. Crowded with harebrained boondoggery and high adventure of brushes with near fatality and permanent injury. Dan knew the old men who sat in lawn chairs at the landing in Chaska. Scooper Reint, Vick Yodel, and Tag Weinert. They smoked cigars and held cold cans of baked beans and dipped potato chips in them to eat. When they saw Dan they'd pound on their armrests and yell at him, "How's Eddie! How's your old pops?" Eddie was dying of Alzheimer's disease before anyone knew what Alzheimer's

disease was. At that time it was just an increasing knowledge
that something was gravely wrong. Eddie forgot the names of
grandchildren. He wet his pants because he couldn't find the bathroom in his house. Scooper, Vick, and Tag weren't surprised. People began to cough at young ages, they lost hands and lungs and
eyes. They died and nobody complained. When Dan said, "Not
good. The old man ain't good," they were already nodding their
heads, expecting as much.

Tag Weinert liked to show me his tattoos. He told me what
he thought I'd look like when I was eighteen. "A looker. A knock-
out. A heartbreaker." I had an image in my head of a large blond
woman, gleaming in a white puffy dress with cleavage and perfectly coy and curling lips. A woman who was in no way connected to me, but a woman whom I would magically become. He
said he'd like to get his hands on me then. He told Dan to get a
big stick because he'd have to beat them away. He advised Dan
of the headache I'd become. Tag was the second person I knew
who had been in jail. I supposed that's where he got his tattoos.
I imagined that they sat around in their cells, rolling up the sleeves
of their black-and-white striped jail outfits, giving tattoos, and
talking about their hard luck.

I'd heard Dan's mother, Joy, tell my mother about Tag one
afternoon in Joy's kitchen. (This being the way I learned just about
everything during those years. I was young enough to pass for a
child too dumb to understand and old enough to know perfectly
well what they were talking about without offering my opinions
and giving myself away.)

It was a big scandal, having to do, of course, with love, betrayal,
and a pretty woman named Lucy (who, without having to be told,
I was sure had red hair and chewed her gum aggressively). Lucy
worked the counter at the bakery in town. She was engaged to
be married to the baker, Hal Barnes, but she fell in love with Tag
instead. Back in love. They'd been high school sweethearts. Tag
had joined the army and was sent to Korea. In his absence, Lucy
had become engaged to Hal. When Tag came home he brought
her a blue silk robe with a dragon embroidered on the back and
her name stitched in white on the front. He drank coffee at the
bakery just to see her. He left extra quarters on the counter when
he left, and once, brave, he kissed her without warning.

Joy stopped there, significantly, "Well we know how the story goes."

She fell back in love with Tag and out of love with Hal. (I had come already to know that this is how love was: this swaggering, swerving emotion that could change and change back again, outside of anyone's control.) Lucy was afraid to tell Hal. Something about his terrible temper. Something about how he once broke the collarbone of a man who got fresh with Lucy at an oven and appliances auction in Minneapolis. Joy spoke hushed, "He may even have hit her."

So it went on. Each day it became more pressing that Lucy tell Hal that she wasn't going to marry him and intended to marry Tag after all. By then everyone in Chaska knew except Hal and a few of his best buddies, "the guys who drank at the Hilltop— Bud Jenkins, Davie Stewart, Ot Grenwold, and the like" Joy said by way of explanation.

"He's there when he finds out." Joy said this like it was the worst part. "At the Hilltop. The way I know is Eddie told me. He seen it all happen because Wert's was closed down, something wrong with the taps, so he and the guys went to Hilltop instead."

Someone joked with Hal about it. Said some wise comment about Lucy working a double shift. "A brick wall falls on his head." Joy smacked her forehead with the heel of her hand to demonstrate. Hal put it all together. Tag hanging out at the bakery, the way Lucy had been acting. "So what he does is starts slugging 'em down. Tells Billy to line 'em up and he slugs them down and the guys are yelling go, go except for good old Ot, who's trying to talk some sense into his head." Joy leaned toward my mother and said, "There ain't no doing that, talking sense to a jealous man."

Joy's face was flushed and smiling like she was telling a good long joke. "He gets so drunk that he can barely walk. Eddie always says the Lord only knows how he was able to drive his truck from that bar to Lucy's house, but he did, and he was a pounding away on that door! Sure enough, there's Lucy inside, crying and yelling at him to go home, clutching onto Tag's arm so he won't go out and get killed by Hal."

Tag shook her off and went out anyway. It was winter, bone cold, but he didn't put a coat on. Hal wasn't wearing one either. They stood in the walkway in T-shirts. Lucy watched them, on her tiptoes, peeking through the diamond-shaped window in the door. Hal swung a few punches at Tag, missed him for the most part. Tag hit Hal square in the face, then in the gut, and took his face and shoved it into the snow. Hal rolled over to look at Tag, but didn't get up. Tag walked back toward the house. Before going inside he turned and yelled, "Go home!"

"But he doesn't go." Joy pressed her hands to her face and stretched the loose wrinkles back from her eyes, making her look younger for a moment. "He stays right there. Lucy starts feeling bad and talks to him a bit through a window. He doesn't say a word. He stays and stays and stays until finally the cops come by and pick him up."

It had been a while by then. A good while, maybe two hours, more. They took him straight to the hospital where they chopped off two of his fingers and all of the toes on one foot for frostbite. "That's why Tag went to jail." Joy pointed her finger and tapped it hard on the table. "Assault or battery. Nineteen months."

What happened to Lucy? She married Tag, quietly in a jail ceremony. She knitted him sweaters, baked him cookies, held hands with him across the table as the guard watched. "Bad fortune looked upon that girl." Joy pronounced. "It wasn't a year that Tag was out before she died in a car wreck." Joy paused for a moment, then brightened up, "But now, Hal, he did fine. Married a real nice girl, Evie Polasky." And that, to Joy, was the end of the story.

But jail. That's what I was most interested in. That's where Tag Weinert went. Jail for making a guy freeze his toes and fingers off. There was a time when I'd believed that in my whole life I'd never know anyone who went to jail. Criminals. But by then, by the age of eleven, I'd already met two. Tag and Dan's brother, Joe, who went in and out of jail for things I only caught whispers of. Stealing a garbage truck, selling marijuana, driving drunk.

They went to the Carver County jail. I knew what it looked like on the inside because in third grade my class had taken a trip there. The warden gave us a lecture first. He made us count off. Thirty-eight of us. He stood a few minutes, breathing in his tight brown uniform, doing the math. "Okay. If we're going to go by the statistics, oh about six of you will serve time in a correctional institution at some point in your lives." He paused to look intently around the room. Hair rose on the back of my neck, terrified he might point me out as one of the future criminals. He stood with his legs wide apart, like a football coach, and his hands folded in front of him. He continued, "Now that does not mean that you can't beat the statistics. It's your choice. Do you want to grow up to be worthy citizens?" We were silent, aghast, sweating. I had a fear of containment. Prison, or accidentally becoming a nun, an unfounded fear since I'd only attended church a few times in my entire short life.

"Ask yourself that question, boys and girls—girls too. Girls are a growing prison population, just a reality of the times." He crossed his arms on his chest. "Ask yourself if you want to be a good citizen. Let's go take a look at the alternative." He led us down a narrow beige corridor, his club and gun wagging along against his hips. He told us to line up single file to walk through one of the cells. It was clean, unoccupied, with two thin bunk beds and a toilet perched white and long as a tulip in the corner. When I walked by the toilet I saw a single cigarette butt floating in the water and felt sure someone horrendous had smoked it. There was a window in each cell where the wall met the ceiling. It was thick as a block of ice and the only thing that could be seen through it were streams of color and light: not really a window at all.

Dan never went to jail, though I feared he would. I saw him siphon gas from cars in parking lots. I knew that he stole a case of Polish sausages from a place where he used to work. Once he pulled our van behind a closed gas station and grabbed two tires off a pile and threw them in the back. He never got caught. My real father almost went to jail for strangling my mother nearly to death, but at the last moment she decided not to press charges. When I brought it up, my mother scolded me. She scolded me in a kind of way that let me know that it was for my own good not to discuss such things. My mother liked to let bygones be bygones. Let lying dogs rest. Bury the hatchet.

My real father never hurt us, Leah, Joshua, and me.

Except for once when Leah flunked first grade and he hit her in the chin with a wrench and she bled all over the carpet in our bedroom until our mother came home and took her to the emergency room for stitches. And a few other times, I suppose. Mostly when we got in the way of some fight between them, or later stepped on a piece of glass that had been broken during one of those fights.

My mother and Dan did not fight in that way, did not fight at all beyond an occasional argument. The first time I saw Dan he was holding Joshua upside down by his ankles, shaking him, as if Josh had some money in his pockets that he was after. He had come to have dinner, to meet us. We lived in a complex of apartments especially for single women and their children. The apartments were small. There was nowhere to put the kitchen table, so my mother cut the legs off and set it in the middle of the apartment. We had to sit on the carpet, our legs folded under us, to eat. This is how we ate, the five of us, on that first night together.

There were no pets allowed, but we had a bird anyway. His name was Canary and he got to fly free through the apartment. In the middle of dinner Canary landed on top of Dan's head and stayed there. We laughed so hard that we couldn't eat. Dan looked innocently at each of us. He asked, "What? What's so funny?" as if he didn't know a yellow bird was perched on his head.

A few months later, again in our apartment, Dan asked us if we wanted to find a house to live in with him. Our mother was not in the room. We loved Dan desperately. He said, "Your mom said to ask you kids." He reached for a magazine from the table. "How about it?" He began to page through the magazine as if he were relaxed and distracted, as if our answer were nothing to him.

Dan was twenty-five. I thought of him as old. He had an enormous sharp German nose and bright blue eyes; eyes like our mother's only more muted. He was the best man I'd ever met.

Joshua began to hop and sing a song, "Yes, yes, yes." Leah looked at me. She was three years older, but by then she had stopped being the one to speak for us. I said, "That would be nice."

Dan was holding that magazine. He looked up at me, "Good. That's what we'll do then." What I remember is that his hands were shaking.

*   *   *

So that is how we came to live in the house with the horse and the blue canoe. My mother and Dan married there, down the hill, under a willow tree beside the lake named Grace. Then my mother's pinky finger got burned and broken and Dan fell off a roof. Bad things happen in threes, that's what my mom always said, so when we were evicted from the house nobody was surprised.

The landlord came one day. His name was Lyle Sweet. Mr. Sweet. He was the only person I'd called Mr. anybody except for my teachers. He had thick dark hair with a wide chunk of gray in the front that made him look as if someone had swiped him by accident with a brush full of silver paint. When I was near him I was constantly on the verge of reaching out to touch it. He wore baggy polyester pants and a button-up shirt with a tie that he loosened the moment he was in our presence.

Dan said, "It's not that you won't get your money. It's just that I got hurt." Dan was sitting in a chair in the kitchen. He had spent the last few months sleeping in a special bed from the hospital that we rented and set up in the living room. He was wearing a white cloth brace around his middle on the outside of his T-shirt. We called it his corset. When his back wasn't hurting too much, he pulled it tight and posed for us like Scarlett O'Hara. He continued, "I'll be back to work soon. I've got this money coming to me as soon as we get the suit settled." He paused. There were troubles. The company wouldn't pay the worker's compensation. His voice took on a quieter, ashamed, more reasoning tone. "We can give you . . ."

Mr. Sweet wouldn't let him finish. "Look, it's nothing personal. You tell me this story like it's personal." He scratched behind his ear where he kept a green pen. "I'm sorry. I know what you're going through."

My mother was washing dishes. She turned to him and raised her voice, "Oh you're real sorry, you're so . . ."

"Don't give me this crap! The point of it is it don't matter to me why you can't pay the goddamned rent." His face turned redder as he spoke. "It don't matter when you can pay it. It matters if you got the cash now. What I wanna know is are you gonna hand me seven hundred and fifty bucks across this table right now."

My mother reached into her pocket and threw a wad of bills on the table in front of Dan. She reached in her other pocket and slammed some coins down. Dan gently counted the bills, ignoring the coins. He held it, slowly arranging it into a neat stack. "Two hundred and seventeen."

"That's not going to answer my question now is it, Mr. and Mrs. Echt. That's just not going to do it, is it?"

"I guess not." Dan said. My mother stood next to him with a wooden spoon in her hand, ready.

Mr. Sweet took a sip of the apple cider my mother had given him and set it down on the nearest counter. He looked at my mother and Dan. "My hands are tied." He pressed his wrists together and held them up. "What do you expect me to do?"

Neither of them looked at him.

Now louder, gaining steam, more exasperated he yelled, "My hands are tied!" Pushing his wrists closer to Dan and my mother he asked again, "What I wanna know is what you people expect me to do?"

My mother turned and went to the sink. She plunged her hands back into the cooling water and began to wash the remaining dishes. Dan stared at the table. Mr. Sweet stood shaking his head for a moment. He grabbed the stack of bills sitting in front of Dan, counted it and put it in his pocket. He snapped his fingers, "I'll take this against your balance due and send you a bill for the rest."

Dan stood up slowly, using the table to help him. He looked about to say something, but didn't. Mr. Sweet cleared his throat and said, "Bye, then. Luck to you." He tightened his tie as he walked toward the door.

We moved into the trailer then. In the trailer perched over the town of Chaska. Over the Minnesota River way off in the distance, over the sugar factory, the egg plant and the plastics factory where my mother's pinky finger got burned and broken, over the pickle factory and the rows of vats full of vinegar and cucumbers and, Dan said, rats.

Dan couldn't work a job because of his broken back. While my mother was at work and we were at school he cleaned the trailer and cooked dinner. He sat on the patio and carved little wooden people out of scrap wood. He made an entire tiny village—a man pulling a sled, a grandmother with her hands on her broad hips, a child bent to gather a snowball. We already had a miniature log cabin we put out each Christmas and, slowly, Dan filled it up. Each week the scene became more complex. There were teacups as small as tacks and warm yellow lanterns balanced on the mantel. He made an outhouse with a slice of the moon on the door and a man inside who sat permanently with his pants down and a bewildered expression on his face. He painted the figures too— the men had burly red-and-green flannel shirts and the women wore rich blue skirts with maybe a pattern of tiny white flowers on the hem.

That is how it was for a brief time in our lives, when I was ten, eleven, twelve.

We would sled on a hill a little way from the trailer. We poured into the trailer, wet and cold and flushed. It was in December, near Christmas. Dan brought a tree in and we set up the tiny village and the log cabin beneath it. We gathered around cradling cups of hot cocoa and pretended we lived in the log cabin. My mother made us fantastic promises. She told us that we would live in an enormous house with a swimming pool in the middle and a horse for each of us to go around on. Dan's hair was still short from being shaved in the hospital, but growing. He told jokes, made faces, tickled us, kissed our mother.

It was dusk, but we let the house grow dark around us. My mother sang. She sang Christmas carols, right through her untrained voice. "Oh Tannenbaum." Any song she could think of that had a tree in it. We decorated the tree with years of ornaments, hours of popcorn and cranberry strung the days before. Dan gave us each a gift: the last ornaments, made by him. There was one for each of us, wooden, with our names carved in the back. A Santa. A candle. Two angels and a reindeer. We each stepped forward, taking our time to hang that last one, then stepped back. We sat, spread out around the tree, hushed. My mother switched the strings of lights on and it was how it always is.

Magnificent.

Our faces glowed like gentle unformed stars. We believed then, at that moment, believed fully that things would only get better and better for the rest of our lives.

IBIZA

Jane DeLynn

I couldn't find a room in the main town on the island, which is
also called Ibiza, so I had gone over to San Antonio, where the
Germans and a few English were. Germans vacation differently
than Americans; they often start out alone but they find other
Germans, they go out for dinner in groups, nobody gets left out.
The English drink lots of beer and beach their fat white bodies
in the sun. They don't get tan, only red, you can hear their hideous
accents miles away. There were no Americans but it didn't matter;
they travel in twos or fours and stick to themselves, the quieter
the place the better. Maybe it's because we don't know foreign
languages and even when we do we don't know how to make
conversation. The Spanish are elegant and disgusted by both Germans and English, though they like the French and Italians, even
the Americans—probably because we're better-looking than the
English and Germans. But the truth is, even when Germans are
good-looking nobody likes them.

To get away from the Germans, I ended up spending much of
my time in the town of Ibiza anyway. The gay bar was there, and
most of the stuff to see. It was past the famous period, but there
were still plenty of hippie dropouts, writing a little here and there,
painting a bit, making jewelry, living on their incomes, selling
drugs. The Americans had gone home, so mostly these were Euro-
peans. I was sitting in a café near the bay when a beautiful girl
of about seventeen walked over to my table and put one of those

little embroidered wool shoulder bags down on the seat across from me. She was blond and thin and almost too young—even back then—for me. But I couldn't really believe she was after my body.

"You don't mind if I join you, do you?" she asked, first in Spanish, then in French.

"*Ah-wee.*" I tried to pronounce it like the French. "*Ça va bien.*"

"Oh. You're American."

"*Sí.* I mean *oui.*"

"I like Americans very much. They are so generous."

"Would you like something to drink?"

"Maybe a little Coca-Cola. It is so very hot," she looked up at the sky apologetically. I noticed her staring at my *jamon serrano*, and gave her half the sandwich. "Thank you," she said. "Perhaps I am a little hungry." She gobbled the food, so I asked the waiter to bring us another sandwich.

"Are you staying in Ibiza?" I asked.

"Yes. Aren't you?"

"No. I got stuck in San Antonio. I couldn't find a place in town."

"That's too bad. I wanted to take a shower." She seemed to lose a little interest in me.

"Your shower is broken?"

"Not exactly."

"Where are you staying?"

"Here and there. With different people."

"Friends?"

"Friends. People I meet."

"Oh." Maybe she did want to spend the night with me.

"If you want, I can ask them if they know of a place here where you can stay," she offered.

"That would be great. I'm sick of the Germans."

She took lipstick out of her little bag and applied it expertly without looking.

"I'll go now," she said, suddenly standing up.

"I could come with you," I said. "Are they near here?"

"It will be just a few moments. You will not have time to blink your eyes."

I did not expect to see her again, but it was very hot, so I was content to sit in the shade and read my book. I was reading stories set in hot and distant places, places like where I was or even more so. I felt like a character in a story, and was almost glad to have wasted my money on her lunch. I looked at the handsome Spaniards around me in their bright shirts. They seemed extraordinarily happy. Franco had recently died, and the entire country seemed to be on holiday.

When she came back I was so engrossed in my book I didn't notice her until I heard her plunk her bag down on the table. "They are not there, but why don't you meet us at the disco tonight?" She gave me directions how to get there.

"What time?"

"Not too late. About one, one-thirty."

"If you want, you can come to San Antonio to take a shower."

"That's a little far to go for a shower, isn't it?" she asked.

I went inside to pay the check. She started talking to the bartender. As soon as the owner went into the kitchen the bartender brought out a huge straw bag which he placed on top of the counter. She took some stuff from her little bag and put it in the big bag, then she took some stuff from the big bag and put it in the little bag. I looked inside the big bag. In it were several pairs of shoes, pants, shirts, a sweater, a makeup case, some underwear— less than I took when I went away for the weekend. "This is where you keep your clothing?" I asked.

"Yes."

"How long have you been here?"

"Four months. Maybe five."

She glanced around the bar, then quickly slipped off her tee shirt and put on a blouse. She was not wearing a bra. There were only a few people in the bar, and none of them seemed to notice this.

The disco was astonishing, a beautiful place with little bridges over water, flowers everywhere. I arrived about one, but it was quite empty. All the drinks were six dollars, even the Cokes. This was ten years ago. A half hour later people began to arrive. You could see from their tans and their clothing and the way they knew each other that they were mostly locals, not tourists. The men looked dazzling in their splendid patterned shirts and the women—in loose but sexy white dresses of coarse island cotton with flat sandals, or tight little skirts with heels—looked even better. At two-thirty I started to leave. But just as I got outside I ran into the girl I had met that afternoon. "Are you going already?" she asked. "We are only now arriving."

Her friends were a motley crew: a man in his sixties, several boys in their late teens, a few women in their twenties and thirties. The men seemed as if they would be interested in men but it's hard to be sure about things like this in a foreign country, the clues are so different. I did not have on the right clothes and they looked me over without interest. "Would you like a drink?" I asked the girl.

"They are very expensive."

"Yes. But that doesn't matter."

"I don't like alcohol. Maybe you would like to smoke?"

We left the disco and went behind the parking lot.

"Hash," I said. "How great. This is so hard to get in America."

"Really?"

"Yes. All we have is marijuana."

"How lucky you are," she said. "I love marijuana, and I'm not, what you say, so 'crazy' about hash?"

"You should live in America, and I should live in Spain," I joked.

"I would like to visit America," she said seriously. "But I have no desire to live there."

I could not blame her. I was in a disco more beautiful and stylish than any I had seen in America, and this was true of the men and women in it too. It was past three, but the place was jammed. From what I could tell, the entire country was in *festivo*— not a fake *festivo*, like we had in America to celebrate things we no longer cared about, but a real one.

"How late does the disco stay open?" I asked.

She shrugged. "Six, seven o'clock. Until the people go home. Nine in the morning, sometimes, if they're still dancing."

By four I could barely keep my eyes open. I asked the girl if she needed a place to spend the night.

"Oh no, I'm not like that," she said. "Anita! Anita!" She ran over to someone a little older than she was and embraced her. I assumed it was an excuse for getting away from me, but she turned around impatiently and motioned me to join them. "This is Anita. Anita,

this is my friend from America. Have you seen Roberto? He owes
me some money." She darted into the crowd.

"You're the one who's staying in San Antonio?" Anita asked me.

"Yes. With the Germans." I couldn't believe the girl had told
anyone about me. If she had, had it been for a purpose? I looked
at Anita more closely. She wasn't especially my type, but I had
already spent several fruitless nights at the gay bar. "Where are
you staying?"

"Oh, you know. Here and there."

"Maybe you would like to take a shower?" I asked.

"Maybe." She smiled.

Anita and I began spending our nights together. I was not particularly attracted to her, but I had been traveling for several months
and it was good to rest and have someone to sleep with at night.
Sometimes we had dinner, but we didn't have much to say to each
other, so usually we just met in the evenings at some café in San
Antonio. We'd take a walk by the water and then head to my
hotel. I'd go upstairs first and she'd follow me a few minutes later,
so I wouldn't have to pay the double rate for the room. She'd slip
out in the morning before me, though on occasion she waited for
me at the café so I could buy her coffee before she left to spend
the day with her friends.

Once Anita brought Luisa, the friend who had introduced us,
to the hotel so she could take a bath. Perhaps Luisa's luck in the
main town was running out. I told Luisa she could use my room
whenever she wanted, even when Anita wasn't with her. Once or
twice she did this, though generally the two girls came together.
Their toilette would usually take at least several hours, because it
was not just a shower or bath but also finger- and toenail cutting
and polishing, maybe a bit of a haircut. Or they would wash their
clothes and drape them over the railing on my little balcony to
dry. Sometimes they massaged each other and I wondered if they
slept together when the tourists weren't around. I loved listening
to them gossip in Spanish, even though I couldn't understand
them. But I recognized a few odd words here and there, mostly
adjectives and names of people and beaches. Sometimes I asked
them what they were talking about, and they would revert to
English for a while. It was always about people they knew: who

was sleeping with whom and where, which rich person could be counted on to take you out to dinner without fuss and which one couldn't. It confused me that Anita didn't pester me to take her out to dinner more, considering that obtaining a free meal was second only in importance to finding someplace to spend the night. I couldn't tell whether or not I should be flattered by the fact she continued to sleep with me even though in some sense I felt I wasn't very interesting to her.

Nor was our sex particularly good. She accused me of being too passive. I didn't like her enough to touch her very much, and I guess in some way I felt that my supplying the room should in some sense compensate for my lack of activity in bed. It disturbed me a little to be thinking the way men do, but perhaps not enough.

"It is Luisa you like best," she said one night. We had started to have sex but stopped in the middle. The kind of hotel I was in didn't have air-conditioning, and I was bothered by the wetness—the sweat of her body and the gunk on my hand.

I debated whether to be honest. "Well," I admitted. "She's more my type. I like blondes very much."

"It's not her real color," said Anita. "She bleaches it. Her real hair is dark, darker than mine."

This was impossible to believe. Luisa had taken enough showers in my bathroom for me to observe her hair and the way she treated it in great detail. She didn't bleach her hair and the roots weren't black. "You mean, bleaches it in the sun," I said.

"No. With peroxide. Always men are fooled by her," she said with some bitterness.

"You're not jealous?" I asked.

"Oh no. I just thought you should know this."

The next time I was alone with Luisa I told her that Anita said she bleached her hair. She laughed. I asked her if her hair was really black.

"Does it matter?" she asked.

"Well . . ."

"I will tell you what you want to hear," she said. "Do you prefer I bleach it or not?"

"I prefer you don't bleach it," I said.

"Good. Because I don't bleach it. Anita's an idiot."

"She sounded like she was jealous," I said. "But I know she can't be."

"Why not?"

"Because she doesn't like me very much."

"Why do you say that?"

"Oh. You know. For one thing, she doesn't do very much to me in bed."

"Do you do very much to her?" Luisa asked.

"Well . . . not exactly."

"Maybe you think because it is your hotel room you don't have to touch her?" She said this without rancor as she studied her hair in the mirror.

"Of course not."

I watched her do her hair. She was trying to put it up in different ways. She was having dinner that night with a wealthy man she had met several days ago. He was in his forties and she had not yet slept with him. She told me she wouldn't sleep with him unless he let her stay in his house for the rest of the summer— even when he was away. She had gotten a little tired of moving around.

"Actually, it's you I'm really attracted to," I admitted.

"Poor Anita. It is always that way. No wonder she hates me."

"She doesn't hate you," I said.

"Oh yes she does. I don't blame her really."

A few strands were loose at the back of her neck. They blew a little in the late afternoon breeze.

"Will you sleep with me?" I asked.

"I told you I'm not that way."

"How could I be worse than that fifty-year-old guy? I'll pay you a little something," I said. "I know you need the money."

"Anita will be angry."

"She won't. Anyway, we don't have to tell her."

"I have to," Luisa said. "She's my best friend."

"Not if it will hurt her." I walked behind Luisa, and bent down and kissed the back of her neck.

She turned around to face me. "All right," she said. "But only if you promise never to tell her."

"Of course. How much shall I give you?"

"Will ten American dollars be all right?"

"Yes." These were worth much more than they are now, especially in Spain.

She walked over to the bed and took off her shirt. "We mustn't take too long," she said, "or I'll be late for dinner."

The stuff we did and the way it was done was pretty similar to what happened between Anita and me, but I enjoyed it much more because I was so attracted to Luisa. She acted like she was enjoying it too, though of course I couldn't be sure. Right in the middle she got up to go to the bathroom. Frustrated, I listened to the toilet flush and waited for the light to shut off under the door. Then I heard her shout, "What time is it?" from the *bano*, and I knew the sex was over.

"*Ocho menos cinco.*"

"Oh!" I heard the water come on.

Back then I considered it bad taste to use my vibrator in the presence of other human beings, so I followed her into the bathroom and sat on the edge of the tub while she washed. "That wasn't too bad, was it?" I asked. I tried to put her hand between my legs, but she pulled it away.

"No. But you must realize, this was a once-in-a-time thing."

"Oh." Of course I had hoped she would fall in love with me. "At least it didn't disgust you, did it?"

"If it was going to disgust me I wouldn't have agreed to do it."

"But you couldn't have known what it was going to be like," I said.

"Why not?"

"You've never slept with a woman before."

"Are you crazy? It's Anita who hasn't slept with a woman before."

"What!" I thought of the casual—no, lackadaisacal—way she had agreed to come home with me that first night. "I don't believe it."

"I knew in her heart she was that way, so I—what is the expression?—'setted you up' with her. It would be better if you were nicer to her," she added.

"She doesn't like me," I said.

"That's not true. She likes you very much."

"I don't think so," I said. "I think you don't like me either, that you're just friends with me because of my hotel room."

"You're wrong. We both like you very much. What is the matter with you, that you are always thinking people don't like you?"

"I don't know."

While Luisa was putting on her makeup there was a knock on the door. It was Anita. She looked at the messed-up bed, and though there was no reason either Luisa or I couldn't have taken a nap, she knew instantly what had taken place and began screaming at Luisa in Spanish. Luisa sat there calmly, still fixing her hair, though every once in a while she tried to put in a word. When her hair was done, she stood up.

"I'm leaving," she said. "Anita, there is no need to be so upset. I have promise you this will not happen again."

"Oh yes. I should believe the words of the daughter of a whore!"

After Luisa left Anita began sobbing. "How could you do this to me?" she kept repeating.

"I told you I was attracted to her," I said. The degree of her upset was surprising, and interesting—perhaps the most interesting thing I had noticed so far about her.

"Why? Just because of her phony hair. That is so silly, when she is such a horrible person."

"She introduced us," I said. "And in many ways she is a very good friend."

"Good friends don't betray you," she said. "I suppose now you will want to sleep with her instead of me."

"I want to sleep with you too," I said, though at the moment I couldn't have cared less.

"She won't sleep with you again. She always does this to people. How much did she make you pay her?" I thought of lying. "Don't lie, because she will tell me the truth—not because she is honest, but just to torture me." I tried not to laugh at the melodrama of her language.

"Ten dollars," I admitted.

"Then you must give me eleven dollars," she said.

"No."

"Why not?"

I told the easy part of the truth. "Because you've been doing it for free."

"*No más,*" she said. "And you must also buy me dinner."

"No."

"Yes."

"No."

"Why not?"

Usually I would have lied, but I was tired and relaxed. "To be honest," I said, "it's not worth it to me."

We stared at each other. She slapped my face. I could hardly blame her. She pulled back her arm as if to do it again, but I grabbed her hand. Our faces were close to each other and so I kissed her, for the first time with passion. Then we began clawing at each other.

"Luisa was right. You do like me," I said, several hours later. The bed was wet with sweat and other bodily fluids, but for once I didn't mind. I felt almost tender toward her.

"Idiot. It was because you smelled like Luisa."

"You're in love with her?" I asked. Once I heard my astonished voice, I couldn't believe I hadn't figured this out before.

"Isn't everyone?" she said, rather bitterly.

EXCERPTS FROM THE SAPPHIC DIARY
OF SOR JUANA INES DE LA CRUZ

Alicia Gaspar de Alba

31 January 1681

My Dearest Marquesa,

Again, I turn my quill toward heaven, where you dwell, and address my thoughts to you, though this time, it is in apology that I speak, not despair.

Birthdays are not celebrated in the convent, as you know, but one does not forget to count the years that pass, especially when a burning comet falls from the Milky Way only three days after one's thirty-second birthday. It appeared during the dark morning hours of the fifteenth of November and we were awakened by the mad howling of the dogs. I knew immediately that it was a comet, nothing to be superstitious about, but Mother Melchora ordered us out to the garden, including the novices, the servants, and the girls, and made everyone kneel on the ground to pray for our salvation.

"It's a natural phenomena, Mother," I tried to explain to her, but she was too terrified to listen to a rational explanation.

"Kneel down, Sister!" she commanded. "Whatever this mystery means, we shall pray for deliverance and forgiveness. You may lead the rosary, Sor Juana. Since it's now Friday, we will pray the Sorrowful Mysteries, in Spanish, please, so that everybody can pray along."

"I didn't bring my rosary with me, Mother," I said, humiliated by her ignorance.

"Surely you know how to say a rosary without holding the beads in your hand, Sister," she said, and I had no choice but to lower myself to my knees and obey her.

But although I scorned Mother Melchora's fanatic interpretation of that beautiful and disturbing celestial light, I did feel as though the comet portended at least one cataclysmic change in my life. And I knew, somehow, because the comet appeared three days after my birthday and two weeks before the new Viceroy's official entrance into México, I knew that the portent was announcing something in relation to the palace. The comet spilled its unearthly glow over the valley of Anáhuac for five nights, and for five nights I could feel the bright orb and tail of temptation blazing a new trail into my soul.

You know what that temptation is, my lady, and you know, also, how long I have mourned you. For seven years I have stood at my window and gazed out on the volcanoes, imagining that you are still alive out there on that road to Vera Cruz. For seven years I have seen myself as Popocateptl, smouldering, silent, capped with ice and snow, speaking to you, Ixtaccihuatl, my Sleeping Lady, in that language of dark smoke.

When I received your husband's letter explaining to me how you had died, so suddenly, the strange pestilence consuming your body so quickly, as if your heart had just stopped pumping out of sadness at leaving this country that you had come to love so much, I felt responsible for your death, in a terrible way, a proud way, believing that you were heartbroken at leaving me. And I swore always to love you; I married you in my mourning, Leonor. That has been the vow I have lived for these seven years, not obedience, not poverty, not enclosure, certainly not chastity (forgive my boldness; as one grows older, one is less ashamed to speak of the passions of one's body).

But now even that vow I have broken. I must confess, Lady; I love another. Never as I loved you, but then, never will you stand before me again; never will I smell your scent again; never will I hear your voice, again; never again will we sit together in the chiaroscuro of our unspoken love.

Leonor, I did not seek to fall in love again. Please believe that. Heavy as the cross of my mourning has been, I was resigned to carry it for eternity, and it is still there, dear as the silver crucifix hanging from the jade rosary that you gave me so long ago. But there is light in my heart again, Laura, after seven years of darkness, though it is only a comet's glow which could never rival the rays of Helios that once burned there.

She is of noble blood, a countess, our new Vicereine, the same age as I. Her name is María Luisa de Manrique, Condesa de Paredes. Although she and her husband come often to vespers in the chapel of San Jerónimo, and afterward stay to dinner in the locutorio, attended by Mother Superior's own servants, la Condesa prefers to visit me alone, on Saturday afternoons, when she arrives just after the siesta with her retinue of young ladies. We share a passion for poetry and philosophy, and, I dare say, the same loneliness and need of friendship. She does not call me Sor Juana when we are alone, just Juana or amiga. She has no compunctions about embracing a nun, though she does tease me for my stiffness. She has the appetite of my young assistant, Concepción, and from the way she eats, I know that she is a woman of passion (and a choleric temper, too!), a woman who is not afraid or embarrassed to take what she wants. (How silly, to be jealous of a plate of dates, to long for the fate of an orange and be peeled by those strong white fingers.)

In such a short time, we have already come to discover each other quite well. There are times when I fear she will read my thoughts, and I get flustered and tongue-tied, a regular lovesick maid, at the possibility of her guessing my true feelings. But if she has guessed, she is not repelled, for she keeps visiting me and bringing me gifts. How she loves my nut cake! In exchange for a loaf of my nut cake, she brought me a microscope, last week. (What an amazing instrument!) She has brought me a harp, a silver quill and a garnet-studded inkwell, an illuminated edition of Don Quixote, an old mahogany box full of fortune-telling cards she bought from gypsies just before sailing from Spain. These, of course, I could not accept. How would I ever explain them to Padre Antonio? As you can see, the woman is fearless, and I suppose that is the trait I most admire in her. She dismisses the gossip of the convent with a flick of her Persian fan.

"The abbess knows that the convent needs to remain on good terms with the palace," she said last Saturday, "and if I choose you as the convent's representative, if I choose to honor the convent through you, you are not responsible for my choices. Let them talk until they grow scales on their tongues, Juana. Meanwhile, slice me another piece of your cake and let us discuss your ideas for this brave and wonderful *philosophical satire of yours.* Hombres necios que acusaís a la mujer sin razon, sin ver que soís la ocasíon de lo mismo que culpais. *Oh please, Juana, I know you haven't finished it, but do recite that wonderful opening verse for me again."*

> Stubborn men who malign
> women without reason,
> dismissing yourselves as the occasion
> of the very wrongs you design:
>   if with unimitigated passion
> you solicit their disdain,
> why expect them to behave
> when you incite their deviation?

"How true, how true, Juana. They create us in their own image and then they want us to resemble the Virgin Mary."

Would that I had la Condesa's courage. But she does not have to live in this house of intrigue and gossip. She does not have to wake up each morning wondering what new tales her servant has wrought overnight, what new chastisements her father confessor will impose on her for keeping her intellect alive. She does not have an abbess censoring her thoughts, a vicaria and a trio of vigilantes taking notes on her actions.

But if I admire her courage, la Condesa admires what she calls my inspiration, the tenth muse, she has baptized me, and of all possible reactions, I can only blush, I, who blush even less than I repent for my sins. Because of la Condesa's admiration for my work, I have become braver, not only in my writing, but in my own feelings for myself. I am no longer afraid of the nature of my love, Laura, this pure and selfless love I once called ugliness. I compare it to that bizarre and blood-stained love that the holiest of my convent sisters profess for Christ, and to the hypocritical love that forks the other sisters' tongues, and I know that my love is far from ugly; it is a blessed thing in this place of so much falsehood and fanaticism. Padre Antonio would deem it worse than ugliness, worse, even than any mortal sin, but he is a man and knows only the laws of men. If he understands love at all it is a man's love that he knows (though men have even designed to dictate the kind of love a woman may feel).

I remember what you said to me the evening that I returned from the Carmelites after only three months in that austere novitiate. I was broken *and certain that you would have me not at your side, knowing what you knew of my inclination. You said: "Love is never a sin, Juana Inés. Love is our very soul, it has no gender." Listen, Lady, to a few of the lines I have written to immortalize your wisdom:*

> *That you are a woman, that you are absent,*
> *these do not impede my love for you;*
> *as you know, the soul ignores*
> *gender and distance.*

And so now, at the age of thirty-two, I am resolved to express my love for Maria Luisa. Any verse I want to write, any gift I want to bestow, any sign I want to give within the bounds of this habit, I shall do it. And it will be so well done, that even when I lie in the earth, outlived only by my scribblings, none shall know for certain what muse drove my hand. None, but you, Leonor.

I have asked Concepción to bring me the brazier from the bath. She is stoking it, now, glancing this way, wondering why I want to burn what I have written. She frowns when I tell her that I am writing to you, that I am speaking to you the way Popocateptl speaks to Ixtacci-huatl, in the language of smoke, but she doesn't question. She knows too much to question.

Receive the dark smoke of my love, Laura, and remember: Your Spirit sleeps at my side.

Your devoted Juana Inés

14 March

La Condesa and I argued about human nature this evening, but what started out as a debate ended in a quarrel. How she hates to be contradicted! She says human nature is innately good, that original sin is but an invention of the priests (let the Inquisition hear her say that, and she will burn in the Quemadero!), and I say that original sin is selfishness, that human nature is innately selfish, a defect that we can never hope to remove, only to control.

"I never knew you were so pessimistic, Juana," she said.

"On the contrary, my lady, my view of human nature is one of the few optimistic views I hold," I told her, "for it is not grounded in self-deceit."

"Do you imply that I deceive myself, Juana?"

"Lady, this is not a personal attack, and you should not feel defensive. We simply disagree about original sin. Surely our friendship is ample enough to allow some disagreements."

"And are you not being selfish, Juana, in expecting me to gainsay my principles and agree with you that disagreements in a friendship should be allowed?"

"I see that we have changed the subject, my lady, but yes, I *am* being selfish, I am expressing my human nature and expecting you to agree with me just as you expect me to be in accord with your views."

"You always twist my words around to your advantage, Juana."

"Now you attack me, Countess."

"I do not see how believing that we are innately selfish is an optimistic view. You contradict yourself, Sister."

"It is optimistic, Countess, because it allows me to do something about curtailing my greed, to be always on the alert for the shadow of greed in my life. I do not always succeed, but at least I am aware of my own shortcoming and, thus, do not burden myself with the cross of guilt when my human nature gets the best of me."

"You do not convince me, Sister."

"I did not think so, Señora."

Easter Sunday

A gift arrived from the palace this morning after High Mass, a crate of startled, gobbling turkeys, one for each nun, and pheasants for the novices. The gift has caused quite a commotion. It's been many months since we've had the luxury of turkey at our tables. Jane is cooking ours now in that rich and spicy chocolate sauce that she makes, and the scent of it makes the roof of my mouth drip. I allowed Concepción to help Jane in the kitchen, today. The girl actually enjoys the tedious work of grinding on the metate. All morning, Jane had her grinding peanuts and toasted sesame seeds and dried red chiles into a powder. Now she sits across from me at her own *escritorio* and I can smell the spices emanating from her hands.

- - - - - -

Pentecost

Padre Antonio came to examine my conscience yesterday. He says he is "distressed" by my particular friendship with la Condesa. He has heard about her gifts and the verses I write in gratitude, and as penance he wants me to go into silence for a month to meditate upon my sins. He warns me that if I continue in my "rebelliousness" he will have to take my case to the Inquisition. Last night, as a consequence of Padre Antonio's visit, I had that old dream of the bishop on the riverbank. In this dream, I can clearly see the bishop's face, and he wears the same round spectacles that Padre Antonio uses, but he has a short white beard hanging from his chin, so I know that the bishop is not Padre Antonio, but perhaps has the same vision as my father confessor. The man is chanting the *Pater Noster.* In one hand, he holds a smoking censer, in the other a bottle of blue water, and I see that I am prostrate before him, my habit stripped to my waist, my back striped with lashes, my hair a mat for the bishop's feet. He is purifying me.

22 September

Another quarrel with la Condesa, today. I still disagree with her interpretation of the comet, and she has involved me in a silly scandal with Don Carlos and Father Kino. Now I have received Father Kino's treatise on the comet, a refutation of Don Carlos' manifesto, and I must respond in favor of Father Kino's ideas if I want to maintain my friendship with la Condesa. She is far too dignified to request it openly, but I believe my loyalty is being tested, and I know, although in reality I agree with Don Carlos that comets are not portents of disaster, but natural phenomena of celestial origin, that I will eventually submit to María Luisa's will, at the cost of my friendship with Don Carlos. It is an unjust test, and she knows it. The choices that we have to make! Unfortunately, I offended la Condesa today with my sarcastic tongue, and now I have promised to be silent. She is twenty times more willful than la Marquesa, and I am twenty times more foolish for her love.

12 November

My birthday again. Thirty-three was the year of Christ's crucifixion, and I feel as though I, too, were nailed to a cross. Three weeks have passed since my quarrel with la Condesa, and still I have not spoken to her. It is my own pride and stubbornness that have crucified me.

later

I can barely write. My fingers tremble. My chest swirls with emotions that I must force myself to conceal. I have received a summons from la Condesa. She bids me to break my silence, to explain why I have cloistered myself in my dreadful pride. That woman could break Padre Antonio's will, despite his diligent misogyny. Now I must finish drafting that verse of apology, and pray that she will come to visit me today.

> And now your grave command
> shatters my mute silence;
> your wish, alone, is the key
> to my respect for you.
>   And, though loving your beauty
> is a crime without pardon
> I would rather be punished by guilt
> than by indifference.
>   Don't ask, then, my stern lady,
> that, having declared my intention,
> I make myself more wretched
> when I was graced with mockery.
>   If you blame my contempt,
> blame also your own license;
> for if you say I am not obedient,

> *I say your mandate was not just.*
> *   And, if my intention is guilty,*
> *my affection is also damned,*
> *for loving you is a transgression*
> *of which I will never repent.*
> *   This I find in my feelings,*
> *and more which I know not how to explain;*
> *but you, from what I keep silent*
> *will infer what I cannot say.*

There, I have finished. There are traces of my wounded pride in between the lines, but let her smell the bitter scent. Why should I hide that I am bitter about betraying my friend, Don Carlos? I have missed her so much, though, and am thankful that she has come to pull me from the cross.

Now I must tell Jane to heat water for my bath, and Concepción will copy the verse in her graceful calligraphy on a gilt-edged sheet. If my muse does not deceive me, I will be receiving a guest this evening after vespers who will resurrect me from the tomb.

NB: The excerpts from Sor Juana's work are the author's own translations.

LATITUDE

Stacey D'Erasmo

Amanda and I worked together in the library near a park I miss. Amanda lived at the pond end of the park. I lived at the zoo end, with my husband, Tim. I worked in the map room and Amanda worked in Reference, which was a joke, because I can't read a map and Amanda couldn't spell. They were stupid jobs we had, the jobs of people who were really doing something else. Except we weren't doing something else, because something else was still hidden all around us, in clues. So we took the sorts of jobs that revolved around lists and proofreading and long boxes of index cards, as if one day these meaningless stacks of paper would spell out HELP to a passing airplane of vocation. Tim had index cards, too—his dissertation, which lay in neat stacks in the office corner of our apartment, each stack with a white notecard on top: "Birth," "Adolescence," "Marriage to Emily," "Marriage to Katherine," "Wars," "Children," "Death." His subject was Henry the 6th, two before the famous Henry and much more bloodthirsty. In my mind's eye, I see myself traversing our park as if it were a sea and I was a fisherman on that sea, rowing steadily from end to end, every day. I am faithful, faithful, faithful like a clock. Tim is at 12, Amanda at 6. I row between them—1,2,3,4,5 strokes. Five strokes back.

One day at the library, a small girl with big glasses approached the desk. "Do you have any maps of central Rhodesia?" she asked.

I opened drawers, checked indexes. "I'm sorry, there is no more central Rhodesia," I told her. "I can only give you half a Zimbabwe with a little Botswana on the side."

"Can you check again?" she asked politely.

I spread my hands wide, in the way adults do when they want to demonstrate to a child or a dog that they have no more treats. "It doesn't exist," I said. "It's something else now."

"Okay, thank you," she said. She put her pink and purple knapsack on one of the wide library tables, sat down, and took out her geography book, searching pointedly through the index for her lost Rhodesia, the undivided land of diamonds and pain she had imagined that couldn't possibly be simply erased, like a problem on a blackboard.

I told Tim about her that night, in bed.

"Who was she more like, me or you?" he asked, kissing my palm.

"You, I think. No, like me in looks but with your concentration. She answered all the study questions at the end of the chapter."

"Did you see Amanda today?"

"Just for a few minutes. We're going to do laundry Saturday."

"It's supposed to rain," he said irrelevantly, folding his glasses and setting them carefully on the bedside table.

I rolled over, turned out the light. "I barely saw her this whole week."

"Whatever, Christine." I felt him tumble away into sleep, resigned.

I married Tim the day I got out of college, feeling like I had gotten away with something, like he and I were suspended above the fairgrounds while everyone else went from booth to booth, shooting and missing and shooting again. Tim believed entirely in me, in himself, in the two of us rising slowly and smoothly up the ferris wheel of life, our cage swaying only a little in the breeze. I was the distracted passenger, afraid of heights, my ticket damp with sweat, unable not to peek at the creaking iron ropes and rusted pulleys.

I also say distracted, because, as I lay so quietly next to my young husband in the dark, I did what I had been doing off and on for ages: I thought about women—one woman at a time, actually, although usually one I didn't know very well. Sometimes it was a woman I had seen on the street or in a movie, a waitress downtown, a traffic cop. A doctor. A woman, one of two, sitting across from me on a bus, with a gym bag. This woman had to be taller than me, and rougher, with slightly tired, experienced eyes—the better to see right into me, like the beam of a flashlight playing over a darkened house. I did meet women now and then who had this particular, experienced look about them; when I was near them I felt much larger or much smaller than usual, much softer, infinitely shyer, and dangerous. With Tim, fair play was paramount; we were the world's tiniest, best-run democracy. But with this woman, I'd be caught like a bird in a net and soon I'd be running through the rain, late for appointments, late for dinner, late for everything.

In my mind, she always started it. She wouldn't take no for an answer, caught up with me in empty hallways or in intimately overfurnished rooms not quite far enough away from the dinner party to which we had both (unexpectedly) been invited. Sometimes she asked me out for drinks while Tim was out of town somewhere; sometimes she asked me over and sat too close to me on the sofa. Sometimes I woke up with her and sometimes I left her in the middle of the night, silently putting my shoes on outside her bedroom door. We met in cafes, in train stations, bumped into one another in museums. She was always waiting for me, always asking. I always said no at first, but then, stranded with her in that house or hallway, I always said yes.

I thought of it, my secret life, as ballast, or unspent wealth, or raw talent. It was my future.

On Saturday, I lugged my laundry to Amanda's. There wasn't much besides windows in her bright, bright living room—a perpetually unfolded futon couch, a leafy, dark-green plant, a wide, round mirror on the wall.

"Shhh," she said, opening the door. "Anne and Jess are sleeping." We went into the kitchen, sat down at the enormous, claw-footed mahogany table that always looked way too big to have gotten in, or ever get out, any of the hollow-core doors. Lying underneath the table were Amanda's pointy, red shoes, the ones with the buckle.

Amanda lit a cigarette and leaned back in her chair. "What a night," she said softly, exhaling. "First, I spend an hour on the phone with my sister Grace, what a mess, my mother's hysterical. Jess comes in and finds me watching *Night of the Living Dead* on TV, totally on the ceiling. Then we go out to the White House, which is supposed to be mixed on Fridays, but really it's all boys and the music sucks. We run into Peter, who's waiting for his date, some boy who always stands him up, so he's in a terrible mood, so of course Jess has to get all over him about politics or something. I drank about five hundred beers and smoked three thousand cigarettes." She put on one of her shoes. "What did you do?"

"Tim made me dinner. We talked about this Berlin thing." Tim wanted us both to apply for summer teaching jobs at a secondary school outside Berlin.

Amanda made a face, "Don't go to Berlin, Christine. You know they're all Nazis."

"I don't know," I said. "Somehow it makes me feel like an Army wife. Let's go before the laundromat gets crowded."

We sat at the back of the narrow, dingy laundromat like bad high school girls at the back of the bus, drinking coffee out of Styrofoam cups, keeping an eye on the line for the dryers, gossiping. Even in college, where we met, there was something post-apocalyptic about Amanda that was terribly attractive to the men and women whom she dangled lovingly and with much soul-searching over the edge of the abyss. For money, she usually did things that required costumes or props—lifeguarding one summer, switchboard operator, construction worker, and, for two bleak weeks once, topless dancer. Most of the time, Amanda was a lesbian, and she said she always preferred the company of women even when she was sleeping with a man. I had always told Amanda about my crushes on women; she would listen, smoking a cigarette, not saying too much. I wondered if she thought I was a coward. One endless winter when I was getting letters from a woman I had met at one of Amanda's parties, I asked Amanda if she thought I should tell Tim. "Life is really long, Christine," she said. "And Tim—" She shook her head. "He has a lot of principles."

So I put the letters in the same battered, private box where I kept my high school poems and third-grade friendship rings and spent Saturday mornings in the laundromat with Amanda, telling secrets. She was just whispering about a violinist she had picked up three nights before and how she had decided to leave before he could get his pants off when she said, "Oh Christ. There's Jane."

"Who's Jane?"

Amanda glanced away, crushing her cigarette in the bottom of her coffee cup. "You remember. Last fall. I sort of had some dates with her and then she kept calling, but I never called her back. Fuck."

I looked at Jane, whom I didn't remember hearing about at all. She was tall and slender with short black hair. She was wearing a sweatshirt with the sleeves cut out and heavy, black railroad-worker boots, but her expression was serene. She helped the woman next to her wrestle open an unwilling box of soap-powder, then emptied a pillowcase full of what seemed to be nothing but socks into a machine.

"She looks nice," I said.

"Oh, yeah, she's nice," said Amanda, as if that wasn't the half of it. Jane offered her paper to the old guy in the recliner who ran the laundromat, then, spotting us, came over and thumped Amanda on the leg.

"Hey, how are you?" she said.

"Fine," said Amanda, blushing a little. "This is my friend Christine."

"Hi," said Jane. "Is this, like, a laundry klatsch?" She winked at me. Amanda didn't see it, because she was refusing to look up. One of my dirty sleeves bobbed soapily against the interior window of the washing machine, like an arm signaling above waves.

"Sit down," I said, scooting over on the wooden bench.

Jane sat down between me and Amanda, stretching out her long legs, running a hand through her hair, which was wet from the rain—Tim had been right. She wore three silver rings on one hand, none on the other, and smelled faintly lemony, like one of those invigorating bath gels advertised on TV, the ones that make women skip through their work day. Amanda began shredding her cup, drizzling bits of Styrofoam, like snow, over the dead cigarette.

"My sister's name is Christine," said Jane, our guest.

"Oh," I said. "I don't have any sisters. Just one brother."

"All my sisters are insane," said Amanda, gloomily.

No one replied. Something in my wash was making an irregular beating, dragging sound and I watched it all go damply around, idly wondering what could be making that noise but incapable of getting up to look. Amanda stared straight ahead, like an accident victim still sitting upright in the wrecked car.

Jane stood up, saying, "I'm going to get a soda. Anybody want one?"

"No, thanks,," said Amanda. "We're fine."

When Jane walked away, I looked carefully at Amanda, my old friend, whose profile was so familiar to me, but whose motives were sometimes still so opaque. There were tiny bits of gray now in her hair, I noticed, the lightest of touches, as if someone had just grazed it with painted fingertips.

Amanda shrugged. "You know, it's not that I don't like her. Everyone likes Jane. But here I am with major sex guilt and there she is with none at all. It's just not fair. I feel like she must be laughing at me."

"Amanda, I'm sure that's not true," I said loyally, but it was a fool's loyalty, because what did I know? Tim called her "The Unsinkable Amanda" to be mean, but she was more like a ship perpetually half-sunk whom teams of divers were forever attempting to rescue. Did I love her? I wouldn't have dared. She was my eyes and ears, a love-spy going out on missions, returning to be debriefed in the laundromat. Did she love me? I never asked, just as I never asked her why the conclusion of every report was deceit, double agents, treason, mayday. I didn't even ask her what had happened with this affable Jane, whom I knew she had never told me about, and who soon returned, undaunted, with two cans of Sprite.

She sat down and handed me one.

During Jane's spin cycle, while my and Amanda's clothes shared a dryer and Amanda talked to the old man up front, perching sympathetically on his recliner arm, Jane, moving closer, told me some things about her life. She was a photographer. She lived alone, which she liked, because it was important for women to learn to be alone she said, and, besides, the last time she had lived with someone it hadn't worked out. What happened? I asked her. She told me that her last serious lover had been Molly, a dancer, who had left a man for her and then left her for a man. I said that must have been terrible, but Jane said that it was a relief by the time it was really over. I didn't know if I believed her. I tried to picture Jane relieved, moving her clothes over to fill up the half-empty closet.

"She's been on tour practically since we broke up. I'm not even sure where she is now. She sent postcards for a while. The last one was from Texas, or maybe it was Alaska." I didn't like ambivalent Molly, I decided, dancing away from Jane over the tundra.

"But when you got involved she was straight, so you must have figured that, you know—" I paused, not quite sure how to go on.

Jane crossed one big boot over the other, meditatively gripping the bench. She closed her eyes for a second and I was afraid I had been rude. But then she opened them again and said, "Well, I'm always up for being pleasantly surprised. But once it happened it was like, okay, goodbye, that's it. I changed the locks as soon as she left."

"Did she try to come back?"

"Just once. I let her, sort of. It was a mess."

Before we left the laundromat that day, Jane said, "You know, I work right near you guys, at Photo Arts. You should stop by sometime." She seemed to be talking to both of us, but I pretended, both arms wrapped around my orange laundry bag with its warm cargo of shirts and bras and Tim's underwear, that she was talking only to me.

On Monday morning, as I sat at my desk with its hulking, antique phone, a little Sphinx on which Tim sometimes called from the Middle Ages to talk about dinner, I wondered how Jane had known I was thirsty. It was sort of a flirtatious thing to do, I thought, breaking open a fresh pack of index cards to make a new continents file, to get a Sprite like that for someone you had just met, and then to hand it to her, as if to say: I know what you want. And Jane hadn't gotten one for Amanda. So maybe it was a subtle dig at Amanda, a very tiny carbonated brush-off. I had caught Jane looking at me as I was shifting wet clothes to the dryer. Amanda had said that everyone liked Jane. Maybe that really meant Jane liked everyone.

In the evening, I sat with *Middlemarch* in my chair near the window while Tim grappled with Henry's military strategies. Tim had made a list of the possible outcomes that might have followed different, better decisions on Henry's part and assigned a point value to each one. So far, Henry was scoring highest for dying young. I imagined Jane leaning against a car outside my building, arms folded, trying to figure out which window was mine. No, too fast. She was probably serenely at home alone right now, developing pictures, and I was just crossing the outside border of the field of her attention, just an intriguing figure in the distance. Amanda's friend. Maybe Amanda had even told Jane about me, in passing, on some evening long ago. "Oh, my friend Christine, she's really interesting, but shy. You'd like her." And Jane hadn't thought much about it at the time, but now she was thinking of me, hanging pictures up to dry, thinking that I had a nice face, maybe. Thinking vaguely that it would be nice to run into each other again. And here I was thinking of her, too, just in passing, reading *Middlemarch*, the book I read whenever I wasn't really reading, sitting across the room from my husband, Tim, who was wearing his favorite flannel shirt, the blue one, which had been worn by both of us so often that it was slowly disappearing.

Eating sandwiches with Amanda on the library steps, beneath a statue of a warrior-queen with flowing marble hair and wild marble horses, I tried to imagine someone with no sex guilt. I asked Amanda if she thought I had sex guilt and she said, "Sex sanctioned by the state is a gray area."

"I might go there," I said, watching the warrior-queen drive on through an ancient storm.

"Where?"

"Where she works."

"Go for it," said Amanda. "Maybe she'll get you a good discount."

I felt too shy to go. I thought of going, dropping by on my lunch hour. Jane would look up. I would smile, wave a friendly little wave. She would be glad to see me, we would chat, and quickly discover that we liked the same photographers, that we had a natural affinity for the same type of work even though she, of course, knew much more about it than I. I would tell her anecdotes from somewhere or other and she would laugh and we would make a date for lunch. And she would be thinking that I reminded her a bit of Molly, something about the way I moved my hands, but then she would put away that thought because it all still hurt, even though she didn't like to admit it.

I thought of going, and in the meantime I began to feel as though I had a sort of Jane-lining under my skin and it grew by pale but tenacious increments every day I didn't go to see her. I felt it at work, as I slid those swirly maps into their long, wooden drawers. I felt it at home, her hands under my hands, her knees beneath my knees, as Tim fought beside his King, hacking the heads off invading Huns. Jane is a comfortable armchair, I caught myself thinking one morning at work, as I stared at all the globes lined up on the tops of the bookshelves, a row of worlds as-yet unspun in the quiet room. I knew what longitude I was on, but I could never remember my latitude. I had always been a single line of possibilities, extending into space.

I stopped by the bookstore where Jane worked, on my way home. She sat behind a high counter, looking happy and kind. She smiled down at people when she gave them their change, as if she was giving them a special gift. A thin man with one earring, the store's owner, I thought, came over to whisper in her ear as she rang up books. Then he gave her a little kiss and squeezed her hand. Jane smiled, then smiled at me browsing through a book on Weegee.

"Hi," she said. "All those people are dead."

"I know," I said, flipping past several men lying on a dirty street in halos of blood. "Do you like him?"

"Sometimes. But after a while, all those corpses, you just get numb. I try to never be numb."

"That's ambitious," I said, thinking of my day struggling to stack relief maps so as not to permanently crumple any mountain ranges.

"I am pretty ambitious," said Jane. "And Sol says I can leave. Are you going to the subway?"

It was more or less on my way. Jane got her jacket and a very large canvas bag with lumps in it—"I bought some lenses today," she said—and we set off for the corner. She walked slowly, asking me about the library, about Tim, my white knight of index cards, my soon-to-be Berliner, probably executing radishes for our salad as I walked down the street with Jane. She seemed to listen carefully to everything I said, as if she were drawing a map of me in her mind.

We stopped at the subway entrance. A slight wind ruffled up the stair as a train approached, but Jane didn't move to get it. "I've been thinking about you, Christine," she said. "I think we should have lunch next week."

A thousand years went by.

"I would like that," I said, as castles fell all along the Thames. Then, "Maybe—why don't you bring some of your pictures?"

"I will," she said, and disappeared down the subway steps, her mysterious black bag, big enough to fit an entire soul inside, slung securely across her back.

That night, I dreamed of a vast, golden wheat field. The wind was moving over the wheat, like a shadow. There were no houses, no highways, no phone lines. It was one of those dreams that you, the dreamer, aren't in. I was hovering above the scene somewhere, in the sky. Then Jane appeared, striding through the field, looking for someone. I realized she was looking for me, but couldn't see me, like Auntie Em in the crystal ball, looking for Dorothy. She glanced around, up, down, as if hearing distant thunder. Then she shook her head, and walked on.

We sat in a crowded lunchtime restaurant, her portfolio open between us, and she told me about each picture, touching me lightly on the hand now and then. I didn't say so, but I was disappointed, a little, because they were so plain. A monk's pictures. Molly was nowhere in sight. Here was a tower. There was a wall. There was an arc. Here was a dog's eye, quite close. There was a woman's arm, gracefully bending. Jane leaned toward me, talking about light and angles and lenses, but what I wanted to ask was: Why this particular wall? What is this tower? Who is this woman? The waiter came and went and I studied her face, her hands. I realized that she was probably a few years older than me; there was a scar on the back of her left hand. Her eyes were green. She carried a little looseleaf notebook around with her for writing down ideas, appointments, phone numbers. It lay on the table now, beside her place. I longed to open and read it, to see my name written there on this day, in this restaurant, at this exact moment. She confided that she worried a lot—plane crashes, natural disasters, finding oneself suddenly alone on a dark street.

She opened her little notebook to write down our next lunch date, my work number.

When I got back to the library, she called to see if I had gotten there all right.

"It's three blocks," I said.

She told me that she had heard on the radio that there was going to be a tornado.

"A what?"

"A tornado, well, it's a possibility of a tornado. I just thought you should know in case, you know, you want to go home early or call Tim or something."

"Jane," I said. "I don't think there's going to be a tornado," but I spent all that afternoon moving worlds out of the way so I could keep an eye on the window.

Every Day and Every Night

Rebecca Brown

Every night before I sleep, I sit in front of my mirror like an 18th-century lady at her toilet. My face is sagged and wrinkled because of what's seeped out of me during the day. It's only a little so no one notices, but I am well aware that I'm diminished. I sit at the mirror and look at myself. Behind me in my tiny room, I live in a very tiny place, I see the dogs. They're partying like in a couple of scenes from Hogarth. Some of them are sprawled across a squat, tubby wooden table in a low-life tavern. Others tipple at high-backed ornately carved chairs in a high-ceilinged drawing room. They're swigging from tankards or sipping from thin-stemmed crystal glasses. A trio of them takes turns sticking their manicured claws down the overflowing blouse of a heavily made-up, gap-toothed, very buxom mongrel. I can see the cracks in the cheap, thick powder this poor old cur has painted on to hide her sags and wrinkles. I try to look away from them, but even when I close my eyes I see them.

When the dogs have had enough of her, they return their attention to me. They glide around me sly as rakes (the lower class ones having fallen down to snooze beside their spit) bowing low, extravagent bows, and arcing their embroidered, perfumed hankies around my haggard face. They nuzzle me with their moist, cold muzzles and nip me with their shiny yellow teeth. I want them to get it over with, but I know not to rush them. I clench my

teeth and hold my breath and try to not feel anything. I'm taut
as a lampshade, stiff as a doll. *I try to not feel anything.*

But I do. They lick me till I tremble and my holes and seams
are opened and I collapse. The air inside me wheezes out. My
poor head topples sideways then my back slumps down. My arms
and legs and thighs get thin. The dogs press me down until there's
only a little air in me, then they put their mouths against my
open holes and suck out the rods. Then, when I'm deflated, they
grab me by their teeth and drag me into bed with them.

They lay all over, on top of me, I feel them walking on me.
My insides press against myself. The dogs do what they will.

Thus every night they empty me. Thus every single night they
fill my bed.

Then every morning, each and every day, they make me ready.
They do what they undid the night before.

When the alarm the dogs have set goes off, my neck jerks up
like a licorice whip and my eyes, pickle bumps on the flat fan of
my face, pop open. My unsupported skin is spread across the bed
like putty. The dogs leap up and drag me to the bathroom. They
slam me up against the tub. I slip over the edge like that watch
in Dali's "Persistence of Memory." I drape my rubbery hand over
the faucet to try to coax the water, but of course my boneless
flesh can't turn the faucet. The dogs, who are very, very clean, as
I am not, they tell me so, help me. One of the dogs who has
been panting, grinning by the door skips up and turns the faucet
with his teeth. He's young and fit, and, oh, so much more agile
than I. In the filling tub I float like a plastic sheet. Then, when
the dogs are ready, they dunk me.

They "wash" me (that's what they call their rubbing, poking,
slithering paws) then squeeze me dry. A couple of them tease me,
tugging me back and forth between them until one of them gets
me in its teeth, hauls me back to the main room and drops me
on the floor. Then I hear them snickering. Of all the things they
get to do, I think they like it best when I ask them for it. Every
day, yes, every single day they make me beg. For what I hate the
very most. But what they know, I know, I cannot live without. So
I beg them, every day, to fill me up. They yip at their daily
victory, which is my daily shame.

The rods are leaning against the bed like mismatched crutches. The dogs knock them down and I, like a protozoan, like the very lowest, crudest form of life, ooze myself over the rods. The dogs find my holes and ram the rods back into me. Down through my middle opening, two longish rods for legs. Then up the same, a slightly shorter one: my back. Then through my mouth: two medium rods for arms. Then, finally, for my head and neck, a stump.

Sometimes, for fun, the dogs put the rods inside me wrong— the long one up my neck so the soft spot in my head nearly bursts, or two mismatched ones for my legs. This makes me even more ugly and deformed and it also hurts, the dogs enjoy it. Only when they've had their laughs do they take the rods out and put them in again the proper way. When the rods are finally in me right, the dogs lick close my seams and holes. Except my mouth which they let me open and close myself. The dogs get a kick out of seeing the stupid things I can put in, and the awful, stupid things I can make come out of it. And I must admit, the dogs are right, my mouth can do and say the stupidest things. I finish by opening my mouth in a big round "O," which looks like a cry of horror or alarm, or perhaps of hope or ecstasy, and I gulp in air. I gulp as much as anyone can. I blow myself up, I'm like a balloon. I gulp until my fingers and toes, my ears and nose, my points, pop out. Then I take one giant, final gulp and seal the place down in my throat that keeps me in and keeps the world out. Then I almost look like someone, like an almost normal, flesh and body human.

I teeter to the mirror where I sat the night before. I always have to readjust myself. I press my tingling fingers to the places I'm not right and pull and push. The canines, who are perfect, sit around me whispering to each other. They comment about every inch of me—my boring, pasty, milk-white skin, my sagging tits, my fingernails that can't do half the things theirs can. They shake their gorgeous heads about my flaws and bark to tell me how I should improve myself. I try to do what they tell me to—to make my eyebrows thin and straight, or pull my nose more long and square, or color my pale, larvae colored flesh. I try to make me look like them, but I can't.

*   *   *

The dogs have put a checklist by the mirror. They make me stand up, naked, so the pack of them, around me in a semicircle, can see me front and back. I am on show, an auction block, a grade-school spelling bee. Miss Dog, a tall thin bitch with particularly sharp claws, strides up beside me. She stands erect on her firm hind legs. She wears very pointed glasses and her ears are tied back in a prim, tight bun. She holds a pointing stick. Briskly, militarily, she sniffs. I try to stand at attention, but I'm a clunky, too-big, awkward kid, a slob. I try to straighten my terrible posture, but everyone knows I'm hopeless. Still, Miss Dog must check the basics. There is the crisp "click" of her pointer against the list as she taps the word "Mouth." Then there's my squeaky answer: "Check."

Another "click." (Eyes.)

"Check."

"Click, click." (Arms, left and right.)

"Check, check."

"Click." (Head.)

"Check."

"Click, click, click, cli—" (Stomach, tongue, thighs, two hands—)

"Yes! Yes! Yes!"

Her slit eyes glare through her specs at me. What have I done wrong? I burble out the proper word: "*Check*, check, check."

Sometimes the dogs write cute things on the checklist like: "Head on Crooked," "Bloodshot Eyes," "The Shakes," and Miss Dog has pointed at it and I have answered "Check," before I notice what it really says. All of them are class clowns; I'm the fool. Miss Dog pokes me with her pointer. I lift my arms and turn my head from side to side so she can check behind my ears and the back of my neck. I'm so unclean. With her pointer she lifts my lips and checks my gums and makes me stick my tongue out. I see how I repulse her in her face. When she has seen what she requires of me, she swats her stick across my ass.

I shuffle, head bowed, shoulders stooped, to the closet. I have to be careful with my clothes. If I wore something with a pin it could prick me, or a zipper could tear me open and I'd deflate. I'm safest in my ragged, soft old sweats. Miss Dog *hates* the way I dress, but allows it as a way to help prevent at least this one particular disaster. The puppies help me button and zip. It's so humiliating, at their young age! But they're so much more dextrous than I.

When Miss Dog nods the briefest nod, this is my permission to go out. I open the door as quick as I can and close it as quickly too. I hurry away from my tiny room and I do not look back.

:

I brought a girl back from the bar. We went to my apartment. Maybe we talked some small talk, but I don't remember, I wasn't paying attention. We went in my building and up the stairs. When I stuck the key in the lock to my apartment I suddenly shivered. I gave this girl a pathetic little smile. Was I hoping she'd see my hesitance, and remember—suddenly—that she had an appointment somewhere else? (It was 2 AM.) Or was I really expecting that I could just breeze out and haul some relatively normal human being back to my place? Before I could do anything, she'd pushed the door open and slipped in the room in front of me. Her hair brushed my face. I could smell the smoke from the bar. She slipped on the overhead light, a bright bare bulb. I flinched. I didn't want her to see them.

She tossed her baseball cap and jacket on the back of the chair and sat on the bed. I sat next to her and she kicked off her shoes. The laces flicked when they fell to the floor and I gasped.

What's the matter, she said.

Nothing, I lied. I looked at the floor.

Well, come on, she said impatiently. She was the kind of girl I used to like. She kicked her shoes off and I heard another click.

I looked down and saw, sticking out from beneath the bed, a claw. The girl was unbuttoning her shirt. I grabbed her shirt and threw it over the claw. Which was now attached to a paw. Which was coming out from beneath the bed. The girl laughed, like my pulling her shirt off was fun.

She put her hands on my shirt to do the same.

No, I said.

Shy, she snickered, like this was part of our fun too.

No, I tried to say again, but she'd grabbed the bottom of my shirt and was lifting it over my head. I yanked my shirt off and dropped it on the black muzzle nosing out from beneath the bed. I held my breath. She lifted her t-shirt over her head. The skin of her shoulders was perfect. Her collar bone was perfect. I looked down and the muzzle threw my shirt off. The girl put her hand on my neck. There was another paw beside the first.

Come on, she said. Then she was on me, I heard them stir and I pulled away.

Relax, she said. I heard them laughing, it was such a classic line. Relax, she said again, a little louder.

I stared at the floor. The paws and muzzle had slipped back beneath the bed. What fucking game were we playing?

She pulled me. There was a growl.

Come on. She was getting impatient. She pulled at my jeans.

I closed my eyes and we fumbled around. I heard our hands swish over each other. I heard the wet sound of the opening of mouths, the clack of teeth, the rustling of the dogs. We put our mouths against each other and opened them.

Open-mouthed, the puppies gasp. They're eager to play, they're having fun. They're playing Punch and Judy, that hokey old where-will-they-pop-up next routine. I feel her mouth, this girl's, and her hands, and I can't see her, I keep my eyes closed, but I see them, their toothy muzzles and pointy ears, their long, pink rolling tongues. Their goofy mugs burst through the paper back-drop on stage. They swing down from a ceiling bar and pop up through a trap door or from inside a traveller's trunk, from under-neath the bed. And I am, still, as always, every time, the wide-eyed fool, the idiot, the clown. My floppy, giant-toed shoes trip me and my dirty, white-gloves hands are thumbs, they poke out from my hips, I can't lift them away, I'm tipped off balance. And I know the bowler hat that crowns me like a pin will not protect me from the bucket of whatever is above the door that I'm about to walk through. I wish someone would stop me, but I don't.

Hey, this girl says, Whoa, and squeezes me by the shoulders. My head is down, my eyes are closed, my body's still moving towards her as if it hasn't heard.

Stop, she says firmly, and pushes my body away.

I pull myself away and roll over on the bed. The room rolls over. I'm afraid I'll step on one of the dogs and piss it off, but I find the floor with my feet and stand up, swaying.

I open my eyes and look at her. She's holding her hands in front of her as if to keep me away. I want to tell her something but I can't. I shake my head and close my eyes again and I see the dogs beneath the bed. Like the kids backstage who play the angels in the Christmas show. But then it's not the cover of my bed they hide behind, it's a curtain, and they're on stage, and the curtain's open and it's their cue, they're front and center and performing. As am I.

The place is packed. (Admittedly, with comps, we had to drag them in.) I'm doing my desperate, sweetest, heart-felt best, but I can't convince them. The dogs don't care that my role is meant to make them cry; they're laughing. They're shaking, doubled over, tears streaming out of their jolly, squinting eyes. They're a bunch of vaudeville comics yucking it up over a corny prank I am the object of. They're rolling around on a garishly lit stage as big as the Palladium. I try to picture a hooked cane popping out from stage right and dragging them back by their necks—no—I really try to picture that hook of a cane inside their ribs and hooking their pebble hearts. But that's a picture I can't make come. I can only see them chortling, their thin black eyelids squeezing out their tears.

I look behind the footlights, and into this girl's eyes as if I could say something to her.

I take a deep breath. And then, with the stiffness of a miserably over-coached pre-teen in a spinster's elocution class, I pronounce: I-guess-you-should-go.

The dogs howl! They burst! Their jaws stretch wide. Their eyes pour giggly tears. They stamp their two-toned shoes. Have you ever heard such a funny thing, they ask themselves in stage-whisper asides. I'm better than the travelling salesman, the farmer's daughter, I'm better than Take-My-Wife-Please. They slap their knees, take their bowlers off and fan their sweaty faces. They stick cigars in their mouths and clap and clap and clap.

Down, I think to myself, *Down.*

Their shoulders shake. They pull wrinkled hankies from their oversized pinstripe suits and wipe their piggy eyes. They blow cigar smoke up into the overhead lights.

The girl is staring at me. I wonder if she can hear the dogs.

I say each syllable slowly, like I'm talking to a foreigner—no—not *to* a foreigner, but like I *am* a foreigner. I-guess-you-should-leave-now, I squack out. *Stop! Down!* I shoo them away from me. They're kicking up their heels and raising their skinny noses and lifting their horrible flabby jowls in song.

I stumble back to the chair this girl has thrown her jacket across. The girl doesn't move.

Their ears perk up, their hats are tipped awry. They pat their bowlers on their heads with their white-gloved paws.

Please, I say. I hold out her cap and jacket to her.

They put their forepaws around each other's shoulders and sway back and forth.

She takes the jacket. Its weight lifts from my hands like a promise I never meant to keep. Their ears are up. Their bowlers bump into the bottom of the bed.

That was quick, the girl raises an eyebrow.

They straggled chorus line of them sways back and forth, clicking their claws to a sloppy, sentimental song.

So long, she smirks.

Their hankies wave good-bye in a Busby Berkely wave.

She puts her jacket on. I hand her her baseball cap. She taps it on her head and tugs the bill down a bit over the back of her neck. She looks at me. I shrug. She gets this look on her face then shakes her head and walks to the door. The dogs press their hankies to their muzzles and blow. I don't even try to say anything because the dogs are blowing into their hankies, loud, high-decibel, fart-sounding honks. Who could hear anything beneath their racket?

Then the girl is at the door.

Stay, I'm thinking, *Please.* But I don't say anything.

She puts her hand to the doorknob. The dogs all grab forepaws and snap their feet together and stretch all the way from stage right to stage left and bow as one. She turns the door handle. One of the dogs, an especially beautiful one, breaks from the chorus to come forward, lift her paws to left and right, the pit, up to the balcony, the light booth. She is a gracious, gorgeous star and she is giving humble-seeming thanks to her loyal, hard-working, adoring company. She opens the door to let herself out. She pauses. Someone runs up with a dozen beautiful long-stemmed roses for her. She smiles a rapturous, yet modest smile, then clasps her hands above her heart. She accepts the flowers and bows. She doesn't turn. She pulls the door closed behind her. The curtain falls. My door clicks locked. There's a click of claws in thundrous applause. Their feet stomp in enthusiasm. Her feet pad down to the end of the hall. Backstage, they're opening and closing dressing room doors, they're shifting sets. She opens the door at the end of the hall. I hear it close behind her.

I see her. I can see her in the back of my head. She's on the landing, she's going down the steps to the first floor. I know just when her hand will touch, it touches, the door. She lets herself out back. I see her step into the alley, into the dark wet night outside. Outside it's raining. Backstage the dogs are peeling off this night's makeup, pulling off their bright white skin with cold cream. She pulls her jacket around her tightly and crosses her arms and lowers her head against the drizzle. In the alley outside the stage door, fans are waiting for an autograph or to touch the hem of a garment or to see the fancy car the chauffeur drives away. She walks out the alley to Howell. There's so much competition for a cab this time of night. Most of the audience have to walk. She crosses 17th then 16th. The dogs stream out of the theater in their tuxes and tails and formals and furs. She gets to 15th and waits for the NightOwl bus to take her back to her apartment where she will fix a cup of tea. The dogs settle down in smart cafes where fine linen napkins are tucked beneath china dessert plates and fancy patterned silverware and coffee cups with saucers. I step to my door and double lock the lock. They order coffee and liqueurs and cakes and bones. I sit down in my chair and take a deep breath. I lift my hands in front of my face; they're shaking. The dogs chat about their stocks and art and chat each other up: Your place or mine? A penthouse at the Ritz? I wish they'd go, I wish they'd leave me alone.

I look over to the bed, at the dark black two inch line beneath it. At first there's nothing, but then I blink and when I open my eyes again, I see: a nose. Then a paw. Another paw. Then more of the head, the lips and gums, the black spotted flap of the gums.

The eyes. Then the two brown dots above the eyes, the square block of the top of the head, the two stiff ears. Then the forepaws stretch and the front legs pull and the claws click and she scrambles out. Then there's another set of paws and nose. Another. More. They scramble out from underneath. The pack.

I expect them to be jocular—they've had a lot of fun tonight—but they aren't. They're quiet and attentive, reverent. Reverently they arrange themselves in a neat little semicircle, then in concentric circles behind that one. They sit straight and still, their backs aligned, feet neat and even in front of them, their sharp ears back, their dark eyes sad as Greco's saints. And like those saints, they're looking up. So I do too.

To the overhead light, a bright bare bulb. The one that's shed its wretched self on my abominations.

I look up and gasp, then clasp my shaking palm to my—empty?—chest.

For hanging from the fixture it is not a light, it is a rope. And from that rope, a thing of red. The dogs look up at it with longing. It's a piece of meat.

It's a part of me. A part of me is hanging there, the toughest little nut of me, my Dolorous, my Verite, my heart.

It's me inside that rope, which is a noose. I'm standing but I can't see what I'm standing on. On nothing? Air? On fear of them? The rope is pulling, slowly, I am stretching up my neck, my heart.

The dogs are underneath, intent and ready.

I'm choking, yes, I can't stay up. The noose is tight around my throat, around my foolish heart. But also, now, I'm someone else, I'm also wearing a hangman's mask, a mercy mask, a mask of shame so I can't see my face.

The dogs are waiting underneath. They know I can't go on like this.

I look out through my hangman's hood and see them and am terrified.

But then I think how this could be a comfort, I could be released.

The dogs have always known what I've not wanted to. The

loyal, patient, prescient dogs were sent to teach, and help me know, and do, what I was always meant.

I hear us say the words to me. I hear us tell me, *Jump, you sucker, Jump, you fool pathetic child, Jump.*

And so I do. I jump.

THIS EARLY

Mei Ng

It is morning and I reach for the brass candlestick by the bed and scrape the wax that dripped down last night. Soon there is a small white pile and for a moment I almost believe it's shredded coconut and want to eat it. I'd be done much quicker if I would just get up and get a knife from the kitchen but I'm not in a hurry. Besides, it doesn't seem right when other people are downstairs chipping away at the icy sidewalk, the frozen steps. All that noise and they've hardly made a dent.

You call to say you're on the way. We hang up quickly as though we can't wait. I brush the wax from my fingers and put the kettle on. Waiting for water to boil is something I don't do. I gather up the garlic skins from the floor, fill the salt shaker, eat a few cashews. There is hardly anything in the refrigerator: a couple of old yams, some lemons, a green pepper that's only starting to cave in on itself. It makes you nervous that I keep so little food in the house.

You walk quickly to my apartment, our morning bagels tucked inside your jacket, close to your body. When you get here, they are still warm so that the butter melts. We both hate margarine. You say, "What if there's a big storm and I can't make it over here, what will you eat?" You've known me a week, but already you know how I hate going out in the mornings.

I try to explain that it only looks like I have no food. In an emergency, I could whip something up. When there's too much food in the fridge I get edgy, afraid I won't get around to it. It's like I'm always waiting for food to go bad, so I can throw it out already.

I wait for the water to really get going before I make the tea. I make your cup first, you like strong tea. I let it steep, then add lots of lemon, lots of honey. Then I make my tea with your old tea bag. I take my tea light, like old ladies at the diner. If it's too strong, I can't sleep at night.

You show me pictures from your trip to China. For a white girl, you look pretty good in your red imperial robe and headpiece, standing by the palace. You hold your neck very still so the headpiece doesn't tilt you over. It's heavier than it looks. You tell me you are angry at your mother for not teaching you Italian, that all you have left is lots of ways to cook pasta and a big family. I tell you my second language is Spanish, not Chinese. As I look at the photo of you by the Great Wall, I remember that your boyfriend is Asian, too, and I wonder if you've got some fetish thing going on. But then you are talking and touching my arm at the same time, and I think: Everyone's going to China these days, it doesn't mean anything. Me? No, I've never been.

The phone rings. The machine clicks on and then there's my father's voice in my room. "Hello, Daisy? Did you go out yet? It's slippery out there. I almost fell down when I go out to shovel. You be careful when you go down your stair," he says. Then he's quiet but doesn't hang up right away like there's something else he wants to say but can't remember what it is. He clears his throat, then it sounds like he's trying to hang up but can't quite fit the phone back together again.

"Was that your father? He sounds sweet," you say.

"My father? Sweet? I guess so," I say because there isn't enough time to explain him. It would take all day, all night even, and you like to get back early.

My bagel is too big and doughy, each bit seems a lot of work. You don't eat your bagel either. We cover our plates with napkins and tell each other how we normally eat, tons and tons. We're just not hungry right now. Maybe later.

We say something about the weather, about how important the right boots are. You are not looking at me, you are talking and looking down at the floor. The more you touch my arm, the faster you talk. Your mouth is moving and I am looking at it.

Later that afternoon, we are on the couch, its velvet worn almost smooth as your skin. You tell me you've never done anything like this before. Outside, it sounds like everyone on the block is chopping ice. There is still so much to break up and push away.

My wrist is thin next to yours. Your arms just a little bigger than mine. I ask you if you work out and you say only at your job, emptying bags of ice into the bin, reaching for bottles on the upper shelf. You say you hate all the people who come to drink in the afternoon but when they don't come, you miss them.

I ask about the scar on your arm, near the curve of your elbow. It's so light you can hardly see it anymore. I put my lips to it as you tell me, "I used to clean my grandmother's chandelier. Her eyes were huge behind her glasses but still, she couldn't see so good. Her hand was always moving on the table, reaching for things she couldn't see. One day when I was cleaning, I moved too close to one of the bulbs. I'm always burning myself." I show you my hands, all the little scars. I don't have to worry about burns, but keep me away from glass.

You say you want a picture of me to take with you. I bring out my shoebox and you pick the one of me in my orange sun hat, running on the beach. It's hard to tell what direction I'm running in.

You put the picture in your bag, then pile on all the layers again—you are well prepared for winter. I hate socks and hats, I can stay in for days. I wonder if I'm getting like my father. He doesn't like to go out of the house, doesn't like putting on shoes, says they hurt his feet. He still dresses every day in a white shirt and neatly pressed pants, but on his feet are those old gladiator slippers.

"What are you doing for the rest of the night?" you ask me.

"Oh, I don't know," I say. "This and that."

"Are you going to read, cook dinner, go out?" you say. You are completely dressed and it's hot in my apartment. I see that you don't want to think of me just sitting here in the same position all night.

"Yeah, I think I'll read, make a little dinner," I say, so you can leave. I listen to your boots going down the stairs, then out the door. There is no sound as you make your way down the icy stairs. I listen for the gate opening and closing, then I start chipping away at the wax again. I am working faster now, digging with my nails. There is more ice out there than anyone is used to.

I saw someone fall yesterday. She got to the corner and slid off the curb. Her legs folded under her and she crumpled gently as though she were tired of walking and just wanted a little rest before going on.

I call home. I want to ask my mother how to make her sea bass with black bean sauce. Not that I have the ingredients, but just listening to how she makes it would be enough. My mother always gave me the best bits. After she drizzled the sesame oil over the top, she'd remove the backbone with her chopsticks. She would check to see if there were any little bones left, then she'd put a good piece in my bowl.

My father answers the phone. He says, "Your mother?" like he doesn't know who I'm talking about. "She went shopping. Again. It's been four hours since she left the house. She took the cart with her. The refrigerator is so full you can't fit anything else in it. There's food all over the house. She buy, buy, buy, then she forget about it. How much can two old people eat?"

The next morning when you come over, it is the same with the bagels. We butter them but don't eat them. Today we don't talk about the weather. Today you're the one to say, "Let's sit on the couch where it's more comfortable." We start ever so slowly.

"I don't know what to do. Help me—you've done this before, yes?" you say.

Have I touched you before—here, and here? No, but I've wanted to for a long time. I don't say this to you.

"Yes? With other women?" you say.

"A little, just a little. A long time ago," I say. I don't want you to think I know what I'm doing either.

Afterward, we are finally hungry. You have dinner plans in a couple of hours, but you want to eat now. Even though it's only afternoon, I cook those two steaks that I had in the freezer. Sweet potato fries and a salad. See, didn't I tell you I had food?

I watch you cutting into your steak and you're not the least bit squeamish. You take yours medium rare. All that blood. You tell me you don't want to hurt your boyfriend's feelings. He is a nice man, you tell me, easy to be with. He shaves before coming to bed so as not to bristle you. You don't know whether to tell him or not. I wonder whether you will eat two dinners.

It is time for you to leave, but we both want another cup of tea. I rinse the cups from breakfast and make your tea first. You drink it so dark. How can you sleep at night? You tell me to use a new bag for myself, but isn't it just a waste if I take it light anyway?

At my mother's house, she makes tea in the old blue-and-white pot that she's had forever. If you want it light, you take the first cup. If you want it darker, you have to wait a little longer. I used to have a teapot. It was ivory-colored, squat and small. First the knob on the lid fell off. Then the spout got chipped and finally the handle. I saved the pieces for a while, meaning to glue them back together.

Downstairs, there are kids going door to door, with shovels over their shoulders. "Shovel your walk, mister? Just three dollars for the whole sidewalk. The steps, too." People have taken to using axes and hammers like they are angry.

It is dark and I light a candle. Just one. The wax doesn't start falling right away. It collects at the top, then pours down all at once. Tomorrow there will be white dots stuck to the floor.

When you tell him about me, he doesn't seem to mind too much. "It's just kissing, isn't it?" he says. With him it's easy, you tell me, he's the boy and you're the girl. You've had lots of practice and you're good at it. When I come to see you at your job, tending bar, I see how much money the men leave on the counter.

It would be mean to leave your boyfriend when he hasn't done anything wrong. He's sweet, you tell me, a nice man. It's not that I think you're lying. I've known lots of nice men; I was married to one. Daniel would cook brown rice for me even though he hated the smell, said it smelled like mouse droppings. But he could never get it quite right. I would tell him to use more water, cook it over a slow flame. But somehow, it was always too hard. I had to put it back in the pot, add more water and cook it some more. But I would kiss him when I did this so he wouldn't feel bad.

You don't tell your boyfriend what you tell me, that when we're together, you don't have to be the girl, the woman; you don't have to be all the women on billboards smiling with their mouths open, their eyes closed. You don't have to hold in your stomach. You can just be a plain old person. This is scary to you, you're not sure how to do this.

One afternoon you say you will brush my hair for me. You brush slowly, starting at the bottom and working your way up. I can tell from the way you hold the brush that you've had long hair before. Now your hair is cut close to your head. As you pull the brush down my back, I remember that Daniel would brush my hair. After a while he could do it like you are doing now, but in the beginning he'd try to undo the knots in one stroke and ended up pulling my hair out. As you brush, slow and steady, I start to cry. You do not stop.

I had a friend once in the sixth grade. Her name was Marianne Shirts and there was no television in her house. I would sleep over, wearing one of her nightgowns that seemed softer than mine and I would brush her hair a hundred times before we went to bed. After we got under the covers we would practice kissing. At first her tongue was a surprise, something I wouldn't have thought of myself. Then after a while, our nightgowns would ride up to our waists and our bare legs touching was another surprise. I was afraid that I would like practicing too much, that I would like it better than the real thing. One night when Marianne turned to me and said Wanna practice, I made myself say no thanks, like she had offered me a hot chocolate or a peanut butter cookie. I stayed up all night watching her eyes move back and forth under her lids.

After you leave, my mother calls me. First, pick a sea bass with clear eyes, not cloudy. When you get home, wash it in cold water, inside and out. Make sure there aren't any scales left on it. Soak the black beans in some warm water. Put the fish in a bowl, chop garlic, scallion, and ginger. Pour a little soy sauce on it, not too much. Then, steam it until it's done, maybe twenty minutes. Heat some peanut oil in a pan until it's very hot, but not smoky, add a few drops of sesame, pour it on top. Watch out for small bones.

Sometimes in the evenings, you go into your kitchen to call me. I hold the phone close to my ear; you are talking softly. I wonder what your kitchen looks like and I imagine you leaning your head against wallpaper that was pretty when it was new but is faded now and buckled in spots. I'm sure that in reality the walls are painted a pale yellow and I try to imagine that, but I'm too busy wondering what your boyfriend is doing while you're whispering in the kitchen.

I know I can't ask you to wait for me, you say.

But wait for you? I say.

You have known your boyfriend for three years but now he feels alien to you. You say that sometimes when you are in bed with him, you close your eyes and pretend it's me. This is not much consolation. When you tell him you want to keep seeing me, he says "Sure, why not?" but then he gets real quiet. You ask him what he's thinking and he says, "Should we catch a movie tonight, or just stay in?" Later when he fucks you, he does it rough and you like it at first. Afterward, he says, "You shouldn't lead that woman on like that."

I would like to ask you why you keep my picture in your lingerie drawer. You tell me it makes you happy whenever you go to put on your bra and there's my face. The picture of you is by my bed. Next to the one of my mother. The one where she's sixteen and her face is smooth and white as the inside of a bowl. Her face isn't really white, that's just powder. It's the picture that made my father go all the way across the ocean in a boat called *The Wilson*, of all things.

"Ma, did you love him then?"

"Nah, I thought he was mean, he looked like a gangster."

"Did you grow to love him, Ma?"

"Love? Chinese people don't believe in love."

It is night and all the shutters are closed. I think of you and even my teeth ache with wanting. I wait for the sound of chopping to stop, but there is so much ice. It's stupid to start waiting for spring this early.

A QUIET ACRE

C.W. Riley

The year that Leslie went away to South America was the year that Joan first noticed her own body. On the eve of Leslie's departure, a secret was lodged in Joan to remain submerged and nameless for the six years of her sister's absence. The night before leaving, Leslie had come to Joan, who was then just sixteen, and lay in bed with her. This was a night of confession. This was the night when Leslie first became a voice in the dark. Among many things, Leslie had told Joan that around women her heart felt as fragile as an egg. For a long time, Leslie explained, she had been uncomfortable in her skin, but now she had a name for her passion, had heard other women say it and had read books about it. Now, Leslie said, she had to get on with her life. That year Joan had been shocked by the changes in her own body. She confronted this in the bathtub where hot milky water encircled her breasts and where new mossy hair floated, clinging to her pubic bone. She held her nose and slid down into the safe silence, where she couldn't feel the persistent bobbing of a secret wanting to rise into the air, where she couldn't even hear the kicking of her own heart. This year, the year of Leslie's return, Joan rose up and took a breath.

Leslie came home from South America just after Christmas. She was familiar and different, looking more, Mom said, like the father who was nothing more to Joan than a grinning figure in a black-

and-white photo and a sparkling pink tombstone in a St. Louis cemetery.

Every spring of Joan's life she, her mother, and Leslie had driven from Illinois to Missouri to help Aunt Edna put in her garden, but for the past six years it had just been Joan and Mom. This year, Leslie drove the station wagon with Mom beside her in the front, reading aloud from a magazine for women, while Joan sat behind, her elbows on the back of the front seat.

Joan watched the blur of fence posts trolling wire along Highway 60 and listened to Mom read. The story was about a woman in a pool noticing a man, the thick black hairs on his chest and his tiny blue bathing suit that formed to his genitals when he climbed, streaming, up the silver ladder out of the pool. While Mom read, Joan touched the nape of Leslie's neck where the fine hairs made a downy dark V. She touched it lightly, separating Leslie's hair into two rows, with one finger. When Leslie's head twitched and her eyes met Joan's in the rearview mirror, Mom's voice quit. She looked up from the magazine and waited. It was as if they had each taken in a breath.

The day before, Mom found out their secret. It had been Leslie's own for a while, but had surfaced in Joan like a jubilant mullet flashing silver on the crest of a wave. Mom came upon them in Joan's room. She opened the bedroom door and must have put one foot inside before she saw. She saw Leslie unfolding over Joan like a starfish and Joan's hip rising, her bent knee falling sideways like an opening clamshell.

Their dressing was a frenzy of legs, arms, and heads poking through tunnels of fabric, backward shirts and inside-out panties. In the kitchen Mom sat at the round glass table. She turned the pages of the newspaper, letting each fall slowly one upon the other. She was not reading. Leslie lingered in the shadow of the hall, leaning against the doorframe. Joan came into the kitchen and put one hand on Mom's rigid shoulder. None of them were able to speak.

Finally Mom reached the last page of the paper that closed like a lip puffing air, and she said, "What would your Aunt Edna think?"

That had been the last word, the last word about what Mom had seen.

Mom began to read again about the wet man in his tiny bathing suit. The woman toweled herself, running terry cloth slowly across the back of her neck, under her arms, and between her thighs while she watched the man leap from the diving board, extend into a straight powerful rod, before tucking into a dive, his pointed hands spearing the water.

From the rearview mirror Leslie's eyes watched.

Joan. A moment ago you touched me. Your finger felt like a whisper in the dark. Your breath, the heat from your body, ripple along the hairs on the back of my neck like warm wind blowing over fescue.

Mother has inserted silence between us.

When Mother's belly was round and pearly pink I hugged her, you. Mother's flesh was between us. And even so, that stretched pad of skin, muscle, and fat seemed thinner than the silence between us now.

I have loved you since I first held you, your body floppy and heavy as a sack of cornmeal. I was like a mother. And Mother was like you, like you now, then. She was a fall maple, yellow hair and eyes like sky between leaves. Mother never nudged me out with her thin elbows, you and I sat in her deep dress and I held the breast while you sucked.

Aunt Edna is an old cornstalk. She is bent and her thin tan sweater flaps like a papery husk in the wind. She once flamed yellow, like you and Mother. She faded, as Mother fades now, to faint fires in her hair. She always held you and stared, knowing and not knowing that you are her mirror. She is Mother's mirror. Mother stares at you both.

I am different. My eyes are not sky, but the confused brown of twigs and leaves in a frozen puddle. I never had the pale silk weed that whipped up from your scalp when you were two. My hair is dark and curly like an oak leaf before it spirals to the ground.

I am like the man we drowned in dirt. And I thought you came from that day, the day we dropped him in the earth. Mother said no, you came from before. You were not even a thing then, just a sack of water. Mother carried her belly in her hands even before it was big, to protect the little sack of you.

At the farm we will lay open Aunt Edna's garden. We will disc her acre, as we have always done, peeling wet, brown soil from the silver saucers to make rows. You will drive the tractor now, as I did six years ago, as Mother did before that. The handles of the planter will chew my palms as I stab the pointed end into the ground. Mother and Aunt Edna will hull hard white beans and break the golden teeth from corncobs like you did six years ago, like I did before that.

Joan was imagining, she realized, that the woman in the story was Mom. She had been picturing Mom standing by the side of the pool in her black one-piece with the hole cut out in the belly. Mom, tanned from summer, eyeing the dark-headed man. The man could easily be Boyd, Mom's last boyfriend who lived with them. Mom didn't marry him because one day after Leslie had turned eighteen he followed her into her room. Mom saw him shut the door.

Leslie told Joan about it that night, six years ago, when they lay in Joan's narrow bed in the dark. Until then it had been Mom and Leslie's secret, a secret that had muffled them, put words into a gaze or a look rather than out on the air.

Mom knocked, but didn't wait for an answer and opened the door. She filled up the doorframe. Leslie was kneeling on her desk chair by the window and Boyd was near the door, his hands in his pockets. Leslie's small bed was between them. For all Mom knew he was in there imparting a secret surprise, or asking a birthday or Christmas question. But Leslie said that it was the way he turned to look at Mom that inflated her suspicion until the doorframe could have bowed and splintered. His face was mottled red and white with fury. His fists filled his pockets.

Boyd had done nothing and that much Leslie told Mom. On the night of confessions, that last night before Leslie left for South America, when their elbows touched under the plaid blanket, Leslie told Joan what Boyd had said to her. It wasn't much. He had become attracted to Leslie now that she was maturing. He could hardly say it and ducked his head like a bashful boy, like he thought he was cute, like he thought she could forgive him. And after he told Leslie he stood waiting, his eyes fixed on his feet. He waited until Mom came in, then he turned in anger, as though Mom was mother to both Leslie and him and had chased them into a private place.

Joan liked Boyd, how he had done the dishes, playing in the suds, as though the task were a novelty and how he hid around corners in order to jump out at Mom, who would scream, making Joan laugh until she nearly wet her pants and how he hugged and kissed good night like sleep was a long journey. But the winter Joan turned twelve, Boyd had somehow done wrong. Nothing was said, but when they went to plant Aunt Edna's garden Mom didn't make the the usual phone calls home. Leslie was moody. Aunt Edna said, "troubled," and she looked at Mom when she said it.

That spring Joan climbed the milk barn roof and peered beneath the shelf of her hand where the South Eighty swelled up like a cresting wave and saw Leslie skipping across the top like a dark bird, her coat open and flapping in the wet spring wind. Below the hill a yellow light burned in the tractor shed where Mom gapped and regapped the plugs for the old Farmall and patched tires like they had never been patched before and never would again.

Aunt Edna held Joan's hand as they walked to the hog pen, each with a coffee can of feed in the crook of her arm. Though Joan was twelve, she blinked in wonder at the sight of Aunt Edna's cracked nails, her thick knuckles, and fingers curled gently around her own hand. It had been many years since Aunt Edna had acknowledged that Joan was still a child by holding her hand. It was this that compelled Joan to confide that Mom and Leslie were both angry at Boyd. Aunt Edna simply nodded, like she knew.

At supper Aunt Edna held a few strands of Leslie's hair between her fingers and told her she was growing up pretty. And for a moment Mom looked at Leslie like she was the first star of night. By the end of dinner, though, Mom was telling Leslie that she was no-good and lazy for walking all of the time and not helping get ready to plant. Leslie ran upstairs and slammed the bedroom door. They heard her feet stomping the length of the bedroom, then back again. Mom sighed and dropped her fork in her plate. Later, Mom threw a sweater over her shoulders and stood out on the back porch in the dark. Aunt Edna went out to get some firewood off of the stack. From where Joan stood washing dishes, next to the window, she could hear the murmur of voices. Mom told Aunt Edna, "I'm getting old." Aunt Edna answered, "Shoot,

who's old around here?" Mom said, "Boyd is leaving." And Joan
bent her head so they wouldn't hear her crying into the dishes.

When they got home, Boyd was gone. The dangerous and
murky issue between Mom and Leslie settled like silt after Boyd
left and they went carefully, as though they might slip and skid
into one another. Mom started handing Joan the tweezers, asking
her to find the gray hairs. They were hard to find in the blond
but some were coarse and curly and flashed like silver wire. Joan
didn't pull them and it became her secret, the preservation of her
mother's beautiful hairs.

The man in the story wouldn't be Boyd. Joan ran her knuckles
across Mom's cheek. Mom caught Joan's hand and smiled as
though she were touching a baby. For an instant Joan saw how
Leslie was Mom's child. Sometimes, in profile, when Leslie bent
her neck to look down at something, her lips slightly apart, a
shade of Mom composed in her face. And this smile, this was
both of them too. Joan stroked her mother's cheek and wished
that Mom had never opened any doors. She wished that Mom
could smile like this all spring at her and at Leslie.

When did we cross the line? Not when you tucked your sweet
head under my chin those spring nights in our big iron bed at
Aunt Edna's. Not when your thin frame grew straight and tall and
you were as sturdy and flexible to hold as a bundle of sticks.
There were no lines then.

You burgeoned at the age of sixteen. That was the last time,
before I fled, that we went to Aunt Edna's together. You were an
unexpected bloom. When the ground, like today, lay long and
soggy brown under surly white skies, you broke open, practically
splitting the seams of your clothing. Your heat crept across the
sheets to me until I had to sit up in that iron bed, holding my
burning face. You had spilled out of childhood. Every trace of
your babyhood had faded like the green from a ripening tomato.

Once, in Ecuador, the feeling of that spring with you returned
to my body, spreading under my skin until I was tight and tender,
sensitive to breath, brushes of hair, or fingertips or glances. I was
with a woman and we had climbed up into the Andes. Just when
my muscles balled up on my bones and my lungs could expand
no more than wispy cirrus clouds, we paused to watch the moun-

tains fall away to the far sky. In the deep distance we sensed, and nearly saw the Amazon valley steaming between the toes of the mountain. White blooms of moisture mushroomed from the shadowy hint of green. Oxygen. Great full gulps of it. Dirt. Black. Fertile. Green and fertile air, great full scoops of dirt. Green.

The Amazon rain forest is a dangerous place, so rich that the dream of a seed might sprout and grow unshakably real. You and I, Joan, are used to ground that yields only what was given us to sow. We've unearthed Aunt Edna's potatoes and shaken dirt from her onions as we gathered them in bunches. We've sown corn and beans, collecting clods on our soles if the spring was wet. We've turned smoking compost and severed orchard grass from its clutch on the field. We felt we knew plenty. But standing on that airless rock, miles above the Amazon, it seemed an easy leap into that grasping green that teems with such we've never seen. So easy to immerse ourselves where plants as big as buildings bust up through the dirt, and the colors are so fine that the only places that they exist are between the lines in the rainbow rays that ripple in the air between leaves that sing silver Sssssss, breath drawn from swelling roots clutched in the cake-sweet dirt.

Anything can hide in that forest. No color is betrayed.

The woman, Ingrid, said she would take me there. Though she brought me many places, the Amazon was not one of them. And later when I lived in Caracas I did not take the invitation of proximity. I never even went to the edge that I imagined to be there, a line of tropical trees creating a definite border. There is no border, though. It's a gradual thing; the forest gets thicker the deeper you go.

Mom paused in her reading. She closed the magazine on her thumb and shut her eyes. They had hit the part of Highway 60, between Poplar Bluff and Mountain View, that rolled like an ocean.

Joan fell back into the seat where she could stare eye to eye with Leslie via the rearview mirror. Leslie was twenty-two the last time they had made this trip together, the same age that Joan was now.

When Leslie left for South America, Joan and Mom both took her to the St. Louis airport where, after arriving early, they wandered under the vaulted ceiling that rolled voices and footfalls out of its curve in a shattered shimmer of sound, like light off of water, a water sound.

And when it was time for Leslie to board her plane, Mom grabbed her by the forearms and pulled her into a hug, like she hadn't done in years. When Leslie hugged Joan hard, she whispered "Don't forget me," as though the door to her room would sink and seal up in the wall, as if Aunt Edna's iron bed would shrink around Joan. They waited until Leslie's plane leaped up into the sky, where it would rise and surface among the clouds.

On the way home Mom, holding a crushed Kleenex to her nose, told Joan that she would depend upon her now because Aunt Edna was getting frail, though Joan had never seen evidence of this. Aunt Edna had never been a robust woman. She was sinewy and solid as a root. Each spring found her the same as ever. But during the six years Leslie was gone, each winter, Mom began laying Aunt Edna in her grave. Each year Mom pointed out Aunt Edna's crumpled feet and knotty toes. She noted the angle of Aunt Edna's stoop. And every spring Mom paced off the garden as though over the past year it had grown ever wider and toward an unmanageable state. And that was when she muttered that though jars of beans and corn, the bags of fresh tomatoes, potatoes, and onions were worth it now, when Aunt Edna died she was going to sell this plot because it was making her old.

As far as work went, Aunt Edna's ritual was changed little by Leslie's absence. The garden was disced, the spinach was planted, the sweet potatoes unburied, and the beans hulled into a tin dish. The first spring without her, Aunt Edna set Leslie's place at the table once or twice without thinking and afterward said, "oooh?" pressing two fingers to her lips and laughing at herself. Mom saw it and cut her eyes at Joan. But Joan, who had never plucked her mother's silver hair, secretly leaving her intact, would not even engage in Mom's secret worry over Aunt Edna's mortality.

Mom stirred, traced the line of print in the magazine with a fingertip. With a wink, Mom took in a breath to resume the story. Joan hunched forward, listening.

In Colombia, Ingrid brought me into the coffee. A polished road took us to a gravel road that took us under the thick green banana leaves and past the spindly coffee plants to where Ingrid's aunt's villa was cut into the groves. We heard music and voices from the grassy slope where there stood three flat houses, one after another like stair steps. There were flowers and bushes blooming, buzzing with golden bees and big, black bees that were as furry as cats. Ingrid's family, a world of people, hung to the shade of bushes and trees or lay in the dapples on the soft lawn, each of them as bright as a blossom, as loose as a leaf, each of them speaking.

Abuela, Ingrid's grandmother, wearing a shirt like zinnias, wrapped her arms around me like a sweet flower garden. Her gold medallion, hard as the seeded center of a sunflower, pressed into my chest. Her bracelets rattled like loose kernels of corn. I thought I was home.

On the way back through the cool vegetable night, after we had swilled aguardiente with Abuelo and the uncles, after we had howled North American melodies under the swinging yard lamps and eaten beef with corn cakes, I could taste Abuela's perfume. It hung still in my nostrils from our hug good-bye. I kept grinning over Abuela's last embrace, soft and sturdy as a haystack.

"My life is a lie," Ingrid told the night. "They all know what I am and who you are with me. But we all pretend and somehow the unspoken is acceptable to them ... more acceptable than my happiness."

Her voice struck like a bolt grabbing the sweet dark, lighting up my eyes, burning out my dreams. And there I was believing that silence was the breaking of an acre, the turning of a furrow and a hole the width of a finger, waiting for a seed.

Ingrid has skin the color of dried cornhusks. She smells of acorns and oak leaves kicked up by shuffling feet. Her hair ran through my fingers like ropes of night. I began to feel kin to her. She called me "hermana."

My mother's lips are the lips I first kissed, perhaps even as I passed headfirst into life. My mother's heart lay first against my head before I turned bottom up. I was the first, even before my father, to draw sustenance from her breasts. I was the first female, since her mother, whose body she loved to touch and kiss. I loved her first.

On a balcony above narrow streets, our hair heaped on our

heads, Ingrid and I said how birth is backward coitus. We held cold Cokes against our sweating temples and broke open taboos, exposing the hollows where a mother's hand had been. Our feet propped on the iron rail, our butts slung in low canvas chairs we talked until dawn fractured the perfect purple night. We talked until that thin sliver of time between absolute dark and absolute light cooled our fury. We had been deceived, mi hermana and me. We had been making counterfeit love while ignoring the very source of our passion.

But we closed the shades and opened the sheets, Ingrid laughed at how all night our tongues had wagged until numb and sober. "We are silly," she said, uncurling, then curling her whole length around me like a vine. When I closed my eyes she said, "Maybe you're tired."

Joan you are an echo, my earliest, dim lusts, my first desire, bouncing at me from the rearview mirror.

Mom read.
The woman who looked like Mom and the man in the tiny blue bathing suit got acquainted when the woman complimented him on his dive. There was an immediate attraction and they conspired to meet at the pool late that night.

Joan thought it was all too easy. Mom stopped reading long enough to glance at Joan as though what she had just read was the best gossip she had heard in years and then began reading again. Joan listened, wondering. Maybe the point wasn't that the woman should worry about constructing a snare. Maybe the point was that they experienced a quick and real attraction that would lead them into complicity. In this case they conspired against the pool authorities, who locked the gates after sundown.

On the coldest night in February, behind the movie theater from where they could see stars flare in the black sky, bits of mica and glass sparking in the asphalt and the very air aglitter with frozen moisture, Joan told Leslie that she wanted to make love with her.

It wasn't sudden. The first moment she saw Leslie again, inclining slightly at the waist, neck arched, head tilted as she watched for her bags to come riding around on the baggage claim carousel,

Joan sucked a breath as though she were rising out of hot bath-water and into a rare and resonate air.

They met at the gates, the man and the woman, giggling like children. Both were Mom's age and feeling giddy from their juvenile adventure. He wore a red T-shirt tucked into jeans under which, the woman knew, was the tiny blue bathing suit she had first seen him in. It was the notion of his suit, this fix on the familiar, that kept the woman from fearing the man, who had become a stranger in his clothes.

Leslie said her ear wasn't used to English yet and for a day or two, after her return, she sometimes started a sentence in Spanish. Her voice was deeper with a trace of an accent. She had cut her hair. Her skin seemed darker.

Joan went where Leslie went. She waited, stretched across the Naugahyde benches in the hospital waiting room while Leslie got treatments for the amoebas she'd picked up in South America, her reason for coming home. Joan hung on her sister's arm when they went shopping and rode with her head in Leslie's lap, feet on the window glass, when Leslie drove the station wagon.

But it was Leslie who had been in Joan's room one night when Joan came in from her bath, rolled in a towel. Leslie's eyes had visited the slope of Joan's neck, the shadow of cleavage, the hollow between Joan's thighs suggested in the towel. And it was Leslie who didn't stay when Joan unwrapped the towel and dropped it like a hanky in the middle of the floor. Those same eyes hovering over the front seat had widened and averted. Those same hands gripping the steering wheel had snatched up the towel. How many times had Leslie scooped warm water over Joan's naked body, or stripped shirts and shorts off of her in preparation for PJs? How many times had Joan held the towel for Leslie as she stepped, beaded with droplets, from her sweet oily bath?

Mom began clearing her throat as she read because the man was peeling the woman's bathing suit off. They were in the water, had climbed the fence and left their shriveled clothes next to a chair. He had his thumbs on her nipples, his tongue in her mouth. She squeezed his big erection while his little blue suit fluttered to the floor of the pool. Joan knew that soon the woman would "put him inside of her," as if the man's penis was his all. She also knew that Mom had been waiting for this part. She didn't read it with relish as she might have, had she been silently absorbing the scene. She did not hesitate and giggle, but read with determination.

Of this, Joan was ashamed. Mom's example, anecdote, a story in a magazine that brought two people hurling over boundaries simply to have eight minutes of intercourse in the silent waters of a deserted municipal swimming pool. What would Aunt Edna have thought of that?

. . . and then your breath and then your lips and then the whisper of your fingers and then your hard hot palm and then your soft, thick thigh and then your hair then your voice. . .

Mom triumphantly closed the magazine. The story ended the next day at the pool, a secret smile when he caught her eye. The last image, his glistening chest as he spread arms wide before arcing into a perfect dive.

Joan flopped backward, arms crossed over her chest, while Leslie's crow's-feet crinkled at her from the mirror. Mother rolled the magazine and popped Leslie gently on the thigh with it and Joan saw Leslie's profile as she looked at Mom, brief, dark against the white windshield.

In an hour or so they would be at Aunt Edna's, sipping coffee and talking about the viscid square of land behind the smokehouse. Mom would pull on rubber boots and tromp among the blunt stalks of dead corn. Aunt Edna would find where she'd left the dried beans, probably on a dusty shelf on the cold side porch. And who knew what Leslie would do, probably walk. And Joan would follow Mom into the furrows, hopping puddles, skirting lakes of rainwater, and when they reached the middle where raspberry bushes grew on the hump, she would simply say, "Let Leslie speak, Mom. Let her speak to you."

Mother, I will till until this garden grinds into my flesh and fills the bubbles on my feet and my palms. I have inherited from you the will to cut this land open and I will help you until you can't be helped, to encourage the thin dirt to yield. Mother, your every grief hangs on my bones, but for you I can only dig a hole, dig a hole and drop a seed. And in time, maybe you'll see what I've seen, that sometimes we don't know what we have sown.

Swimming Upstream

Beth Brant

Anna May spent the first night in a motel off Highway 8. She arrived about ten, exhausted from her long drive—through farmland, bright autumn leaves, the glimpse of blue lake. She saw none of this, only the grey highway stretching out before her. She stopped when the motel sign appeared, feeling the need for rest, it didn't matter where.

She took a shower, lay in bed, and fell asleep, the dream beginning again immediately. Her son—drowning in the water, his skinny arms flailing the waves, his mouth opening to scream with no sound coming forth. She, Anna May, moving in slow motion into the waves, her hands grabbing for the boy but feeling only water run through her fingers. She grabbed frantically, but nothing held to her hands. She dived and opened her eyes underwater and saw nothing. He was gone. Her hands connected with sand, with seaweed, but not her son. He was gone. Simon was gone.

Anna May woke. The dream was not a nightmare anymore. It had become a companion to her, a friend, almost a lover—reaching for her as she slept, making pictures of Simon, keeping him alive while recording his death. In the first days after Simon left her, the dream made her wake screaming, sobbing, arms hitting at the air, legs kicking the sheets, becoming tangled in the material. Her bed was a straitjacket, pinning her down, holding her until the dream ended. She would fight the dream then. Now, she welcomed it.

In the daylight she had other memories of Simon. His birth, his first pair of shoes, his first steps, his first word—*Mama*—his first day of school. His firsts were also his lasts, so she invented a future for him during her waking hours: his first skating lessons, his first hockey game, his first reading aloud from a book, his first . . . But she couldn't invent beyond that. His six-year-old face and body remained unchanged in her mind. She couldn't invent what she couldn't imagine.

She hadn't been there when Simon drowned. Simon had been given to her ex-husband by the courts. She was judged unfit. Because she lived with a woman. Because a woman, Catherine, slept beside her. Because she had a history of alcoholism. The history was old. Anna May had stopped drinking when she became pregnant with Simon, and she had stayed dry all those years. She couldn't imagine what alcohol tasted like after Simon was born. He was so lovely, so new. Her desire for a drink evaporated every time Simon took hold of her finger, or nursed from her breast, or opened his mouth in a toothless smile. She had marveled at his being—this gift that had emerged from her own body. This beautiful being who had formed himself inside her, had come with speed through the birth canal to welcome life outside her. His face red with anticipation, his black hair standing straight up, electric with hope, his little fists grabbing, his pink mouth finding her nipple and holding on for dear life. She had no need for alcohol. There was Simon.

Simon was taken away from them. They saw him on weekends, Tony delivering him on a Friday night, Catherine discreetly finding someplace else to be when Tony's car drove up. They still saw Simon, grateful for the two days out of the week they could play with him, they could delight in him, they could pretend with him. They still saw Simon, until the call came that changed all that. The call from Tony saying that Simon had drowned when he fell out of the boat as they were fishing. Tony sobbing, "I'm sorry. I tried to save him. I'm sorry. Please, Anna, please forgive me. Oh God, Anna. Oh God, I'm sorry. I'm sorry," his voice fading away as the phone slipped from Anna May's fingers and fell to the floor.

So Anna May dreamed of those final moments of a six-year-old

life. It stunned her that she wasn't there to see him die when she
had been there to see him come into life.

Anna May stayed dry, but she found herself glancing into cup-
boards at odd times. Looking for something. Looking for something to drink. She began to think of ways to buy wine and hide
it so she could take a drink when she needed it. But there was
Catherine. Catherine would know, and Catherine's face, already
so lined and tired and old, would become more so. Anna May
saw her own face in the mirror. Her black hair had streaks of grey
and white she hadn't noticed before. Her forehead had deep lines
carved into the flesh, and her eyes, her eyes that had cried so
many tears, were a faded and washed-out blue. Her mouth was
wrinkled, the lips parched and chapped. She and Catherine, aged
and ghostlike figures walking through a dead house.

Anna May thought about the bottle of wine. It took on large
proportions in her mind. A bottle of wine, just one, that she could
drink from and never empty. A bottle of wine, the sweet, red kind
that would take away the dryness, the withered insides of her.
She went to meetings but never spoke, only saying her name and
"I'll pass tonight." Catherine wanted to talk, but Anna May had
nothing to say to this woman she loved. She thought about the
bottle of wine: the bottle, the red liquid inside, the sweet taste
gathering in her mouth, moving down her throat, hitting her
bloodstream, warming her inside, bringing the sensation of life to
her body.

She arranged time off work and told Catherine she was going
away for a few days. She needed to think, to be alone. Catherine
watched her face, the framing of the words out of her mouth,
looking into her exhausted eyes. Catherine said, "I understand."

"Will you be all right?" Anna May asked her.

"Yes, I'll be fine. I'll see friends. I'll start cleaning out the garden.
I'll be waiting for you. I love you so much."

Anna May got in the car and drove up 401, up 19, over to 8
and the motel, the shower, the dream.

Anna May smoked her cigarettes and drank coffee until daylight. She made her plans to buy the bottle of wine. After that,
she had no plans, other than the first drink and how it would
taste and feel.

She found a meeting in Goderich and sat there, ashamed and

angered with herself to sit in a meeting and listen to the stories and plan her backslide. She thought of speaking, of talking about Simon, about the bottle of wine, but she knew someone would say something that would make her stop. Anna May did not want to be stopped. She wanted to drink and drink and drink until it was all over. *My name is Anna May and I'll just pass.*

Later, she hung around for coffee, feeling like an infiltrator, a spy. A woman took hold of her arm and said, "Let's go out and talk. I know what you're planning. Don't do it. Let's talk."

Anna May shrugged off the woman's hand and left. She drove to a liquor outlet. *Don't do it.* She found the wine, one bottle, that was all she'd buy. *Don't do it.* One bottle, that was all. She paid and left the store, the familiar curve of the bottle wrapped in brown paper. *Don't do it.* Only one bottle. It wouldn't hurt. She laughed at the excuses bubbling up in her mouth like wine. Just one. She smoked a cigarette in the parking lot, wondering where to go, where to stop and turn the cap that would release the red, sweet smell before the taste would overpower her and she wouldn't have to wonder anymore.

She drove north on 21, heading for the Bruce Peninsula, Lake Huron on her left, passing the little resort towns, the cottages by the lake. She stopped for a hamburger and, without thinking, got her thermos filled with coffee. This made her laugh, the bottle sitting next to her, almost a living thing. She drove north, drinking the coffee, with her father—not Simon, not Catherine—drifting in her thoughts. Charles, her mother had called him. Everyone else had called him Charley. Good old Charley, Good-time Charley. Injun Charley. Charles was a hard worker, working at almost anything. He worked hard. He drank hard. He tried to be a father, a husband, but the work and the drink turned his attempts to nothing. Anna May's mother never complained, never left him. She cooked and kept house and raised the children and always called him Charles. When Anna May grew up, she taunted her mother with the fact that *her Charles* was a drunk. Why didn't she care more about her kids than her drunken husband? Didn't her mother know how ashamed they were to have such a father, to hear people talk about him, to laugh at him, to laugh at *them*— the half-breeds of good-old-good-time-Injun Charley?

Anna May laughed again, the sound ugly inside the car. Her

father was long dead and, she supposed, forgiven by her. He had
been a handsome man back then, her mother a skinny, pale girl,
an orphan girl, something unheard of by her father. How that
must have appealed to the romantic that he was. Anna May didn't
know how her mother felt about the life she'd had with Charles.
Her mother never talked about those things. Her mother, who
sobbed and moaned at Simon's death as she never had at her
husband's. Anna May couldn't remember her father ever being
mean. He just went away when he drank. Not like his daughter,
who'd fight anything in her way when she was drunk. The bottle
bounced beside her as she drove.

Anna May drove north and her eyes began to see the colors of
the trees. They looked like they were on fire, the reds and oranges
competing with the yellows and golds of the leaves. She smoked
her cigarettes, drank from the thermos, and remembered this was
her favorite season. She and Catherine would be harvesting the
garden, gathering the beets, turnips, and cabbage. They would be
digging up the gladioli and letting the bulbs dry before packing
them away in straw. They would be planting more tulips. Catherine could never get enough tulips. It was because they had met
in the spring, Catherine always said. "We met in the spring, and
the tulips were blooming in that little park. You looked so beautiful against the tulips, Simon on your lap. I knew I loved you."
Last autumn Simon had been five and had raked leaves and dug
holes for the tulip bulbs. Catherine had made cocoa and cinnamon
toast, and Simon had declared that he liked cinnamon toast better
than pie.

Anna May tasted the tears on her lips. She licked the wet salt,
imagining it was sweet wine on her tongue. "It's my fault," she
said out loud. She thought of all the things she should have done
to prevent Simon's leaving. She should have placated Tony; she
should have lived alone; she should have pretended to be straight;
she should have never become an alcoholic; she should have never
loved; she should have never been born. Let go! she cried somewhere inside her. "Let go!" she cried aloud. But how could she let
go of Simon and the hate she held for Tony and herself? How
could she let go of that? If she let go, she'd have to forgive—the
forgiveness Tony begged of her now that Simon was gone.

Even Catherine, even the woman she loved, asked her to forgive. "It could have happened when he was with us," Catherine cried at her. But Catherine didn't know what it was to feel the baby inside her, to feel him pushing his way out of her, to feel his mouth on her breast, to feel the sharp pain in her womb every time his name was spoken. Forgiveness was for people who could afford it. Anna May was poverty-stricken.

The highway turned into a road, the trees crowding in on both sides of her, the flames of the trees leaving spots of color in her eyes. She was entering the Bruce Peninsula, a sign informed her. She pulled off the road, consulting the map. Yes, she would drive to the very tip of the peninsula and it would be there she'd open the bottle and drink her way to whatever was waiting for her. The bottle rested beside her, and she touched the brown paper, feeling soothed, feeling a hunger in her stomach.

She saw another sign: Sauble Falls. Anna May thought this would be a good place to stop, to drink the last of her coffee, to smoke another cigarette. She pulled over onto the gravel lot. There was a small path leading down to the rocks. Another sign: Absolutely No Fishing. Watch Your Step. Rocks Are Slippery. She could hear the water before she saw it.

She stepped out of the covering of trees and onto the rock shelf. The falls were narrow, spilling out in various layers of rock. She could see the beginnings of Lake Huron below her. She could see movement in the water coming away from the lake and moving toward the rocks and the falls. Fish tails flashing and catching light from the sun. Hundreds of fish tails moving upstream. She walked across a flat slab of rock and there, beneath her in the shallow water, saw salmon slowly moving their bodies, their gills expanding and closing as they rested. She looked up to another rock slab and saw a dozen fish congregating at the bottom of a water spill—waiting. Her mind barely grasped the fact that the fish were migrating, swimming upstream, when a salmon leapt and hurled itself over the rushing water above. Anna May stepped up to a different ledge and watched the salmon's companions waiting their turn to jump the flowing waters and reach the next plateau.

She looked down toward the mouth of the lake. There were others, like her, standing and silently watching the struggle of the fish. No one spoke, as if to speak would be blasphemous in the presence of this. She looked again into the water, salmon crowding

each resting place before resuming the leaps and the jumps. Here
and there on the rocks, dead fish, a testimony to the long and
desperate struggle that had taken place. They lay, eyes glazed,
sides open and bleeding, food for the gulls that hovered over Anna
May's head.

Another salmon jumped, its flesh torn, its body spinning until
it made it over the fall. Another one, the dorsal fin torn, leapt
and was washed back by the power of the water. Anna May
watched the fish rest, its open mouth like another wound. He was
large, the dark body undulating in the water. She saw him begin
a movement of tail. Churning the water, it shot into the air,
twisting his body, shaking and spinning. She saw his underbelly,
pale yellow and bleeding from the battering against the rocks, the
water. He made it! Anna May wanted to clap, to shout with elation
at the sheer power of such a thing happening before her.

She looked around again. The other people were gone. She was
alone with the salmon, the only sound besides the water was her
breath against the air. She walked farther upstream, her sneakers
getting wet from the splashing of the salmon. She didn't feel the
wet, she only waited and watched for the salmon to move. She
had no idea of time, of how long she stood waiting for the movement, waiting for the jumps, the leaps, the flight. Anna May
watched for Torn Fin, waiting to see him move against the current
in his phenomenal swim of faith.

Anna May reached a small dam, the last barrier before the calm
water and blessed rest. She sat on a rock, her heart beating fast,
adrenaline pouring through her at each leap and twist of the
salmon. There he was, Torn Fin, his final jump before him. She
watched, then closed her eyes, almost ashamed to be a spectator
at this act, this primal movement to the place of all beginning.
He had to get there, to push his bleeding body forward, believing
in his magic to get him there. Believing, believing he would get
there. No thoughts of death, of food, of rest. Only the great
urging and wanting to get there, get *there*.

Anna May opened her eyes and saw him, another jump before
being pushed back. She held her hands together, her body willing
Torn Fin to move, to push, to jump, to fly! Her body rocked
forward and back, her heart madly beating inside her chest. She
rocked, she shouted, "Make it, damn it, make it!" Torn Fin waited

at the dam. Anna May rocked and held her hands tight, her fingers twisting together, nails scratching her palms. She rocked. She whispered, "Simon. Simon." She rocked and whispered the name of her son into the water, "Simon. Simon." Like a chant. *Simon.* Into the water, as if the name of her son was magic and could move Torn Fin to his final place. She rocked. She chanted. *Simon. Simon.* Anna May rocked and put her hands in the water, wanting to lift the fish over the dam and to life. As the thought flickered through her brain, Torn Fin slapped his tail against the water and jumped. He battled with the current. He twisted and arced into the air, his mouth gaping and gasping, his wounds standing out in relief against his body, his fin discolored and shredded. With a push, a great push, he turned a complete circle and made it over the dam.

"Simon!" Torn Fin slapped his tail one last time and was gone, the dark body swimming home. She saw her son's face, his black hair streaming behind him, a look of joy transfixed on his little face before the image disappeared.

Anna May stood on the rock shelf, hands limp at her sides, watching the water, watching the salmon, watching. She watched as the sun moved behind the lake and night came closer to her. Then she walked up the path and back to her car. She looked at the bottle sitting next to her, the brown paper rustling as she put the car in gear. She drove south, stopping at a telephone booth.

She could still hear the water.

ANGELS AND MINISTERS OF GRACE

Blake C. Aarens

The effort to keep one's mind blank. To live without thinking, to breathe without thinking. Inhale-pause-exhale.

The snip and click of scissors. Why don't they just use clippers?

Because this way is more humiliating.

Blank mind, even breath.

Tufts of nappy-natural hair. Free-falling to the shoulder. To the lap. To the floor. The tufts transform themselves into brown-skinned angels. Trailing coarse black curlicues as they ascend.

But what becomes of the processed hair on the floor? Freed from the confines of artificial straightness, the follicle rebels. It writhes on the floor, reclaiming its kink.

Footsteps in the corridor. A guard passes. Pauses. Takes in the scene and mourns.

"All that pretty hair."

The mind becomes an unwritten book. Blank pages. The prisoner turns another. Takes a deep breath. One of the few remaining.

It is done. Scissors fall to the table. Strange. The prisoner hears no sound. Reaching up to touch the unceilinged head, the prisoner finds barest stubble. Vulnerable to the elements: Earthwaterfireair. Electricity. Long moments before the flesh of wrist meets the bite of metal. Handcuffs the prisoner had forgotten and flown past.

Once more the confines of the body. Rump on chair, feet on floor. But starting at the nape of the neck—such openness. The prisoner returns to the *exposed head. Sneaking as if to a heavily guarded runway. Take off. Taking self out of self. Escape is imminent.*

But a hand on the prisoner's shoulder catches the last foot of spirit. Slams it back into the body. Broken, yet whole.

The prisoner looks up into black robes topped by a white face. Gnarled red hands clutched around more blackness. The good book.

"Do you wish to confess your sins, my child?"

The priest's body expands to the contours of late pregnancy: bloated belly and full, heavy breasts straining the fabric of his robes. No opening made for birth.

"I am not your child."

"We are all of us God's children."

"You're not god."

"I am his servant here on earth."

The prisoner almost laughs, almost feels.

"Can you tell me what hell is like? No, nor heaven neither 'cause you ain't been there. Can't answer my simplest question, but would presume to know the complexities of my life."

The prisoner turns another blank page.

"Can we go now?"

The last walk. Shuffling in shackles. Ancestral memory. Somewhere far off in the distance, the faint sound of African drums. Another chair. This one with arm rests. Like a throne, the prisoner thinks, settling in.

A metal cap. The soul once again has a ceiling. There is no escape. The switch is thrown and a finger of lightning arcs across the room toward the prisoner.

In the moment of contact not only is the ceiling blown off, but the whole house of the spirit is uprooted. The arms of life let go and the scream of all screams leaves the prisoner's throat.

"Brenda! Brenda, wake up!"

Her baby brother Nathan Lee materialized above her; an angular face, skin the color of toffee, full lips. His heavy lidded eyes more weary than worried. She turned away from him and encountered Rafert's urn on the shelves across the room. Rafert. Their elder brother. Housed for all eternity in eighteen inches of hand-painted blue glass from Mexico.

"It was about him," Nathan Lee accused.

"No. No, it was about me."

"It's been ten years, Brenda. Let it go. Let him go."

:

Brenda turned on the water in the tub. Just the cold. She stuck her hand in the stream until it ran frigid enough to send a shudder up her entire arm. She fought the urge to clench her fist against the chill. The vague brown of her palm blanched white; the muscles in her hand began to ache and throb. The pain was good, a point of concentration. Brenda stepped quickly into the shower. She braced herself between the tile wall and the nubbly glass of the shower door. Lifted the latch to divert the flow to the shower head. The gasp of contact. Needles of ice on her skin, chilling her to the bone. Numbing her mind.

Brenda wasted no time. She soaped her body. Rinsed. Got out. She dressed in the first thing she grabbed from the closet and went to the kitchen to make breakfast.

Her father found her standing at the stove. Every burner in use.

"It's either the heat or a hard night at your pillow," he said, bringing his wheelchair up alongside Brenda and laying a hand on the small of her back.

"What?"

"You didn't curl your hair."

Brenda cracked eggs and thought of chickens, of her father an overprotective hen. "I'm fine, Daddy," she said. "Pull yourself up to the table; I'll bring your plate."

He turned to the table; she brought him his breakfast: eggs lightly scrambled, home fries, a pool of butter in the center of a larger pool of grits, and bacon. She stared at the food as she set the plate down in front of him.

"You want anything else, Daddy?"

"No, this is fine."

Brenda kissed the bald spot at the top of her father's head, turned, and went back to the stove.

Still in pajamas, Nathan Lee stomped into the kitchen. He went directly to the coffeepot. Two lumps of sugar, one big splash of milk, five ice cubes. Enough coffee to fill the remaining seven inches of his mug. He threw himself into a chair at the table.

"Well, good morning, Mr. Nathan."

"Sorry, Daddy. Good morning. Guess I'm kinda groggy. My sleep got all broken up last night."

"Your sister made breakfast."

Brenda brought Nathan Lee's food to the table and her own plate. He kept his hands in his lap until she stepped away. The air moving between them was all the touching they did. "Sunny side up like you like them," she offered.

"In this heat, I coulda been happy with cereal."

Irvin Casey looked at his son over the top of his glasses. Brenda sat. The three bowed their heads. Brenda's eyes were the only ones open.

Irvin Casey cleared his throat—making room for the prayer to come out and the food to go in. "Gracious Father, make us truly thankful for the food we are about to receive, for the nourishment of our bodies for Christ's sake. Amen."

Brenda and Nathan Lee stared at their plates and ate in silence. Irvin stared at his children. Watched Nathan Lee dip the toast into the eggs into the grits and into his mouth. Two times. Then bite into the bread. Brenda ate each item separately. With a spoon. A bite of grits. Then egg. Then potatoes. Nibbling between each mouthful at the bacon in her hand.

"Pass me the hot sauce," Irvin said to his children.

Brenda and Nathan Lee both grabbed the bottle. Both let go. Both watched as the bottle fell and sauce spilled all over the tablecloth. Both reached their napkins toward the spill.

"I'll get it, Brenda," Nathan Lee said. It was an order, not an offer of help.

Brenda balled her napkin in her lap and picked at the last of her breakfast.

"I got a final in the calculus class tomorrow, so I'm gonna work late tonight to make up the time I'm gonna miss." Nathan Lee brought his cup to his mouth and waited for their responses.

"You been studying, Nathan Lee? You ready for this?"

"Yeah, Daddy, I think I am."

"Brenda? You work with this professor? He not gonna be too hard on your brother, is he?"

"Who's teaching it?"

"Damn, Brenda. I been in the class all summer!"

Brenda set down the strip of bacon she'd been eating. Made circles of oil with her thumb and forefinger on opposite sides of her napkin. Said nothing.

Nathan Lee snatched his plate off the table. He skidded it onto the counter and left the kitchen. Brenda picked up the crown of her soft-boiled egg. Plucked the little bit of white out of the shell. Stuck it in her mouth and sucked on it. She got up from the table and rinsed her plate in the sink.

"I'm going now, Daddy. Tell Nathan Lee there's potato salad and ribs left over from last night for him to take for lunch. I'm going to the gym after work, so if you don't want to wait for us to eat, have Mrs. Blackwell fix you something."

"Naw. That's all right. I'll wait for y'all."

Brenda grabbed her own lunch. Kissed her father on the cheek. Headed for the front door with him following behind her. She picked her purse up from the hall table as her brother came bounding down the stairs. She shouldered herself into speaking to him.

"Bye, Nathan Lee. Have a good day. There's leftovers from the ribs I barbecued last night."

"I think I'm gonna use my lunch hour to catch up on sleep." He disappeared into the kitchen.

Irvin unlocked the screen door. He touched the small of his daughter's back one more time before she left. He stood in the doorway watching as she walked to her brown '78 Toyota wagon and rolled down the windows. Nathan Lee came up behind him and he moved out of his son's way. Then reached out to grab his arm.

"Nathan Lee?"

"Yeah, Daddy?"

"When you gonna get past shoulda and stop punishing your sister for her pain?"

"When she get ready to realize I lost him too." He pulled his arm gently from his father's grasp. "I gotta go, Daddy. I put a chicken on to parboil, don't forget to turn it off, okay? You get hungry waiting on me to get home, have Mrs. Blackwell make you something." He walked out the door.

At the sight of her brother coming out of the house, Brenda threw her car into neutral. Let it free-fall down the driveway. Nearly ran into Mrs. Blackwell's car. She turned the ignition, yelled an apology out the window, and sped away toward campus. Nathan Lee followed in his black van. Irvin Casey looked up at the cloudless sky and sighed. He wiped the new-formed sweat off his face with a worn handkerchief.

:

Netta Jean Blackwell's cream-colored, mint condition, '75 Monte Carlo glided up the driveway. Gravel crunched beneath the white-walls. The car stopped and a big-boned, high yella, tree of a woman emerged from inside it. A woman with sternness and softness. With a no-nonsense grip on her nursing bag and a starched white uniform. With laughter in her eyes and in the roll of her belly.

Well, now Irvin James, you lookin' mighty sorrowful this mornin'. Like them children a yours might not be comin' back tonight. And where Miss Brenda rushin' off to so quick? Never seen nobody in that muchofa hurry to get to work. Humph. But the sooner they clear out, the sooner I come in and set to work takin' the frown offa that forehead and the knots outta them shoulders. I come to put a smile on your face and a li'l somethin' special in the resta your body.

Irvin James Casey was caught in the light of Netta Jean Blackwell. He sat stock still for the examination of her eyes. The swift and flowing rush of his desire cleared his mind of the worries of the morning. And of the will to move. He had to be told to wheel out of the doorway and let her come inside. When her eyes were no longer on him, the lure of her let go of his limbs. He reached out and cupped the curve of her rump as she passed in front of him. Felt the power in her hip and groaned a deep baritone in his chest.

"Jus what you think you doin', Irvin James?"

"Jus sayin' good mornin', Netta Jean."

"Talkin' with your hands again? I done told you bout that."

You done told me a lotta things. Like what a man can do to make a woman moan and sigh when he ain't got no control over his legs nor what

God done put between 'em. You done taught me how sensitive be my hands and this bare spot on the top of my head. And how to put my lips to yours and take your breath in.

"I be needin' a bath this mornin', Netta Jean."

"Humph. Only thing dirty bout you is your mind."

Irvin guffawed. Netta Jean set her bag down and went to Irvin's bedroom to strip the bed. She lifted one big pillow. Shook it out of its case. Brought the crumpled cotton to her face and through the wide-spaced nostrils of her fiercely forward nose, breathed the scent of Irvin's sleep. At his grunt of desire, she smiled a full, gap-toothed smile.

"You say somethin', Irvin James?"

"Naw, Netta Jean. I'm jus sittin' over here tryin to stay outta your way."

You sittin' over there steady watchin' the way I'm gonna go you mean. Lookin' like you could use some lovin'. I know what day it is. Bet your children breakfasted on angry words this mornin'. And you sat there strugglin' to give 'em somethin' more wholesome to eat. Gotta be wore out tryin' to nourish hardheaded Negroes intent on eatin' poison. Come on over here and get some of this I got for you.

"Clock ain't yet reached eight and already it's hot in here."

Netta Jean opened the top two buttons of her uniform. She bent one dimpled knee and rested it against the bed. Leaned way over to strip the far corner of the fitted sheet off the mattress. Felt Irvin's gaze warm the curves of her full figure. His eyes mixing in the heat already building between her legs.

Ain't yet time to put the kettle on though.

Irvin checked the fingernails on his right hand. Flexed his big arms. Sat up taller in his wheelchair and lifted the broad muscles of his chest. He matched his breathing to Netta Jean's. From the place over her heart, and deep within her lungs, and down between her thighs, he breathed the energy of her sex into his upper body. He moved himself forward in his mind and saw his mouth at the perfect height to suck her titties when she leaned over. Like she was leaning now, the wide expanse of her behind straining the fabric of her white cotton uniform.

Unhh, unhh, unhh. Woman lets me play with her. Lets me sit here watchin' her with her dress half-unbuttoned. Actin' like she all alone. Woman, you

*know how glad I am you gotta patient nature? And no shame bout makin'
your pleasure known? Netta Jean. Netta Jean.*

"I'm gonna do them breakfast dishes now. You comin' Irvin
James? Reckon we can see bout that bath once I get the kitchen
cleaned up."

The widow Blackwell led the way with her arms full of bed
linens and a practiced sway in her ample hips. She set the bundle
down by the stairs and took Irvin's plate to the counter. Turned
the chicken off and laid it to cool in the lid of the pot. She filled
the sink with hot soapy water and washed the dishes with her
bare hands. She rubbed egg yolk out of the lip of a plate. Pressed
kernels of grits between her fingers. Rinsed the soap off and
watched the wet seep into her skin.

Irvin leaned toward those working fingers. Knew firsthand the
wonders they could perform. On a stiff neck. An aching back.
And sometimes even on a reluctant penis—disconnected from the
brain that might urge it into thickness. Into hardness. He thought
he felt a whisper of arousal between his legs. He let the thought
be enough in the absence of real feeling. Let the desire in his
chest, in his hands, in his mouth take him back to remembered
hard-ons. His sex tight against his belly. His legs bowed to give
it all the room it needed. His hips rocking the bed. And the
woman beneath him. Or bent over the arm of the couch in front
of him. He rested his hands lightly in his lap and closed his eyes.

Netta Jean sensed his settling. "You not fallin' asleep on me, are
you?" she asked over her shoulder.

He kept his eyes shut. "Naw, Netta Jean. I'm jus sittin' here
thinkin' lustful thoughts."

"I gotta thought or two of my own."

"I bet you do."

Netta Jean turned from the sink to look at him. Took in his
bowed head, the steady rise and fall of his chest, and his hands,
upturned and wide open on his lap.

*Wanted him the first time I massaged them big hands. That broad chest.
Them arms like thick brown poles. Them mannish hips that had seen so much
lovin' now still and shy. Wished I was food the first time I watched him eat.
Grateful for the heat of a jalapeño. For each taste of somethin' sweet. Each
creamy swallow of butter. Wanted to take your tray from you right then and*

there. Ask you to try a new dish. This one I been cookin up for the last fifty years.

Netta Jean dried her hands on a towel and walked silently across the kitchen. She pressed her bosom into Irvin's face and startled him into a deep inhale. His mouth opened before his eyes did. Opened and closed over her nipple through the fabric of her uniform. His insistent sucking left a wet spot. His love bites sent a tingling deep into her flesh. She pressed the 'V' of her pubic mound into his knees. Grabbed the back of his wheelchair. Brushed her lips over the exposed flesh of his head and whispered his name into his own ears. She told him of the sensations he gave her as a gift shared between them. She dragged her nipple from between his teeth. Let him see her shudder.

"You ready for that bath now, Irvin James?"

"I been ready."

THE BUTTERFLY

Jenifer Levin

During the larval period the corpus allatum dominates. Its secretion, juvenile hormone ... *controls molting as the larva progresses through several growth periods* ... *Meanwhile, secretory cells in the brain produce* brain hormone ... *which is actually secreted by the corpus cardiacum. Its target, the prothoracic gland, responds by secreting* ecdysone, *which favors the development of adult structures* ... *The continued dominating effect* ... *eventually influences the adult emergence.*

—*"Metamorphosis in a Butterfly"*
From Biology: The Science of Life

There is that second where you seem to hover over the water like a haunting ghoul, in motion, yet inside the motion it feels infinitely slow. The entry headfirst, always, arms then, hand press strong, sure, outsweep, kick, both legs together, not from the knees but the hips. Hands arms down, elbows bent just so, and in. Sweeping. Up. Sweeping. Kick again. Then over the water neck and chest, shoulder swing, arms rotate, hip flex, in motion but slow it feels, so slow, every breath and drop an agony, a triumph, arched over the water like a fierce haunting ghoul, repetitively attacking, fearful, bursting for entry.

Pretend you're ghosts! coaches would yell, grimacing, baring

teeth in endlessly bad cartoonish apings of something awful. Headfirst! Rrrrrr!

Big kick! Baby kick!

When we were both little age groupers trying to win medals,
my brother Jonathan and I swam butterfly.

Later, the boys adopted a different chant.

Win! they yelled. Wine! And women!

Over the years Jonathan's gotten used to my being gay.

Queer, I correct him sometimes, taunting, tender. Or, you know,
lesbian, dyke, tribade, muff-diver.

He's even gotten used to me defiantly donning a yarmulke during Passover seder, a prayer shawl for Yom Kippur.

What he once said he'd never get used to, though, were all
those big, sunny, friendly, fair-haired Nordic-looking girls I used
to bring home for family gatherings, one after the other.

They're all-American sexy, I'd observe. That's why they make
you nervous.

No, he told me. But it's like you keep picking them up in some
special store that sells these perfect, pretty, good-natured WASP
jock types; you know, you finish with one, then you trade it in
for the next latest model. Throwback wish fulfillment, Josie. To
make up for all those swim team types you secretly lusted after
when we were growing up. Runt.

Well, runt I was. The overt invert, family disaster in more ways
than one—full of desire, generally lacking talent. Jon? He was
Golden Boy, full of talent, but—and he *knew* that I knew—generally lacking desire.

Sure, I shot back. We *both* secretly lusted after those girls, Jon.
But *I* am the one who gets them.

He scowled, blushed.

See, it's true.

The family Benvenisti? Small. Abramo can trace his lineage back
to the Golden Age of southern Spain, but has few relatives. Sarah,
a Holocaust survivor, has none—none, at least, since the death of
Yanos. Out of mutual loneliness and loss my parents created a son
and a daughter, two dark-haired, hazel-eyed, faintly olive-skinned
children. Jonathan. Josefa.

He. And me.

Yanos was my mother's cousin, from some God-forsaken little nation that, not too many decades past, had merrily sent its Jews off to death camps. We called him Uncle. A quiet, broken man, he had bad teeth and visited on weekends. He and my parents would sit companionably in the front room, not saying much. One Passover seder, when I was six and Jonathan seven, he drank too much, took us down to the basement, undid our various buttons and zippers and poked his fingers everywhere. They were stubby fingers, I remember, the nail of the right thumb missing. Then, smiling, he dropped his pants and showed us what an Auschwitz surgeon had done.

If you tell anyone, he warned, I'll say how bad you both were. We never did tell.

Over the next few years, mostly on holidays, I'd see him, sometimes, in a breath-held sideways glance, descending into or emerging from the basement with Jonathan. Smells came to me: sweat, must, aging flesh. My brother's eyes seemed dulled and red. Later, for days afterward, he'd be unusually silent.

When I was ten and he eleven, Yanos died. At the funeral my brother and I stood stiff and silent in our good dark clothes. Afterward, on the little lawn at home, we tried to catch fireflies. Jonathan found and killed a toad. Then he stole some matches, and set the corpse on fire.

In general, Jonathan had a lot of success in the medal quest. I did not. We were just a year apart and, until adolescence, about the same size. But life happened. He continued winning the 200 butterfly; I entered a permanent slump. He was handsome, and shone. I was not, did not. Trophies, good grades, high school popularity, a macho bravado that left everyone wondering why he never dated—all these were his. Chasms spread between us.

Coach expected him to get a scholarship somewhere, somewhere good—a couple of Division I schools were definitely interested. We needed it—he did—God knows, we were not rich. Then, about thirty-five yards into a very important 200 final, leading the field, he stopped dead, floated back to the starting block, got out of the pool, and walked away.

He never did go back.

A week later, in his advanced chemistry class, someone set a
desk on fire. They never found out who.

That afternoon I skipped practice and went home early. My
brother was down in the basement, plugged into a Walkman.
Some overhead bulbs had been turned on. In dull light you could
see the stairs littered with butterfly wings, with their dead wingless
insect bodies.

Jon, I said, what did you do?

He glared defiantly and removed the earplugs.

Nothing, he said, just got curious.

Curious about what, Jon?

What things would look like. After.

I still swim, but only recreationally.

Family visit—my first with Maddy. In the little girl's bedroom
that once was mine, Maddy tells me what she thinks. A mixture
of compassion for and condemnation of my family. Oh, sure, she
sees their good points. But she won't forgive them for being so
goddamned blind. For not asking questions, at least, when the
failures and troubles began. And Jonathan? Well, he doesn't like
her, she can tell. Something wrong there. He's handsome and
dangerous, she says, the proverbial ticking time bomb. She isn't
sure she can like him, either. Although, for me, she will try.

We kiss. Talk about kisses. First times. She has been with many
men, but her first kiss was with a girlfriend at the age of ten, and
she knew then it was women she would love. Unless you count
Yanos—should you?—I have never been with a man. She tells me
what it's like; but, I confess, it seems unintriguing, perfunctory.
It's *her* flesh, her smell, her touch that I want, that make me burn,
that make me want to give her every kind of pleasure.

Maddy, listen: Here, in my childhood home, I will tell you
more. How, for so long, love seemed willing to pass me by. High
school summers spent lifeguarding on the beach, watching transparent globs of jellyfish cluster along mellow shorelines like tundra,
car hoods along the parking lot road twinkle like mirages in the
waves of heat rising from polished fenders.

Beach umbrellas speckled the yellowish sand, colored monster
mushrooms. Kids screamed and tossed plastic shovels at each
other, complained loudly about the orange and green pails whose

handles seemed always to twist off irreparably, sobbed that yet another beach ball had drifted out too far, rainbow stripes dotting a circle on the horizon, the circle growing smaller and smaller until it disappeared altogether. They'd capture snails, stuff them in sand castle chambers for torture and death. Under umbrellas their mothers creamed sun-sensitive noses. I'd watch from a high white lifeguard perch, wondering how it was that these children, who had no Uncle Yanos, were so willingly curious about cruelty and murder.

Weekends the college kids were there with forbidden six-packs, rolling crotch to crotch on their towels. Weekends, all the fathers were there, dragging mats and heavy picnic baskets, tossing cigarette butts ash-down in the sand. Above all this I'd stare from my white ladder chair—one of four along the beach. At its base, a cherry-colored surfboard. After each shift I'd take it out, paddle a half mile or so. My skin baked reddish brown and had a dusky glow. I used plenty of tanning cream, though, rarely removed my sunglasses, and was the only female on my shift—which, for some reason, suited me fine. One of the other guards was Jonathan. I'd watch high school girls go by that summer, watch them cluster around the base of his chair, stretching their arms to brush against the rungs, laughing in high, delicate trills that abruptly ended. The male lifeguards were youthfully muscular, casual on their thrones. It was a Catholic town, a WASP town, a factory town, and most of them were blond, pale-eyed; against the whitewashed white and gray background, my brother glowed darkly, like some dream lover from a romance novel you'd buy in grocery stores, so all the girls watched him with a fear-tinged lust. They didn't know how damaged he was, how far away from them all. How his seemingly tantalizing remoteness was no put-on, but the very best he could manage; how their approach made him shudder inside, afraid of what anyone coming close might do, of what he might do to them. Once in a while he'd deign to take part in some conversation. Mostly, like the other boys, he flexed biceps and pectorals, pretending to ignore the girls and the dense summer heat.

Watching his anguish, I felt, for the first time, my own—my absolute difference from that pack of young women who adored him. Although I didn't yet quite comprehend its meaning or origin,

I was unutterably apart from them somehow, absolutely alone. Love had passed me by. The thing they talked about in locker room showers, giggling, blushing; the thing these oblivious blond high school girls felt following my poor crazed brother along the sand—this love was of no interest to me whatsoever. The thought of it failed to stir me. When I tried to imagine it, I was left with a feeling of emptiness.

By August, my skin had turned a deep, burnished chestnut. So had Jonathan's. I rescued two drifting beach balls before the season ended.

Maddy, listen: At college I tried out for the swim team but didn't make it. Had few friends. Studied something socially contributive and utterly uninteresting. Caught myself, sometimes, trying to gaze through the faces of other young women, mind's eye peeling the makeup from them to reveal fresh skin, unveiled cheekbones, untouched lips; sometimes, in this kind of reverie, I'd feel slightly embarrassed and wouldn't know why. Winter Sundays brought me face-to-face with unavoidable loneliness. Dull papers completed for the week, readings done, I stared through cheap dormitory windows dripping icicles and felt the ache of despair inside. One Sunday I decided to work it off, as in the old days. I packed some necessary items and was soon trotting through white drifts on my way to the field house, once familiar territory. It was late afternoon; the pool would be nearly deserted. Wind froze my face. I blinked against the flakes blowing down from trees and limbs, walked as fast as possible. Only in quick motion would the internal gnawing rest. I was glad to be heading for water.

In the changing rooms of some sports-minded colleges, lockers stretch forever. They're usually gray, or lemon-colored, or the color of orange peels. On off-hour winter afternoons there is only the sound of footsteps ringing along concrete, echoing on metal; the sound of a shower head dripping at lonely, maddening intervals; a clang of locker doors being pressed open, canvas athletic bag set on wooden bench with a gentle thud. The lighting always bleaches skin of color. Wall-length mirrors are fogged near sinks and showers; when clear, they reflect relentless pallor. Water, sweat, deodorant, the smell of hair and damp clothes, the obliterating scent of chlorine, hang unstirring in the air. When you're alone in such a place, you feel two big conflicting things: enclosed, yet revealed.

I hurried through the ritual of hanging clothes, suiting up, selecting a towel and cap, spitting into my favorite old high school goggles, passed under a solitary shower in the row of unused stalls just outside the pool area. Good to come on a Sunday; as I'd thought, the place was nearly empty, only one other swimmer there. I watched her in appreciation. She was performing quick butterfly repeats, lots of 50s, action methodical and rapid, the stroke nearly perfect, supremely powerful, electrifying—drops flashed silver from her fingertips before each plunge forward, head looping down gracefully before the arms, everything else following like the rounded, raised, descending limbs of a dauntless, haunting ghost. Water trailed after her in uniform ripples.

I wondered if I'd seen her before. Decided no; this was someone from the team, maybe, but no one I knew. A thin lifeguard lazed in his chair at the far end, reading. Even from twenty-five yards, I recognized the lime green textbook cover for Biology 101. But my gaze went back to the swimmer, who was resting briefly now between repeats, goggled eyes fixed on the time clock and fingers settled gently against her neck's pulse, counting.

I slid into sterile turquoise water. Began a slow warm-up that went nowhere. Every now and then found myself glancing up, expectantly, watching. The swimmer had switched to longer repeats, each interval as well-paced as a metronome.

I finished a lackluster workout that was, nevertheless, a little relaxing. When I pressed up and out of the pool, she was still busy a couple of lanes over—this time with perfect fifty-yard repeats again—and, you could see by the clock, she was right on the money. This was immediately humbling but somehow pleasing, and I retreated to the showers, soon back to the long, deserted locker room, dripping clean and naked onto a towel spread bench-wide, shaking out my lycra cap, drying goggle lenses, sorting through a bag for skin cream. The mirror steamed slightly, reflected some blurred image back. I avoided looking that way. Mirrors bothered me. Still, whenever I did look, sideways, as if stealing, I realized how much I wanted her to appear from the shower entrance behind: that swimmer with the electrifying butterfly, looming suddenly into life on land. The mirror fogged. I felt

my heart pound with a different, brutal thud. Outlines of a suited
body had indeed appeared, as hoped for, plain white towel thrown
over one careless, smooth broad shoulder.

I turned. She was in a dark suit. She still wore cap and goggles
and, approaching the mirror, looked like some strange, blank,
faintly cruel creature from space—head smoothed to bright round
baldness, eyes obscured; she looked strong and bold, almost strut-
ting as she moved with chest wide and breasts proud, nipples
erect, pointing forward. I turned back clumsily to my skin cream.
Blushing. Felt water drip from cheeks to towel. Stole one last
blurred glimpse of myself and the woman, strange swimmers in a
mirror. Then, suddenly, became aware of subtle burning in the
corner of one eye. A tear slid silently out to join the rest of what
speckled my face. It hit me full force then: that I was alone, and
filled with desire.

This seemed, suddenly, to be the source of all dark things: the
hollow ache that kept me up at night; the pain of family, of
childhood. Without knowing why I raised my head again to the
mirror, gazed fully at it—not at myself, but at the anonymous
swimmer who stood there staring coolly at both our fogged images. Silly me. I couldn't have known how much it showed on my
face: desire. That desperate, pained yearning for love, however it
might come; the look must have left my face open and raw for
the first time in years. And then, because of this or in spite of it,
and for just one racing second, I saw something else bloom on it:
a certain torn beauty that was no longer adolescent; that some
woman, somewhere, might love.

First times take us by surprise. All this was news to me. So I
couldn't have known, couldn't have seen how clearly it was
witnessed.

The other woman turned slowly. There was something regal in
the motion, haughty, almost calculated. She approached with
calm, slow steps that slid gracefully on the damp floor tiles. Entirely female and familiar, and at the same time unknowable: a
creature from the water with eyes obscured, head rounded
smoothly by a cap that thousands wore. She was well formed, but
completely unidentifiable—as anything but a woman and a swimmer. Close up her features seemed blander still, with that cruel

alien quality. Desire and cruelty hovered in the damp air, hovered over my own broad shoulders, my upturned face.

Then it melted.

She leaned down in one smooth motion and her transformation was complete: from brutal water creature to angel of mercy. Dripping hands planted firmly on my shoulders, she kissed me full on the mouth. And a thrill rippled through—the otherness of the touch, sudden invasion of an unknown tongue against my own— it rippled up and down my neck and along my spine in a continuous wave, caused my ears to burn, forced my nipples instantly erect, thighs to shiver strangely as they never had before.

Had I thought about it logically, maybe I would have been a little appalled—that all the handsome, sometimes friendly boys and men I had seen in my life had failed to arouse me; while this anonymous woman, with whom I had no discernable connection, could move me to the edge of some unidentified high and glorious cliff by a mere touch of wet lips and tongue.

But I thought of nothing then. There was only sensation, and it washed through me quickly. Some locker room door groaned open down an aisle. The kiss ended abruptly. Then my angel of mercy retreated, hovering remotely away along the length of mirror. She turned without a single look back, vanished among the rows of lockers.

I walked in the snow that night. Slightly demented. That love would show its face to me this way—I had trouble absorbing it. It had been disguised, really, by water apparatus, cut short by the creak of door hinges. Entirely outside all the rule books and regulations—a love of which no age groupers' coach would have approved.

I am crying a little. Maddy licks the tears.

I just got all wet, listening, she says. Get on top of me, baby.

Here, in my childhood room, the bed creaks up and down.

We are all getting older. Jonathan's thirty-three now. And, he says, beginning to understand why Mom and Dad always carried on so much about the importance of family. Nowadays, he says, he feels that way too. Wants to reconnect—with them, with me. He tells me that, in therapy, he has learned how love is good. He has become less dangerous, he thinks, to himself, to others.

We will see.

He's itching for accolades, I can tell: about to finish his residency at a good hospital. Engaged to marry—a woman! Shoshana!—who is visiting relatives in Tel Aviv now, but would otherwise be here, with us all, for the weekend.

I have a name for his bride-to-be: GIT—the Gorgeous Israeli Tease.

She seems to make him happy. Or, at any rate, proud.

Me? I finally decided what I wanted to do, and passed the EMT training course. Blood doesn't bother me. Neither does pain. They have rotated me to the day shift.

Also, I have love now—I have Maddy.

And I have this dream: Maybe my brother and I are approaching neutral ground again; closeness, even. Without fear. Envy. Pity. Yanos. The butterfly.

In early middle age, maybe, we'll be friends.

In between, though—somehow, in a way neither of us understands—there is Maddy.

One of your *shiksa* types again, he says.

It isn't really true—at least, not like before. All those other women I showed off to prove some point. That, one way or another, I could fuck them; whereas maybe he could not. But this woman, I love.

We are married.

My wife? Yes, actually. Plump filling in the contours of a sturdy, once-slender body, her short-bobbed fair hair starting to streak now with gray. She has a terrific face marred here and there by old acne scars. Wears makeup and loose-fitting flowery dresses. Everything set off by big bright cool evaluative eyes that take no hostages.

And Maddy, too, is here for the weekend.

You and Maddy are really going to like each other, I promise.

Mom's busy in the kitchen, Dad rustling around the front yard. I stash our overnight bags. Quietly, in a big chair in my old bedroom, Maddy sits.

With his whiskey sour half-finished, Jonathan tries to break the ice. I rummage inanely through hangers in an empty closet, letting this first thing that is happening between them sound a little faintly in the background.

"Hiya, Maddy."

"Hi."

"Can I get you anything?"

"No thanks."

"Well, I'm glad to finally meet you. My sister says we'll like each other. Not that it matters—I mean, so long as *you* like *her*."

She leans forward, eyes full of a strange humor he cannot quite recognize. "I *love* your sister, Jonathan."

"Good. Well. That's good."

"What about you?"

"Me?"

"Do you love somebody?"

"As a matter of fact, I do."

"Good," she says. "Lucky for your patients."

Uh-oh.

The bed is right there; he sits, probably warily. "My patients?"

"Sure. You're going to be a surgeon, right?"

"*Am*," he says—it comes out bitterly, and I wonder why. "I already am a surgeon."

"Oh, okay. Say you had to go under the knife. You wouldn't want somebody fiddling around inside *you*, would you, who didn't know the first thing about love."

"I guess not."

My brother suspects the bitch is patronizing him, but can't really tell.

My Maddy—yes, she *is* a bitch. One of the reasons I fell for her. Flip side of all that softness that can pull you right down on top and inside it, so that you never want to leave. It's her armor— the bitchiness, I mean, the femme ferocity—a bulletproof vest covering her, and me.

I do worry for his patients.

Maddy smiles then. So gently. I can tell without looking. It's an engaging smile, female soft, the teeth imperfect but white.

She helps my mother prepare dinner. Sarah protests—but it's for show. Despite herself, she likes this—girlfriend? lover?—this *wife* of mine, Maddy's easy female chatter, the expert way she

slices vegetables gently, how she cores the iceberg lettuce with
one deft whack on the side of the sink, washes everything thor-
oughly, cleans up after. The details of survival—sleep, sustenance,
sanitation—are important to Sarah, more important than anything
else, not just women's work but the life and breath of the world;
and, after all, she ought to know. I hear them talking through
walls, around corners, yakking away. My mother senses that, in
some way, Maddy is also a survivor. They share much more than
they'll ever consciously know. Both have done just what they had
to do, at times, to get by. In retrospect, some of the things they
had to do were rather unpleasant; one might even say, immoral.

But who sets standards of morality, these days? God? The same
God who watches holocausts, and all manner of suffering, with a
cool, indifferent eye? Who watched our Uncle Yanos in the
basement?

I'm not impressed.

Later, we dine. Roast beef. An intentional or unintentional
slight—I've been vegetarian for years. On the other hand, a way
of honoring Maddy. I watch her, and Jonathan, over a mountain
of string beans. Catch Maddy examining his handsome, sullen
face. Like sister, like brother, she is thinking. But my features are
less smooth than his, even though I'm younger, bitten by harsh
dyke things and by sorrow here and there, tangible and intangible
loss you'd think would show on him too by now, craggy and sharp
where Jonathan's are rounded. Out of my eyes' corners, I notice
him glancing back; and, I notice, so does Maddy. He's looking a
little smug, my brother. Adding the pieces of her up; surmising—
correctly—that the mascara probably hides a few of the blocks
she's been around.

This sneaky evaluation is something my Maddy has come to
expect from men. Frankly, she says, she finds it a bore. Granted:
the truth probably wouldn't make appropriate dinner conversation;
but, were my brother to openly ask, Maddy would have no problem telling him about the years she spent jerking guys off in
massage parlors to make a living. And that, sure, she does more
middle-class things nowadays to pay rent, clerical, secretarial,
whatever. But she's never been the type of girl to lie much, or to

suffer undue shame about the past. Women do what they have to do to get by at the time. No more, no less.

Jonathan has puckered lines of worry across his forehead. Maddy, who sees everything, has already seen this. I know what she's dying to tell him: Honey, what you need most in your life is a good blow job. Trust me. And, by the way, that gorgeous, full-lipped, selfish-eyed girl I've seen in photographs—the one you're about to marry—will probably never give you one.

If only that were the answer.

Thankfully, it is his problem. Not, bless Maddy, his sister's.

My mother and I put food away, clean dishes. Maddy's making friends with Dad, trying to charm him, and every once in a while, through the splash of green cleansing bubbles and running water, I can hear her laugh echo faintly from the den.

Dutifully stacking things in the drainer while my mother washes and rinses, I'm thankful for this older woman's quiet dignity. For years, now, she has accepted my sexual destiny with seeming serenity—certainly without comment. Maybe it's due to a lack of willingness to confront painful truths. On the other hand, there are some truths better left alone; they tend to caper around more freely, these truths, when they are not shoved right into your face. Sarah's difficult life will not be made more complete, by any stretch of the imagination, if I bothered to tell her that, for the last decade or so, her only daughter has been buckling leather harnesses around her hips, attaching silicon rubber dildos of various sizes thereto, and using this equipage to enthusiastically fuck other women as often as possible.

Had Jonathan turned out gay, I think, certain truths could not have been so successfully avoided.

What then?

Would my mother's life have been enhanced by knowing exactly what her sole surviving relative did? Would she understand that it filled her children's lives with sorrow? Dimmed her only son's bright promise? But that it did not, did not, did not make me queer? That loving women have healed me; being queer has been my salvation? That my goddess, my angel, was a woman swimming butterfly? So that what I am today, what Maddy and I have together, makes up the beautiful and triumphant part of things—not the tragic?

That Jonathan is still unhealed? And dangerous?

All talk of this seems, somehow, easy to escape. A man tried to destroy me, but a butterfly saved me; she did not save my brother. This would be difficult to prove. He's done nothing but kill a toad, set a fire, quit a race, gone through med school. A bright and golden boy. Who once I knew. Who once I loved.

Should I go to the police? Tell them, Look here, I have a feeling that my brother, upstanding citizen, outstandingly handsome heterosexual male specimen, up-and-coming doctor, is insane? That he may do something terrible, someday?

Should I tell Shoshana?

No one would believe.

In the end, maybe there is little we can do about anything. We're a private species, with plenty of secrets. If humans were meant to live in controlled fishbowl environments, we'd all have been born guppies. And I don't like anyone, even Sarah, staring at pieces of *my* life that, after all, I cannot really change. Why should he.

My mother has a deep intuitive understanding of certain things: basically, there are qualities that never change. People can be bad sometimes, or good. Full of ignorance and terror, or full of curiosity.

Curiosity itself can be healthy or psychotic. Your average doctor is curious about prolonging life; your average Nazi doctor about prolonging death.

She told me, once, that each child begins life full of energy and fear. At life's end, she said, we are less afraid, but also much more tired. So that being a death camp survivor, in the final analysis, could not make you better or worse than anyone else; just a good deal more exhausted.

And I love her for this, though she doesn't know it: things like personality, psychological trauma, sexuality or lack thereof, are, to her, a drop in the bucket of life. It's the bucket itself—the living, breathing life—that she knows is important. In her own damaged European way, Sarah is totally *cool*. Always sees the big picture.

Although the details, like Yanos, do tend to elude her.

*   *   *

We're finished washing and stacking and drying. The door to the den's closed. Jonathan is in there, Maddy says, with my father, having some kind of a man-to-man. We women share tea, Maddy and my mother hunched close in a weird conspiratorial silence at the kitchen table, I near the door in my tilted-back chair, ankle over a knee, boylike.

What are they doing in there for so long, father and son? My dad, I think, is comfortable in his armchair. Schnapps swirling in a shot glass. He'll drink it slowly, the way he did every night of our childhood, swishing each meager mouthful up against the insides of his teeth with a liquid clicking sound, as if it's his last taste of schnapps on earth. A late-night rerun of the "MacNeil/ Lehrer Newshour" or something will disturb the den's low-lit serenity—some news broadcast, always a news broadcast, for he likes to know, to know, to know. Even though, as usual, mostly terrible things have occurred during the last twenty-four hours; even though, as usual, he can do nothing about any of it. Abramo muttering at the screen, shaking his head. The conversation will go something like this:

"Bastards. Kill them all."

"Who, Dad?"

"Better yet, let them kill each other. Bunch of Nazi scum. How does it feel, scum? How does it feel, now that you don't have the Jews to kick around anymore?"

Jonathan will know without looking: Bosnia. When he settles onto the sofa, though, Dad turns it off. Silently wishing that he does not have to go through all this fuss; he wishes Jonathan and Shoshana would just elope. But raises his glass in one thick, steady, workingman's liver-spotted hand. "Cheers."

"Cheers."

"Your mother wants me to talk to you about the wedding."

Gifts. Money. Arrangements. Invitations and exclusions. I still know my brother—at least, a little. Alarm will prick his spine. And everything he's been meaning to say—Look, Dad, I thought I'd tell *you* first, Shoshana and I have decided to elope! And oh, by the way, remember Uncle Yanos? Well, he raped both your kids in the basement; I think it made me crazy!—will desert him in a kind of panic. In his mind he'll see himself diminished, a small, frail boy, racing futilely around a windy lawn to retrieve the shredded pieces of a firefly, a toad, a childhood, of some important document.

On my childhood bed, Maddy and I are getting there.

When my brother walks along the hall, past the basement door, past the mostly closed door meant to hide us well, he stops for a second to watch. It's not something he was meant to see, for sure. But there he is, anyway, curious, and here we are—never mind that the bed's made and our clothes on—practically in flagrante delicto. Maddy on her back, face turned passionately against a pillow, legs spread to straddle me as I rock, gently, smiling, between them. Every once in a while her lips part, a soundless moan. Her eyes are closed. When they flick open to see the shadow he makes in the partly opened crack of doorway her hand, which has been spread across my back, beginnings of sweet urgency, flex warning, and the motion we're making together stops.

Jonathan flees. Down the hall to his own room with a face burnt red. Probably half-aroused, half-nauseated, I think. And wishes like hell he hadn't seen us—the close, almost delicate, generous motion of two women's bodies pressing into one another, prelude to something unspeakably exquisite. What will he do? Turn on a lamp, grab the thumb-worn copy of Gray's Anatomy from a bedside table, searching out ligaments, tendons, cartilage to cut.

But it's too late. Flushed and blushed we're standing, Maddy's chasing him. I follow out into the hallway, stand listening, watching, halfway between my childhood bedroom and his, right in front of the shut-tight basement door, a tired and violent no-man's-land, stuffy with memory.

She leans into his room.

Under makeup, Maddy blushes. The steely eyes are furious.

"What are you, some kind of creep?"

"Me?"

"You. I saw you looking."

"Why don't you two just close the door then, Maddy?"

She pouts. And he must wonder, intrigued by the utter female prettiness of it, if she does that to get her way with me sometimes, too—and, if so, does it work?

Yes, Jon. And—yes.

When she speaks, though, any vestige of childishness has vanished. I listen, amused, deperate. "Okay, Jonathan. You and I are in serious trouble already, I can tell. Are we going to work it out or not?"

"Work *what* out, Maddy?"

"You. Me. Our relationship."

I can imagine him: Putting his hands up half-mast, as if staring down the barrel of a gun that hasn't been cocked yet. "Whoa there, whoa! *Your* relationship is with my sister, doll!"

"Yes. Right. And therefore, with you. Has it occurred to you, at all, that we're in-laws?"

"In-laws?"

"Sure, you know, like that wife of yours will be, whenever you do all the brouhaha—Well, Josie and I are married, too."

"What? You mean, ceremonially?"

"Yes, sure, and in our hearts." Her left hand flashes, extravagantly; there it is, second to last finger, what I gave her, band of gold.

"Three weeks ago, Jonathan. Central Park. Some friends read our vows. Then we went down to City Hall and registered—you know, as partners—"

"You can *do* that?"

"Oh God, honey, get a life!"

"How do you like that. She never even told me."

"She almost called. Then she cried. She loves you, Jonathan—you should hear how she talks about you sometimes, it's as if, growing up, you were *everything*, you anchored her to the world, and you didn't even know it. Personally, so far, I think you're a sick, selfish, narcissistic fart. But if *she* loves you, I have to consider the fact that maybe you're worth loving. So you and I have this choice, now—are we going to break the ice? Don't we have to? Because one thing I won't let anyone, anyone in the world do, is hurt her. Not you, not me, not anybody! I'd scratch your eyes out, mister, if I thought you'd even try."

I imagine him, staring at her with that look he wears instead of defeat, a mixture of hate and admiration. For a moment, there's silence. In which I know, somehow, what he will not say: that, like me, he just wants to be home again sometimes, safe and sound;

that there is no home for us anywhere, anymore, and maybe never was, unless it be inside ourselves.

When he speaks, the words echo toward me down the hallway, smiling, vile, off the cold locked dust of the basement door.

"Christ, Maddy. Next time you want to break the ice, remind me to bring my blowtorch. Or my scalpel."

I retreat for the night. Before all this, there was the hot wet feel of sex about to happen; now, given the opportunity, I would rather shoot thorazine. But Maddy insists. Partly out of desire, I think, mostly out of stubbornness and pride—she's not about to let my family desexualize us, she says, not now or ever, not if *she* has anything to do with it. Which, of course, she does.

I do what I can in the way of submission, knowing that tonight it will soothe her ego: letting her touch me a little, but not inside. She accepts that. Whispering in my ear never mind but to fuck her, fuck her, please.

Well. I can always do that.

I wonder if Jonathan hears us through the walls, if he even listens. If it arouses him, or sickens him; makes him think of Shoshana, or old races, or of butterflies. If he can love his woman, too, and please her, and make her moan; and if sometimes, as Maddy has taught me, she has taught him the sweet power of surrender.

Later, Maddy sleeps. I stay awake. Listening for what I think might happen, rustlings now, and footsteps.

I am Jonathan's sister, for sure. Almost a twin—in some ways.

Since the thing with Yanos, neither of us have ever slept well. Tonight, insomniac or exhilarated, full of psychotic or sane energy or both, we cannot possibly sleep. I listen through walls. Hear my brother tossing. Throwing off blankets and throwing on an undershirt, pulling denim cutoffs over his boxers. In my room, I do the same. Sitting then standing, carefully, while this lover sleeps. Lacing up smelly old running shoes with holes in the toes. I follow after him the way I've done all my life, runt trailing bro, like a cub following papa bear's scent down the hall, through flimsy locks and rusted screen doors, until both of us, runt and bro, queer and straight, disappointment and triumph, are out in the night; but only he believes he's alone. Crossing wet grass, following pockets of light spread by streetlamps.

Jonathan moves quickly across lawns, skirts hedges, wiggles through rusted-out holes in aluminum fences, follows old paths into narrow clusters of spruce and maple. He does it by instinct, and I follow—or is it something more deeply ingrained than conscious memory? How many times did we do this, as kids? Shortcuts. Vaulting lightly over one barrier or another, to get where we wanted to trespass. The one place where, yes, both of us were forbidden.

Back then, when it was a mostly WASP and Catholic town of sparse privilege and unspoken genteel prejudice, the place we are heading for was restricted. Now, they've let in some Jews, and an Asian or two.

Still, even in the old days, nothing ever kept us out at night. A few stone walls. Bridged barricades. Past fading signs saying PRIVATE KEEP OUT or MEMBERS ONLY, across the falsely rolling green and sands of a man-made golf course. Parking lot. Club dining room. Pool house. Over a waist-high freshly white-painted barrier. My brother vaults, and I watch; he lands right next to the lifeguard's chair and the smell hits him, hits me: damp northeastern breeze of late summer, grass, chlorine, concrete. It stretches off into the dark, touched only by a leaf here, a bug there—fifty meters of water, this specially preserved enclave into which, as kids, equally excluded, we trespassed with terror and glee.

Jonathan pulls off shirt and shoes. When he unzips the cutoffs they fall, loosely, simply, and he steps out of them clad only in boxers and hint of a beer gut. The floating lanes have been taken out and coiled heavily on land, many hours ago. The rectangular expanse of water is all his now, he thinks, undivided sideways, lengthwise. All his. And mine. He sticks in a toe.

"Come on, Jon. Go for it."

My voice should have startled him into turning around; instead, he dives. Luckily, into the deep end. There is that slight almost unfelt rush of the air. Up a little, over, down. Kick back with the legs. Head aiming between the shoulders now, a little lower, deep. I vault the waist-high fence. Settle cross-legged by the side of the pool, watching this man, my brother, who once I loved, who once

I knew, splash like a boy in the water. He shuts his eyes and I feel it with him, gushing past his ears, up his nose, torturous, chilling, wet. How, in the first moment of contact with the substance, his life rolls behind both eyelids like a stunningly fast videotape: Mom Dad Josie Shoshana. A dog we had once, long ago. Crushing bright leaves in the autumn. Does he think of trophies won? Youth passed? The 200 fly? Uncle Yanos? Childhood, lost? Does he even remember. Now he's bobbing up, opening his eyes—chlorine stings them, I know—shocked to be breathing. Racing dive. Not bad, he chuckles, and we both feel it—his surprise, easing away. Not bad, no not too bad, for a weird doctor with a beer gut.

"Right, Jon. Just a touch too deep."

"Shut *up!*"

"Hmmmph." I sit motionless at the side of the pool. If there were any lights, he'd see me smile.

He treads shakily, doesn't sink, then relaxes and the movements get easy. All there, after all, in the muscles. When your mind forgets, the body remembers. Wind rushes through his lips, through mine.

"So you got married, huh?"

I nod. See him catch it, barely visible, a motion like a sound. "And you didn't even tell me."

"Well, Jon. It was kind of private."

"Bullshit."

"Okay, okay. I just got afraid. I mean, afraid, okay? But also tired."

"Tired?"

"Mmm. Yeah. Of explaining myself. Do it enough, it hurts, you know. And it does get boring."

He dips his face in and blinks, arms moving slowly, effortlessly, as if he is in a perfect time warp, young again, and strong. Used to the water now aren't you, my brother, and it no longer feels foreign, just faintly refreshing, summer warm, life itself. Like something you were born to.

"Shit, Josie. That—lady of yours. She's quite a character."

"Maddy makes me happy."

"Well, she loves you."

"Oh," I say, softly, "I know."

"You're lucky. Tell me something, do you ever think about it?"

"Love?"

"No. Yanos."

I shake my head. Then sigh. "Oh, all the time. Mostly with murderous intent. But the kick-in-the-balls-of-it is, Jon, that the motherfucker was so damaged himself. One holocaust that never stopped, right? It went on going, came right into our lives."

"College, one year—"

"Yeah?"

"I got charged with shoplifting. Surgical supplies, books, psychiatric diagnostic manuals—I wanted to find out some name for what I was. That's where you queers are lucky, ducky: You've got a name. And it's not even in the DSM these days."

"Well, it isn't an illness, schmuck. Other things are."

Warm drops fall from his lips when he laughs. "God, Josie, I stole so much! Anyway, they sentenced me to ten hours of community service and a month of counseling. The month turned into years. It's under control now, too."

"Maybe you shouldn't get married, Jon."

"I'd never hurt Shoshana."

I think: Run, Shoshana, run.

Alone in the water, my brother sobs. He speaks freely, like a kid, telling me he's remembering a bunch of things now, winter, his senior year of high school. Short course. Indoor. That particular meet—an important one, yes. Division I coaches watching. His race. 200 fly. One and a half laps and he thought of Yanos, pulled up dead in the water, mid-lane, went vertical and treaded and watched seven other boys splash ahead into the future. Then surfed slowly to the wall, pulled himself out, and quit, just walked away. Somewhere, off in the background, he heard me yelling— for him, at him—heard my wounded cries. As he walked past the bleachers, head down, eyes trained on the wet tiled floor, he was careful to glance up once at me—in rage, in a kind of unspeakable triumph, eyes blazing something horrible: Look, they said, Hitler won.

What glory it would have been, he knew now, just to finish a thing out. How he had learned, finally, to respect and admire me—not because of my losses, really, but the way I had handled them. How it had buried itself inside him since—that fear, that terror, the suspicion that, whatever the upcoming crisis, he would not have it in him. How it had formed and deformed his life.

I know that some of this is bullshit. But, out of respect for the way he is trying to get close to me again, I keep my mouth shut.

"You remember?"

"Sure, Jon."

"Lap and a half. Christ. I have never forgiven myself. Not in all these years. You still swim sometimes, huh?"

He waits in the dark now—for something. I search inside to give it. Find it missing. Know that he is lost, and the hour too late; I cannot save him. Queer, straight, both dealt the same damage. One of us survived. Who would have thought, looking back, that I'd be the one?

"Josie?"

"What, love?"

"Before I hurt her, I'll kill myself."

Is it my imagination, or does something inside him, some last vestige of brilliance and of love, surge up, break apart? It's shining between us now, a little ball of fire, anger, compassion. Final shreds of sanity he has used to fight his pain. It will burn itself out quickly, in the night. Before it does, though, he will use it, ride it. Offer it to me as a gift. I see this all quite clearly. Watch him see it, too. Maddy's right: he's the ticking bomb, waiting to explode. At the same time, he knows what I know. But the last great wish is love.

"Win!" he sobs. Then: "Wine! And women!"

My doomed brother ducks under and surfaces, breathing air so hot it must feel like fire on his tongue. Then he turns away from me as I sit cross-legged there in the damp and dark, faces the night-obscured far-off end. Maybe, I think, he can feel me grin. Two hundred long ones. In that second we are part of the same flesh and blood again. And both of us know, too, just what it is he'll do—now, right here; and later.

"I love you, Jon."

But he's silent. Beyond all that now, and waiting for permission. I cry inside. I let him go.

"Okay, sweetheart. Swim."

Butterfly.

He takes the last breath of the world. Dives under with all his dangerous male might, dolphins perfectly, surfaces, feet together, big kick baby kick, arms and shoulders spanning the dark wet like a terrible vast-winged bird.

TATTOO

Carla Tomaso

"Hurry up," Eleanor shouts at my bedroom window. She is outside loading the car and I am taking my time fixing my hair which is thin and needs a lot of work. Ten minutes before this the zipper on my pants broke so I had to start all over again getting dressed, which meant I had to repack my suitcase as well. Not a good omen, any of this, for beginning a two-week vacation with someone you've never travelled with before. I glance once around my bedroom with exaggerated nostalgia as if this is the last time I'll ever see it. Then I begin to wonder why I go anywhere. I'm anxious for a week before the departure date, it takes me four days to adjust to the new place, and when I get home I invariably get sick.

But Eleanor is standing in my doorway now, smoking a cigarette. She is short with a round freckled face and lavishly curly gray hair. She is not afraid of anything. She has been married three times and has a tattoo on her wrist that she got on her last vacation. Supposedly it didn't hurt. It's of a butterfly because she's a Gemini, Eleanor has explained, and Geminis ride the breeze. I take that to mean that she doesn't stay with any one thing too long. She had it put on her wrist so she can cover it with the face of her watch when she's at work (she's an ophthalmologist not far from the university where I'm in administration). We met at a meeting of Adventuring Women, a group that organizes outdoor vacations for women who, for whatever reason, don't want to be with men. Eleanor's reason is that she is sick of them.

"Now hurry up, Nikki, or we'll hit the commuter traffic," she says. I'm moving slower than usual because it's so early in the morning and Eleanor is making me nervous.

"The zipper on my pants broke," I say. "Maybe we shouldn't go." As soon as I say it, I want to take it back. Eleanor's mouth twitches, just slightly, but enough to let me see I've hurt her feelings. "Oh, you know how neurotic I am," I tell her. "Don't pay attention to anything I say." I hate to belittle myself just to make Eleanor feel better, but it seems easier than telling her the truth, which is that I'm scared to spend a whole two weeks alone with her. We have a pretty nice friendship as it is; we talk on the phone once a week and take long walks in the mountains on weekends when it isn't rainy. Why push it? Spending a lot of time together is only asking for trouble. I'm a lesbian and she's not, so there's no romance, thank God. And no judgements either. She once said to me, "I envy you. Going to bed with a man is just plain stupid."

"Carry this, would you?" I say and hand Eleanor the Sportsac garment bag I bought for the trip. We're taking her car, a comfortable but small gray Toyota, so I've had to decide carefully what I'll need. I hand her the bag but I don't let go when she tries to take it. I stare into her green eyes for a couple of seconds. I notice for the first time that her left eye seems to be more brown than green and I wonder crazily if this asymmetry is what caused her to go into ophthalmology. She returns the look but then realizes her cigarette is burning her fingers and turns to find an ashtray.

"What the hell is wrong with you today?" she says, finally just grabbing the bag from me. "You having your period? I hope not. It's a mess bleeding on a vacation with hotel sheets and gas stations. I'm glad I'm through with all that shit." She walks downstairs to her car with my bag over her shoulder. The bottom hangs practically to the ground.

Everything in my bedroom except for a pair of sheepskin slippers is put away. I decide to leave them out so I can think of them, while we're hundreds of miles up the coast, waiting for me to come home. I walk downstairs and check all the doors and then go outside where Eleanor has just finished packing the trunk.

"You want me to drive?" I say as she puts my suitcase in the backseat. "Wait. You like to drive, don't you?"

"Yeah," Eleanor says, getting into the driver's seat. I climb into the other side and put my seat belt on.

"Should I run back in the house and get some apples or water?" I ask her. "I didn't even think of it."

She starts the motor. "Don't worry about it," she says. I can see the butterfly on her wrist because she's not wearing her watch today.

"It hasn't faded at all," I say. The wings are bluish green and the body is red, outlined in black. It really looks like it belongs there, like it's a miraculous freak of pigmentation, not something put on with a needle.

"You ought to get one," she says. "A crescent moon, maybe or a scorpion. That's what you are, right?"

"What?" I say.

"Sign of the zodiac," she says. She speeds up to get through the yellow light and I push down the floorboard with both feet.

"Yeah, November," I say. "I'm supposed to be sexy and vindictive. Fiercely demanding of loyalty."

"Where'd you find all that out?" she asks, like it's funny I should know that stuff.

"Somebody gave me a birthday card with it written on the inside," I say. Actually I'm pretty interested in astrology and I like being a Scorpio, even though I think I act more like a Libra.

"We couldn't be worse for each other," Eleanor says, laughing. "This vacation we're going to get you tattooed." The way she says it makes me feel like a head of range cattle. "You're going to come back from this vacation with a beautiful work of art on your butt," she says.

"Why my butt?" I say. All I can think of is the time my mother got me vaccinated and it hurt so much I didn't speak to her for three days afterwards.

"Why not?" Eleanor says merging neatly into the slow lane of traffic. "It's as good a place as any and it doesn't show, unless. . . ," she looks at me and winks. I think it's kind of mean to bring that up when she knows for a fact that it's been two full years since I've been to bed with anybody.

"But it's so permanent," I say. I'd heard they could take off tattoos but I knew the outline would still be there no matter what they did. "What if I change my mind later?" I can't imagine anyone wanting to tamper with their body. It's like saying you're God.

Eleanor runs her butterfly hand through her curly hair. "I think you should get a crescent moon with a little star in the concave part," she says, finally. "That fits you just right."

Eleanor drives as if we are in a tremendous hurry and after a couple of hours of strained reminiscences about terrible family vacations we stop at an ARCO for a fill-up and the bathroom. Eleanor buys an Almond Joy and I get a soft ice cream cone even though it's only ten o'clock in the morning. Then we get back in the car and start driving again. I begin to feel better about going on vacation. I pretend we're on our way to take a spring hike.

We talk about this woman, Roberta, whom we knew from our first Adventuring Women canoe trip. The thing about her is that she just married a man and on the canoe trip she was so homesick for a woman that the leader had to canoe her seven hours back to the parking lot where she had left our cars. Eleanor thinks it's a lot weirder than I do, but that's probably because she's so off men at the moment. I almost ask Eleanor if she's ever had any homosexual inclinations, but I decide we're on a vacation together for two weeks and why get into that?

At about noon we pass an old tourist attraction I remember driving by when I was a kid and we were going on vacation. It was a family-type restaurant, as I recall, and in front there was a recreation area for kids with slides that ran through the bodies of giant fiberglass animals. Sort of like a MacDonald's but bigger. For example, if you climbed up the elephant's back, you entered the slide at its head and shot out through the trunk. All that's left is an empty lot with a two-story gray/green dinosaur standing in the middle. Part of the dinosaur's skin has fallen off and I can see the wooden framing inside. Before I think to tell Eleanor we've sped past it. She's going seventy-five.

Finally Eleanor takes us to a truck stop restaurant. Without warning she just pulls off the highway and into the parking lot like that was our exact destination all along. It is four thirty in the afternoon and we're only an hour or so from the cabin we've rented on the edge of the Pacific Ocean. "I'm sick of driving," she says, "and I want some onion rings." We climb out of the car and stretch our backs. Eleanor lights her second cigarette of the day. She always seems to know what she wants which probably made it both easy and hard on all her husbands. I admire her for it. I hardly ever know what I want; all the possibilities have so many sides.

"You've been very nice about not smoking," I say. I put my arm around her and we walk into the restaurant. There's a good solid feel to her and because she's about three inches shorter than I am, it's a little like she's holding me up.

"I don't notice so much when I'm driving," she says, dragging deeply.

We sit down at a booth next to the window and order cokes and onion rings and just as the waitress is walking away, repeating our order to herself as she finishes jotting it down, Eleanor calls to her, "Make that to go, would you?" The waitress, a large woman with jet-black hair the color of a piano stool, turns around and glares at us. The management has dressed her in a pink fifties waitress uniform that hits above her dimpled knees and makes her look like a joke. I think she is worried about her tip but when Eleanor smacks down two dollars, she seems satisfied and takes our order to the kitchen.

"I don't like this place," Eleanor says. "Too many men." I look around for the first time and notice about a dozen men, a couple at tables talking, but most of them solemnly smoking and drinking coffee at the counter, not even looking our way.

"Oh come on," I say to her. "Nobody gives a shit. Please let's stay in here. I'm just beginning to get over the sensation that we're still moving."

"I suppose you like the artwork," Eleanor says, lighting another cigarette. She points at the wall where a blonde dressed in a black bikini two sizes too small for her is drinking water from a garden hose. The cashier, a small, dark-haired woman, is ringing up a paunchy truck driver directly beneath the woman's rear end. "How would you like to be strung up like that, like so much meat?" she says.

"Of course I don't like it," I say, "but I'm on vacation and I don't want to get all worked up about every little sexist thing we run into." I lean back on the bench and feel proud of myself for saying exactly what I want to. I'd gone through a period of feminist rage a couple of years before and now, probably because of exhaustion, I've trained myself to look straight through the billboards, and magazine ads and everything else, like they're all just so much stale air.

"Little sexist thing!" Eleanor shouts. "Let's leave," she says and begins to stand up.

"No," I say, "please." I must be giving her just the right look because she stamps out her cigarette and then walks over and says something to the waitress. "Thanks," I say when she sits back down.

"Want to play a game?" she says. "Want to see how long it takes one of these assholes to get up and come over here and try to join us?"

"That won't happen, Eleanor," I say. "Everybody's tired. It's five o'clock on a Monday afternoon and all anybody can think about is getting home."

"They're thinking about sex and trashing women, take my word for it." She taps the table a few times with her index finger for emphasis.

"I hate the way you do that," I say.

"I've been around a lot longer than you and I've known a lot more men." She pauses. "And they're all the same."

"So what's it matter how many I've known if they're all the same?" I say. At this moment, the waitress returns with our onion rings and two glasses of water.

"You decided to stay," she says. "Good idea. The Interstate gets real bad at this hour. Last night on top of everything else somebody's car flipped over and burned up. We were stuck for ninety minutes without moving and I'm claustrophobic." She takes a bottle of ketchup out of her apron pocket and puts it next to the onion rings.

Eleanor bites into an onion ring and I begin to think about how you never know what people are going to come up with to be crazy about. Here is this perfectly normal looking waitress who hates closed-in spaces. "So what did you do," I ask her, "about the traffic jam?"

"Oh, I just got out of the car and walked around it a few times," she says. "It helped that I knew I wasn't really trapped. I mean I could of just left the car there and run down the off ramp any time I felt like it."

And Eleanor with her thing about men. And me with my . . . what? My phobia about being with anybody for more than a few hours at a time?

The waitress leaves and Eleanor pushes the plate of onion rings at me. She has already made quite a dent. "What are you thinking about?" she asks me.

"My parents," I say.

"Oh," she says. "Forget it." I take an onion ring from the plate and curve it through the little mound of ketchup Eleanor's put on the side. "I thought you might be homesick," she says, real seriously. I can't tell if she's making fun of me or not so I let it go. The truth is just at this moment I am missing my two cats who are probably staring squinty-eyed out of their cages at the cat hotel where I took them last night. I'd tried to tell the night manager their personalities but she looked so bored I just sort of trailed off and left the phone number of our cabin.

"She didn't bring our cokes," Eleanor says.

"I'll catch her eye," I say, for some reason feeling responsible. I turn around to see where the waitress is and I notice that the man three booths behind us is staring in our direction. Because there's nobody in the booths between us, he sees me looking and glances down at his plate. The top of his head is bald in a perfect circle about the circumference of an English muffin. I think of a target. "I don't see her anywhere," I say. "Just drink the water for now. She's bound to come over this way soon."

Eleanor is nervous about getting the cokes, as if she's worried about losing money on them or something. She smokes a cigarette with one hand and eats an onion ring with the other. I can tell she's not thinking about anything except where are those cokes.

"These are good," I say, biting into another onion ring. The batter is light and crispy and the onion tastes sweet.

"People write guidebooks about the best dinner food to buy on vacation," Eleanor says, looking over to the cash register to see if the waitress is there. Then she puts her cigarette out.

"You on vacation?" a voice says. The balding man has suddenly appeared at the end of our table.

"No," Eleanor says, not even looking up. It's as if she sensed that he was on his way over. There is a silence. The man is trying to size us up. Not in a mean or sly way, but just as if he should ask something else or go. Finally he smiles at Eleanor.

"Yes you are," he says. "I heard you talking about vacations as I was passing by. I'm on vacation too."

"She lives a couple of miles south of here and I live a couple of miles north. We meet once a week for onion rings half way in between," Eleanor says. Now she's looking at him with her jaws clamped together tight.

The man continues smiling at both of us. He has lovely large white teeth. He's wearing a light blue cashmere pullover and gray corduroy slacks and he reminds me of a guest conductor or a psychiatrist, definitely not a masher. I can't understand why Eleanor's putting us through this.

"That was really an untruth," she says, straight at his white teeth, "intended to blow you away. We have all the company we need."

"I'm sorry," the man says. "I was just on my way to pay the bill and I heard 'vacation' so I thought we might exchange notes. I'm heading north to escape the smog for a month."

Suddenly the waitress comes up behind him, smiling, as if she's terrifically pleased to find him there. She has the cokes. "I forgot your cokes," she says, moving around him so she can put them on the table in front of us. "Am I too late?" she says.

"Yes," Eleanor says and nods at the plate of onion rings which is empty.

"Are you joining them?" the waitress says to the man. "You want her coke?" and she puts one coke in front of my place and one to my right where he would be sitting. Then she puts the bill on the table. "Tell the cashier to take the cokes off the bill if you don't want them," she says and goes to check on another table.

"We're leaving now," Eleanor says, standing up.

"Of course," the man says. "I'm Don Peterson." He walks with us to the cash register. I stand to the side while Eleanor pays. I notice that she doesn't tell the cashier to take the cokes off the bill. "People always say that diners have the best food," Don says, waiting to pay behind Eleanor. "Somebody even wrote a guide-book about it."

I begin to feel sorry for Don Peterson and ashamed of Eleanor for treating him so badly. I begin to think that there's something wrong with me for being her friend. "Sounds lonely," I say to him, out of the blue, and he looks at me as if he doesn't remember who I am.

"What?" he says. Eleanor glares at me fiercely but I can't stop now.

"Going up north by yourself, to get out of the smog."

"It's what I want to do," he says, and leaves it at that.

Don Peterson has a convertible Mercedes and it is parked next to Eleanor's Toyota. "My one extravagance," he says, patting the door. "I've always hated the heavy libidinal thing Americans have for their cars but it's heaven to drive." Then he gets in, backs it out and waves at us. "Have a nice vacation," he shouts out the window as if nothing has happened, as if he just had a delightful talk with two women he'd never met before. We get in Eleanor's car and follow him out onto the surface road.

Eleanor is driving much slower than she was before we stopped. She merges into the middle lane of the freeway and stays there. Don Peterson's Mercedes is about five cars in front of us. "Men think we should be grateful for the interruption," she says. I look straight ahead. A huge bug splatters its guts on the windshield just my side of center. I stare at the yellow and red goo. Eleanor doesn't talk for a while which is just as well because I can't seem to decide how I feel about anything.

Finally I look over toward Eleanor and it's like she's punched me in the throat because she's crying. Not hard but just enough that the tears are falling down her cheek and landing on her blue cotton shirt. I look away and stare at the squashed bug on the windshield, wondering what the hell I should should say. I've never seen her cry before.

From the right, a four-wheel drive jeep, license plate TOUGH, cuts in front of us. I shout "Watch out!" just in time and Eleanor slams on the brakes.

"Jesus," she says. "The waitress was sure right about the traffic."

"Eleanor," I say.

"What?" she says. She's stopped crying but there are still little puddles of tears caught under her eyes. "You want to change your tampax? I did sort of rush out of the restaurant fast."

"No," I say. "Actually I don't even have my period."

"I thought you said you did." she says. "I've been under that impression all day."

"I've decided to get the tattoo," I say.

"Hot damn," she says. "If we go down to the boardwalk right when we get into town, it'll have time to heal while we're still up here. We'll buy some Vaseline at the drugstore."

"But you got yours someplace else," I say, trying to remember where she went for vacation last year.

"That's ok," she says. "These places have to be licensed. Besides, I'll check out the equipment, to see that it's sterile and all that. I won't let anything bad happen to you."

She turns toward me for a moment and one of the old tears slips down her cheek. She wipes it off with the back of her hand and smiles.

Suddenly I feel dangerously euphoric. The sensation sweeps over me that from now on all the messes in my life are going to be just as easy to fix as this one. I say, "Well, get going," and without any hesitation she merges into the fast lane and all of a sudden, at seventy-five miles an hour, we're flying past everybody on the road.

DREAMING BIRTH

Linsey Abrams

"Things look at us as we look at them.
They seem indifferent to us only because we look
at them with indifference. But to a clear eye all things
are mirrors, and to a sincere and serious eye
everything is depth."

—GASTON BACHELARD

"Will you help me vacuum?" my mother asks one Saturday morning after breakfast.

"All right," I say, grumbling about my status as assistant housekeeper. We pull the Hoover out of the hall closet, and my mother walks first into the living room while I drag it behind.

"What's this?" she says, bending over to pick up a piece of paper from the floor. It is folded. It has her name on it. "I wonder what it is?" she says again, curious.

"It's probably a note from Daddy," I say. "Telling us where he is this morning." As she unfolds it, I plug in the cord, turning to ask. . . . Ashen, she hands me the piece of paper. And her hands to her stomach, my mother suddenly vomits in the center of the rug.

*   *   *

My father's a man you can have faith in. Even my mother goes to him when she needs advice, though, if possible, she likes to come to her own conclusions. In bed at night, a performer of mental gymnastics, my father seeks to outwit any problem my mother might mention. He thinks about it deeply, picks it up like a barbell, turns it around in his mind, hoping to raise it above his head with the straight arm of solution.

Today, as it happens, just when we could use his muscular shoulder to lean on, he's not here. The weightlifter is out of town. Still, he calls the hospital every half hour from phone booths. He has twenty dollars' worth of quarters and dimes in his suit jacket pocket, which makes it bulge.

Any news? he asks the floor nurse.

Your wife is still in labor, she answers. It will be at least another several hours.

All right. I'll call back, he says, and he hangs up.

My father's apprentice, I lay out the facts for myself like a set of weights. This is what I know about the birth canal: others are excavated, dug out (the Panama, the Suez . . .); this grows itself hollow from the inside out. The atmosphere here is the gray foam of clouds. This is the dark and tubular cylinder of a gun barrel, and I'm the bullet waiting for my mother's trigger finger. My head in readiness, my mother cocked for birth.

My heart beats to her contractions. I snap my fingers to her pulse. Her muscles are the straitjacket I wear; she encases me like a tunnel with light at the end. I want to see this light, and my head will lead me: cue ball of my opening shot, football helmet of my first forward rush. Bald round planet in search of a halo. But what, exactly, are all these things? I wish my father would call back and tell me how to be born.

(My father lay next to us in bed.

What if there's something wrong with it? he asked.

I kicked him through my mother's belly.

Warren, my mother told him, the doctor says everything is fine.

I mean what if it has only one arm? he said.)

If these are my arms, I have two. I have ten toes. Is this too many?

More facts: I'm going to hear jazz. I'm going to taste martinis. I'm going to make love. . . . I'm going to watch plants go dancing.

I'm going to listen to a time bomb tick. When? I'm exhausted, dispirited.

Speculations: If my mother has given up hope, false alarm, she'll say. It's clear that Angela has decided against being born after all. . . . But this isn't true. I'm getting anxious. I do a flip to try to calm myself.

And what if our doctor is incompetent or a drug addict, even, hooked on his own prescriptions? Or what if he's not here yet? They'll have to send a caddy out to the ninth hole at top speed, ducking golf balls as he runs. If the doctor makes it to the hospital in time, perhaps it's we who are late, speeding through traffic in an ambulance at full siren or stopped for a red light in my grandfather's Packard.

What, if by a miracle, the birth is successful, and in a case of mistaken identity, the nurse delivers me into the arms of the wrong woman on the morning she's to leave the hospital for home? Her milk will taste like brine; I'll refuse to drink and grow weak. Neighbors will speak of her bad habits. She'll figure in her husband's nightmares. My own mother wears dresses in the latest styles; she makes them herself on the Singer. Sailors whistle at her in the street. She and my father will jitterbug until almost sunrise just five nights after our return from the hospital. But what if they've claimed someone else instead? Surely my father will recognize me first and set the nurses straight.

Into the nursery he'll stride, in search of his daughter. He'll thread his way through row upon row of babies, like a farmer in the field looking for a particular hybrid he has invented himself. Perhaps he'll tire slightly because there is something happening during this time called the baby boom and not a single crib is empty. But he'll persevere, and when he arrives at my side, This is Angela, he'll say.

(Ros, do you want a boy or a girl? my father asked.

I have no preference, said my mother. But perhaps a girl would be nice. To go with Benjie.

When they grow up, we can do all sorts of things together, he said.

We'll have a foursome for bridge, she replied. We can play mixed doubles.

A child in the arts, a child in the sciences. You can take her to the ladies' room. I'll take him to the men's. . . .

It will be so convenient, said my mother. But what if it's not a girl . . . if it's Arthur instead, after my father?

Then we'll put a wig on him, my father said.)

Arthur. In a long horse's mane. How I rode him like a jockey down the final stretch, outdistancing all the other possible contenders one by one, until just before the finish line when I rose in the saddle, leapt from his back, and hurled myself before him over the wire. How we set off for my mother's affections in two identical, gassed-up cars, just after my father's single sperm found its mark, how I altered Arthur's road map imperceptibly, gave him false directions at the genital junction of the legs and sent him off. To where? Arthur behind my ears, Arthur under my fingernails, Arthur in the tiny cracks between my toes. Still, I'm the luck of the draw, and my mother will know it's me.

Suddenly I'm jingling like the change in my father's jacket. I'm the coin seeking to escape my mother's pocket. I'm tumbling falling doing somersaults reversing my direction with a twist of the hips. I'm an expert diver, slowing my descent. I'll make her wait a second longer how she'll hold her breath how she'll wonder if ever I'm coming. Is this a child, she'll ask herself, who will never be born? Sinking. Swimming. Pirouetting. Leaping down her . . .

I'm on my way, I shout. The walls of her vagina muffle the sound. Can she hear me? My mother awaits me; she anticipates my arrival; she's received the message of my kicks and spins. I'm shooting down her, my mother like a slide, and when I reach midair, a cork shot from the popgun of her thighs, I'll find her.

I'm wearing my mother's cervix like a hat, like a pair of eyeglasses, like a belt, like an anklet. Now the anklet is the doctor's hand; his hand is the hook I dangle from, bait for my own life, target for the slap that inflates me like a tire. Breathing is like speeding. My mother's eyes are the green lights, her two arms the tender roadblock of the criminal who longs to be caught. "Angela," she whispers. Red and wet with blood, I rest my cheek on her breast.

Waking up is knowing that you have been asleep. I sleep much more than the average person, the one who wakes early to a stomach of worries. It's time to sleep again when the mother sings. All my mother's melodies sound the same, but the lyrics are varied: "Don't sit under the apple tree with anyone else but me. . . ." "Oh it's a long, long way to Tipperary. . . ." "Speed bonnie boat like a bird on the wind. . . ."

When my father joins in, I sometimes hear harmony, but after a few bars my mother always changes to his tune.

"Baby," he says. "Can't you stay on key?"

"No, I can't," says my mother, "but, after all, you didn't marry me for my singing voice."

"I sure didn't," he says, and he puts his two hands on the sides of her head and gently combs through her curly, thick hair with his fingers. This is affection. Then he kisses her on the lips. This is affection, too.

They blow me kisses from the doorway. Kisses are in the air. The light's extinguished with a quick flick of my father's finger. Kisses are lurking in the dark.

Soon sleep will cover me like a mask, and if you remember what it has been like to be asleep, this means you've been dreaming. My dreams are a saga; the mask is always changing its features, transforming itself through a lineage of faces. I've dreamt my family from the first kiss.

Today, all day, I've been dreaming about my grandmother's wedding, about the train trip she took with my grandfather to California for their honeymoon. She can't get over how here the sun *sets* on the ocean. . . . About how they stopped off in Mexico City, to visit their friends Patrick and Llewelyn at the embassy, which is where they bought the silver brooch. I've dreamt through 1926; my mother has just been born. My grandmother says the brooch will be her daughter's marriage gift.

My grandfather is a Methodist. He doesn't smoke or drink, and while he passed out no cigars after the delivery, this is not to say that he wasn't pleased. My grandmother is weak from childbearing. She lies in bed under a flowery, hand-sewn quilt and realizes that she must have no other children. The doctor has told her so.

The dream continues and the mask's hue changes; my mother is a blue baby. When she grows up, her favorite color will be blue to remind her how narrowly she escaped an early and tragic death.

The next week a pair of movers came into the bedroom and took away the big mahogany bed, replacing it with twins, light, the moving men said, as feathers. But the two beds weighed on my grandfather's mind.

During her convalescence, my mother's mother passed the time quilting an identical cover to the one she had made for her nuptial bed and a miniature copy to adorn the crib of her daughter. For a year or more, the three of them slept side by side by side in the close bedroom of their familial circumstance.

Once my grandfather rolled over to face his wife and daughter, his bed was on the end, nearest the door, lest a burglar might enter. He got up in his bare feet then and stood above my grandmother's bed until she opened her eyes.

Do you think? he asked.

No, said my grandmother, but she threw back the marriage quilt and moved over for his body beside hers. He kissed her on the throat and slept the whole night through with his arms about her waist. He dreams of the long, full skirts of his youth, of the parasols and hats trimmed with bright ribbon bands. He sees her in her high school bloomers, captain of the girls' marching team:

I've set my cap for you, he told her one night.

And what a nice cap it is, said my grandmother, who was shy in receiving compliments, and while he traveled to St. Louis and Cleveland, selling soap powders and pastes, she finished high school and started playing the piano for the church. She gave recitals; she taught young girls their scales; she accompanied opera singers in Boston. When later her daughter turned out to have no ear for music, she was disappointed, but by that time she had grown older and realized that there were fewer things to sing about than when she had been young.

In her twenty-seventh year, she received a letter from Chicago, return address the YMCA where her husband-to-be had taken up residence almost a year before.

Dear Viola [she read],

Chicago is windy and colder than Alaska this time of year, and I think it's about to freeze me solid. I need a new overcoat to replace the one I came out here with. Would you order me one at Sweeney's? Same

size. Only don't have it sent because I'll be there to pick it up on
December 15th. I'm coming home for Christmas and for good. I'd be the
warmest guy in town if you'll marry me in the spring.

Yours,
Art

In the return mail, she sent him a letter with a single word
printed at the top of the page. Then she sat down at her piano
and wrote a song. The lyric was simple:

> *Yes, yes, yes. [she sang]*
> *Yes I will marry you.*
> *I have waited.*
> *I never dated other beaus.*
> *Now I'm slated*
> *To be mated to the one I chose*
> *Long ago.*
> *Yes, yes, yes.*
> *Yes I will marry you.*

The musical composition was intricate. She repeated the lyric
over and over, using it backwards, arranging it in counterpoint,
deleting every other word, interpreting it in all the different ways
she could think of; she made a sort of chorus of the yeses, and
every bridge was a yes, yes, yes.

That night she took from the trapdoor of the piano bench every
sheet of music it held. She played each one through and all the
rest she knew by heart, not skipping one movement, one verse,
one repeat. She played feverishly to an empty house, and her
performance was flawless. When she finished, for a single moment
she made the keyboard her pillow, and anyone entering the room
just then would not have heard the few quick sobs beneath the
jarring chord her forehead had played. She shut the piano then,
turned off all the lights, and went up to bed.

My brother has learned to burp. He has added burping to his
repertoire of noises.

"Stop burping, Benjie," says my father. To my mother he says,

"Not a word out of him yet, but he can make every sound in the book. He'll probably grow up to have an enormous vocabulary."

The dog is eating the chocolate cake. From my high chair I spy the dog eating the chocolate cake. From my crow's nest, the dog out in the sea of the kitchen is eating our dessert.

"Damn," says my mother as she runs to the clatter from the dining room. "Shotsy," she cries. "No." The dog scampers on her short legs back through the dining room, her dachshund snout camouflaged in chocolate frosting. But it's a poor disguise; the ruse doesn't work. Daddy chases the dog and puts her out the back door. Daddy has an eye for camouflage.

Here behind the curtains of my eyelids, my mother has imagined it a changing room, having shed her smocked dress, her wool skirt with the matching V-neck sweater, her black cap and gown for a suit. My mother has grown up.

On the lapel of her suit is pinned a small beige button. Yellow is for basic security clearance; gray is for the next level up, permitting access to more important documents and otherwise restricted areas of the building; green is for selected congressmen and policy advisers. But sporting a beige button, there's nowhere you can't go, no information you can't be privy to. Beige is for the President, the battle strategists, the Ph.D. specialists, and, of course, the generals who even in peacetime bustle in and out of the Pentagon. My mother's color is beige. My mother can be trusted with secrets.

Beige is also the color of Gwen's uniform. Gwen is my mother's roommate in Washington. Gwen is a marine.

So what's going on, Roslyn? she asks over dinner. They don't tell the enlisted man anything. . . .

Sorry, says my mother. She knows that although Gwen has a claim to beige, she is not top-secret beige. The truth is, Gwen, I'll have to go to the grave with what I know, some of it.

That's sort of romantic, isn't it?

Yes, says my mother, who in spite of her commitment to her country and the war effort is a young woman at the time, too.

Well, what if somebody got you drunk? asks Gwen. And tried to pry information out of you? A spy or someone. In the throes of love . . . They find this funny.

I'd never marry a spy though, says my mother. She sighs. Marriage is on her mind.

(Will you wait for me? the sailor asked her in the dream yesterday. He held her close with one hand; the other held his white hat. I mean, will you not say yes to anyone else until you talk to me first? He chuckled. I wish you weren't so popular, he said.

But his gray eyes reminded her of two portholes looking out on fog, and she started to cry; she buried her face in his shirt; she saw torpedoes coming through the portholes, silver invitations for the whole ocean to follow inside, to in turn swallow up the tiny ship that had swallowed it down, gulp after gulp. She looked up. His shirt was all wet. I will, she said.)

By the way, says Gwen. I met some handsome marines today. Two. Really? says my mother.

They're at Cherry Point, says Gwen, in training. But they fly in once a month. They have our number.

Of the two marines, who do call, my mother likes best the one who is my father. He tells her what it is like to be an airplane navigator. We have a complicated instrument panel, he says. But if it fails I know how to chart by the stars. I'll tell you a secret, he says: I often fly the President himself.

He explains to her all the particulars of his work. My mother, because she is good at hers, doesn't tell him anything.

If only I could go overseas, he says. Besides, on the tests, I'm particularly good at sighting enemy positions from the sky, especially those that are heavily camouflaged. My mother is glad that he's not overseas. My mother, the keeper of secrets, tries to disguise this. But the camouflage expert, he sees right through her.

Rub-a-dub-dub, three men in a tub: Benjie and I, mum in the middle. She holds me upright. "Just like a convoy," says my mother. "Want to do the dead man's float?" she asks Benjie. He tickles her back, lowers his face into the water, and blows.

I'm an only child, my father said on his next trip.

So am I, said my mother.

I was born in Savannah and both my parents are dead, he told her. When I was twelve, my mother expressed the desire to move from the farm where we lived, so my father set her up in a house in town, and he and I stayed on at the farm. But I visited her often. It was a quick train ride.

My father owns a soap company, my mother told him. My mother was once a pianist. I graduated from Bryn Mawr last year and I'm twenty-two years old.

I'm twenty-seven years old, he said. I went to college for one year when lack of money prevented me from continuing. I was going to be an engineer.

I'm going to be a lawyer when the war is over, she said, if they start accepting women at law schools.

My mother was very well educated, he replied. When I had to leave school she was especially disappointed. My father, on the other hand, figured I could do it the way he had. He told me I could jolly well teach myself. My father would often sit with a bottle of whiskey until sunrise, reading, when he'd get up from the chair, change his clothes (he was a very particular dresser), and head off for the railway office where he worked.

My father doesn't drink at all, she said. We're Methodists.

I'm an agnostic, he told her, and I've been in barrooms all over the world. When I was twenty, when I left school, I became foreman in a cotton mill. And there was nowhere to go from there, no possible promotion, so I packed my things and went to sea. I shipped out. When you're in port, all you do is drink. . . .

I'm fluent in French, said my mother. I was a government major, and great literature makes me weep.

I cried for the first time, he told her, when I received word of my mother's death. We were docked in New Orleans, lucky thing for me, so I just followed the rails to my father's office, and we buried her together. When he died, I packed up his personal effects, sold the rest, and withdrew the hundred dollars that was in his bank account. It was cancer that got her. And he drank himself to death. I would ask you to marry me, he said, only I'm married already and I have a son.

And I'm engaged, said my mother. To someone overseas.

This is how they fell in love, and as it was already eight o'clock in the morning, my father put on his cap and left.

When he arrived at the base to report for duty, he sent his wife, whom he hadn't seen for several months, a telegram (asking for a divorce), which my mother received later that day (the words

were different but the message was the same) as notification from
the war office of her fiancé's death at sea. As she lay awake that
night, she reread all the sailor's letters and invented what their
life together might have been like. My father, in his bunk, willfully
recollected the two years of his marriage.

My grandmother and grandfather are peering over the railing
of my crib. Smiles and waves like a bon voyage from a cruise ship
deck. My grandfather has a package. He's unwrapping it. Is it
for me?

"See how pretty she looks in it," says my grandmother. "It kept
pretty well, didn't it, Arthur?"

"That it did. That it did," says my grandfather, tucking it under
my chin.

"It kept pretty well. Just like us," she says and shakes her head.
"Did you remember the other present?" He nods and I shut my
eyes for sleep.

"I wonder if we should have waited for some appropriate occasion," I hear him say.

I'm getting married, my mother told first her father, then her
mother, when she called from Washington. She has had trouble
getting through; all the circuits are busy. The war is over. Today,
when the news was announced (although my mother knew a few
days before), a general picked her up in the street and twirled her
like a top, danced her around like a crazy waltz. And she kissed
him, although it's my father she plans to marry.

The bomb has been dropped on Hiroshima where the heat was
so intense it caused the flowers to bloom instantaneously, like the
ones on the quilt that covers me now. The war is over

To whom? asks my grandmother, thinking of the sailor drowned
in battle. She can't imagine who my mother might be marrying.

His name is Warren, he's southern, and he's a marine, says my
mother. And we're not getting married right now (she hesitates)
because he's in the middle of getting a divorce.

You bet you're not, says my grandmother, and she hangs up
the phone with a bang. This hurts my mother, who never, herself,
expected to get married under such circumstances.

My grandmother starts packing right away. My grandmother is planning a trip.

He's uneducated, she tells my grandfather after the letter arrives. He even has a child. We had such plans for Roslyn . . . and besides . . . She looks at him. We gave up everything for her.

I'm mad about you, says my father.

I dream about you, says my mother. When he's there, he spends the night on the couch because if, by mistake, he gets her pregnant and his divorce is delayed, they'll be in big trouble.

We'll be poor at first, he says. I've got to support my son.

When is your discharge? she asks.

In ninety-seven days. Will you marry me? he asks her again.

Yes, she says, as usual. They are always asking each other to get married. They propose to one another all through their engagement, waiting for the divorce. They're storing up yeses for the times ahead.

Will we always be in love? my mother asks.

Oh yes, says my father, gleaning another to store away against the future. He won't think about his first wife; he won't think about his parents' separation. He knows that being in love dictates that every proposal must be the first no matter how many times he asks her. It is the continuous present, a vacuum.

Will you marry me? he asks every day on the phone when he calls her up.

My grandmother has taken up residence in Mexico City with her friends Llewelyn and Patrick. She's been visiting for three months. She will not help with the marriage plans.

I'll come home on the day of the wedding, she tells her husband in a letter. My mother shops for her wedding dress, the invitations, alone. My grandfather sees to all the details of the reception.

Marriage. Ha, says my grandmother.

Some work and some don't, says Llewelyn. But the truth of it is, you never can tell at the beginning anyway. That's the time everything looks rosy.

At the reception, everyone is red in the face from drinking or dancing, or just because it's warm for June. My parents are having such a good time they don't leave their own wedding until three in the morning. My mother dons a new suit for their escape. Her fingers miss the beige button, searching her unadorned lapel while the rice pelts them.

I wake up in the same pose in which I left my mother in the dream, pausing on the stairs leading down from the reception hall. My hand is clutching the lapel of the flowered quilt my mother slept under as a baby. The silver brooch, which she never received, is in my fingers.

All in all, things are going smoothly, says my mother.

As smooth as my Uncle Clayton's whiskey, says my father. Home brew. Benjie is balanced in his lap. He's testing his son's reflexes: tickling his feet with a ball of cotton, holding a pocket watch to each of his ears to make sure he can hear the tick, waving different-colored swatches of material they're considering for the new couch cover in front of his eyes. He seems to like yellow best, says my father. What a kid. He picks up a textbook from the arm of the chair.

Want another? asks my mother. A second one?

Yes, he says.

I mean right now, says my mother. Right this minute.

You bet, baby, he says.

At my father's graduation from business school, he wears a cap and gown. In just a few months you'll be needing a style like this, he says, placing his hands on her slightly rounded belly.

I'll take it in any color other than black, says my mother.

Wait till my first raise, he says, and the next week he starts out as a management trainee in an electronics firm. The apartment will definitely be too small for a family of four, so the moving van is ordered and it drives out of the city to a small white house where the family of three awaits it.

Benjie learns to walk. At my father's thirtieth birthday party, the punch is so strong that two people pass out. One of them is my father. From joy, he says.

OLD SOULS

Carol Anshaw

July 1990
New York City

Jesse is standing at the cabinet in her carrel in the literature stacks, filing away notes on Flannery O'Connor for a book she's writing about the influence of illness on certain twentieth-century American writers. In this research phase she has become both mesmerized and profoundly depressed. There are times when she wishes she were writing instead on the influence of puppet shows on certain American writers, the influence of clowns tumbling out of small cars. Hurled cream pies.

These back stacks are among the few truly quiet places in Manhattan. They look out onto an ivy-clogged courtyard, a souvenir from another New York. The only sounds are internally generated ones—the occasional rustling of papers being gathered up, the soft thwack of book covers being shut, a constant fluorescent hum. But now there is a sudden rush of air, the sharp clank of a bangle bracelet hitting the shelves, followed by Kit sailing in breathless. Finding Jesse, she stops short, her elbows lofting a little as she slams out of forward, into neutral. She often arrives this way, as though she has been missing for years, shipwrecked and given up for gone, but now—astonishingly—here!

In fact, it has been less than three hours since they last saw each other. Jesse looks down. She doesn't like Kit to see how strongly she is affected by her; it seems a little absurd even to Jesse.

Anyone could walk back here, although it is summer and Friday and late in the afternoon, and so probably no one will. Still, Jesse feels the dead atmosphere of the room begin to crackle a little with risk as Kit presses her back against the jutting handles of the file drawers, tugs her shirt free, and runs her hands up Jesse's back and then around, tracing her breasts.

"I think," Jesse says when her mouth is freed up, "that if I get fired from a tenured position, I'd especially like for it to be on account of the morals clause."

Kit puts her hands behind Jesse and pulls her in.

"Maybe we'd better go home," Jesse says. "Start our vacation."

Kit nods, kind of hearing.

They walk on an angle through the Village. Kit gets stopped by a flurry of teenage girls. Jesse thinks, boy, teenage girls these days sure look like hookers. Then she notices one of them negotiating with a guy in a delivery van and realizes these girls *are* hookers. They are also fans of Kit, and want her autograph.

Kit is an actress of sorts. She plays Rhonda, the vampy intensive care nurse on a terrible hospital soap. Five days a week, she has to Rhonda around in an extra set of eyelashes and outfits that are as provocative as possible within the limitations of their also being white uniforms. Wardrobe has also worked up a sexy nurse's hat for her.

When she first came on the show, Rhonda was almost immediately given a juicy euthanasia subplot. She was accused of pulling the plug on an intensive care patient, an old guy who only days before he died, changed his will to generously include Rhonda. Since this story line was resolved, though (it turned out there had been an inadvertent mix-up in medication charts), for months all the scripts have let Rhonda do is lurk suspiciously around the medicine room, and vamp through her mirrored apartment in slinky hostess gowns and earrings that hit her shoulders, entertaining married doctors. Kit was worried they were going to write her character out entirely, but now she's gotten a break. Rhonda has shot the latest of the married doctors after he laughed at her ultimatum that he leave his wife.

This week, she has been busy scrubbing bloodstains out of her carpet, dragging the body out in the dead of night to the river, where, before pushing it over the bridge railing, she tied dumbells to its wrists and ankles. Without a corpse, Rhonda's guilt is going to be difficult to prove, and Kit figures she has at least several months more of employment while Rhonda acts coyly innocent in the face of strong suspicion. The show is taped two weeks in advance, so they can write her onto a back burner and she can slip away to Missouri tomorrow for a few days, and go home with Jesse.

While the teen hookers are pulling scraps of paper from their oversized purses, Jesse ducks into a small record shop and buys a tape for the trip. When she comes out, the girls are gone, but have been replaced by a middle-aged woman and her mother, trying to cajole plot revelations out of Kit—specifically whether Dr. Silva and Louise the hospital administrator are really the leaders of a satanic coven. Wordlessly and rudely—it's the only way—Jesse pulls Kit free and off up Christopher Street.

"Next time anybody asks me for an autograph," Kit says, "I'm going to say, 'Well, where's your autograph hound then? I only sign stuffed hounds and leg casts.'" Kit doesn't—can't, really—take her celebrity seriously; it's only based on a moderate-sized part in a daytime drama, and some commercials for a dandruff shampoo. If she's at all pretentious—and this takes a bit of wine and some prompting—it's about her aspirations, which hover in Meryl Streep range.

"I'm going to cook tonight, something special," she says now.

Jesse draws a fingernail across the inside of her own wrist, miming the opening of a crucial vein.

"Be nice," Kit says.

They kill each other with kindness in the kitchen. Both of them are deadly cooks. Jesse is bonded to her godmother's red plaid cookbook from the fifties. Everything she makes is baked for an hour at 325 and covered with white sauce and sometimes crushed potato chips, or molded in freezer trays and topped with mara-schino cherries.

Kit is of an opposite persuasion. "Civilization has advanced be-yond the plaid book," she says. She careens into the elaborate and exotic. Cuisines from the fourth world, the deepest folds of the

Himalayas. She shops in the darkest of ethnic groceries, rummages through the dusty cans on the back shelves, the inscrutable plastic-shrouded items lurking in the smoky depths of the freezer. She has involved, labored conversations with shop owners, then with their ancient mothers brought out from curtained back rooms. By this time, Kit is taking notes on check deposit slips, buying additional, amazingly authentic condiments.

The end result of these flurries goes like this: Jesse arrives home. The hallway of their building has a malevolent odor. She immediately worries that Mrs. Levine in the garden apartment—the oldest person Jesse has ever seen outside of those yogurt ads—has finally expired, and everyone has been too busy or self-absorbed to notice.

But the peculiar smell only gets stronger as she climbs toward her own apartment. Inside, the odor is almost visible. Several pots burble ominously on the stove.

"What is it?" Jesse will say, skipping past the pleasantries.

"Well . . . you like steak, don't you?" Kit will say in a desperately cheery voice.

"I like steaks when they come from cows," Jesse says. "Cows who, when they were alive, lived in America."

"Well, this is just the Burmese version."

"Kit. If there's lizard in any of those pots . . ."

At this point Kit's eyes begin to water up.

"Oh no," Jesse says, rushing over to hold her. "There really *is* lizard in one of those pots."

"But *only* one."

"Don't cook," Jesse says when they're inside the door. "It's way too hot. We'll go out."

Not right away, though. They fall onto the futon, pulling off some of their clothes, forgetting the rest.

A while later, Jesse asks Kit, "Are you about to come?"

Kit nods.

"Can you not?"

Kit laughs. "Maybe. Just."

Jesse stands and pulls Kit off the futon. "Come on. We'll be back. Later. Now though, you'll have something to think about during dinner." Jesse holds Kit in a light sexual thrall. Who knows how long it will last. And anyway, Jesse figures all the real power is on Kit's side of the equation.

When they get back, they drag the futon up onto the roof, near the washtubs of potting soil in which Jesse is cultivating an urban garden of hybrid tea roses. The petals, deep red in sunlight, now look black and give off a heavy night musk. Here, Jesse and Kit begin again, then sleep under the stars and above everyone's music. Then wake and watch the moon travel across the deep black sky.

The next morning, Jesse takes the mail key downstairs. It's only eight-thirty, but Carmen stands in her doorway like a lesser goddess of the demimonde, backed by dim lights and a thin haze of blue smoke. Lou Reed is on the stereo. Samuel, her boyfriend, is lounging on the sofa. He owns a few laundromats, which seem to spin and tumble along on their own. Jesse thinks Carmen and Samuel might be the ultimate party animals, that they could write their own weekly column for the *Voice*, just about what happens in their apartment.

Once Jesse went down to borrow a screwdriver, and Carmen and Samuel were starting the day with one of their panatela-size joints and offered Jesse a hit. Why not, she thought, and then lost the whole part of her life that happened between exhaling and finding herself at the checkout counter of the Korean mini-grocery down the street, having just bought three Hostess chocolate fried pies.

"You'll be back when?" Carmen says now.

"In a week. We're going to see my mother. In Missouri."

"Ah," says Carmen, closing her eyes and smiling dreamily. "The Show Me State."

It astonishes Jesse, the things people know.

Later, she's clipping a borrowed fuzz buster onto the visor of the rental car while a couple of teenagers, unasked, squeegee the already-clean windshield.

"No thanks," Jesse says to the palm sliding through the open window in front of her face.

"Man you shoulda said something *before* we did such a nice job for you."

"I'll leave you something in my will. It'll be like that gas station attendant and Howard Hughes."

Coming originally from a small town, Jesse is given to just the sorts of mildly witty comebacks that get people knifed in their hearts every day in this lower end of Manhattan. This time, though, the fates conspire kindly around her. Kit comes down the front steps and gets in the car just as a coplike vehicle rounds the corner (it turns out to be something bogus like environmental patrol), and the squeegee guys sulk over to the curb.

Jesse clicks her tape in as Kit pulls out. It's Springsteen's *Nebraska*. "Open All Night" comes up.

> *Fried chicken on the front seat*
> *She's sittin' on my lap.*
> *Both of us poppin' fingers*
> *On a Texaco road map.*

Kit smiles from deep inside the ethos of "trip." For a couple of weeks now, she has been expressing longing for "the road," and making statements like, "Living in New York is like living in an extremely interesting shoe box." And now she's R.T.G.—ready to go—in traveling clothes. Hawaiian-print bermudas and a T-shirt that says I EAT MY ROAD KILL. She has her blond hair gelled up and back into some kind of surfer retro. She looks like Jan, or Dean. "All *right!*" she says, pushing her shades up onto the bridge of her nose, shifting into third with just her fingertips as they ramp onto the interstate, pinky-tapping the turn signal as she glides across three lanes.

"Are you nervous? About bringing me?" she asks Jesse in southern Ohio. They're sitting across from each other in a big booth in a restaurant–truck wash along the highway. The restaurant part is the Home of the Dorisburger. Jesse is stretching her bent arm over her head, trying to pull out the kink inside her right shoulder blade, an old weak spot, a vestigial reminder of some punishment her body absorbed during its training days. She shakes her head in response to Kit's question, lying. She has no idea how she's going to mesh Kit with Missouri. Plus there is so much stuff that now seems necessary to explain.

"Don't go crazy with this," Kit says, seeing that Jesse is fretting. "Everybody always feels like their family scene is too weird to translate for someone in their present. You don't really need to tell me anything. I probably won't even see any of the bad stuff. Everyone'll be nice to me just because I'm with you. And I already think you're the most wonderful person in the world, so you don't have to worry about my opinion of you. It's locked in." She taps her heart with a forefinger.

"Still . . ."

"Okay," Kit says. "Go ahead and wrestle those old alligators of your past. But don't worry about me. They're your alligators, they won't bite me."

Every time Jesse comes back to Missouri, she tries to prepare herself, get the issues lined up, sorted out, internally addressed so she doesn't get ambushed by them when she's there. This, of course, never works. Once home, the same faulty systems kick in—everything out of whack and running full steam at the same time. She is almost immediately sucked into trying to impress her mother, and trying to dismiss her. Feeling far above and beyond New Jerusalem, and at the same time romanticizing it like crazy. Longing to be instantly away, and alternately to stay forever, spend her days with Hallie, move with her and William into a house with a wide porch on Broad Avenue.

"What's chicken-fried steak?" Kit says from behind a giant laminated menu. "Does it have chicken in it, or what?"

"Oh, honey," Jesse says, thinking of the week ahead.

Kit and Jesse have been together half a year. One night Jesse was supposed to have dinner with Leo Swift, who teaches all the Victorian courses in the department, and is far and away her favorite colleague. Leo is how she imagines the Bloomsbury boys were. Maynard Keynes. Saxon Sydney-Turner. He seems to her a true scholar. Always lit from within over a connection discovered, an influence discerned, always bearing down on a monograph deadline, pressing into the night as though the world will awaken the next morning in urgent need of coffee and literary criticism.

They share an office in the department's basement quarters, and often when Jesse arrives in the morning before a class, Leo's presence is still hanging around in the air. Peppery cologne, dry-cleaned wool, butterscotch. So she knows he's at most an hour or two gone.

One morning into the second month of a terrible broken heart Jesse was languishing with (she hoped in a quiet way no one was noticing), he asked if she would like to come to dinner with him that Friday.

"There's a new restaurant on Thirteenth Street that serves food of the Southwest. Do you think that would be interesting?"

And then on Friday, he asked, by the by, if she'd mind if his niece joined them. Something, nothing really, made Jesse think the niece would be a girl, a teenager. And so she wasn't expecting a woman, wasn't expecting a dyke, and especially wasn't expecting someone so blond and tan and better-looking than regular people to such a degree and in such a put-together way you knew right off that the looking good was part of what she did for a living.

Jesse wanted to resist being influenced by this. She didn't like to think looks played a big part in what attracted her to other women, although when she thought about it, the bookstore owner and the flight attendant and the taxi driver–performance artist and the investment analyst and the house painter, and one of the two radiologists (she met one through the other) on the slightly longer than she would like (now that they comprised her past, her permanent sexual record) list of women she had been involved with were actually quite good-looking. But still, none like this.

"Flake off," Kit said when she sat down, looking seriously into an invisible camera. It was the name of the product, and her tag line on the ads. "I'm supposed to say it in a sexy way. No mean feat." She had just landed a five-commercial deal as spokesperson for a dandruff shampoo. The night turned into a small celebration of this small piece of good fortune, in spite of Jesse being a little pissed at Leo for not giving her fair warning about this matchmaking, and in spite of her being leery of Kit's looks, and the fact that she was an actress, which seemed almost to guarantee self-absorption.

At some point probably too early on, Jesse could feel herself throwing caution out the window and running all her internal red lights. She began letting herself sink into deep focus on Kit, who was just smiling and sitting down and acknowledging Leo's introductions and saying "flake off"—performing perfectly ordinary social mechanics in a perfectly unflashy way. Yet at the same time, occupying the available space with molecules that were traveling faster than normal, achieving higher density. Everyone else's had to shift a little and rearrange themselves to make way. Jesse was made goofy by this, and then somewhere around the second margarita, Kit began to reply in kind, paying an elevated attention to whatever Jesse said, responding to her remarks as though they were particularly droll or perceptive or whatever.

Oh boy, Jesse thought, staring for way too long at the puddle of salsa on her plate. And then felt a flush run through her entire body when their fingertips brushed, not quite accidentally, amid the blue corn tortilla chips.

And then later, when Leo was insisting on picking up the bill and Jesse was thanking him and saying good night, Kit was coincidentally heading just Jesse's way and so why didn't they get a cab together? And then why didn't Jesse come up, Kit had some Kona coffee she'd just bought herself as a treat.

In the time it took the creaking freight elevator to ascend the five floors to Kit's loft, Jesse, traveling on a light gloss of margaritas, figured, What the hell, if there was a seduction going on, why not co-opt it? She pressed a hand against the scarred metal wall next to Kit's head, leaned in, and kissed her.

"This is so—" Kit started to say.

"Oh, come on. Not *so*."

Two weeks later, Kit left a toothbrush of commitment in the glass on Jesse's sink. A month after that, Jesse sublet her small one-bedroom and Kit sold the loft, so they could start fresh in a place that was neither hers nor hers, but theirs. Aided by Jesse's shrewd scouring of ads and following up of leads, and Kit's ridiculously wonderful salary, they got a small but pretty apartment on a relatively quiet block off West Broadway. Of course, this was pure recklessness in Manhattan. The romance could expire, and Jesse could be out on the streets, looking for an apartment half as nice as the one she'd just given up, which had taken her two years to luck into. At first, she was impressed with her own daring. Now she worries it was ridiculous impulse, and that it has added another weight on Kit's side of the delicate balance. Too much when added to her also loving Kit too much. "Too much" being more than she suspects Kit loves her.

In the past (with the exception of the heartbreak she was nursing when she met Kit) Jesse has always been light on her feet through the course of relationships, and at their ends, halfway out the door before the other person could even get up from her chair. With Kit, though, her steps are slowed and softened, as though she's walking through loam. There'll be no running away. She'll stay until Kit ends it, probably even past that for a while of wordless calls to Kit's phone tape, of turning up at restaurants and parties where Kit might be found, while trying not to appear to be looking for her.

Loving Kit strips all the coating off her nerves. It wasn't until after she met her that Jesse took her first Valium, or saw "Painting with Pamela," which is on cable at three-thirty A.M. Now, when she waits for Kit to show up at the apartment, she sits in the window looking down, counting people who come around the corner, stopping at one hundred and going back to one again. Feeling as though she has eaten and is trying to digest something large and made of rubber. It's a lot like the Olympics. It's the first time since those hundred meters in Mexico City that she hasn't felt any buffer between her and the sequence of events she walks through which makes up "her life." This is probably good, a step in personal growth. She hates it.

While Kit has settled so easily into the relationship, Jesse can't seem to come down off the romance of it. This is rattling. She sees herself as a grounded person. She really listens to her dental hygienist when she advises flossing every night. She's a hard grader on student papers and tries to be critically rigorous in her own writing. She sees things in terms of moral dilemmas and winds up pressing on with this sort of conversational tack even when people don't want to hear it, when they just want to dance.

In the abstract, she would say love should be an extension of respect, and yet she doesn't think anything as rational as this accounts for what she feels about Kit. She worries Kit could tell her she secretly dumped toxic wastes in rivers at night and Jesse would still love her, that what she really loves is not Kit—not who she is, certainly not how she looks, the aspect of her that initially attracted and frightened Jesse and which now seems so integral, she couldn't say if Kit is good-looking or plain, only that she is Kit-looking. Rather what she loves is how Kit makes her feel. Lighter, aerated with something like thrill. And she worries that it's way too late for her to be feeling this. It's goony. It's as though, at thirty-nine, she's on her way to some cosmic prom.

Fifteen hours of interstates, and Jesse, now behind the wheel, turns with a wide sweep of headlights across tall grass, onto 54 heading southwest. For a brief flash of crossroads—Kingdom City—the night is white with the arc lamps of gas stations and minimarts, drawing into their light an edgy population jacked up on Cokes and coffee and maxing the speed limit.

"Look," Kit says, pointing as she emerges from sleep. They're coming up on a trailer park with a lit neon sign. MEADOW ESTATES–CHRISTIAN FOLKS IN MOBILE HOMES.

Jesse just says, "Mmmm."

"Guess it's pretty hard to get fireworks around here," Kit tries again as they pass the twentieth tourist-trap tent-store. "Or walnut bowls."

"Mmmm."

"Ah. We must be getting close. To where the heart is."

"Where I can never go again," Jesse says. But Kit has guessed wrong about what is preoccupying Jesse. She isn't looking ahead to her mother's house, where the kitchen light will have been left on for their middle-of-the-night arrival. She is looking farther along the loop, to when they get back to New York and Kit will leave her.

She's pretty sure about this. For the past month or so, maybe a little longer, Kit has been seeing someone else on the sly. Jesse has no proof, just feels it, like a light breeze coming in from an open window off to the side. She knows, for instance, that she will not be the recipient of the postcard of Imogen Cunningham's "Unmade Bed" she found yesterday in a card shop bag under Kit's keys on the dining room table. She's not sure who *will* get it. Most likely Yvonne Scherr, who plays Mandy, the tough-talking paramedic on Kit's show. Jesse can't stand to imagine Yvonne coming on strong. The girl is wired for vamping, has smoldering looks at her command, like Shanghai Lily. She brings her own web. It's the sort of fooling around Kit would think is fun for a while. Jesse suspects this trip is Kit's farewell offering, that the bad news will be delivered when they get back.

They're on old Highway 4 now. Rabbits and raccoons skitter off the thin gravel shoulders, unused to being disturbed at this hour. The night offers no relief from the inferno they drove into around midafternoon. It's as though the heat was merely absorbed by the ground, which is now releasing it back into the air. Jesse can feel her back drenched against the velvety upholstery of the car; her foot is prickly from being pressed so long against the accelerator pedal. The lights bounce off the reflector letters on the sign:

NEW JERUSALEM—7 MI
EULA GROVE—23 MI

She cruises past the city limits sign.

Kit opens the glove compartment so she can see Jesse's face by its light. "Is it weird? Being back?"

"Yeah, that. Kind of nice, too. In a weird way."

She points out the feed store and the houses of a half dozen families she knows. Past the courthouse-library. Past LUNCH. Past what used to be the dry goods store but is now a video rental shop. The Set & Style has its sign flickering in the window, pale white connected letters: REALLY GOOD PERMANENT WAVES THAT LAST.

She drives as though the car is a vaporous phantom rather than a large piece of steel. She takes three red lights as though they're yellows before Kit comments. "Hmmm."

Jesse takes a corner with style. "I lived here seventeen years. Unless someone dies or starts having a baby, I can tell you we're not going to see anything moving at this hour but us."

"I can't believe your mother's sleeping through all this," Kit says after they've dropped a suitcase and rattled the handle of the screen door forever, trying to fiddle it open, and then crashed into a wheeled cutting board cart in the middle of the kitchen, which Jesse doesn't remember being there before.

"Oh, I think we've probably woken her by now," Jesse says. "But she won't come down. She'll want to wait until tomorrow. She'll want to be fixed up proper to meet you, someone new."

Her mother's notions of fixing up have little to do with attractiveness, more to do with old, set forms—short perky hairdos, "daytime" fragrances, slips under dresses, nylons even in deepest summer, handkerchiefs (never Kleenexes). At one time emblems of respectability, these are now also symbols of holding one's own, keeping back from the slippery slope, of stains on a hem, dust on a bookshelf, mold on a shower curtain. From there it's straight onto the skids of lipstick applied without a mirror, pajamas worn into the day.

Jesse hasn't been back here for three years. She is coming now for her mother's sixty-fifth birthday, and her retirement after forty-two years of teaching English at the high school. There will be a party tomorrow afternoon in her godmother, Hallie's, backyard. Nearly all the guests will have known each other all their lives.

There's a note stuck to the refrigerator door with a magnet that's also a laminated card of uplifting verse about kitchens and friendship. The note says, "Have a snack. I've left warmups in here."

"What are warmups?" Kit says eagerly.

Jesse sees that she thinks they are something specific, something regional and delicious, like fritters. She hugs Kit, then disappoints her. "It's just what they call leftovers down here."

Kit opens the refrigerator and looks in, then pulls back out with an accounting. "Fried chicken."

"From the Colonel." Jesse knows without looking. "I'll fix you up a plate."

She starts puttering around the kitchen and gets killed with crummy sentimentality going through the drawers and cabinets, coming across all the old stuff. The plate with the picture of Bagnell Dam painted on it. The scoop they won for naming the new ice cream flavor at Gilley's Creamery one summer—Passion for Peach.

"Bring it on up with us," she says as she hands the plate to Kit. "I'm wiped."

They drag their bags up the stairs with soft thumps. At the door to her room, Jesse puts her hand on the knob, then turns and tries to prepare Kit. "It's kind of a shrine. I mean, I put it up, of course. But even now, my mother doesn't take it down. Which is so weird. She always just dismissed my swimming, always made sure to point out to me what a waste of time she thought it was for anyone with brains. She never came down to Mexico City. So you figure this out. Of course she's very tricky in giving approval and holding it back. She gives just enough so you understand the other ninety-nine percent is being withheld."

"Maybe she was secretly proud and just couldn't show it to you directly," Kit says.

"It's true I gave her an odd sort of status around here. I didn't come up with a husband or grandchildren, but they named the junior high after me."

"I didn't see that."

"I'd die. I took the long way around so you wouldn't. Come on," she says and pushes against the door.

"Oh boy," Kit whispers. "King Tut's tomb."

The room is filled with gold and silver, colored satin—ribbons and medals and trophies, statuettes of girls in modest bathing suits crouched on starting blocks, electroplated into an eternal present tense, poised for the report of a gun that will never go off.

Kit walks around slowly, like a tourist. She homes in fairly fast. It's hung from a couple of carpet tacks pushed into the plaster—a silver medal on a heavy red, white and blue ribbon. Next to it is a yellowed newspaper photo of Jesse on the second highest, the left of three staggered platforms. All three girls on the platforms have damp hair, arms filled with roses, and smiles brought on with the first ebbing of adrenaline. They have just proven, minutes before this picture was taken, that they are the three fastest women in the world at getting through a hundred meters of water.

"How'd you ever come down off this?" Kit says.

"With quite a thud, I'm afraid," Jesse says.

"What's this?" Kit says now. Jesse has her back turned, pulling a sleep shirt from a canvas duffel. Still, she knows exactly what Kit has found—another photo. Everything inside her jams. Kit holds up the picture in its black wood Woolworth frame. It's an odd photo, taken from behind. Jesse and Marty are both wearing sweatpants pulled on over their tank suits. They are standing side by side in an atmosphere of aftermath, their arms draped across each other's shoulders, waiting for some next wonderful thing to happen.

Kit guesses, "You and the girl who beat you. What's her name."

Jesse turns and tries to gather up a few words. Even a few will do. But she can't. She sits on the narrow bed in this obscure defeat. Kit sees there's a problem and takes charge. She comes over and pushes the bag onto the floor and crawls on top of Jesse. She pins Jesse's wrists to the old chenille-covered mattress and lowers herself until her mouth is on Jesse's ear. "I love that you have something this important you can't tell me about."

Much later, Jesse sits on the floor of her mother's bathroom, in the bluish glow of the shell-shaped light fixture over the mirror. She's drawing a weak chill out of the side of the tub with the heat in her cheek. Her eyes are closed, and behind the lids, everything has already gone to aquamarine. She has shot back a few million moments to the one in which she's slapping the tile at the end of her lane, surfacing to see what the fates have written. Pulling off her cap, shaking her head to drain the water from her ears. As though not being able to hear is the problem, when of course it is actually not being able to know. Looking over at Marty, who's also just breaking through, from the white-noise rush of the water into the cacophony at poolside, the hard, dry surface of the rest of the world, where they will be judged. They have already done what they came to do, won the medals they came to take, made the times that will enter the record books. But what times? Which medals?

And then Bud Freeman is hunkering down in front of Jesse, putting up two fingers, his face free of expression from years of practice at bearing news both good and bad. And in this split second of finding out she has lost, Jesse realizes she was utterly convinced she would win, that all along she hadn't really given any weight to the possibility of losing. It won't take a scaling down of expectation to accept this defeat, but rather a substantial reconstruction of her notion of herself. And she must accomplish this in the next few minutes, before she's out of the pool and dried off and sweatsuited and ushered smiling (the smiling is imperative, imperatively expected) up onto the staggered pedestals, positioned slightly lower than Marty. Who, in the next lane, has just received the flip side of Jesse's bad news, who in her pure joy at having taken the gold is reaching across the lane markers toward Jesse, putting a long arm around her shoulders. She can feel the hot flush of Marty's skin under the cold film of water.

"Told you," she shouts, although in the din no one will hear her but Jesse. "We've won. All the fastness, it's ours."

And for a brief moment—the one Jesse needs to carry her away from the pain scissoring into the wall of her heart—she believes this, buys Marty's version and feels herself being pulled into the next lane, then borne aloft, the two of them arcing into the air, then backflipping into the water, somersaulting along the bottom, skimming the aquamarine floor.

From here, the color of the memory bleaches up to white, the dead white of the night before. Down in the showers on a wide bed of fresh towels they've scattered on the tile floor, then fallen onto. It's late. Everyone else is upstairs, held in restless, pre-race sleep. In their collective unconsciousness, they are all winning their events, all of them. The beds of this dormitory are filled with gold medals, gleaming like coins overflowing treasure chests.

Floors beneath them, Jesse is lying very still under Marty, feeling the full press of her, taking on her imprint, committing her body to memory. The small, hard breasts. The wide span of shoulder, wider even than Jesse's. Today was Shave Day, a ritual among women swimmers—the *psshhh* of foam, glint of blades across this shower room as months' worth of hair was whisked away to eliminate its infinitesimal drag in the water, to make the body the smoothest, most aquadynamic set of planes possible. And now she is feeling these planes, Marty's hot and dry at the same time, against her own.

She looks over Marty's shoulder, down the long length of the two of them, for they are both tall girls with great, long reaches. When they are swimming, their arms seem to catch the water as though it's a field of a million aquamarine dragonflies. Although they are both fair by nature, a blonde and a redhead, they are extremely tan from summer training and in this peculiar moonlight, against the white of the towels and the tile, their limbs are black.

Jesse's specific sensation in this moment is one of thrill ebbing into safety, of having vaulted over a high bar, and fallen onto a feather bed. The small tugs of doubt about Marty—that maybe this friendship did not come up out of pure impulse and mutual desire, but was calculated, planned—these fears slip away now. Jesse, who is seventeen and touching and being touched for the first time, thinks no two people can be this close and have any secrets from each other.

By the time Jesse wakes up, she is alone in the bedroom, the Imogen Cunningham card propped on the pillow of the other, empty, twin bed. "Try to know me," it says. "Don't make me up. K."

There are traces of coffee and conversation in the air. Her mother and Kit are downstairs in the kitchen. From where Jesse lies, it sounds like everything is humming along nicely without her. The rhythms, the lilt and fall, seem pleasant and superficial. Kit is probably being charming, making life in New York sound "My Sister Eileen-ish," life as it hasn't been lived by anyone in Manhattan for forty years. A whirl of working girl wiliness and colorfully eccentric neighbors and rounds of parties featuring fascinating, but alas impossible, men. Jesse's mother has so far shied away from visiting New York, and so these fictions would be easy to perpetrate.

Jesse doesn't, though. She isn't out to her mother in an explicit way. They've never had a "talk." On the other hand, she has never lied outright, or concocted boyfriends. And she told her mother when she moved in with Kit. And now she has brought her lover home.

When Jesse gets downstairs, she sees she was wrong. Up close, the rhythms are not good. Now she's sorry she stayed so long in bed, then in the shower.

Her mother is standing at the stove, waiting by a tea kettle rattling its way to the boil. With age, she is becoming a stark figure, the sort of old woman who frightens small children. She is nearly as tall as Jesse, five eleven or so, and has perfect posture, which only adds to the looming effect. She has always considered her height an attribute rather than an oddity, won Tallest Girl ribbon one year at the Mullen County fair, was never bothered by towering over Jesse's father.

She is thinner every time Jesse comes home, now has the rangy look of the farm women she has always felt superior to. At the moment, she looks even more severe for being tense. Her mouth is pulled tight, tucked in at the corners. Something has gone wrong. Jesse tries to smash through whatever it is with a lot of entrance. She gives a hug and gets back an awkward yank around the waist. Her mother has always been uneasy with physical show. If they were alone in this kitchen, Jesse wouldn't even have tried. But in front of Kit, she doesn't want to seem like Camus' stranger.

"Now that's a sophisticated haircut," her mother says, eyeing but not touching the vaguely New Wavey style Jesse has been wearing for a while. The translation is that she finds it ridiculous, arch. "What do you call it?" The unanswerable question is one of her mother's specialties.

"Am I too late for the good stuff?" Jesse says by way of not answering. This question, too, is a charade. There *is* no good stuff. Her mother hates to cook, did as little as possible until she was rescued by the arrival of frozen foods and prepared dinners and carryout. She had the first microwave in New Jerusalem. She drove all the way to a railroad siding sale in Arkansas to pick it up.

Now she opens the freezer and pulls out a stack of frosty boxes. "I've got blueberry pancakes. Scrambled eggs with sausage." She lowers her glasses off the top of her head and reads from a package. "Western omelette."

"Pancakes sound great," Jesse says. Her mother opens the box, pulls back the shrink wrap, pops in the tray, slaps shut the door of the microwave, and speed-types commands on the panel of buttonless buttons on the front. She wipes her hands on a dish towel, and sighs, "There." Like Julia Child coming off the sixth vigorous kneading of the croissant dough. "Coffee?"

Jesse nods and watches another teaspoon of instant go into another cup set next to the two already waiting for the water to boil. She can tell that Kit is trying hard. She is wearing loose white walking shorts and a pale blue polo shirt. She has her hair blown out in a soft young-wife style. She's trying to be the most muted and acceptable version of herself possible. She doesn't know something has already gone terribly wrong.

Kit goes upstairs to get the present she has brought, which she refers to as "a little bread-and-butter gift." She has now profoundly entered "country." In the time she has been down here, talking with Jesse's mother, she has already picked up a trace Missouri accent. On the stairs coming down, Jesse heard Kit asking her mother about local crafts. The girl has quilts on her mind, and jams from quaint berries, goose and elder. At thirty, Kit still sees experience as something gift-wrapped in small packages, just for her. Sometimes this aspect of her seems irresistibly ingenuous. Other times, Jesse longs for her to be fifty-five and Piafesque, someone whose high living is past and anecdotal and expresses itself now mostly in regretting *rien*.

Kit is upstairs long enough for Jesse to lay out a few openings, to give her mother a chance to spill what's bothering her.

"It's a longer drive than I remember. Actually, each time it seems to get a little longer."

"You said she was an actress. I thought, Shakespeare. I don't know. Why didn't you say she was that homewrecker on the hospital show?"

"Oh, Ma. You don't watch that stuff?!"

The lines pull again at the corners of her mother's mouth, giving it an artificial set, like that of a ventriloquist's dummy.

This was the same look, given in this same kitchen, which had caused Jesse to abruptly cut short her last visit, which was supposed to be two weeks long, but ended with her leaving on a night bus to Kansas City after just five days. An unscheduled departure in response to the moment when Jesse's mother, after having disparaged all the important aspects and accomplishments of Jesse's life, looked down over the top of her cup of instant coffee and wondered aloud if Jesse wasn't developing thick ankles, taking after the blunt-shaped women on her father's side.

It was immediately following this remark that Jesse went upstairs to her old room and packed as people in B movies do when they're on their way out of a stormy argument or disastrous marriage—stuffing everything into suitcases with no folding, no concern about tossing shoes in on top of white shirts. Sitting on the bulging cases to get their zippers closed, then exiting the house with the detonation of a slammed door.

Jesse came out this time determined not to mention this last visit. She actually expected that, because of it, her mother would be on her best behavior. It looks like that's not going to be the case.

"We have a committee at church," she says now, assigning to a higher authority responsibility for her not being able to accept Kit. "S.O.S. Save Our Sinners. We write letters to the shows, the networks. We ask them to take off characters like hers and put on families that reflect Christian values."

Jesse tries for a serious nod, but her mother can smell her amusement, and makes a small, angry sound, a tiny click deep in her throat, and turns away to wash out a couple of glasses with a complicated looking soap-dispenser brush.

"She's not the person she plays on the show," Jesse says, because she can't not defend Kit against any attack, even one as nutty as this.

"Well, I'm sure, but she gives people ideas," her mother says, not letting go now that she has purchase. "Sets a bad example. How'd you even meet a show business person like that, anyway?" she asks now, fixing Jesse with a whammy.

"I teach with her uncle," Jesse says, then wonders if this sounds warm and family-oriented, or like Humbert Humbert recalling how he met Lolita. She watches her mother turn back to the sink and sweep into the soapy water a spatula and spoon rest that says "Spoon" on it.

"Look . . ." Jesse starts, feeling a flash of being up to this. By directly coming out to her mother, she can at last go on the offensive in this conversation, rattle her mother's cage by speaking the unspeakable, break the regional code of polite conversation: that when something is unpleasant or difficult to talk about, it is simply placed on a lower shelf of fact by not mentioning it.

"You don't have to tell me," her mother says. "It's on all the shows. Donahue. Oprah." And that's that. Her mother reaches over and tugs the quilted cozy over the toaster and shuts down the subject.

"There's something important I need to discuss with you," she says, further dismissing Jesse's sexuality as too trivial to bother with even while it is too unseemly to mention. A neat trick. She slaps the pump on a bottle of lotion. Too much shoots out and she comes over and strokes the excess onto Jesse's hands. "Darrell and I want to take a long trip this fall," she says. "See the West, in his van."

"What's the S.O.S. going to say about this?" Jesse can't resist.

"I don't care how old you are, I won't tolerate a smart mouth."

Jesse waits.

"We're fixing to get married. Around Labor Day."

Jesse doesn't say anything for a beat too long.

"I know he's not your father. I'm just asking you to respect my happiness."

Jesse thinks for a second. "What are you supposed to say to the bride? I've forgotten. Not congratulations."

"Best wishes."

"Well, you've got mine," Jesse says.

The microwave pings. Jesse goes over, takes out the breakfast. She inhales the steam, which smells like absolutely nothing, then looks up and asks her mother, "What about Willie?"

Her mother sits down across from Jesse, the way the women characters do on Kit's show when they are earnest and anxious. "I was hoping you could take him on for a while. The home's all right so long as he can come here on weekends. They take care of the basics there, but . . . I mean, they miss a lot of what's really important. Nobody smiles when he comes into the room. You know. I wouldn't want to leave him there for months on end. He wouldn't starve, but he'd surely wither a bit." She stops, then adds, "I just want you to think about this."

Jesse nods, dragging the side of her thumb across her lower lip, thinking. She is pretty sure right off that she'll do it, even though it will turn her life upside down and shake the change out of its pockets. Kit is thudding down the stairs. Jesse lowers her voice. "Let me talk to her when I can find a right time, will you? I mean, don't mention it just now."

Her mother tightens up again and says, "Whatever."

Kit's present is a sampler of fancy teas. Lapsong soochong, gunpowder, China green. Jesse's mother eyes the brightly colored tins as if they were ticking. "Why, how interesting. I'll have to give a tea party."

Jesse's heart cramps for Kit, her face lit up with what she thinks is success.

Jesse's mother pats the tea tins and looks up at the wall clock.

"You girls better run on over and fetch William. I've got some party clothes here for him. When he comes out of there, it looks like he got dressed at a rummage sale."

"Does he know I'm coming?" Jesse says.

"Yes, but I only told him yesterday. Otherwise he builds up to too much of a pitch."

On the drive out, she tries to imagine Kit going along with the plan for William, but can't. Kit came down from upstate New York—Syracuse—because she thought Manhattan would be "hot." Hot is not living with your lover and her retarded brother, probably way out in Brooklyn to afford enough space for three. No, Kit will go with Yvonne Scherr, who inherited a place in the Dakota from her parents, Broadway costume designers. She has parties where everyone tries on her large collection of hats. Kit will definitely go with the hats.

Dismissing her as callow is one of Jesse's hedges against the moment when Kit will leave her. Another is trying to think back on things Kit has said that weren't really all that interesting, or funny. She's trying to put as much cushion as possible between her and the falling stone slab.

Of course, Jesse also realizes that she may be turning up the volume and color simply to make things more interesting. A long-standing tic.

Everyone of course refers to Walnut Farm, where William lives, as the nut farm. Local boys rush up the drive on their bikes, hurl a few insults like rolled newspapers, then peel back out, fishtailing through the gravel as they go. William and his friends, the younger crew at the house, don't seem to take these too much to heart.

They wave back at the boys—variously waving to them and waving them away—then take their insults and turn them on each other in what seems to Jesse a pretty sophisticated defusing mechanism. They call each other "retard" and "dope" and mock each other's idiosyncrasies, as they see them. This is selective appraisal, though, what they consider goofy. For instance, while they seem to find making faces—crossing eyes, waggling tongues, wiggling ears—extremely witty, they consider pratfalls childish. They play to each other a lot and don't let themselves be intruded on too much by an outer world that is always out of synch with them.

The home stands behind an enormous sloping lawn. It is an old farmhouse and a large barn. It's a working farm. Under supervision, the men and women who live here raise vegetables and a small summer cash crop of corn. They keep a dozen milk cows and a coopful of chickens. William likes it here pretty well, he has friends. But he is also always eager by Friday afternoon to come home for two days of a more concentrated sort of attention, a more direct kind.

Everyone is out on the lawn, playing a loose, heat-induced, dreamy variant of baseball. Jesse and Kit get out of the car and sit on the hood to watch. It's as though someone here heard a game or two on the radio, and they're working off that. There are way too many fielders, maybe ten, William among them. And two batters, standing a ways apart. The trick seems to be who'll get pitched to.

"Well," Kit says. "Why not?"

Jesse is smiling with having been discovered. William is loping across the lawn, through the middle of the game. The other players aren't too bothered by this, no more than they are by the sprinkler fanning away in the middle of the field.

She watches William coming toward her and floods with feeling. She can never see him plain and simple, for what he is. He always comes wrapped in their shared past. Jesse's growing up was, unavoidably, a lot about Willie. Because of him, modifications had to be made constantly, the center moved from where it ordinarily would have been, over onto him. Money had to be siphoned off for schools, special programs. Attention had to be paid by all of them in huge amounts to carry him over his frustration at not being understood, not understanding.

And Jesse—by virtue of being normal, regular—was discounted for being so privileged, expected to excel because how dare she not, given such an advantage. She was also expected not to disappear exactly, more to recede into a neutral state of transparency, to not quite fully exist. And so although Jesse loves her brother so much she can feel the muscle of her heart spasm slightly in moments like this, on first seeing him after an absence, she also resents him for having taken up all the available childhood in their house.

He looks less like himself than the last time Jesse saw him, more like a generic retarded person. One of the drawbacks of institutional living, she guesses. He is heavier and walks like his friends, flatfooted, fiddling his fingers in front of him as he goes. It's the walk of a thirty-six-year-old man who has never worn a suit or driven a car or negotiated a deal.

"Boyohboyohboy," he's saying as he approaches. He picks up speed, starts running full-tilt toward Jesse. Then stops short by a few feet and stands there twitching with shyness, running his thumbs back and forth under the waistband of his brown pants.

"Well, excuse me, but have you seen my brother, Willie?" Jesse says.

This sends his gaze rushing with shyness to the ground.

"The last time I saw him, he was wearing blue pants. He did look a bit like you though, I must say."

"Me."

"But no," Jesse says, putting a Jack Benny hand to her cheek and looking him over. "He had long hair."

William runs a hand over his hair, which is cut in a sculptured way Jesse hasn't seen before.

She pats his small belly. "And my brother didn't have this."

He giggles and she gives up the game, letting herself get crushed in a hug. "Oh, Cowboy." then she pulls back a little to make introductions. "This is Kit."

William nods with sureness and says, "From Ferris."

Ferris is the grade school Jesse went to. It's still there, a block from her mother's house, a fortress of sooty brick and small windows designed to intimidate children. William didn't go there. By that time, they already knew he wouldn't be going to regular school. He would walk Jesse to the corner in the mornings, and be waiting there for her when she got out in the afternoons. The duty girl on that corner was Kitty Hanes. William remembers the most amazing bits of nothing from a million years back, and then goes out forgetting he has put on socks but not shoes.

"No," she tells him. "A new Kit."

But he has become distracted by the baseball game. Everyone is in an uproar. Three or four people are running the bases clockwise. Everyone is clamoring for order, but of many different sorts.

When they finally get him into the car, Kit climbs in back, deferring to William, who then gets in back with her anyway. Jesse chauffeurs them back to her mother's and listens over her shoulder.

"I know a lot about you," Kit says. "Jesse talks about you all the time."

"How?"

"Oh, Willie this and Willie that."

"Willie what?"

"Willie's the best."

In the rearview, Jesse sees his eyes flutter lightly shut, which is what they do when he's blissed out. She wants to stop the car and get out and lift Kit over her head. Buy her all the flowers in some shop. Make her a little cheese soufflé.

THE BAY OF ANGELS

Carole Maso

Sophie, seven months pregnant, stands before the ditch she is about to be shot into at the Treblinka concentration camp. This is the opening of a longer work that takes place in the feverish, hallucinatory moments before Sophie's death.

Roses and apples and snow continue to fall while the living carry their keepsakes: their small bouquets, their trophies, their testimonies, their diplomas and scrolls—and pale birds swoop. Roses and angels, the century, fall on the horizon, and snow. Feel them now as they move slowly into you. Their sweet and round—everything for a while—and you are getting, you are—undeniably—you are getting sleepy. Roses and apples and snow, angels, while the living in this place cradle their symbols and myths, their bowl of infinite tears, their fierce bouquets, their inventions—all they have made: pyramid and wheel, lint brush and paper clip, knit 2, purl 3, their names: Sophie and Rachel and Rose and Petra and Hannah and Hildegarde, Renée Benededetti, Mavis O'Malley, Fisher, Shoemaker, Goodman, Rosenbloom—their pockets overstuffed with apples and roses and poems. They've wrapped them in brown paper so that they might survive, placed them in the shelter of shoe or museum or leather box. And they remember their stories with longing: *we used to take the rabbit path.* Photographs in lockets

and locks of hair. *You had the most beautiful*—But you are getting
sleepy now. Roses the century and so many apples ... angels.
Songs written for a duduk in the time of Christ. And you are
getting sleepy as apples and roses move into your pale bird bones:
they are hollow, they are lighter than air and snow. You are
sleepy ...

... And now the Madame. The mad concierge, with spinning
wheel and metronome approaches through angels and snow, with
hatbox, with pendulum and rose, chalice and motive and oblivion,
ditch and glass and hanger and forceps.

Help.

Feel your opaque bones which remarkably, even here, still emit
small quantities of light, get sleepy now, heavy with snow and the
century which undeniably falls while the unborn drag their empty
baskets of souvenirs and roses, their silver baby cups engraved
with tears, and the living with their oaths, their vows, their slang,
their desperate code. Limoges will stand for help, and danger will
be called The Closed Book. And death is near will be called Rien
à Faire. Peas in a Pod will mean the coast is clear. S.O.S. will
mean meet me please, it's urgent—at the Hôtel de Ville. And
Stabat Mater will stand for look after the child should anything
happen.

And the living carry their kettles, their hot water bottles, their
compasses and barometers. And the living, wearing disguises
trudge through the landscape of the dead and *say never mind—
cherish whatever has been left behind*. A rhyme from the Hundred Years
War, a song: *I never thought you'd leave in Spring*. A memory: we
made perfume in the garden while our father watered the roses
and wept. Tears continue to fall. Cling to your pencils. Hold out
your small cups.

And when I tell you the story of Pierre and the cafe it will
mean Run! Go quickly and hide. It will mean I am afraid.

Rosy angels and apples and roses and all we loved continue to
fall like tears, move into your bones, mementos and bouquets,
while they weep and bargain and plead and she appears dressed
in a little Chanel suit and veil, carrying her wishbone, her black
hourglass and metronome, counting the snow, and the centuries,
while apples and roses, and you are—you are, aren't you?—sleepy.
And okay, okay you are pregnant and hungry, and there are roses

to tend—but not now—even those who love you would say as much, and it is and you are getting undeniably sleepy now—while the living try to nudge you awake with promises of bon bons and tobogganing, the Etude #12, the Symphony #3, their dreamy catalogs and you're undeniably moved by them but who can resist the Madame with her bobbin and abyss and book of numbers and sleepy now.

Une femme chaque nuit
Voyage en grande secret.

And the living with their pettiness and greed, their small and large cruelties, their harnesses—their thread and lampshades, and alligator handbags. And the men with yellow hair collect blood in their little blood collectors, and vowels in a jar. And the living with their brothels, their New York publishing houses, and locks without keys and you are getting sleepier. Sleepy. ShhhShhh. Go to sleep now.

And I ask the men with yellow hair, why do they put up their windshield wipers when the squeegee men come? And the living bow their heads in acts of contrition and the living say forgive us and forgive us our trespasses and the century shatters. And the Madame says come with me and *entrée libre* and roses. And apples and snow which I try to catch on my dreamy tongue: I was always hungry there.

And the living say: twelve fish. And eleven are the stars in Joseph's dream. And ten are the commandments and I am getting sleepy. And the living carry their miracles. *In the beginning was the word* ... *On the seventh day* ... *And in the desert* ... And the living stripped of everything still say, still whisper: *When we get there,* and *it's as if as if*—and then no more. And the living will soon be dead. And the living, madly scribbling will fall into procession. Life may be a cylinder of tears then, or the sorrowful mysteries, or flowers pressed in a closed book. Life may be a heart shaped box or a blindfold or the closed book the women are forbidden. They can never open it. But the men say never mind. And the living pack their suitcases of roses and diplomas and apples and snow and whisper, *when we get there* and they wait for their instructions in the gray square.

And she says to me hurry as I pack my last alligator bag, and put on my sun hat. And she says very chic, very smart, and she says you are getting so very—

Sleepy. Roses and dark apples and the century falls into your innocent lap. And you remember once more late coffee and oranges and a sunny chair. And the baby you've carried these long months about to be born into roundness and snow. She takes her pendulum and sighs, your breasts like bread, she says. Your belly. . . . She takes out her blurry numbers, her box of fat snow and says count with me, count backwards with me into oblivion or love, into the *as if*, and *if only* and *last hope* with me, as the century shatters all around us and the living become the dead and pale birds swoop. Breathe, breathe—

Deeply now. Dissolving.

Almost but not even. Leave this life. Why is this night different from all other nights? Leave this life behind. Say bye-bye, say bye cruel world. And she holds the closed book in her hands. Say good-bye undeniably cruel and beautiful world. Just walk away Renée. Walk away now.

We used to take the rabbit path.

She engraves no fear on my forehead, no harm on my forehead in snow. Count backwards now. Count apples. Count roses into forgetfulness. Most undeniably beautiful world where we used to— say good-bye.

And nine are the months of childbirth. And seven are the days of the week. And you are getting sleepy. She takes out her metronome and thorn. She takes out the third inversion of the seventh chord and goes down one note a perfect fifth lower. She takes out her black hourglass and catechism, she reads Lamb of God and World without End. She plays the murdered chord, touches my round belly and says please forgive us, someone forgive us our sins. The century falling and roses on an unmarked grave. Best to—What was your name there? she asks.

Sophie, I say. Best to count backwards. Sophie. Best to forget. She holds up an enormous flash card: TEN

TEN

Ten. Where you were happy. Breathe deeply now. Yes, where Father would do his funny walk that would make us laugh so hard we fell in the grass. His black overcoat. His hat . . .

Where there was do, re, mi, where there was a,b,c and world without end. Where I learned to write my name: Sophie. The thrilling, the dangerous S. Where I was left breathless.

And the living carry their precious alphabet. Their nominations and prizes, their laurels and accolades. Their diplomas.

Mother I've gotten triple stars on the end of term exam!

When Mother was so proud.

And the living with their monuments, their tributes. Yes, Madame says, putting her feet up, their monuments: the North Pyramid of Senefern; Dashur, that was our pleasure. The Temple of Luxor. The Sphinx of Chephren decked in royal headdress, false beard and cobra brow ornament. The Baths of Rome. The Baths of Greenwich Village. The pagodas and pallazzi and pallazzini. Bauhaus, apse, forget about it. Gaudi, Frank Lloyd Wright. The Eight Great Wonders, the Six Senses, the 32 Temples, the 1,578 Pleasures, leave this life. Everything ever made. You are getting—

The Bridge of Sighs. The Hôtel de Ville which was our paradise—the endless corridors of desire—more and more and little more—your milky skin and honey. I was always hungry there, where we were left breathless every time. Once more *con brio* and *entrée libre* and *l'amour fou* and we were alive.

NINE

Nine. At the table, table songs. The table that held more food than we could ever finish. Bread and fish. Goose and hen. Apple butter and strudel. Rejoice. May I have more? And the apples and honey and wine that lit the night. And we danced in a circle. The Madame remembers the dervishes, the line dances, the minuet, the tango, the two step. Ecstatic dancing to nonsense texts. To klezmer and prophets. Celebrate. Hold hands in a circle. And my sister, Rachel singing. She had the most beautiful—

My milk bottle, my chatterbox. What did you learn in school today, my dear one—Sophie? The laughter, our happiness, bread rising silently in the dark, a circle dance, table songs we sang by heart.

Where Mother was so proud: *The joy has been in watching you grow. The joy has been in loving you.*

And roses continue to fall. And apples. Apple butter and strudel in the warm kitchen while outside snow fell. And out the wavy glass snow collecting on his shoulder—a shoulder you loved. Father with his shovel and glove. He grew roses. We made perfume from petals and rosewater. Snow continues to fall. And ashes, ashes. Let them all fall, the strange one with the pendulum, with hook and eye, says. Glass that shatters. Sorry, she whispers but you are sleepy. And the mad dervish sings a drugged lullaby, leave this life, and the glass whispers, leave your precious life behind. And the table songs you knew by heart. And all human thought. Quaquaqua she says and dogmatic rationalism. Radical empiricism, transcendental idealism. The Cartesian Circle, the Golden Rectangle, a priori, Madame chants, epistemology and you are getting sleepy. The role of virtue, forget about that, Kierkegaard, Kant's Imperative, the young Hegel, the old Marx, Spinoza and geometry, forget about Heidegger already. She goes up an octave, shrill, *forget about free will!!!* God speaks his eternal No to the world. For Christ's sake forget about God. Dasein and Entfernung. Gerworfenheit and Gezundtheit.

"That we are still not thinking stems from the fact that the thing itself that must be thought about turns away from man, has turned away long ago," Madame reads from the Heidegger pamphlet. So don't worry about it.

a) Nothing is. b) If something was, it could not be known, c) If something could be known, it could not be communicated. EIGHT.

EIGHT

Given the existence as uttered forth in the public works of Puncher and Wattmann of a personal God quaquaquaqua with white beard quaquaquaqua outside time without extension who from the heights of divine apathia divine athambia divine aphasia loves us dearly with some exceptions for reasons unknown but time will tell and suffers like the divine Miranda with those who for reasons unknown but time will tell

SEVEN

Your alphabet was Roman. Your numerals were Arabic. Your language was English. Or was it? Once in your language there was a word for longing and wandering and sadness. Once there was a word for black stallion. Once there was do, re, mi and a, b, c. Ring around the Rosy. And roses. Once there was a book.

Check in your name here. Your place of birth. Your handful of dates. Hand in your passport. Your Michelin Guide. Your video and MCI cards, your library—and the card for the piscine.

Once we sang. Once we came to this square of gray dirt and sang.

She was knitting a baby blanket with pink wool when the men followed us up the rabbit path home after our game of Hide and Seek. The little cat asleep in the basket.

When I enter a cafe in search of Pierre and he is not there, he is no more not there because of my expectation, than he is not there when I had not thought of him.

And she babbled her apple vowels in any order they wanted. The air grows vaguely sweet. Yes, he grew roses. Check in your name, your place, your licenses and pedigrees, your small dates.

Snow falls. Snow falls all over the world tonight. Say goodbye. In your language there were one hundred words for snow. Five. Five. No not yet, six. Six, then.

SIX

Windows and mirrors and crystal, good nacht. Candelabras. The Venetian chandelier and lamps and glass trays and eyeglasses *but how shall I see, my vision is weak?* Her collection of demitasse cups. And the window that framed the shoulder you loved. And the glass flowers. Her small ornamental birds . . .

Shatter. Limoges. A border of roses.

And the Madame magnifies her metronome and pendulum. Pumps up the volume. Give over, give over now to tick and tock. To quaquaqua. She opens the box. Let snow fall like silence on your pretty, on your drowsy, your undeniably sleepy head.

Water was your pleasure once. So what? You loved to listen to your sister talk about the birds. You swam across the lake. She and Father would follow you in a boat.

I never thought you'd leave in Spring.

Love might be a circle or a chandelier, but not here. Or dancing—your hand entwined in mine. Your happiness may have been an S or an 8 or the sign for infinity. Dried fish or a wurst or a knish. Candles on fire. A bit of Schnapps. Your happiness one day may be a word for black stallion or a Mercedes or the TGV or the sleek autobahn or Berlin Alexanderplatz—but not now. A toboggan or a boat. Or the roses. He grew the most magnificent—

Winter roses and the century continue to fall. You can stop your wandering. You can stop your wandering now.

Love might be—And the little cat Schnitzel comes back after—after so many days away we took her for dead. And her shining fur and that first glimpse, after complete resignation, after hopeless—through the pane of glass—come home in the snow—ice and stars on that radiant frame.

Mamma, come quickly to the window, she is back!

And his return, and the snow on his shoulder after the Many Years War. Home.

Your language was German. Your color was red. Your day of the week was Saturday. In your language there was a word for wandering and sadness and homesick. A word for black stallion. Your number was three. You had the most beautiful singing voice. Younger sister. You could call the birds from the trees.

May I interrupt this quaint revery for a moment, she laughs? The Madame stands by with her tar and feathers. Blood sausage and embers and looks at the dead. They were once my friends. Come with me she says come with me to five where you will not starve, where you will not die.

FIVE

Where we will not starve. Forget the dead who are so hungry they cannot close their eyes. They bite down on air. Sitting at the long table. Biting down forever on air. And they can never close their eyes . . .

. . . They used to say after a particularly bitter winter that it made the spring all the more tender and dear, all the more sweet.

In the fragrant, wild, rainy springtime. It could have been the day of your birth. The house covered with roses again. The brass water tap turned green. The snails have left their shells. Black trees on a green mountain. Birds swooping

Let it all fall—a) nothing is; b) if something was,

FOUR

I wish we had the time to have Rachel tell you about each bird, where they are from, where they migrate to, the habits of each . . .

THREE

Where there was fa, sol, la, ti, now the silent table.

Where there were table songs sung from memory, now the silent table.

Where there were the apple vowels that once saved you oooooh and ahhhhh and ohhhhhhh, now the silent table.

TWO

When they came from behind the trees while we were playing Hide and Seek and followed us through the woods and up the rabbit path home, I understood it as I hadn't before: the x was on my house.

ONE

And now like a cat gone out on a long journey and come back, your second lids close, and then your first, and you are asleep finally at the silent table and you rest your head. Mamma and Pappa have gone—nothing can be done.

And the glass shatters backwards into silence. One. Where the open graves suture themselves closed into beautiful earth, undisturbed. And the river flows free of blood for once.

And the kicking and healthy child on the verge of her birth floats back into remoteness, curls back into a circle—you will remember none of this—just as well.

I was seven months pregnant there.

But she is up to her elbows in red, now wielding her mad forceps, her tongs, her claw. Her fishbone and kill. Singing a Stabat Mater. *Almost but not*

And she says, the Madame pleads, the maker of angels begs, You will remember nothing. At the number after One ... I was seven months pregnant there, you will remember none, nothing of this. *Almost but not*. And there's blood everywhere and she waves her pincers and star magic and wand. *Almost but not even*. Have mercy. Apples and snow and roses are falling. The century. The child falling forever. Have mercy on us.

And the Madame catches the *almost but not*, the seven months in a hat box, falling.

Almost but not even a baby yet. Angel. And it falls kerplunk into the hat box. We all fall. Rien à faire. Nothing can be done now. And the mother stands, falling.

And we, invisible for a prolonged moment embrace in that all but evacuated square. Where has everyone gone? Say goodbye.

Falling. My daughter forever. Where are you?

Once there was almost a child with apple cheeks conceived in snow and she was called Rose.

Apples and roses and snow. Angels at our feet. *Mercy.*

You will remember nothing. Zero. Zip. Nothing now. And she is waiting there in the place after One. And she takes off her red soaked gloves and she shakes my hand and smiles—coltish, coquettish and girlish and blushing a little. *Enchantée.* She asks, What is your name? I shrug. Says, What were you called there? I shrug. Says, What was the configuration of your village?

I do not know.

What do you remember?

Stabat Mater and autobahn. We were going to go to the— numbers that descend. She smiles and opens her palm. A bon bon. Inviting me to the place where we will not starve.

What was your name there?

I shake my head no. I do not know.

She sings, "Hail wind from afar, desert and you, forgetfulness!"

And now like a cat having used up only a fraction of your possible lives—your light—

My Remoteness, My Amnesia, she says—the only place still possible to live. Her hands flutter across her face and she offers

bittersweet chocolates, bits of honey and apple and nuts. Bon
bons. Come here my Sweet. And she is clucking and cooing and
taking teeny, tiny baby steps backward. Baby steps. Bon bon steps
backward. *Baby.* This way that way yes, here, yes, no, as we step
and step and she says go lightly, and she says heads up and she
says come quickly, step gently, and we traverse over fields and
fields and fields of the dead. And she says go lightly, they were
once my friends. And darkness streams from the open eyes of the
dead. We'll need a torch, she says. And the dead say Someone
shaved our heads at night while we were sleeping. Someone collected the gold from our throats and we will no longer sing.
Someone stole all that could be stolen.

Father would do his funny walk—of course.

And the Madame says with her notebook and abacus, step
quickly, come quickly. She brandishes a butterfly net. She says
bon bon and yo yo and figure eight. She says home and safe and
soon we'll be home.

And the dead shall be called Invisible Cities and Rien à Faire.
And the Madame says *Ça Suffis*, and *Entrée Libre*. She says Come
quickly and Faster, but then stops.

Yes, she hisses, but is it you? Is it really you? She asks me for
the note I have carried all this way in my shoe. And she points
her torch at it while the dead without opus number recall table
songs and sweet wine and ask what was our crime? And the dead
who are, dear God, now everywhere just want to know. And she
cheers and applauds and does a pirouette. Reading again and again
the note written in a language of stars and glass. In a language of
dots and dashes. Shatter and flame. In a language of ash.

I follow her, this moonwalker, to the soon we'll be home. To
the soon we'll be at the door called No Harm, the door called
Safe. Over this path of shattered glass.

I step over last stories, songs, wishes, recipes, requests, questions, small leather boxes, candles on fire, arms and legs and heads,
and bottles of Schnapps.

The skull sings a boating song. *Alone at last with you, rowing ...
twilight approaching ... the willows ...*

Shut up, she screams. Shut up already! And she turns to me,
step quickly, go lightly.

And the skull remembers her mother. Such beautiful hair. Each night. One hundred strokes.

She writes No Harm in a language I do not understand on my forehead. She writes No Fear. And she suddenly notices my luggage. We'll need a chariot, a chariot, a chariot for your bags, all the while taking little baby steps, cha cha steps back. Baby. *Viens ici*, my sweet, my pet, swinging vaguely in my direction the butterfly net. *Hurry*.

Come with me I promise you anything you want. Dancing boys and minty drinks. Odessa. Nice and Antibes. A spa! Anything you want. She's shameless. She says I like your sun hat, but I know Madame would say just about anything to get me on to that chariot.

What do you recall?

I remember only the mystery of book and rose. Rose and baby snow. A shock of red. Numbers that descend.

She smiles, I promise you memory one day.

I remember Hide and Seek and forceps and thorn. And red and red. And the x.

The Madame whirls around midnight wearing micro mini and veil, alb and stole, and pumps and lines she has painted up the backs of her legs, saying the darkest evening of the year, cradling skulls, weeping, checking pulses with a gloved hand. Numbers that descend. Chaque nuit, une femme—

Madame is exotic—night blooming. Beautiful in her Houdini suit. She sings a mad aria: HURRY. And the dead say bring us back. Let us dance. And the dead say listen to us for once. And the dead say write this down and get it published. And Madame screams *Enough* in a voice of dissolving lines and shattering glass, Maria Callas and baby blanket and Diamonda Galas, as the numbers drain and the hatbox turns red. The voice of five, four, three, of blood and frogs and cattle disease, of boils and hail and darkness and I promise and I'm sorry and I promise and no harm now and life without end.

The x was on my house.

And apples like heart beats continue to fall. She says hurry now, into the chariot. She says what's this with the sun hat and where the hell do you think you're going anyway? And quaquaqua and her legs dissolving no, and she shrieks as the snow turns to rain and the dead become deader, *hurry!* And the living with their vows and promises, their half-baked schemes, their novels and French lessons and charm schools, and guidebooks, their footnotes and postscripts, their small escape hatches.

She coaxes me onto her foul rag and bone shop, singing in a falsetto, *we're peas in a pod! We're Fred and Ginger, we're Cagney and Lacey, we're—we're—*And I collect my alligator bags in the night in the rain in my ridiculous sun hat and step onto the horseless carriage. What choice do I have? And she whispers Safe and No Harm and Home. And she makes a cross in ash on my forehead now. She turns on the torch. Lifts her half glasses from her breast. Sighs and squeals. Gurgles, coos, laughs. Does a triple pirouette. My beauty, my future, my savior, *my best idea yet!*

What were you called there?

I shrug.

She holds my small forgetful hand in hers. What was the configuration of your village?

I do not know.

What can you remember?

Nothing now. How odd.

Excellent! she says and does another spin. My Beautiful Forgetfulness.

And she settles into the rickety chariot and puts on her kidskin gloves. Repeat after me, she says. *The rain in Spain stays mainly in the plain.* As flip flops and forceps and bikini bottoms and bon bons tumble out of the chariot. *The rain in Spain* . . . And the child Picasso appears for a moment drawing infinity and figure eights and the dead whisper Guernica there. Again: *the rain in Spain stays mainly* . . . *I think you've got it!*

She revs up the chariot, and a squeegy man comes by wanting to clean the window for some bread, and she puts up her windshield wipers and screams, GO!!! as the glass shatters and her voice does the forty lashes.

She prepares for departure. Only at midnight, she whispers, only on the new moon which is no moon at all. And no stars. Shall we take the upper or the lower corniche?

What are angels, she asks, shining her torch.

I shrug.

What were you called there?

I do not know.
Say Petra.
Petra.
Say Petra, again.
Petra.
Say Petra.

She snips a glittering lock of hair and smiles pure gold and places it in an envelope. *This must be my lucky day.* Say life everlasting. She opens a black catechism: say world without end.

What is the true cross, she asks, thumbing madly. She screams. Raises a small periscope. Checking the darkness for danger. Prepare for blast off! In the new moon which is no moon at all and all the stars out. Roses continue to fall. Don't linger. Don't linger quite so long. They are alas—they are undeniably dead, sadly, yes, *for God's sake dead!*

How many angels can dance on the head of a pin?

Une femme chaque nuit,
Voyage en grand secret.

What is your name?
I forget.
Say Greta. Try Greta.
Greta.
Say Greta again.
Greta.
Try Gretchen.
How many angels . . .

She peers through the periscope at something and shrieks into the black rain with her red veil and fang, with her garlic and cross. *You're a collaborator's collaborationist!!! To the manor born! Groomed since birth for the post! You're a one trick pony. A wolf in a sheep suit. I know all about it. I heard it through the Arab's telephone.* And she whispers blood sausage, and she whispers how much and she whispers, what have you done for me lately? And she exchanges hair for bread, gold for bread, anything for bread. And she holds up the metronome and bargains for time—and the black hourglass shatters.

The true cross may be a wishbone or an x. Numbers that de-

scend. It may be the stain left on the sheet or the apple vowels
that saved her—

When I enter a cafe in search of Pierre and he is not there—

The true cross may be the pregnant woman standing, her arms
outstretched—before the pit she will be shot into. The true cross
may be the Stabat Mater or the Madeleine qui pleure. The true
cross may be the book the women are forbidden ever to open.

The true cross may be a woman with no home, who hoists her
child into the air pleading for money or just a morsel of food—
an apple, some bread, in one of your cities. The true cross may
be a tortured figure hanging upside down so that his Shylocked
pockets can be emptied of everything.

She holds up her bony hand and cackles. She says she carries
a bit of the true cross in her ring. She says when we get there
and she says if you're good—she's got papal vestments galore, just
wait and see!

It may be 1945 or 1993 or 222 or 12 BC or World War I. It
may be the end of the world or just the middle, and the skull
sings a boating song. Remembering the Seine and moonlight. And
the French say j'ai faim and the French say cassoulet and pomme
frites. Pâté and pâte brisée. And the French say send more Tabasco
Sauce when you get a chance. Fewer American films.

And the dead have four questions and three cups and five sorrowful mysteries. And the dead carry the sixth book of the *Aeneid*:
their words are shadows now and they long for their long distance
telephone cards. And the dead recall the true cross as they chew
forever on an imaginary mutton leg. They are so hungry, still.
And the dead remember the true cross: chemotherapy and shock
treatment and ddI. And some of the dead remember being in the
capriccio of health—except for one thing: someone was hurting
them. Or they were starving or—

Gas pellets release a strange perfume. *It's as if—as if . . .*

And the dead ask what was our crime? That we sang, that we
loved sweet wine? And the dead cry.

Someone stole all that could be stolen.

The skull says when I was a boy we used to take the toboggan
up to Mount Ararat . . . And in the spring that same mountain
covered with wildflowers.

And the skull sings a song of Odessa ... *pearl of the sea* ...
Remember me ...

And the Madame weeps and performs mouth to mouth and
Stabat Mater—Late magic and recruitments and resuscitations.
And I'd like to do a little CPR on you, she grins, a little mouth
to mouth on you my sweet she says with glee, and dreams of her
after-hours bars and redemptions and charms. And the dead whisper we are smoke, and Madame says enough already and enough
already with the jokes.

And the dead gnawing on an imaginary mutton leg—
Bite down on air. And the silent table. And the quiet.
There was a child once ...

The joy has been in watching you grow. The joy has been in loving you.

And the dead whisper, set us free now. They used to carry their
miracles. Their faith. Grace. Go to the desert and pray for your
true name. Take back the vowels. And take back the consonants
too. And the dead hand us back the alphabet and they say help
us if you can; they say do something—or nothing—and shrug.
And the dead whisper we are tired now. Let us go.

And the dreaming dead, crucified to a wishbone think *when we
get there* ...

I never thought you'd leave with the roses in bloom.

Love may be a child. Conceived in joy. Imagined with hope.
Someone stole our beautiful hair ...

And the dead shall be called Rose and Rosen and Rosenberg
and Rosenbloom. And the dead shall be called, God help them—
God love them for once—they shall be called Invisible Cities and
Rien à Faire and Rabbit Path.

They used to say after a particularly bitter winter that—you
know.

The inevitable nostalgia for 10.

The true cross may be the healthy and kicking apple child,
shattered. Or the black book, unborn in them, that they are forbidden forever to open.

The true cross is the vowels and the vowels she spoke. When
the men came with yellow hair and red breaking on their arms,
she feigned ecstasy every time—*oooooh* and *ahhhhh* and *ohhhhhhh* so
she would be spared. And the men came back with yellow hair
over and over for more.

Someone stole all that could be stolen.

What is an angel, she asks?

A woman x'ed to a bed.

In the all but evacuated square.

The angels shall be called Rachel and Nathan and Sophie and Sol. And the angels shall be pictured holding goblets and chalice and waiting for Elijah or Godot to show. They are so patient.

Tears have fallen for centuries. Cling to your pencils. Hold out your small cup. Dream.

And the angels shall be called pagoda and pyramid. And the chorus of angels shall be called Cambodia. And children of Cambodia. And the chorus of angels shall be called Sarajevo. And Children of Sarajevo.

And the angels shall be called Egarian, Kavafian, Bedrosian, Zakarian, Agoyam, Sarkisian and they shall play duduks instead of harps and they shall dance again.

The angels shall be called Alphabet and Song. Pray for us. And the angels shall be called Baby and Baby Blanket. Hear our prayer.

The true cross is the silent table where we are asked to sit quietly forever. And the true cross is the stain left on the sheet in the shape of an "a" or a "u." Une femme chaque nuit pinned on a bed of vowels.

The true cross is the body of a woman nailed to a closed book.

Please take my hand for a moment, and come here to this feather bed: under the eiderdown, the duvet, the perfumed sheets, the pillows plumped—come close—and before we go any further—before you admire my loops and curves and curls, take my hand and whisper in my ear, tell me

What was our crime?

The x was on my eyes. The x was on my mouth.

But the angels shall be called Desire and Peas in a Pod and Chatterbox. Sophie and Ava and Rose. And they shall live on the earth again some day. And they shall dance.

And the living press apples and roses to their breasts remembering. Snow falls all over the world tonight. Close your eyes.

What is your name?

Say Greta. Try Greta.

What is your name for now?

Greta.

Or Hildegard. Say my name is Hildegard.

What are angels?

Say my name is Hildegarde and I shall live forever.

And the angels say like your mother once did when you brought home triple stars, despite the force of the closed book, despite the persistence of x—you can fly.

What is an angel? Madame asks.

Say my name is H. and I shall never die. Fill in the blank. Write it: My name is Hannah and I shall never die.

She pulls me toward her. She whips out a box of gossamer and glitter and wings. What is an angel she sings? She bats her lashes and puts on her aviator glasses. She passes me a box of haloes and snow. Drink this she says: a rainwater Madeira, a peppermint Schnapps. Drink this: a triple espresso, a cup full of tears. What is an angel, she weeps, and I sing Do Re Me Fa Sol La Ti. And I say A E I O U & L M N O P. What is an angel? she cries. And we are flying.

AUTHOR BIOGRAPHIES

Blake C. Aarens' writing has appeared in literary journals and anthologies, including *Aché: A Journal for Lesbians of African Descent, The Best American Erotica 1993,* and the nonfiction anthologies, *From Wedded Wife to Lesbian Life: Stories of Formerly Married Lesbians* and *Virgin Territory.* She is currently completing a novel, *Cowards of Conscience.* She lives in Oakland, California.

Linsey Abrams is the author of three novels, *Our History in New York, Double Vision* and *Charting by the Stars,* from which "Dreaming Birth," the story that appears here, is an excerpt. Her stories, reviews, and essays have appeared in *Mademoiselle, Christopher Street, The Review of Contemporary Fiction* and numerous other publications. She is on the faculty at Sarah Lawrence College, and a writer-in-residence in the graduate program of the City College of New York. She is the founding editor of *Global City Review.*

Carol Anshaw is the author of the novel *Aquamarine.* Her work has been anthologized in the *1994 Best American Short Stories.* She reviews books for publications nationwide, and won the 1989–1990 National Book Critics Circle Citation for Excellence in Reviewing. She lives in Chicago.

Beth Brant is a Bay of Quinte Mohawk from Tyendinaga Mohawk Territory in Ontario. She is the editor of *A Gathering of Spirit,* and the author of *Mohawk Trail, Food & Spirits,* and *Writing as Witness.* The past recipient of an Ontario Arts Council award, a Canada Council grant, and a National Endowment for the Arts Literature

Fellowship, she is currently working on *Testimony From the Faithful*, a collection of essays about land and spirit. She lives in Michigan.

Rebecca Brown's most recent novel is *The Gifts of the Body*. Her previous work includes a book of stories, *Annie Oakley's Girl*, and the novel-in-stories, *The Terrible Girls*, a finalist for the Lambda Literary Award. Her work has been translated into Danish, Dutch, and German, and enjoys great critical acclaim in England. Her work has also been adapted for the theatre in England, Scotland, and the United States. She lives in Seattle where she writes and teaches part-time at the University of Washington, Extension. "Every Day and Every Night" is from a longer work in progress called *The Dogs*.

Ana Castillo is the author of several books, including *My Father Was a Toltec and Selected Poems*, the novels *The Mixquiahuala Letters* and *So Far From God*, and a new work of nonfiction, *Massacre of the Dreamers: Essays on Xicanisma*.

Stacey D'Erasmo is a senior editor at the *Voice Literary Supplement*. Her fiction has appeared in *Boulevard* and the *VLS*.

Jane DeLynn is the author of the novels *Don Juan in the Village*, *Real Estate, In Thrall*, and *Some Do*. Her fiction and essays have been published in a number of magazines and newspapers, including *The New York Times, The Washington Post, Tikkun, The Paris Review, The Advocate*, and in the anthologies *High Risk, Bad Sex, Infidelity*, and *Testimony: Contemporary Writers Make the Holocaust Personal*. She was in Dhahran, Saudi Arabia, for two months during the Gulf War as a correspondent for *Mirabella* and *Rolling Stone*.

Mary Gaitskill is the author of BAD BEHAVIOR, a collection of short stories, and TWO GIRLS, FAT AND THIN, a novel.

Alicia Gaspar de Alba is a native of the El Paso/Juarez border, and recognizes herself as "the first Chicana fruit of her family." Her full-length collection of poems "Beggar on the Cordoba Bridge," appears in the volume *Three Times a Woman: Chicana Poetry* (Bilingual Press, 1989), and her first collection of short stories, *The Mystery of Survival* (Bilingual Press, 1993) was awarded "Premio

Aztlan," an annual prize for emerging Chicana/o fiction writers. Her writing has also appeared in several anthologies of Chicana/o and Latina/o literature published in the United States, France, Germany, and Mexico. She received her Ph.D. in American Studies from the University of New Mexico in 1994. Currently, she lives in Southern California with her lifemate, Deena Gonzalez, and is a founding faculty member of the Cesar Chavez Center for Chicana/o studies at UCLA.

E.J. Graff grew up moving around the Midwest. When she was eight, her family settled in Beavercreek, Ohio, where they were the only Jewish family in the township. Since 1979, she has lived in the Boston area. Her stories and essays have appeared in such publications as *The Iowa Review, The Kenyon Review, Ms., New York Times Magazine, Out, The Progressive, The Women's Review of Books,* and in several anthologies. In 1993 she received one of the Astraea National Lesbian Action Foundation's Emerging Writers Awards.

Stephanie Grant's fiction was read on the nationally broadcast radio program, "Selected Shorts" and has appeared in *AGOG* and *Beet.* She is curator of "In Our Own Write," a reading series for emerging queer writers at the Lesbian and Gay Community Services Center in New York City and has just completed her first novel, *The Passion of Alice Forrester.* A native of the south shore of Boston, she currently lives in Brooklyn.

Judith Katz received a Lambda Literary Award for her first novel, *Running Fiercely Toward a High, Thin Sound.* Her second novel, *The Escape Artist,* will be published in 1996. Born and raised in Massachusetts, she currently teaches Women's Studies and creative writing in Minneapolis.

Mary La Chapelle is the author of *House of the Heroes and Other Stories,* for which she received the PEN Nelson Algren Award. Raised in Wisconsin and a long-time resident of Minnesota, she currently teaches creative writing at Sarah Lawrence College in Bronxville, New York.

Jenifer Levin is the author of four novels, *Water Dancer, Snow, Shimoni's Lover,* and *The Sea of Light;* her short stories have been widely anthologized. She has written for *The New York Times, The Washington Post, Rolling Stone, Ms., Mademoiselle, The Advocate,* and taught fiction writing and literature at the University of Michigan. Having worked, studied, and traveled in Europe, the Middle East, South America, and Southeast Asia, she currently lives in New York City.

E.J. Levy earned a degree in history from Yale University in 1986 and has worked as an editor and freelance journalist. Her articles and book reviews have appeared in, among other places, *The Nation, In These Times,* and *The Utne Reader.* She was formerly managing editor of *The Independent,* a national monthly for film- and videomakers, and was founder and editor of *A Common Language,* a lesbian and gay newspaper for Northern New Mexico. She is completing a novel.

Carole Maso is the author of four novels, all of which will be reprinted in paperback in 1995: *AVA, Ghost Dance, The Art Lover,* and *The American Woman in the Chinese Hat.* She is currently at work on two novels: *Defiance,* to be published in 1996, and *The Bay of Angels.* She is on the permanent faculty at Columbia University.

Kristina McGrath earned her MFA in writing at Columbia University. She is the author of the novel *House Work* and her stories and poetry have appeared in *Harper's, Paris Review, Iowa Review, Yale Review,* and numerous other journals and anthologies. Her fiction won a 1989 Pushcart Press Prize, and a 1993 *Kenyon Review* award. Having lived in San Francisco and New York, she now resides in Kentucky, where she is a contributing editor of *The American Voice,* a national feminist literary magazine.

Lee Ann Mortensen won a Fellowship from the Poets & Writers Exchange Program in 1993. Her writing has appeared in *Ploughshares,* the *Mississippi Review, Quarterly West, Inscape,* and *The Student Review,* and she is now finishing a novel called *Strip,* the first chapter of which is "Not Quite Peru." She has been the Fellowship Coordinator for *Writers @ Work,* and is currently an assistant professor of English at Utah Valley State College.

Mei Ng is a writer living in New York.

Jan Ramjerdi is an assistant professor at California State University, Northridge. Her work has appeared in *Denver Quarterly, The Little Magazine,* 13th Moon, *Quarterly West,* and other magazines. She is currently completing a virtual hypernovel, *RE.LA.VIR,* and has a collaborative novel in progress, *Geosynclines,* about Death Valley and the Northridge Earthquake.

C.W. Riley, an Ozarkian, received her MFA from the University of Alabama. While in New York City, she was an active member of Lesbian Avengers. Also, she taught English and writing at Polytechnic University, Parson's School of Design, the College of New Rochelle, and others. She now lives in poverty in Las Vegas, New Mexico, with her partner, Lisa, hoping to concentrate on her writing.

Pamela Shepherd's work has appeared in *Passages North, The Taos Review,* and *Conceptions Southwest.* She is a graduate of the MFA program at the University of Washington, and the winner of the 1990 Poets & Writers "Writer's Exchange." She lives in Taos, New Mexico, where she works as a New Mexico artist in the public schools, and teaches English at the University of New Mexico.

Cheryl Strayed, formerly Cheryl Nyand-Littig, grew up in rural northern Minnesota. Having lived in Dublin, New York City, Texas and Oregon, and traveled extensively, she now lives in Minneapolis. Her writing has won several awards. She is currently writing her first novel and working as a waitress.

Carla Tomaso is a writer and teacher whose short fiction has appeared in *Common Lives, Lesbian Lives,* and in the anthologies *Unholy Alliances* and *Voyages Out I.* She is the author of two novels, *The House of Real Love* and *Matricide.*

AVON BOOKS TRADE PAPERBACKS

MEMOIR FROM ANTPROOF CASE 72733-1/$14.00 US/$19.00 Can
   by Mark Heplrin

A SOLDIER OF THE GREAT WAR 72736-6/$15.00 US/$20.00 Can
   by Mark Heplrin

THE LONGEST MEMORY 72700-5/$10.00 US
   by Fred D'Aguiar

COCONUTS FOR THE SAINT 72630-0/$11.00 US/$15.00 Can
   by Debra Spark

WOMEN AND GHOSTS 72501-0/$9.00 US/$12.00 Can
   by Alison Lurie

BRAZZAVILLE BEACH 78049-6/$11.00 US
   by William Boyd

COYOTE BLUE 72523-1/$12.00 US/$16.00 Can
   by Christopher Moore

TASTING LIFE TWICE: LITERARY 78123-9/$12.00 US/$16.00 Can
LESBIAN FICTION BY NEW
AMERICAN WRITERS
   Edited by E. J. Levy

CHARMS FOR THE EASY LIFE 72557-6/$12.00 US/$16.00 Can
   by Kaye Gibbons

THE MEN AND THE GIRLS 72408-1/$10.00 US
   by Joanna Trollope

THE LEGEND OF BAGGER VANCE 72751-X/$12.00 US/$16.00 Can
   by Steven Pressfield